A MARRIAGE OF INSECTS

a novel of the World Tree

Bard Bloom

PADWOLF
PUBLISHING

ALSO BY BARD BLOOM

-THE WORLD TREE ROLE PLAYING GAME
by Bard Bloom & Victoria Borah Bloom

To Vicki, for everything I know about marriage,
and a good deal about insects, too.

A Marriage Of Insects
a novel of the World Tree Role Playing Game
© 2007 Bard Bloom
www.world-tree-rpg.com

cover art © 2007 Maggie Hogarth

design and book layout by Howling Pixels

Padwolf Publishing, Inc.
www.padwolf.com

ISBN: 1-890096-36-9
Printed in the U.S.A.
First Printing.

AN ORDINARY DAY AT WORK

Nethry Chrestilium was not her name. She had put her real name aside when she started working among the monsters and wild folk. She knew that she would be doing things which most primes would call foolhardy or wicked, and she did not want her real name attached to them. So she had, in essence, folded it up and packed it away in a box at her parents' house, wrapped in cheap silk, to pick up again when she retired.

But her retirement was a long ways off — if it ever came. She knew quite well that for every colleague of hers who retired, three died at work. She worked in the most dangerous territory on the upper branches of the World Tree, outside the heavy walls of magic around the cities, outside the largely tamed farmlands and countryside on the flat tops of the world-branches. Sometimes she worked in the Verticals, the unconquerable wilderness on the sides of the world-branches, never more than thirty miles away from even the safest city. At the moment, she worked in the Lenwynt, the primordial forest that filled the five hundred miles from distant Araldy to her native city of Byronny. In ancient times, the goddess Lenhirrik might have claimed it as her personal territory, never to be civilized. The goddess had been a motionless wooden statue for decades for unknown reasons, but no sensible prime would gamble that she would stay that way.

She hiked along the crest of a hill, trotting now and then to keep up with her four companions. They were Gormoror, brawny and strong and ursine, and even the shortest of them was a head and both ears taller than her. They and their small tribe lived in the Lenwynt, travelling, hunting, never building homes, never civilized; Lenhirrik paid them no particular attention.

"C'mon, city Rassy. You think you're the equal of a War-Bannu, and you can't even keep up with us in a walk? I don't expect much from you in a fight then," mocked Runderax, and broke into an uphill trot, her loincloth flapping over her short tail.

Nethry had to run, but did not fall behind. She was much relieved when Runderax stopped at the top of the hill and poked around in the brambles by the edge of a bluff.

"Hey, Rassy, once you're done panting, come look at this. Carcanofex footprints. Don't often see those."

Nethry flicked her ringed tail away from the eager thorns of a bramble-bush, and crouched by Runderax's side. The print was long, showing four toes with their blunt claws clearly, and the brambles around it were not disturbed. The Gormoror pointed. "Look there. That's the *left* foot. The right foot would have to be about there — " she gestured to the empty air. "Not much else could have left a print like that. Carcanofex don't care whether they're walking on land or sky. And they go right through wood as if it weren't there. Ddirmion's got a leather noose. They can't go through that."

Nethry nodded. "Ah, thank you for the lesson. I am a warrior equal to your best ..." She did not think she was that good on her own, though with her equipment she was probably a better one. In any case, Gormoror appreciated boasting. "... But not such a tracker."

"We'll sell the horn for a fair bit of money ... Hey! I know how you can make yourself useful and earn your share, city Rassy. Take the horn to Byronny and sell it there."

"A double share, then, for I'll do as much as any of you in the fight, and more," said Nethry with a calculated laugh. She stood up and brushed her face with a hand. The black mask around her eyes always looked lopsided unless she was careful to keep the fur flat, which annoyed her no end.

A deep booming Gormoror cry of pain shook the summertime air behind them, followed by a pair of battle-shouts. "The War-Bannus may be mighty in war, or they may not, but I don't think you snuck up on it, Runderax," said Nethry.

"That we did not! It attacked us from the rear, the cowardly air-rabbit," shouted Runderax, and ran back towards the cries. Her axe was made of bone, hardened by the best spells the unsophisticated War-Bannus could cast, but it was longer than Nethry was tall, and Runderax whirled it over her head and warbled a gleeful bass song as she charged. Nethry needed all her breath for running.

The carcanofex looked almost silly: a scaled kangaroo, with a long spiral horn protruding from the center of its chest, hopping and bouncing among the Gormoror. It fought well, though; as Runderax and Nethry arrived, it leapt at one of the other Gormoror, putting its full weight and the full strength of its hind legs behind its chest-horn. The Gormoror fell over under the carcanofex's weight, howling, pierced through his left lung. He was used to such wounds, and he slipped a leather noose around its neck as it was stabbing him.

In a moment, the carcanofex was surrounded. Two of the Gormoror were wounded, but still filled with the lust for battle. The others, unhurt, shouted insults at the carcanofex. It squeaked insults back: "Wicked greedy Gormoror! Stop murdering at me!"

Nethry saw a chance to double her gain from the battle, a gain which had nothing to do with money. She stood by the side of the brawl and shouted in Runderax's ear, "Let it go, Runderax!"

Runderax laughed. "Coward of a Rassimel! I shall do no such thing!"

Nethry flung her sword down, and peeled off her enchanted glove that was more dangerous than her sword. "Runderax, I challenge you to an honor-duel for the life of this person." She used a generous word for "person", a word which included many monsters as well as primes.

Runderax frowned at her. "Nethry, what are you saying? I'm far stronger than you. And you'll get a share for taking the horn to market."

Nethry drew a dagger: wooden, but edged with valuable copper. "Runderax, I challenge you for this: Take the rope off the carcanofex. As long as I stand against you, the carcanofex can run free. When I fall, you and your warriors can chase him again."

Runderax laughed. "Nethry, you are battle-mad!" That was not a bad thing among the Gormoror. "Very well." She turned to the carcanofex, and proclaimed, "This slip of a Rassimel is being your champion. We won't strike the first blow against you until I have defeated her. If you attack, though, we shall strike the second blow — and the last one!"

The carcanofex grunted, "Crazy murderous robber primes!" He looked at Nethry. "I, who am Tuku, accept your assistance!" The Gormoror took the rope off of him, and he leapt away into the air, hopping on the wind, passing intangibly through the trees.

Runderax looked after him. "Cursed coward of a monster. We can't chase him that way!" She scowled at Nethry. "Let's see what kind of a fight you can give us, now you've made us lose our prey *and* our prize." She put her battle-axe down, and drew a heavy bone dagger, more suitable for social combat.

Nethry smiled. "I'll leave you bloodier than the carcanofex would have!" She fought with all the skill that the best weapons-masters in Byronny had taught her. But weapons and war were in Runderax's blood, and the Gormoror was the stronger. After some minutes, Runderax, bleeding from a dozen wounds, slammed her blade through Nethry's heart for the third time. Nethry fell, unconscious and dying, just as she had planned.

* * *

Runderax kneeled by Nethry's side, panting. "Ddirmion, could you heal the Rassy? I'm too aching to do a good job of it."

Ddirmion nodded, casting an unsophisticated spell with moderate force. Nethry opened her eyes and sat up, alive again, her wounds barely closed. "Runderax, you *do* fight reasonably well after all. I challenge you to a rematch next year."

Runderax laughed, a Gormoror war-cry that echoed from line-hill to line-hill. "She wakes up and the first thing she does is challenge me again! Well done, city Rassy, you're almost as brave as a Gormoror." She threw her arms around Nethry, picking her up and whirling her around; when she set Nethry down, each was thoroughly smeared with the other's blood. "You don't fight half badly, either," she said, noticing how badly picking up the Rassimel hurt.

Nethry smiled, and slapped Runderax on the back as hard as she could, grinning to herself. The best way to win Gormoror friendship is on the battlefield, and the more pain the better. Nethry pressed her advantage, suggesting the second-best way herself. "Well then, I've got brandy in my backpack in your camp, but this wasn't a brandy sort of fight: I'll trade you brandy for mead."

Runderax laughed. "I'll drink with you, little Rassimel. I'll drink you to the ground!"

And she did, too. By the fourth horn of mead, Nethry couldn't have stood even if she hadn't been injured. Nethry thought about seducing one of them, as the third-best way to win Gormoror friendship, but she fell asleep before she made up her mind one way or another. It was no great matter: when she woke next morning, aching terribly along with everyone else, she and the War-Bannus were the best of friends — as far as the War-Bannus were concerned, at least. Which is what Nethry had been after all along.

* * *

Two days later, Nethry took the path to the carcanofex's home. She was alone, without a Gormoror to make her run, and carried a small linen bag where she had carried a leather noose last time. At the top of the hill, she called out, "Tuku? It is Nethry, the Rassimel who fought a Gormoror for you...."

The carcanofex popped his head out of a pile of logs. "Hello! I am called 'Tuku'! You know this already! I thank you very widely for that rescue! Those violence-lovers were for to kill me!"

Nethry nodded. "You're quite welcome, Tuku. I am Nethry. The Gormoror were eager for your blood, but they could be almost as satisfied by a good fight, so that's what I gave them."

Tuku asked, "Did you kill her?"

Nethry grinned. "Oh, not at all. I lost — she killed me. The Gormoror healed me, though."

"Healing, yes ... Do you have a healing spell, O Rassimel? They wounded me rather, and I'm not well yet."

Nethry nodded. "Oh, certainly." She was hardly an expert healer, but all Rassimel have somewhat of a gift at Healoc, and her employers had equipped her well. Tuku's remaining wounds vanished like water on a hot griddle.

"Well, then, you're a mighty helpful Rassimel, and a kind one to boot," said Tuku. "I don't know many primes personally, mind you, but I do have to wonder *why* it is you've been so kind to me?"

"I'm an explorer and gatherer, a trapper and adventurer," she said, leaving out one vital detail. "I prefer to travel alone, really."

"In the Lenwynt? This is wild land for primes! Even the Gormoror go about in bands or groups or packs!" said Tuku.

"Well, that they do. And that's why I was kind to you: in the hopes that you'll be kind to me if you ever notice that I need it. In case I get into a fight with one of your more vicious neighbors, like, perhaps you could rescue me ... or perhaps just give me a safe place to rest for a day or two if I need it."

Tuku nodded. "That's just a fair thing, Nethry! I'd be glad to."

She smiled. "And maybe one more thing...?"

Tuku curled his tailtip. "Now that sounds like a prime: there's always one more thing, but it's the hard one! You'll be wanting me to risk my life fighting the scyanturge in Soohoon with you, I know it!"

She laughed. "I'm not like that. I was wondering if I could leave a bag of glirries and puruulska pods with you for a week or two, so I don't have to carry it. It's not so heavy, but it *is* bulky and fragile. I'd hate to crush half my profits in my sleep!" She offered him the small linen bag.

He blinked, relieved. "Why, that's nothing at all! I've got a whole strong line-hill to hold up your bag of glirries! I bet they can hold up its weight!" He hid the bag in a hollow in the middle of an ancient arken trunk. "Nobody that wood's a solid for can get that, not without chopping the tree down. I'll get it right out when you go."

"Several gleaming thanks to you!", said Nethry. "Oh ... and, *is* there a scyanturge in Soohoon, or is that just a figure of speech?"

"Oh, there's a whole scyanturge, right there in Soohoon! I met her! She's named Aulihemm Bremm, she's got a thousand thorns around her, she's scary and devastating and terrible, and I won't be going to fight her at your side even if you save my life nineteen times!"

"I won't be challenging her either, Tuku." Nethry was fairly sure she was lying to Tuku, but that was a matter for later. "A friendly fight with a War-Bannu is enough death for one week. Where *is* Soohoon, though? It seems like an excellent place to stay away from and never visit."

"Oh, Soohoon is down at the bottom edge of the world-branch! It's just where it curves under and the Verticals become the Underneaths! It's in a great big gall, a bubble of bark for a wall! With a little hole for a door!"

"Dangerous upon dangerous. The Flats are bad enough, in the Lenwynt."

"And Gormoror make them every bit worse!" chirped Tuku.

She shared some candied fruit from Byronny with him, a treat that rarely got to the Lenwynt. They gathered thick starchy petals and nuts, and they caught an unwary wudgeon, and they had quite a pleasant lunch together, and they chatted about life in the Lenwynt. Nethry asked Tuku a few delicate questions about Aulihemm Bremm, but he knew less about it than she had learned from her other friends already. By midafternoon, when Nethry headed off towards Byronny, Tuku called her friend.

She grinned to herself, as she hiked along. She had picked up two useful contacts in the Lenwynt, in two very different social circles, at only the cost of a bit of blood and a bit of candied fruit. Neither had told her anything particularly useful or important, and perhaps neither one ever would. But one informant out of a dozen would, sometime, have something vital to tell her. So she made as many friends as she could, and she exploited them carefully. Most primes would think badly of her for that, but most primes did not know how much the information she gleaned protected them.

THE TAWLOWNS' WEDDING

The wedding was held in Dorly, on a gently-sloping hillside, on which horses and guntries had been forbidden to graze for several weeks for entirely practical reasons. The new triad was to be named "Tawlown", the next on the list of two hundred or so traditional Herethroy triad names in use in the area. The hillside commanded an excellent view of the goddess Virid in her manifestation as a spray of silvery leaves in the higher sky, if one looked up, and of the neighboring world-branch Dentheia and all its twigs, if one looked out and down. The sky was clear and the day was warm, which pleased the guests. But the sun was dim that day, and it dripped huge teardrops of blazing solar fuel off one side. A celebration that should have been bright was darkened with flickering shadows.

Most of the guests were Herethroy, from the villages being joined or their neighbors. Three hundred people strolled or sat, nibbled a dozen varieties of stuffed vegetables, or conversed in the fashion of farmers everywhere about weather and crops and spells for storing vegetables or evicting pests. Their chitin shone like matte emeralds and sapphires in the dismal sunlight, and those that could afford it showed off inlay-work of copper or yulexion or gold. Everyone wore their best, for they were wealthy by farmers' standards: tight-fitting silk embraced arms, legs, and the middle limbs that can serve as either. The co-lovers and some males wore confectionary painted leather hats rising between their many-jointed antennae, or short capes of painted lace, or tied glittering ribbons between each pair of knobs on their tails. The women dressed less flamboyantly but no less elegantly.

A wedding of the lower nobility must be conservative, so the trio getting married wore nothing but ribbons. Boragette Norrow's parents were glad of the custom; zie had recently developed the habit of stripping off whatever clothing they managed to get zir into, and clambering around on furniture or people, as naked as the day zie was hatched. Ribbons, at least, could be tied tightly enough that zie could not get them off. They pleased zir, rather to zir parents' surprise, and zie stayed quiet for most of the morning admiring zirself in a glass, and coercing everyone who came nearby to admire zir too. By the time of the actual event, though zie was overwhelmed by the crowd and the pomp, and stayed quietly by her father or sather. Despite being told many times, zie was too young to understand zie was one of the three people the occasion was ultimately about.

Casamint Imbarr found the ribbons entirely too much fun. He spent most of the morning trotting around waving his four arms and yelling, "I'm a Zi Ri! I'm a Zi Ri! I'm flying! I'm flying!". Several collisions with guests and one with a huge square wooden bowl of honey-wine earned him a collection of parental scowls which he did not notice. His sather, the Baron Teamary, gave up and levitated him around, which did nothing to calm him down but at least limited the damage he could cause.

Marjoram Rowns was old enough to understand, barely, that she was getting married. She had gotten the impression that her husband and mari would be her only playmates for the rest of her life. Since they were younger and of the weaker and thus less interesting sexes, she had found this displeasing enough to be worth an extended tantrum the day before. Her father Amberstripe disapproved of tantrums, and lectured her at length that this was her only chance to get married, and that she was lucky to have a chance at all. Her mother pointed out that the heirs of Great Barons rarely go unmarried, girls or not, but that it *was* her only chance. In the end, she was quieted down by the gift of a strength-spell, and stayed up late the night before the wedding grafting it onto herself so she could cast it. She was quiet and full of yawning on her wedding day, which displeased Amberstripe less than tantrums.

The ceremony proper was to take place at noon. Count Fressis Farwinn himself delayed it by a third of an hour. He had lost his notes, and was only barely starting to learn the duties that came with his quite fresh title.. He was a Rassimel, not a Herethroy, and as one of the few mammals at the event felt somewhat out of place. For one thing, he was head and antennae shorter than everyone else, and rather less elegant of movement, though among Rassimel he was considered tall and graceful.

After some frantic scrabbling through luggage and gifts and other peoples' coats, his wife Narina discovered them under a pillow in their coach. She brushed his fur until the mask around his eyes looked almost symmetrical and the rings on his tail were actually ring-shaped, straightened his waistcoat, extracted a stray hen's feather from one of his earrings, kissed his muzzle, and sent him off to perform the wedding.

By this time, the guests and celebrants were practicing patience. The guests, being farmers, were quite good at it. The bethrothed, being children, were not so good. Count Fressis strode with all available dignity to the triangle of candles, their light greatly amplified by a local pyromancer for a daytime ceremony. Casamint's flailing tail hit Boragette in the face. Boragette immediately started crying. Marjoram, with a very responsible expression on her face, cast her strength spell and whacked Casamint's shoulder with a candlestick hard enough to be heard in the back row of guests. Casamint burst into tears and ran out of the triangle to hide behind Teamary. Boragette scolded zir fiancée-cum-defender soundly, if incoherently, for behaving badly. Marjoram grunted and stomped off. Casamint tugged a storybook out of his sather's bag, and insisted on being read to. Count Fressis stood alone in the triangle, doing his very best to look in command of the situation.

After another third of an hour and a great deal of effort by parents, the affianced were all calm enough at the same time to have some hope of remembering their parts, and the ceremony could proceed. It still wasn't entirely peaceful or proper — while they walked around the triangle on the trail of grain, Marjoram squeezed Casamint's hand hard enough for him to yelp and flee for his storybook again — but with some effort and some generosity of interpretation, all the parts were performed and the wedding was made proper and perpetual in the sight of the laws of Pennypell, the customs of all of Araldy, and the opinions of relatives and neighbors.

The children themselves knew nothing about the matter.

* * *

After the ceremony, the newlywed Tawlowns were officially consummating their marriage. For children, this involved nothing more intimate than taking much-needed afternoon naps at the same time in different rooms, which was, by a polite fiction, considered entirely sufficient. Their parents discussed what to do with them next. As a courtesy, they invited Count Fressis to the discussion, on another polite fiction that the future of three of his barons-to-be would be any concern of his.

Baron Seven-spikes Norrow started the negotiations in the way that tradition required, despite vehemently disagreeing with it. "I should think all three of them would be best off living here, in Dorly. They must learn to live as a triad, and grow up to be proper Herethroy and all, and Dorly is as good as anywhere for that and better than most." The other barons said their own versions of the same thing, recommending their own home instead of Dorly.

Seven-spikes calmly said, "Upon further consideration, I must disagree with all of you, and with myself as well. My own marriage — forgive me, Wisteria and Arkenta — has been somewhat flawed, in ways which various scholars say are typical of marriages where the triad grows up together. If you are a child with your wife and mari, it is hard to see them as ... if I may be permitted a rudeity and a vulgarity ... your consorts. They seem too much like your siblings. So I say that our children ... the Tawlowns, I should call them now ... should not live in the same place for some years." He held up a well-thumbed copy of a popular book on childrearing for the upper classes.

Fressis sighed, and tugged his black-furred ears. "Why did you marry them at all, so young? I had a three-year engagement and didn't have the actual wedding until I was, to be quite vulgar about it, quite interested in other Rassimel. I can't imagine getting married any younger. And nobody thought the worse of me for it: it was quite a suitable match, not like a commoner's love-match. And Narina and I were old enough to be civil to each other. Those poor babies are going to be miserable together, unless they're terribly lucky."

Amberstripe looked to the count, and said quite blandly, "It is the traditional thing to do."

Fressis flicked his tailtip. "Well, the other marriage I performed was between young adolescents, age twenty or so. And yes, they were Herethroy, and yes, one of them was a baron's heir or I wouldn't have been invited to do the ceremony. It may be traditional but it's hardly required."

His wife tapped him on the shoulder. "Fressis? I do think you should come try some of these spinach and pea pies. They're quite good."

"Narina, forbear, if you please. I realize that I am quite concerned about this."

"Not as concerned as you should be about the spinach and pea pie, Fressis," said Narina. She took his hand and led him away from the barons.

When he was safely by the buffet table, pie-plate in hand, he curled his tailtip. "What was I doing wrong there, Narina?"

"Oh, recommending that they not do something they have already done, and something that's entirely their concern, for one thing. But I think that they've their own reason to marry their children so young. They can all call themselves 'Great Baron' now, because their heirs collectively hold four villages, and their grand-heir will actually *be* a Great Baron."

"The Rowns are already Great Barons: they have Comblefree and Corster. And 'Great Baron' isn't worth *that* much more than Baron, is it?"

"The Rowns must be delighted to have two sets of new and reasonably well-off relatives. They lost a good deal of money on making silk, or, more accurately, not making silk. And the difference between 'Great Baron' and just-plain-Baron may be slight to a Rassimel who's been calling himself 'Count' since the actual Count first taught him to talk, but I daresay it means a great deal to them. Teamary had her recent court-case delayed for a week, when Great Baron Moliante invoked precedence."

"You would understand such things quite well!" Narina had been a commoner, the daughter of the glassmakers' guild of Pennypell, before her engagement to Fressis.

She nodded. "I'm afraid I do. Now, if you want to justify your title for the day, you could defend the village from some ravening monster from the Verticals — what's that? no? none are currently ravening? Then I'm afraid you must indulge the other guests in small talk about, oh, the goddess Lenhirrik having just turned herself to wood, or the latest border dispute between Byronny and Drysselwyn on the other side of the Lenwynt, or something else outside of their immediate farmerly concerns."

He looked across the field at Teamary, still discussing the rearing of married children. "That Herethroy's immediate farmerly concerns got her an advanced degree in theoretical opera at the Pennypell Academy. I'm not sure I could keep up with her."

"Well, there are three hundred other guests with whom you *must absolutely* talk with first," said Narina. Fressis sighed, fortified himself with a large bowl of grated radishes in honey and cream, and got started. It was several hours' hard labor, with many desserts. When it was over he was glad to leave Dorly, and the entire countryside, until the next marriage or funeral of a noble.

In the end, the three families agreed to try the most radical of the scholars' advice, and let the newlyweds grow up to adulthood, thirty years of nine months each, before starting their marriage. It was the approach with the fewest miserable case studies — since it was the newest, and the fewest people had tried it.

And for decades, they had nothing more to do with one another.

OOSTMARINE'S FUNERAL

> *To the family of Oostmarine, formerly named Shark-of-Swords and before that Darjie, on the bank of Pesengue Pond near the old wall in Lowmont, miserable news. Oostmarine was slain beyond the power of our magic to heal by the nycathath reaver Bherva-Charion, though by his deeds Bherva-Charion was himself slain. We shall bring you his body and his personal effects in a day or two shortly following this letter.*
>
> *In shared sorrow, Rajel, which is to say the pro-Baroness Marjoram Rowns Imbarr Tawlown, and Arrhwy, a Sleeth.*

Oostmarine's family and relatives were as completely gathered as a group of Orren could be on short notice. His three wives, wearing the blue-grey ribbons and dark veils of the traditional mourning costume, sat with his corpse. They held his cold hands, retelling in bitter whispers the complicated story of their marriage, with its pursuits and its breakups, its half-dozen other Orren who had gotten involved with one or another of them, and its final fatal compromise that he take one month a year to go adventuring.

Arrhwy, with a traditional Sleeth's disdain for social matters no matter how important, had found the only large puddle of sunlight in the room, and claimed it for her own. The sun had just rolled out from behind the main trunk, a bit roll'gainst of trunkward, so Arrhwy's puddle was splashed across the top of a low wall in front of the door to the kitchen. Arrhwy took up most of the wall, her hind legs straddling it, her head resting on her forepaws. Her half-lidded eyes lazily followed the waiters as they brought out chalices of cold, over-brewed tea, but her ears swivelled this way and that to follow the conversation. She was probably the only person in the room who could hear Oostmarine's wives talk.

Rajel not only had some idea what etiquette was, but felt obliged to use it. She sat at a table with half a dozen Orren. Her blue-grey chitin was remarkable in a room full of ottery brown fur, but it matched the mourning ribbons well. On an ordinary day, the Orren would wear clothes with too many bright colors, but for the funeral they wore their oldest and dingiest, and sloshed them in pond-muck for additional somberness.

"Did he die well, my son Oostmarine?" Tavernat, Oostmarine's father and the organizer of the funeral, sat on Rajel's left and asked questions in a loud voice, so that everyone might hear and remember.

He had asked her that before, in private, and she chose her words carefully this time. "He did, to be sure. The nycathath Bherva-Charion raided Pangrelliton village and stole farming-charms and an ancient lead statue beyond price. The bestiaries say that six skilled warriors, or even eight, are required against a nycathath. Oostmarine persuaded the Baron of Pangrelliton that the three of us alone could recover their lostments, and he, I, and Arrhwy pursued him into the Lenwynt.

"Oostmarine devised a subtle plan, whereby the three of us could sting Bherva and weaken him. We would fight in an ancient forest, where the trees would foul his wings and he could not fly. We would alarm him with dangers. A nycathath can do much more with one cley than any prime can, but they have very few cley. We prepared several surprises ..." She looked around the table, to see an assortment of distresses on the Orren faces. Evidently nobody else in Oostmarine's family was an adventurer. "... but I shall not bore you further. It was a very good plan. It would have to be, to persuade Arrhwy and myself to fight a nycathath with only three of us." She did not mention that Oostmarine's share of the planning was the smallest of the three, nor that Oostmarine's indiscretions had left him easily blackmailed by the Baron of Pangrelliton. Such details were better off dead with him.

"And it nearly worked. Arrhwy lured him to our trap, where Oostmarine and I waited, invisible, and an ancient rotten tree waited, quite visible. And, when Oostmarine's spell had tumbled the tree on Bherva-Charion, and Bherva was dazed for a moment, Oostmarine's great bravery and ferocity as a warrior went to his head, and he leapt over the tree and struck the nycathath a terrible clout..." She decided not to mention the details; the funeral-goers did not seem to be the sort who delighted in hearing of entrails spilling out. Nor did she mention that the plan called for Oostmarine to hide as their potent but sluggish spells took effect upon him. If he had waited, he probably would not have died.

"In any case, it was a vicious and a terrible battle. We had not intended to fight to the death, just to retrieve the goods of Pangrelliton, but Bherva left us no choice." Bherva had killed Oostmarine, and then killed him thrice more after Oostmarine's protective talismans restored him to life; but the last of those exhausted those talismans, and that death was final. This was the same treatment as is given to the worst traitors and doorwayers. Arrhwy and Rajel were in no mood to spare Bherva, though at the end the nycathath pleaded to be allowed to surrender.

"In the end, I would like to remember Oostmarine as a great hero, as clever as any Orren, but as brave as any Gormoror and as fierce as any Sleeth." Arrhwy, on the wall, flicked her tailtip at that phrase. "I know several of you tried to turn him aside from the adventurer's profession, but he chose to stay in it, and he was one of the great ones." That was entirely exaggeration, such as is acceptable at funerals. Oostmarine had been reasonably good, though Rajel and a hundred others in the region were just as good, and Arrhwy for one was undeniably better.

The Orren nodded, and Tavernat gestured for Rajel to sit. Oostmarine's mother stood up next, and told her own stories of Oostmarine's childhood. From the sound of it, he had been an adventurer from the day he was born, which had been, impetuously, rather earlier and rather more dramatic than the midwife had intended. "And it wasn't enough that he went and came out in the middle of a field, but then he goes and squirms into the cookfire when he's only two hours old." Probably her stories were no more accurate than Rajel's, of course.

The waiters brought out the main course. The food itself was fine enough: grilled blackscale eels stuffed with parsley and butter, thin slices of raw zabouf and steamed occarfish, a salad of pondweed and crisp slices of fruit dressed with wine older than Oostmarine. The presentation was suitable for a funeral. The plates were crude slices of tree-trunks, not the polished and lacquered square wooden platters that the restaurant usually used. The food appeared to be thrown on the plates in rage and despair — except, of course, it was thrown in exactly the same way on every plate.

Rajel nibbled on the salad; Herethroy cannot digest meat. The Orren man on her right poked his eel morosely once or twice with a fingertip, and scowled at it. "Not to your taste, either?" she asked him.

"Not that, but I don't much feel like eating just now. I've never really enjoyed funerals, truth to tell," he said.

"Not many people do, I should think," she said. They talked briefly about Oostmarine. He was Oostmarine's uncle, and had taught Oostmarine swordplay as a child, and he was more than a little distressed that Oostmarine died with a sword in his hand.

"It's a bitter business, adventuring, isn't it? I read in the broadsheet about Vaxsedhonie Varnouv, a mighty wizard from Lowmont, getting herself killed and a Glory of Flokin lost in the depths of the Lenwynt. Just last week, too. Horrible week for adventuring there, it was."

"I found it so," she said. A bitter silence followed.

To fill the silence, he asked her, "And what of yourself, O most fierce of Herethroy? Do you have any spouses waiting for you somewhere, or dreading a terrible letter about you?"

"Why, I suppose I have," she answered. "Not that they're waiting for me, nor dreading a letter. I daresay they've mostly forgotten about me."

"Ah, you're a second wife, then, and lucky to be married at all? I must say that I am glad to be of a species with equal numbers of the sexes — and only two sexes at that. Such marriages as we have, we have for love and not for arithmetic," he said. Rajel let his rudeness pass; it was a funeral, after all.

"No, I'm a first wife. Only, it was a child marriage — for reasons of titles and nobility — and I haven't seen my husband or mari since then," she said.

"Ah, so they're not sitting at home waiting for you."

"I suspect not. I suppose they might be pining away for me — I truly have *no* idea what they've done since the wedding — but if they are, they've been singularly reluctant to write me letters or send me news," she said.

"Are they far distant from you, then?"

"They're from a farming village off by Pennypell, and, oh, a long day's walk or a very very long day's walk from where I grew up," she answered.

"They should have visited you, then!", he exclaimed, suddenly indignant on her behalf. He seemed glad of a chance to legitimately show some emotion other than sorrow.

"Well, I scarcely visited *them*, either." she said.

"Well, they should be the ones coming to you, shouldn't they? You *must* be the pro-baron," he declared. He started to stab a bit of eel and parsley with an ivory skewer to eat.

"I must, must I? And why is that?"

"You're the woman, which is the most plentiful sort of Herethroy. Why would they choose *you* as a child if not for you having a title?"

"I wasn't *that* horrible as a child. But, yes, I'm a pro-baron. All three of us are, though, so there's nobody that the others should come to." she said.

"Ah, a trio of barons. What towns?" he asked.

"Corster and Comblefree, for me. Dorly for Boragette — she's my mari — and Yazelton for Casamint," she said.

"Hah, I'm right after all. You're a pro-Great Baron. Or a Great pro-Baron, is it? I'm not really used to nobility myself."

"Pro-Great Baron. And we're all very petty nobility: we own the land, but we're not very important and not very rich."

"Well, I must say that I *am* glad that Oostmarine had gotten up there in society, going off and killing terrible ravaging monsters alongside a great-pro-great-baron and all!" Rajel glanced over at their partner, who had intimidated the waiters into giving her two dinners. She was happily levitating bits of fish to nibble on and apparently ignoring the entire funeral. Adventuring alongside a Sleeth would probably negate any cachet that adventuring alongside a pro-Great Baron would bring, but Arrhwy could be ignored at the funeral as easily as she could ignore it.

"Oh, I'm hardly the most important or notable person who knew Oostmarine ... or who depended on him, for that matter. We did a thing or two for Ilzatheinen, quite an important wizard in Lenkasia, and we rescued some children in the household of the Count of Pirriauthe, also in Lenkasia." Lenkasia was Lowmont's neighbor, and the most honored city on the branch.

"If I were a count, I'd keep careful track of my children! For that matter, I'm a carpenter, and I *do* keep careful track of my children! Or I did, but they're all grown now," he exclaimed, and inquisitorially skewered a slice of occarfish.

"Actually they weren't the count's children, they were the count's head-chef's children. In any case, the count personally thanked us and had us as guests for nearly a week." Rajel suspected that Oostmarine got even more familiar with the count than she or Arrhwy had done, but that story, and a half-dozen stories like it, was best not said at his funeral.

The conversation continued to wander around for an hour or two, with the Orren periodically getting excited enough to eat, but always returning to Oostmarine and suitably bowdlerized versions of his stories. The waiters took the plates, and replaced them with bowls of intense bittersweet tea ices, and then with first-rate fish balls and arcs of onion grilled on the ugliest skewers that could be purchased anywhere in Lowmont.

Then Tavernat produced a terrible thunderclap — from a bound spell; he was not nearly good enough at magic to do it himself — and everyone gathered around Oostmarine's corpse to say their final farewells. Oostmarine (which is to say, his wives) formally thanked them with generous gifts of his more treasured possessions. Rajel was given a leather glove with a respectable enchantment of flight. Arrhwy was given one of the healing talismans that had tried but failed to save Oostmarine.

* * *

After the funeral was formally over, Rajel went home with Oostmarine's family, to give such comfort as she could, and get some comfort herself. There was not much to be given or taken. Oostmarine's wives dwelled for a long while on the unanswerable, unendurable question, "Wasn't there anything you could have done to save him?"

Oostmarine's uncle finally rescued Rajel from them. His price was high: she had to babysit three distressed Orren toddlers for two hours. Despite having more hands than there were toddlers, she found it no easy feat.

Arrhwy, of course, felt no social obligations, and slipped off for most of the day. Her oldest son Lyonder lived in the forests around Lowmont; the two of them shared stories for a full hour before she got up in the middle of an old joke and wandered off. Her son shrugged, and went to sleep; the visit had been long and friendly by Sleeth standards. Arrhwy tracked down one of her son's Sleeth neighbors, propositioned him demandingly, and coupled with him in an ear-aching serenade. She spent less time with him than she had with her son, and left him licking blood off four long shallow cuts on his flank. Sleeth are not kind to their lovers.

In the evening, they met back at their hotel. The Cantilevered Cabbage looked nice enough from the outside, and charged accordingly, but the rooms were shabby and the straw in the mattress hadn't been changed in far too long. Rajel sat heavily on the old mattress, more exhausted after the funeral than she had been after the fight that made it necessary.

Arrhwy shrugged, an elaborate shrug from her ears to her tail tip that conveyed leagues of unconcern. "If it bothers you enough, go poke the night clerk with your sword until she comes up here and changes it. It does not bother me, for I was not going to sleep in the bed in any case."

Rajel thought a minute. "Not worth the fussing. I'd rather get to sleep sooner."

Arrhwy sat, lifting a hind leg awkwardly so that she could lick herself clean. She winced as she did. "He claws me, and I do not even notice. I am getting old and careless, Rajel."

"Lyonder clawed you?", Rajel asked.

"No, no. I do not ask the name of the tom-Sleeth who claws me. I just ask for the better thing that tom-Sleeth are good for, rrai! But afterwards I have cuts on my rump."

"Well, didn't you claw him?"

Arrhwy peered oddly at her partner. "Why is this a question to be asked?"

"It *would* be fair of him to claw you, if you clawed him," said Rajel.

"Hah, wife bug! This is the foundation principle of your marriage, no?"

"Hmph. What do you know about my marriage?"

"Until you mention it to the uncle Orren this morning, I do not know that you are married at all! Never do you say this to your very helpful and friendly Sleeth!" laughed Arrhwy.

"Well, you never asked much about my life. And besides, I barely remember it myself." muttered Rajel.

"Perhaps also you are the God of Fire and do not tell me that?" said Arrhwy, her ears pricked up.

Rajel waved her antennae. "I think that's Flokin's job. The upper ranks of the lower greater nobility are as close as I get to godhood, and that's none too close no matter what some of them say. My title and my three-hander can kill a brace of rongon. Without the title I can only kill a pair."

"So, if on our next fight you die, what am I telling your family? Also how am I finding your family?"

"I haven't any idea of what to say to them. And you'd go to my parents' village. You *do* know where that is, don't you?" said Rajel.

"Comblefree, near Pennypell. This much I know, for this much you tell me early on. But these are your parents. These are not the people who leave scratch marks on your rump." said Arrhwy.

"Nobody leaves *scratch marks* on my rump. Scratching through my chitin would be rather excessive, even by Sleeth standards. Not that I'd couple with a Sleeth," said Rajel.

"You should try! I am available every few weeks. For you I make the special bonus offer: I wear leather paw-shoes so I remember not to scratch you afterwards," said Arrhwy.

Rajel tossed a handful of stale straw at her partner, who swatted it out of the air and ripped at it with her teeth. "Arrhwy, you *know* I'm decent and cisaffectionate."

"OK, I do not ask you any more. Until the next time I am on heat of course. Between now and then, what do we do?"

"Sleep," said Rajel.

"I am an expert at sleeping ... " said Arrhwy

"You certainly are. You slept through the entire funeral," said Rajel. This was unjust: Arrhwy had slept through less than half of it.

"... but even I do not sleep for weeks or months! I am the old Sleeth, I do not have so long to live any-the-more, I do not wish to sleep all so long!"

"Well, perhaps we could go back to Comblefree and let me try to track my mari and husband down? I'd rather like to meet them before some awful monster kills me. I can't imagine that they'd be as sad as Oostmarine's wives, but it might be nice if they at least *noticed*," said Rajel.

"Now you must sleep! You are being very the morbid insect, Rajel."

"I *have* been at the funeral of a good friend and companion all day. This leaves me more more morbid than, say, slinking away early on and finding fornications," said Rajel.

"Hah, you are jealous!"

"Hah, I am envious. You found yourself a nice same-species person. I should go find myself a nice same-species person. Or two." said Rajel.

"Ah, so we go back to Comblefree to set about gratifying your enormous yet finicky lust!"

"To at least **meet** my spouses," said Rajel.

"Hrarhu, to meet them and considerably more. They are cheaper than your usual lover, because you are married to them. Other options are cheaper still, of course," said Arrhwy.

"It's not *just* for the fornication. I'd like to have a chance to actually *be* back home and married and all, like a reasonable Herethroy, before I get killed like Oostmarine. Now go to sleep, will you?"

"Rrai, I am already asleep!" The Sleeth sprawled out on the floor by the fireplace, her tail thumping dust from the threadbare brocade cushion of the archaic armchair.

LETTERS FROM RAJEL

There was no Postal Guild hall in Dorly, of course. Once a week or so, when there was some other reason to go to the city, one of the villagers would stop at the post office in Pennypell. This week it was Chicory's turn to do that errand, and half a dozen others for Baron Seven-spikes Norrow and the village as a whole.

"Oh, frumbles," said Chicory. "It's time to plant the hosh. If I don't help out, it'll take everyone else twice as long."

"You are an excellent farmer, Chicory, but I doubt me that you're the equal of *ninety* others," said Boragette. "The equal of five or six, anyone in Dorly must agree with, but I doubt that even your most devoted admirer would say you were the equal of much more than a dozen." Zie curled one antenna coyly, in case there was any doubt who that admirer might be.

"It's still not right!"

"Well, it's my turn to run the kitchen, but I think I can switch days with my mother. I'll come with you! We haven't been alone together nearly enough," said Boragette.

"Now *that* is worth missing the plowing for!"

Wisteria, Boragette's mother, had hardly missed how Chicory and Boragette looked at each other, but zie trusted zir coun's propriety to a substantial degree. In any case, with only two of the sexes around, the worst improprieties were unavailable.

Chicory and Boragette walked to Pennypell on four legs, holding upper hands. They were the picture of two-thirds of a Herethroy triad. Boragette was pretty, nearly six feet tall, with rose-colored chitin and delicate spikes at the edges of zir face and wrists, and transparent spots on zir antennae that caught the sunlight. Chicory was rugged, with a heavy mottled chitin that looked like bark; she was a full foot taller than Boragette, and bulky where Boragette was slender.

The first few errands were easy enough, and there was even some point to having Boragette along. Boragette helped Chicory avoid buying low-grade jersany for the price of high-grade in the market, and chatted about weather and walking-trails with the elderly Lord Moliante at his townhouse while Chicory delivered three large jars of pren marmalade.

After a lunch of grilled onions and fennel buns, the couple strolled to the Postal Guild. Chicory peeked into the courtyard, where the enchanted mirizcatlin tree hung with round flat leaves waiting to be written on; but she knew few people outside of Dorly, and had never had occasion to write a letter herself.

Boragette had visited the Postal Guild many times before, and knew the customs. Zie strolled to a Cani clerk selling paints and brushes to those who needed to write letters. "Hallo! I'm from Dorly, here to see if we've any mail." Zie handed him a scarf-full of fresh prens.

The Cani spilled the fruit into a basket behind the counter, mingling it with several other villages' produce. "O Herethroy of Dorly, this week it pleases me to earn your bribe three times over. There's something about prices of leeks and garlic, something about a Boragette's wife surviving, and something about your Baron's creditor agreeing to more generous terms." Dorly's gifts of fruit were not nearly large enough to keep bored guild members from reading their mail.

While the Cani was getting the actual letters, Chicory peered at Boragette, antennae flattened nervously. "What's this about your wife? I had hoped she'd ignore you forever."

Boragette shrugged. "I haven't any idea. This is the first time she's tried to say a word to me, I think." Zie squeezed Chicory's lower hand. "I can't imagine that it will be anything for *us* to worry about. I imagine she just, oh, got stepped on by a horse or something, and thinks I might have heard the news."

"You're Boragette? Then this is for you." The Cani handed zir a mirizcatlin leaf. Several days ago, it had grown on a tree in a similar hall in Lowmont, but now it was covered with large, sloppy painted words. Boragette read out loud:

To Boragette, greetings. I am returning from some moderately dangerous circumstances, and I do think it is time that, as we are married, we behave accordingly. I request that you come to Comblefree as soon as is convenient. Your wife, Rajel (Marjoram).

Chicory winced. "Frumbles and fuming frumbles! I don't like that a bit! What will you do, Boragette?"

"The first thing you must do is accept my apologies," said the Cani. "If I had known it was such a bitter matter, I would have been more gentle with it!"

Boragette put on zir bravest voice. "The second thing we must do is leave the Postal Guild, and go on to the Bank of Teleporting Hexagons, and finish my father's errands, Chicory. After that ... I have to think." Chicory nodded, slipped her arm around the juncture of Boragette's thorax and abdomen, and stayed close to zir as they finished up their town's business in the city.

The sun's flame dwindled and flickered towards sunout as they walked back to Dorly, and they had no errands to distract them. "What right does this Marjoram or Rajel or whatever-she-is have to drag you away from home like a mule dragging a goose, Boragette?"

Boragette did zir best to stay calm. "Well, she's the oldest of us, so I suppose she could take the lead because of that. She's the woman of us. Since women only marry once, they're supposed to look out for the one triangle they're in. And she's the highest-titled of us, with two villages. Those have to count for something, I should think."

"What are you going to do?"

Boragette shrugged helplessly. "I can't see all that many choices. Go to Comblefree and see what she wants, I imagine. What else could I do? I traded days with my mother, but I don't think I can trade *wives* with anyone."

"You could marry twice, Boragette."

Boragette squeezed zir lover's hand. "Eventually. Once my first marriage is all working properly, I'll ask for it. We'll need to find a man, too."

"Oh, I know where to find one. You're married to him! What could be easier?"

Boragette squeezed again, a bit desperately. "I haven't met Casamint since the wedding, Chicory. He might not like the idea."

"Aw, I'm sure it'll be easy."

"I wish I were that sure, Chicory. There are a lot of people who'd have to agree before I could marry you. I know my marriage was designed to make us higher-ranked nobles ... and you don't have a title at all."

"If I marry you I'll have a title," said Chicory. "But that's not why I want to!"

"I know it's not... but that title doesn't count. Anyone would, who married me."

"Oh. Right." said Chicory, her antennae drooping.

Boragette touched zir girlfriend's mid-arm. "I have no idea whether they'll be helpful or antagonistic, whether they'll want me to stay aristocratically single-married or let me double-marry ... whether they'll care if I have a girlfriend outside of marriage, for that matter. Maybe they each have their own true lovers, and the three of us can get together once a year in Comblefree for a picnic or some such, and I can be with you the rest of the time."

"I don't think so. Sounded to me like she was she calling you to her bed the way I call a guntry ewe over. To the ram, to get tupped and preggy as soon as possible."

"Chicory! That's a horrible thing to say!"

"Well, it's a horrible thing to do, too."

* * *

The performance of Tiraad's *Anscoletto Wriggling on the Hook* closed with a fierce if haphazard fandango of all five dancers, while their singers sang old love-songs to the tunes of traditional dirges. The musicians stood up on their balcony, thereby breaking the invisibility spell that had kept them hidden throughout the opera. The stage crew strolled out and picked up furniture, sets, and the occasional performer: it was not what a formal opera house would have done, but it was a tradition for Pennypell Academy's drama students.

Casamint and Skirret held middle hands, ostensibly to stay together in the crush of the audience leaving the theatre. Skirret snagged Wilsamander's hand as well, towing the Rassimel towards the door.

"I think it started to make a bit of sense this time," said Casamint. Pennypell's operatic tradition involved concealing the true plot of an opera in layers of obtuse symbols and lapidary riddles.

"You're ahead of me, then," said Wilsamander. "I don't think I *ever* would say that an opera made sense 'til at least the third time I saw it."

"Well, the bit isn't very big. But, well, I'm pretty sure that Anscoletto died in the middle of the second act, when all those red things showed up," said Casamint.

"I'm pretty sure Tiraad was using Pelshquentine symbolism, so he'd show a red ribbon to indicate death," said Skirret. "And there was a flurry and a half of red things. A red teapot, a red sword, a red cardboard horse, a red cardboard snake, a red candle, and any number of other things. Nothing like a ribbon. As if Tiraad was taunting us with suggestions of death, but not actually killing him off."

"One doesn't ordinarily need to be a student of natural philosophy to try to decipher operas... indeed, this is the first time it's helped me a bit," said Casamint. "But the red snake was a specific kind of snake, being very thin and marked with two long light-red stripes down each side of its back." He grinned at Skirret, and let her fill in the puzzle

"There wouldn't happen to be a kind of snake called a ribbon snake, would there?" she asked, antennae curled outward in a grin.

"There would indeed. A little and unimportant sort of beast, but definitively wearing the word 'ribbon' in its name."

Skirret laughed, and hugged him with her left-side arms.

"Oh, Tiraad is trying to be a bit too clever with that one," said Wilsamander. "I think we should shower him with overripe carrots tonight. Or whatever means 'too clever' in Pelshquentine symbolism, at least." The composer was a student and somewhat of a friend of theirs, and they knew where he was likely to celebrate that night.

"It's not *too* clever if someone can figure it out the second time through. Even if the someone is Casamint," said Skirret.

"Oh, Casamint's not the smartest student in the academy. Probably not even the tenth-smartest. He's clever enough, but misses things right in front of his nose," said Wilsamander.

"I see things right in front of your muzzle though, 'Mander!" said Casamint. He held a hand in front of Wilsamander's face and created a head of cabbage in it.

"Don't you have *anything* better to do with your cley, Casamint?" asked Wilsamander querulously.

"I'm sure he and I can think of *something* to do with it," said Skirret lasciviously.

"Herethroy use cabbage for body-play?" asked Wilsamander. "Never mind. I think I would prefer to leave such matters for the natural philosophers and the pornographers. If, indeed, there is a difference."

"The difference is small but significant," said Casamint, "though I, too, wonder what Skirret might have in mind. She rarely if ever so much as offers to use vegetables on me. Triremes and other warships are a more common choice! She is very feminine, and not likely to be found in a kitchen."

Skirret cut the cabbage in thirds with her pen-knife. "Well, just as a bit of a snack for the person with the right sort of genitalia, is the tedious truth. The other one will have to find someone of his own species, I suppose."

She handed one to Casamint, who smirked, another to Wilsamander, who scowled, and kept the third for herself.

"I haven't achieved body-play with anyone in quite some time," complained Wilsamander. "And that was a very drunk and very adventurous Thalassa."

"Thalassa, the Orren girl with the necklace of white spots, and, by reputation, the scheme to try out every mammalian male in the Academy?" asked Skirret.

"Well, yes. The very one. It was a very drunk and very adventurous 'Mander, too", said Wilsamander.

"I suppose that cross-species encounters don't matter quite so much when both species are mammals," said Casamint. "I am glad this Thalassa restricts her predations, or I should dread winding up in a mammal's bed!"

"Oh, don't be so provincial, Casamint," said Skirret. "I'm sure that mammals can be almost as romantic as Herethroy."

"Hah! Two-thirds as romantic at most, for they lack one sex — and very appealing one, at that. Perhaps I am provincial, but I must say that the thought of a Herethroy tripling or even coupling with a mammal is *rather* disgusting," said Casamint.

"So I can't entice you into inviting 'Mander to sharing our pleasures some evening, Casamint?" said Skirret, her antennae curved wickedly.

"Only if I am so drunk that I cannot tell him from a co-lover!"

"Never fear! By the time you were that drunk, you would be unable to do anything of note, or to remember your failure! Also, *I* would be even more drunk, or I would be far, far away," said Wilsamander.

"Oh, enough of this," said Skirret. "Casamint is still from Yazelton, and he may be from Yazelton for years to come."

"Aren't you from Yazelton too, Skirret?" asked Wilsamander.

"Yes, but I am *far* more urban and urbane than Casamint," said Skirret.

"Perhaps so! In any event, your allowance is twice mine, for all that my mother is the Baron of Yazelton and yours is a simple cheesemaker." said Casamint.

"Simple cheesemaker, hah! Our family cheeses are complex and subtle — as proved by the prices that are paid for them in the Transwynt."

"True, true. This extra income grants you many urban pleasures which I require to wash the remaining bits of farm-soil off my spirit!"

"Are you begging for another evening's entertainment with me? At my expense?" asked Skirret.

"I should hope for more than just one!"

"I shall consider it! Fortunately you are a tolerably pretty bug, and a tolerably clever one, or I should dismiss your request out of hand," said Skirret.

Wilsamander stomped ahead, the leather wings on his shoes flapping against the boardwalk. "I have heard you two say that dialog every two days for the last three months. At least be original, if you are going to desecrate my innocent — which is to say 'lonely and loveless' — ears with such tedious and workaday romantic spittle."

Skirret and Casamint looked at each other. "Do you happen to remember the Pelshquentine symbol for a once-married Herethroy man finding a Herethroy woman appealing, Skirret?" asked Casamint.

If the Pelshquentine school had any such symbol, Skirret certainly didn't know it. She invented a convenient one on the spot: "A broken ink-block in a wooden box, naturally."

"Ah! How fortuitous that you broke my ink-block earlier today!" said Casamint, and displayed it in all four hands, in the manner of an opera dancer. Behind him, Wilsamander started singing the song of the evil wizard from *Anscoletto Wriggling on the Hook*: a sprightly jig melody with words portending terrible wickedness. All three of them laughed, and went to a favorite cafe for further pleasures.

* * *

Casamint scowled at a pair of letters, each of which displeased him more than the other.

> *To Casamint, greetings. I am returning from some moderately dangerous circumstances, and I do think it is time that, as we are married, we behave accordingly. I request that you come to Comblefree as soon as is convenient. Your wife, Rajel (Marjoram).*

and

> *Dear Mhebb and Casamint. I am tired of working one hour or two hours after noon. You hired me for two mornings a week. Mornings end at noontime. You are paying me for two mornings a week. You are not paying me for one hour or two hours after noontime. Even when I ask. I will not work for you any more. — Gremmet*

Skirret and Wilsamander jumped when Casamint slammed his books on their table, scattering papers and thin strips of wood. "Casamint, what's been tugging your antennae today?" asked Skirret, getting up to embrace the other Herethroy fondly.

"I should never, never have shared an apartment with an Orren. Better no roommate and no servant than a roommate and a servant — or, 'til we find another one, than a roommate and no servant."

"Gremmet gave notice, then? He didn't seem the most fond of you two," said Wilsamander, fidgeting with his ringed tail.

"Gremmet gave no notice when he quit. Mhebb gave no notice when she slapped me with a dead fish. Marjoram gave no notice when she summoned me. Nobody notices me these days *except* to give me no notice."

"Who would Marjoram be?", asked Skirret. "The only Marjoram I know is four years old, and if you're at *her* beck and call, you're less of a Baron than I thought."

"My wife Marjoram is the Marjoram it would be. She's not from home. She's Marjoram Rowns Imbarr Tawlown. She signed her name Rajel though."

"I had almost forgotten that you are a married man, Casamint. You hide it so very well!" said Skirret.

Wilsamander quirked his ears. "I'm a city Rassimel, and the country Herethroy customs are a mystery and a half to me. You're Casamint Imbarr, aren't you?"

"I'm Casamint Imbarr, and you know it. Marjoram — Rajel — you can call her what you will. I should call her 'My Lady Wife'."

Skirret took Casamint's mid-hand. "She's a Rowns. They're famous country nobility. And Casamint's practically a Great Baron."

Casamint beamed. "Between the three of us, we're heirs to Yazelton, Comblefree, Corster, and Dorly."

Wilsamander nodded sagely. "Therefore you are more rich and powerful than your finances or your clothing would suggest. I must remember to extract more money from you at long-chess or at cards when you get back."

"Back?", asked Casamint. "I'll be here tomorrow evening, and it is I who will extract money from *you*, ringtail."

"Perhaps, on the extraction. But you were summoned on no notice, so I thought you'd be dashing off from Pennypell as fast as Gremmet dashed off from your service," said the Rassimel.

"Oh, that. No, she wrote me on no notice. I'll go to Comblefree early next month, after examinations, and miss the next term of classes."

Wilsamander smirked. "Ah. She wrote you on no notice, and you resent this. You ordinarily expect your wife to send you a letter explaining that she will send you a letter? Do you expect a letter explaining that you will soon receive a letter alerting you to a letter, as well? How far on does that go?"

Skirret waved a strip of wood. "It's his new secret scheme for immortality, cheaper and easier than any great enchantment. From Professor Ochirion's mathematics class, you see. He wants the whole infinite series of precursor letters, you see. And whoever heard of someone dying before he received a letter from his wife? So this way he'll put off his death to infinity."

Wilsamander balanced one strip on top of another, badly. "He's got it backwards then. The letter arrived at a definite moment in time; the infinite series must therefore extend into the past. This will render him infinitely young. Which explains why he's so cross today: he's an infinite baby, up infinitely late past his bed time."

Casamint snatched Wilsamander's strips before they fell. "Samand, that doesn't make sense — it doesn't even make *nonsense*. I don't like to be dragged off to some little village when I could be here over the break, trying to decipher the latest opera written by a *real* composer. They say that Slio Slossimass is writing something new — something she has not done since *Empty Sun* and *Crippled Fingers*."

"Right, she was off fishing on Lake Popostaber, or some such?" said Wilsamander. The conversation drifted to the arts, leaving servants, marriage, and studies behind.

DEATH OF A MONSTER

The inspector clicked her claws on the closed door. "Lord Secretary, a moment of your time, if you would be so kind."

A little Cani girl answered. "Oh! Good morning, Inspector Nethry. My mother's mate is in the pool. He'll be dressed shortly."

Nethry Chrestilium crouched, muzzle to muzzle with the girl, curling her many-ringed tail. "Oppet, do tell him that it's more important than sometimes."

"I will, Inspector Nethry!" She darted back into her family's longhouse, which also served as the office of Byronny's Lord Secretary of the Lenwynt and two other important government buildings.

Not too long after, Muspis Pororn emerged, his deep golden fur limp with half-dried bathwater, wearing a suitably dignified bathrobe. "Good day to you, Inspector Nethry. Oppet says it's deathsomely important."

The Rassimel woman curled her tail. "Some few deaths have already happened, and some more are going to happen. The main question is, whose?"

Muspis smiled, his tongue lolling out of the left side of his muzzle. "Why, that's easy: the duke and the top three generals of Drysselwyn." Byronny and its erstwhile colony Drysselwyn were bickering about a few villages on their border.

Nethry smiled. "Oh, excellent. If you'll just sign a requisition for enough money to hire them to go fighting a terrible beast in the Lenwynt, I'll attend to the details straightaway."

"Unfortunately I fear me that there's not so much money as that in the city's whole treasury, much less my budget. Perhaps you could had some cheaper plan in mind for ... well, why don't you tell me what it's for?"

"Certainly, though I'd rather do it a bit more privately than your living-room with half a dozen of your husbands and wives and mates and spouses and whatever other degrees of marriage you have listening in."

He blinked at her; usually she was happy enough to do state business in his living room. "Oh, dear. This **must** be serious."

She nodded gravely. "Yes."

Nethry was pleased. Muspis Pororn was a scion of a powerful family in Byronny, and he had been appointed to the office of Lord Secretary of the Lenwynt two years ago. He had never actually been to the Lenwynt in person; that vast stretch of uncivilized, uncivilizable forest held no appeal for him. In the first year of his appointment he had tried to actually propose strategies and suggest projects, many of them disastrous. More recently he had learned that his job was a sinecure, and that Nethry and her scant handful of colleagues knew their territory and had better plans than he ever did.

"This is about, oh, a third or a half of the unpleasant reports I've ever given you. "

"I *do* hope you're going to explain to me that each one was a separate and wholly unrelated accident, Nethry."

"You know I am not, Lord Muspis. The best I shall do is explain all with a single, solitary monster," said Nethry.

"Am I permitted to hope that it is a single but very insidious conlee?"

"You are certainly permitted to hope that your single conlee somehow disguised itself as a scyanturge. Disguised to the extent of doing all the wickednesses that a scyanturge could. Nonetheless, I shall expect you to help me as if it were a scyanturge, not a conlee."

"Nethry, dear Nethry, I am perhaps the least potent Cani on the branch. My eyes are weak. My fangs are blunt. I haven't used a spear since grammar school. My most aggressive spell is one to delay the onset of orgasm. I am hardly the one to go off and challenge some terrible beast of the Lenwynt!" This was not strictly true.

"Simply administrative help, lord," she said with a grin.

"That much I can do, and most powerfully! Tell me what you need. For that matter, tell me what a scyanturge is. I vaguely remember that they have eight bodies spread over hundreds of miles, but I'm confusing them with something else, aren't I?"

"That would be a chromodon, which would be bad enough. No, this is a scyanturge: a body like a stretched-out Gormoror, with hundreds of thorns floating around her, and seven fearsomely strong spells in her eyes. An old one would be one of the most dangerous threats on the whole World Tree. Aulihemm Bremm is a young one, barely mature, trying to establish her place in the society of monsters."

"I do try to be optimistic, Nethry, but you are making it very, very difficult. I shall surely note this the next time I consider what to do about your excessive salary. Unfortunately for my poor aching budget, I will have to count your results, too... You *did* say you had discovered a few more things about this Bremm creature and her deeds?"

"She has destroyed a great many skyboats, two dozen or more, to start with. She has killed or evicted various of the calmer and friendlier inhabitants of the Lenwynt. She has slain the great wizard Vaxsedhonic Varnouv, and looted the Tilmarth Note from her. She has even destroyed the Vilarvil Safari Company's adventure resort, in Drysselwyn. She flies or teleports wherever she wishes in our land, and is getting bolder about it," said Nethry.

"Another hope disintegrated by scyanturge eye-bolts! I do hope that you have some plan for dealing with her, Nethry, or I shall be quite entirely hopeless."

"I have some ideas, though they will be little comfort to your budget. Indeed, they will gobble greedily at the military budget as well — ours and Drysselwyn's, if you can manage it."

He lowered his tail in a smooth arc behind himself. "Since their lands, too, are being attacked by the piratical personage? Well, we are not *quite* at war with Drysselwyn at the moment, and I suppose a bit of a common enemy could be politically useful... Fortunately I have a half-cousin-in-law married to their duke, so I should be at least able to at least utter a few poignant cries before they reject our requests. You *will* come to Drysselwyn and explain what's going on, Nethry? I'm sure to get rollward mixed up with roll'gainst, and the sky mixed up with a cupcake."

She grimaced; she was more comfortable with the etiquette of monsters than of ducal courts. "Well, of course."

And so it was done: not cheaply or quickly, but done. A military skyboat of Byronny was disguised as a trading ship, with a dozen of the greatest warriors from each city-state on board, generously supplied with protective spells and even more generously supplied with healing. Nethry was on board; Muspis was in Drysselwyn, Aulihemm Bremm took the bait, and arrogantly waited eight seconds to decide to flee after she realized that it was a trap; but by then it was too late. All the soldiers died at least once, five of them past all healing. It was a very, very cheap victory over a scyanturge, for all that it cost more than the last war between Byronny and Drysselwyn.

Nethry herself was created a marchioness for her part in it, one of the few people in the Transwynt who did not have to purchase her title for lozens. When her brother pointed that out, she complained that she had purchased it for blood, and that lozens would have been cheaper were she inclined to waste them on such nonsense. Transwyntian titles, unlike Araldean, show that the bearer has power and wealth; they do not come with any of their own.

HOMECOMING

Great Baron Amberstripe Rowns, lord owner of Comblefree and Corster, was picking caterpillars off his apple trees at noontime, with half a dozen other farmers. With a typical farmer's economy, this task served two purposes. For now, it would keep the apple blossoms from being eaten. Later, he would drown the caterpillars in peppered wine, and sell them in Pennypell, where Rassimel who wanted a little extra meat for cheap, spicy flavor would buy them.

He heard his daughter before he saw her: the metallic slapping of her armor against the huge sword on her back. He clung to his ladder with his hand-feet, and shouted, "Girl, where did you get all that metal? If you've mortgaged my villages I'll pry you out of your chitin and roast you over a slow fire!"

She looked up at him. "Earned some spare cash. Bought 'em myself."

"Earned some spare cash, did you? Doing what, pray tell?"

"You *did* send me to Talliper's Academy of Weapons to study weapons, right? To save the expense of hiring a knight protector, after a few years?"

"Study them, yes. Spend a fortune on them, no. These are peaceful lands — nothing that comes here *needs* a three-hander!" He noticed Arrhwy for the first time, barely more than a green and black shadow beside his daughter's horse. "And who's *that*? You were supposed to replace the knight, not *hire* one. And certainly not a Sleeth."

Arrhwy smiled broadly at him. "Also am I equally pleased at the meeting of you!"

Rajel snorted. "Father, this is Arrhwy. She and I are just back from killing a nycathath in the Lenwynt. He had been raiding villages in Lowmont. Nothing much smaller than this sword could have broken his armor."

Amberstripe pulled a caterpillar off a blossom, pinching it too hard and squashing it. He scowled and tossed it over his shoulder. "Marjoram, you've gone and gotten overtrained, and so far over your head I can't see your antennae. I sent you to train enough in fighting so you could help protect your villages — leading farmers with their spears and staves against bithorga, perhaps, or prarl or jaran-jabow. You should not be challenging nycathath or nendrai or scyanturge! You may be a disobedient spendthrift, but you are still my daughter and I do not want to hear of you killed by some horror."

Arrhwy captured the caterpillar with Sleeth's innate Ruloc Corpador magic, levitating it in front of her face, and snapping it down. She sprawled in the clover at the edge of the orchard and started grooming her fur, yawning a mouth full of ivory daggers.

Rajel scowled back at her father. "You didn't say, 'get half-competent and then stop.' You said, 'Don't let these lessons be a waste of my money.' So I took a few little fighting jobs for a little bit of spending money. And to make sure I was getting good value from the lessons. Turns out I was."

Amberstripe jammed another caterpillar into his jar. "Recall further that I cautioned you against gambling. The distinction between rolling dice for lozens and risking your life for lozens is slight. Staring gods, but I'd rather you rolled dice, Marjoram."

Rajel remembered Oostmarine's glove, and flew up to join him grooming the tree. "Father, call me Rajel. I was careful. I'm always careful."

He scoffed. "You're a wastrel and a squandrel, not some angry warrior princess from some stories, and I'll call you by your proper name. You're using cley for levitation right now, when Virid gave you six limbs for climbing."

She wiggled her fingers triumphantly. "Father, look sharper. With magic sense."

He inspected the glove. "Enchanted, is it? A lovely lozen that must have cost you. You've been battering around in the Verticals, haven't you been? You shouldn't be wasting money or cley or your life. Especially not your life."

Her feeling of triumph limped and died, and she turned her head aside. "It didn't cost me a terch, father."

"What then, Marjoram? Your honesty, if you stole it? Your blood-innocence, if you took it from someone you killed? Enchantments are not cheap: if the price is not this, it must be that."

She disentangled a caterpillar from a blossom, and put it in her father's jar. "We found it in a klegsnaesh's hoard."

"And..?"

"And our companion Oostmarine got to use it. The nycathath killed him, though. It's mine now."

He was gracious in victory. "I see. I trust the lesson is not lost on you."

She spread her antennae. "It already wasn't lost. I wrote to the other Tawlowns. They should be joining us here in a few days."

His eyes brightened, and he waved his antennae. "You did? Excellent! I was expecting to have to order you to do that." He started climbing down the ladder, and called to the woman on the next tree. "Calamus, you're in charge of this now. I've family matters to arrange, and noble's matters as well."

Arrhwy stretched, rending the innocent turf with her claws, as Rajel flew back. "Your father expects grandchildren tomorrow. Does he get them?"

"Not this year even if we start immediately. I don't know that we will."

* * *

A noble co-lover making a formal visit needs accompaniment. Not a chaperone in the sense that an Orren might need, to keep zir from getting distracted and arriving hours too late and covered with seedpods or whatever. Not a companion for companionship's sake, as a Cani would prefer. Simply someone to be strong in case strength was needed, or to block dangers with spear and staff.

Chicory would not have been a suitable choice. Boragette chose Tarragina to be zir companion, a middle-aged spinster who had lost an upper hand to a falling arken tree the preceding autumn, and who had thus been relegated to lesser jobs. Tarragina sang on the road in a deep voice like honey flavored with hops, choosing songs with complicated choruses to distract Boragette from thinking about the evening.

By midafternoon they saw the peaked roofs of Comblefree painted a pale orange, amid tall flat aileaf trees. Calamus, atop the apple trees, saw them too, and ran on four legs to join them and greet them to town.

"Tell me about my husband and wife," said Boragette to Calamus, after the introductions.

"I've nothing to say about your husband, for I think he's never been to Comblefree. Marjoram — Rajel she calls herself now — has been away for two years or three herself. I don't know her anymore either, for she clothes herself now in shiny steel and has a Sleeth at her side. She always was a strong one, and fiercer than a farmer."

"She sounds heroic," said Tarragina, "Very feminine if you like that sort of style."

"She is, that," said Calamus.

Boragette rubbed dust off zir carapace with a scrap of chamois, and thought about Chicory. "What's she like as a farmer?"

"Oh, when strength is good for farming, she's a good farmer right enough. She and I were clearing a field that had gotten grown up with gelmolen vines when it was fallow, you know, and Marjoram was worth any two other women there, and her not fully grown then. But when attention is good for farming, you'd best get someone else. She doesn't weed well. Doesn't have the love of the soil in her, I don't think. But you'll see for yourself in a shortly. She's over there, next to the Sleeth."

"At least she's not wearing armor," said Tarragina.

The Sleeth's ears flickered; Herethroy could not have heard conversation at that distance, but Sleeth senses are excellent. She stood up and stretched, and tapped Rajel's foot with a forepaw and pointed at Boragette. Rajel adjusted her tights and shirt to show off the viridian dots on her blue-grey chitin, and strode towards Boragette as if towards a battle.

* * *

Rajel's voice was deep and nervous. "Be welcome here at Comblefree." She was fairly sure that the delicate rose-chitined co-lover was her mari, but she didn't recognize zir. Behind her, the Sleeth smelled her nervousness and chuckled unsympathetically.

Boragette at least was sure of who zie was talking to. "Thank you, my wife ... Rajel? Marjoram?"

"I go by Rajel these weeks. Marjoram's too sweet an herb for a warrior's name."

They paused for a moment, looking at each other. Arrhwy prodded Rajel in the thigh again. Rajel blinked, then pointed to the rollward wing of her sather's house. "We'll be in there for a bit. I think we'll build a new wing, on that side, facing the pond."

"Oh!", said Boragette. "I hadn't realized that you'd intended me to move in just yet. Or that ... this were the right place to move to."

"We've got to start sometime," said Rajel, a bit downcast. She had picked the best place by her standards, and hadn't realized that the other two might have opinions as well. "It might as well be today."

"Perhaps when our husband shows up we can make plans."

"He said he'd come early Thory," said Rajel. There was another grating pause. "Well, mother never taught the proper way to invite someone into zir own house. Come in ... would you like plue or tarrissy?

"Yes, if you please."

"The kitchen is there..." She scarcely needed to point; no other building in the village had four chimneys, nor as many people around it. "They'll be working on dinner, but there's always food to steal."

Boragette spread zir antennae. "We have to steal it?" Customs varied from village to village, but zie had never heard of a place where the residents didn't feed each other.

"Well, no, we don't... that's an adventurer's way of speaking, is all it is," admitted Rajel, as they strolled between pale orange buildings. Boragette stopped to run zir finger over the curves of a gargoyle's wooden face, dripping a bit from the previous night's rain.

* * *

In the kitchen, six cooks and an uncountable number of children were at work or play: shredding leaves for tarrissy, browning onions in sweet butter in leather pans over low fires, simmering leeks and mushrooms and mashed nuts for soup. A short chubby co-lover with white antennae and an off-center red-purple dot on her chest's chitin was cutting circles of sweet dough for some architectural dessert.

"Sather, this is my wife Lovagette. Wife, this is my sather Beetheart."

Boragette spread zir antennae. "Boragette, most people call me...."

Rajel curled her antennae. "Right. Boragette."

Beetheart smiled, and took Boragette's mid-hands in a floury grasp. "I remember you, of course! It's a delight to have you move to Comblefree at long last, so that my hero of a daughter can stop living like a wild monster and start raising a proper family at home."

Rajel curled her antennae tighter. "Mother!"

Boragette flattened zir antennae in embarrassment verging on shame. "... I don't think we've got precise plans yet ..."

"Oh, how could you not, a beautiful young slip of a cosi like you. I'll wager parsnips to parsley that you've had boys and girls begging after you for years." There was nothing save friendliness in Beetheart's smile, but Boragette's heart sank.

"We're here for a snack, is all. Boragette's had a long trip today, and sunout's not for hours yet," said Rajel.

"The leftovers from lunch are on the back table in the snack nook, as they have been every day since your birth and two centuries before that, Marjoram." Beetheart pointed with a rolling pin.

Rajel stalked through the kitchen as if the table were an unwary foe, without seeming to realize it. Boragette followed, clinking her chitinous knee against a hanging ladle by accident, nearly running into a zooming girl carrying a quadruple-armload of immense carrots.

By the time zie got there, Rajel had picked the largest two bowls and scooped them full of lukewarm sticky plue. She handed the larger to her mari. Boragette blinked at it: twice what zie could eat at a meal.

Rajel misinterpreted the gesture. "It's our village's recipe, or one of them. The white things are roundnuts, the dismal greenish color comes from pondygreen and chopped spinach, and the little red flecks are bits of dried currant. I don't know what the brown squares are."

Boragette said, "Black-turbans, cut square. We use trompes-de-miel in Dorly. They're sweeter, so we don't use any dried currant."

Rajel put a big handful of slightly wilted tarrissy on her bowl, and another on Boragette's. "Huh. You know how to cook? Beetheart runs the kitchen. I suppose you will after she retires."

Boragette picked a few shreds of tarrissy, and rolled a little ball of plue in them. There was no vinegar on the table, so zie ate it plain. It didn't taste quite right to zir: currants and black-turbans gave a coarser flavor than trompes-de-miel. "Oh, anyone brought up as a proper co-lover will know how to cook, a little."

Arrhwy poured through the kitchen, nose to the floor. She claimed the one padded armchair in the snack nook, sitting up primly and curling her tail around her paws, peering at Boragette from two cold striped emeralds. "You are Boragette. Rajel does not introduce me, I think because she is nervous and she forgets. She does not get nervous when she fights a nycathath, but she gets nervous when you come here. Be happy! You are more dangerous than a nycathath!"

Rajel had rolled her own porridge-ball, and dipped it in a sauce of pondygreen and wine and onion. She flicked it at Arrhwy's broad muzzle, her expert hand moving faster than Boragette could follow. Boragette chirped and scrambled off zir chair backwards — Sleeth were dangerous; an angry one could kill two unarmed Herethroy with ease.

The Sleeth, unaccountably to Boragette, did not get angry. She licked at her muzzle, but couldn't reach the porridge. Instead she poured off the chair and rubbed the plue off against the cleanest part of Rajel's dark orange kilt. Rajel scritched her behind the ears affectionately.

Boragette spread zir antennae. Zir wife was more comfortable with a Sleeth than with other Herethroy — even ones she was descended from or married to. Was zie going to spend zir life competing for attention with a near-monster?

The Sleeth chuckled. "Rajel is not always the very gracious Herethroy, so I introduce myself. I am Arrhwy. With Rajel I kill this and that, and so we are not so poor and she has money to buy you candles and candies and canning tools."

"You're her ... what?"

"I am her adventuring partner. I ask her every third month for more, but she only does Herethroy and not very many of them."

If Boragette had grafted Hiding in Nowhere, zie would have used it then; zie crouched in zir stool and gaped for a response. Rajel simply flattened her antennae. "Arrhwy, you're not supposed to say things like that to my mari! There are manners to these things!"

Sleeth can look intensely, corrosively innocent, when they want. "If you do not like what I tell zir, you should tell zir some things of your own, then. Starting maybe with who I am."

"Fine. Boragette, this is Arrhwy, my adventuring partner. She's thirty years and more older than me, and she was looking to retire soon, or mostly retire. I'd offered Comblefree, or wherever we end up."

That was the first scrap of good news zie had heard in Comblefree. "Are you planning to retire from adventuring too, then, Rajel ... wife?"

"Father — he's the baron here — wants me to. I was expecting I'd be the protector of the village, with Arrhwy. That would save us the price of hiring a knight. Maybe I'll go on a minor bit of an adventure now or then, keep the blood moving and the sword-arms limber."

She was more excited at that prospect than she had been by meeting zir, Boragette thought. "I suppose I should be glad that you won't be running off to terrible dangers all the time."

Rajel clicked her fingers on her leg-carapace. She hadn't realized that her spouses might care about or even notice any future adventuring. "Not to change the subject, but ..." She paused, desperately trying to think of a new subject, "Do you want to share a bed with me tonight, or shall we wait on that a day or two?"

Boragette wilted as much as zir carapace would let zir. The question was kind enough — they would have to arrange such things — but discussing it in a kitchen with listening villagers, in front of a Sleeth, did not please zir much.

The Sleeth, surprisingly, helped zir. "Rajel, you do not pay enough attention to my lessons in finding lovers. Walk up to chosen person. Tap the genital region with tail. Ask for what you want. Do not wander around the question with 'share a bed'. If you want mating, ask for mating!"

Boragette blinked at Arrhwy in astonishment and embarrassment. "Really?"

Arrhwy grinned at Boragette. "That is the easy way with my own species. I think your wife is imitating me: doing the same with *her* own species. She spends too long being the great adventurer, imitating being the Sleeth. Maybe you and a husband teach her how to be Herethroy some more."

She leaned aside, and Rajel's second porridge-shot splattered on the back of her chair. "Rrai, already you are starting, Boragette! The terror adventuress I know does not miss!" Only the Sleeth laughed.

* * *

Rajel and Boragette did share a bed that night: a pile of straw-stuffed bags big enough for three Herethroy comfortably, coarser than would be comfortable for a species without chitin. They did not touch each other, nor did either watch as the other changed from day-clothes to night-clothes. Rajel fell asleep almost instantly, with the expertise of one who has stood many watches. Boragette curled up as far from zir wife as zie could, and wrapped zirself in loneliness, and got lost many times on zir way to sleep.

THE WRONG MUSHROOMS

Beetheart was trying zir best to be gentle to Boragette, but in the wreckage of the evening zie was not having an easy time of it. Amberstripe and a dozen other Comblefree elders had come to the two of them, saying some variation on, "There are new mushrooms in the plue. This is undoubtedly pleasant." Beetheart knew exactly what they meant, in the subtle idiom of Comblefree, though Boragette only suspected: that the Dorly-style plue that Boragette had made was not acceptable in Comblefree, and that zie would have to work harder to fit in.

"Trompes-de-miel go with sautéed bitter greens, or stewed pears, or on steamed carrots, or crushed with roundnuts as a sauce. They do not go in a dinnertime plue. Only black-turbans go in plue. With currants."

Boragette spread zir antennae. "When my mother taught me to cook, trompes-de-miel went in dinnertime plue."

Beetheart scowled. "You are living in Comblefree. You must learn the ways of Comblefree. Do not seek to break our shells and re-shape us in the images of some village fifteen miles distant! We are not so easily changed! It is you who must change to be like us!"

Boragette scowled back. "Eating one sweet mushroom instead of another now and then is scarcely killing you and resurrecting you! In Dorly we often made plue in the style of some other village!"

Beetheart crossed both sets of arms. "Boragette, you come from a very wild and liberal village, but Comblefree is exceedingly traditional. Here we have a long heritage to honor! Rallannah Rowns made dinnertime plue with black-turbans in centuries past. We make dinnertime plue with black-turbans today. Our great-grandchildren will make dinnertime plue with black-turbans in centuries future. And, speaking of which, are you pregnant yet? You have been married for years!"

Boragette stomped a foot-hand. "Oh, staring gods! I am not!"

Beetheart waggled a finger in zir face. "Don't take that tone with me, Boragette. You may be a pro-baroness, but I am the mari of the current baron, and the head cook, and I will not accept a single insult! We expect grandchildren from you, and in no long time."

Boragette scowled back. "Well, you should have assigned some man from the village to stud duty, if you can't wait until my husband is back from school."

Beetheart lowered zir antennae. "Boragette. That was not called for. Perhaps you should find some useful task that is not in the kitchen, in the future."

* * *

Rajel and Arrhwy did not knock when they came in. "Boragette? Why are you in bed in the middle of the day?"

Boragette uncurled somewhat. "Oh, hallo. Your sather has banished me from the kitchen."

"Is this about the plue from last night?" Rajel sought frantically for some words that would comfort her mari. "I didn't mind it at all — I'm used to all sorts of strange concoctions of plues, from inns in the city to whatever hosh-grain sludge I can cook for myself over a campfire."

"It must please me that you are so tough as to be able to endure my cooking." In the subtle idiom of Dorly, "It must please me" meant almost the opposite.

Rajel sighed. "It really wasn't *bad*. It was just foreign."

Boragette sat up in bed and hugged zir knees with all four arms. "Rajel, Dorly is only in the next county over... I know Comblefree has deep traditions, but Dorly's traditions are just as deep. I can't toss them aside just because I travelled fifteen miles."

Rajel shrugged, and unbuckled the strap of her huge sword. Arrhwy sprawled off to the side and started licking the dust off her flanks. "I've travelled a lot more than that. You get used to all sorts of customs."

Boragette looked away as zir wife started stripping her dusty clothes. "I haven't travelled at all."

Rajel grunted. "Maybe we should."

Boragette was surprised to discover that zie was less afraid of going somewhere new than of staying in Comblefree. "Perhaps we could ... Beetheart was also after me to give zir grandchildren."

Rajel spread her antennae. "Don't ask me now. I'm not nearly ready for that."

Boragette said, "I didn't ask! I don't do everything zie asks — I don't even make *plue* right..." Zie drew the covers over zir knees, and buried zir head in them.

Rajel blinked at zir. Arrhwy reached over and prodded her with a forepaw. "Zie is your mari. You are zir wife. Go be comforting."

Rajel sat next to Boragette, and put an arm around zir shoulder — awkwardly, as it was only the fifth time they had touched. "Boragette, it'll be all right... they're not such bad people really..."

Boragette leaned against zir wife's chainmail, zir limbs still tight with despair and discomfort. "I feel so alone in Comblefree."

Rajel thought about that a bit, then nodded. "I do too, since I came back. I'm not the girl who would be gentle, anymore."

Boragette laughed bitterly. "Well, soon our school-bug of a husband will come. Then we'll all three feel alone together."

THE END OF CASAMINT'S TERM

The month of Hispis had three days left, and the last of those days would bring examinations. At sunout Casamint, Mhebb, Skirret, and Wilsamander were draped over the ragged once-blue couches and teetery chairs in the common room of the apartment Casamint and Mhebb shared. The dregs of the last four pots of kathia had been poured into a wide flat wooden basin on the table, and Wilsamander had put butter, two kinds of pepper, flour, and heated it over a small conjured fireball.

Skirret speared a segment of squash on a wooden skewer, and swished it around in the kathia sauce. "Casamint, even now I can see your carapace bulging. You have filled it too full of mathematics and fondue."

Casamint ran a foot-hand over Skirret's bumpy tail. "Oh, shush. I'm enjoying this studying as I never have before."

Mhebb rubbed her eyes, then stood up and hopped a circuit of the room on one foot. "Savoring the agony of studentry, stocking up on it in the stark and terrible face of a few months of relaxation in the well-armored embrace of your wife and mari?"

Casamint spread his antennae, and recited with a few modifications from Parvamesh and Gozander, "Mourn for me, O my comrades, for I descend from the happy Flats of studyness to the wearying woesome Verticals of wedlock."

Wilsamander grinned. "Not bad. Still, the sun's gone out. There's a way to bring yet more happiness to these scholarly Flats." He took a horn bottle out of his sachel, and swished it around. "You *do* have four clean chalices in here, Casamint?"

Mhebb snorted. "'Casamint' and 'clean' in the same sentence? Samand, you should be boiled for heresy, stir-fried for semantic incongruity, bisected to learn the making of proper divisions, and expelled from the academy."

"That's one of his main charms, though," said Skirret with a grin. Casamint, who had been rinsing four wooden chalices, shook one over Skirret's head and another over Mhebb's. Skirret lapped at the dripping water and moaned a languid mocking moan. Mhebb shrank four inches, then got control of her natural shapeshifting and returned to her ordinary shape to thump Casamint's armored thorax with a notebook.

Wilsamander passed out a handful of thin flat bits of wood, and the four devoted themselves to their books, occasionally grinning and copying a phrase from a textbook onto a stick or eating a bit of fondue. After a third of an hour, Wilsamander ceremoniously thumped the heel of the bottle on the table. "Gentleprimes, scholars, the time has come wherein you will reveal the fruits of your studiomantic researches into each others' true nature."

The sticks were piled together, and shuffled. Skirret drew first. "Skirret is...", she said, and then read her stick, "... a technique for making devices that heal more than one person at a time." She looked at Mhebb. "Mhebb, that's tedious. Aren't there any interesting identification sentences in there?"

Mhebb shook her head sadly. "Not very. If I'd've known Samand were bringing a bottle I'd have studied enchantment in the afternoon, and be coming up with peculiar and eccentric identification sentences from history class now. My turn, isn't it? Mhebb is... She drew a stick from the pile. "... a harbinger of unwanted spiritual renewal in several of Slossimass' operas."

Casamint snickered. "I can't imagine Mhebb harbinging anything at all worthwhile. Casamint is ..." He read a stick. "... trapped, fenced in on all sides by horribly distorted prime figures, with overemphasized sexual attributes."

The other three laughed. Skirret said, "No better description of his wife and mari has ever been given, nor could be — of this I am entirely sure!"

Casamint scowled. "Don't be jealous, Skirret. Who wrote this... It must have been Samand, for it's Rassy writing. How on the branch did you get *that* from a book of Mrasteian history?"

Wilsamander lifted the spine of his book: Paintings and Sculpture of the Tender School and their Successors. "I got sick of reading history two hours ago. I've been on art since then." He flipped back a few pages, and read the whole sentence, *"The bird of hope is trapped, fenced in on all sides by horribly distorted prime figures, with overemphasized sexual attributes."* "And no, I didn't even think about your marital problems, Casamint."

Casamint looked over Wilsamander's shoulder at a full-page print of the painting of the bird of hope. "That's hideous. It's your turn, Samand."

Wilsamander drew a stick. "Samand is ... used to clean fungus off the sides of water-boats."

Mhebb grinned. "He should be."

There was a moment of silence, then Wilsamander opened his bottle with a loud pop, and filled Casamint's chalice. "By virtue of the authority vested in me 'cause I brought the liquor, I do hereby proclaim that you got the most laughter and thus, therefore, consequently, and ensuantly, you have to drink."

Casamint sniffed at his chalice, then grimaced and drank it as quickly as he could. "Gah! Cheap vodka and ... what?"

Wilsamander said, "The very cheapest vodka that ever I could find; bitter honey; a couple ground cherries; a bit of tascernel perfume."

Casamint shook his head. "I'm sure everything will seem funnier to me after one slug of that. Be prepared to drink a goodly amount of it yourself!"

Samand smiled. "That is, indeed, the plan. Gentlefriends, you have nine minutes to find more identification sentences." Mhebb slammed her enchantment book, and picked up her history book, and the evening rolled on.

* * *

Casamint was not in the best of moods. His Academy friends had given him a going-away party, which was pleasant enough, but Skirret had declined to spend the night with him, as she had the several previous nights. When the carriage stopped at what absolutely had to be Comblefree, he tossed the driver a decagonal amber coin. "Ten lozens, as we had agreed."

The driver reached her hand to catch it, missed, and took a few steps over to pick it up with a mid-hand. She gave Casamint a sour look, and clambered up to start untying his pile of tapestry-sided baggage from the top of the coach. A few farmers, their carapaces shining deep reds and subtle blues under soil-smeared linen clothes, strolled over to help.

One of them smiled. "You must be the pro-baron Casamint, come to behusband our pro-baroness Rajel, now, mustn't you?" Casamint nodded, and the farmer went on. "I am Calamus, often the vicar of your father-in-law. These are Effedrian and Bluesways."

Casamint curtsied, swirling his hand in the style of noble students. "I am, as you have so delicately discerned, Baron Casamint, here at the summoning of my wife and mari." He was not yet Baron Casamint, though custom permitted him to use the title that would someday be his.

The farmers looked coldly at his manners. He waved his antennae in small circles, as one does to servants. "I do hope one of you know what you'll do with all this baggage."

The farmers scowled at each other, arranging things without needing to speak. "I'll just be taking these to Rajel's chambers, then," said Bluesways.

Casamint nodded curtly. "That would seem to be their destiny, wouldn't it? And mine as well?"

Bluesways nodded. "I'm afraid so, lord. There's more than one hands-load here. I'll just be getting a cart." She ran off towards a nearby shed.

Casamint watched her run. "Eager woman, I must say. Does she run everywhere she goes?"

The two farmers shrugged. Calamus said, "I would hardly know about that, lord. If you'd be happy to wait here for a moment, I'll tell your wife that you've arrived." She and Effedrian headed off without waiting to see if he was happy.

Casamint climbed into the coach to collect the book he had been reading on the trip. He ignored the leaves that had wrapped his lunch, and the pile of husks of roundnuts: the driver could clean those up just as well as he could, and, unlike him, she was getting paid for her labor.

Bluesways returned with a mucky wheelbarrow, and started tossing his baggage into it. "Follow me, lord," she said, and picked up the handles.

* * *

Bluesways kicked the bedroom door open, her hands full of baggage. Boragette was sitting on the side of the bed, embroidering sheaves of hosh on a ceremonial headband by the light of a half-open window. Surprised by the crash of the door, zie stabbed zirself with the needle; its ivory was too soft to penetrate her chitin, but it broke in three parts.

The farmer dropped Casamint's bags unceremoniously in a corner, and left to get another load. Casamint himself strode into the room as if he owned it. "Oh, hello there. Making yourself useful?"

Boragette curled zir antennae. "You're my husband, aren't you?"

He smirked. "If you have the great fortune to be Boragette, then yes, I am. If you have the terrible fortune to be Marjoram and look like a cosi, then, again, I am. Otherwise it could be arranged, if you're quite the persuasive one. I'm only married once."

Boragette blinked a bit. "Well, I'm Boragette. Your luggage rather reeks, doesn't it?"

He sniffed. "Something reeks, but I had thought it was just the delightful countryside air. I miss Pennypell already!"

Bluesways carried another big load of luggage into the room, and dropped it at Casamint's feet. Casamint crouched to look at it. "It has gotten a bit stinky."

Bluesways looked down at him. "I'm afraid the only remaining wheelbarrow was the one for carting manure." She walked around him to fetch the last load.

Casamint stood, crashing his hands against the chitin of his hips, antennae lowered. "What an utter fool that Bluesways is. Bad enough that she covers my luggage with manure, but it's tapestry. Cleaning it out will be a bother and a half." Boragette shrugged, and used a minor spell to repair zir needle.

Casamint walked around in front of her. "Could you call the servant for me? I put everything in those dashed mucky bags, but I'll swim in vinegar if I take them out and hang them up again."

Boragette looked up at him. "It's the start of summer, Casamint. Most everyone's off working the hosh planting."

He rapped his fingers on the wall, looking at the carving darkly. "They would be."

He glanced intently at Boragette, who stabbed zir needle into the headband. "I think Rajel meant that closet to be yours," zie said, pointing with the tip of zir tail.

"Well, I think you should help me unpack," he said.

Zie looked up at him. "I'm working on the hosh harvest myself. This is the prize for the first-finished sower."

He sighed wearily. "I really don't want manure all over myself."

"And I really don't want manure all over the prize headband. The villagers dislike me quite enough already."

"Do they, now? They accuse you of being disagreeable and unhelpful, perhaps? For no reason I could understand, of course!"

Zie scowled at him. "They accuse me of coming from Dorly, of not learning up their own customs without having been told."

He shrugged. "Oh, that. I've lived most of my life in Pennypell. I should think that one Herethroy village was much like another. Small, rather uncultured, and twice-rather tedious."

Zie stabbed zir needle through the cloth fiercely. "Tell them that, and you'll be lucky if you get no worse fate than manure on your luggage. But wait 'til I've gone home."

Casamint sighed, and turned to pick up the first of his bags. He yelped in surprise: a green and black Sleeth was floating half a yard over them. "Great ancient demons! Who are you, and what the thunders are you doing above my luggage?"

Rajel answered from the doorway. "That's Arrhwy, my adventuring partner. I'm Rajel, your wife."

Boragette smiled faintly. "They sneak around rather well, don't they?"

Arrhwy smiled. "Hallo, Casamint. I am above your luggage so I do not get my fur dirty from being on it. I do not wish to waste a cley cleaning it. Nor do I wish to lick off from my fur what Bluesways has given you as a homecoming present."

He glowered around. "Are you all going to twit me for some mistake some bumpkin of a farmer woman did?"

Rajel snorted. "You all but begged her to, the way they're telling the story in the fields."

He lashed his tail as well as a Herethroy can. "She did it on *purpose*?"

Arrhwy peered at his tail. "She does it on purpose. There is much laughing when she tells people. Everyone thinks you are the elegant dandy from the city, full of fancy gestures and silly ideas from books, who does not like to get himself muddy with farmwork. A Herethroy who is wanting to be Rassimel, is what they laugh about you."

He scowled at the Sleeth, then looked at his wife. "Well, they're your people. I rather wish you'd do something about it."

Rajel shrugged helplessly. "It's a bit petty of an insult for cleaving her in half with a three-handed sword. Aside from that, they're their own people. My father's still alive, and even if he weren't, I've turned at least as foreign as you and Boragette."

He lowered his antennae. "Fictional ancient demons devour the lot of them. I'm spending a whole term here?"

Rajel put her hands on her hips. "We *are* married, do you remember?"

He flung himself on the bed. "I could hardly forget about it these last two weeks. I was such a fool. Seduced by a plate of candy and a red hat."

Rajel smiled. "Ah. I got a Strong Arm spell, and I've used it many's the time, too."

Boragette looked at zir spouses, aghast. Zie stuck zir needle carefully into the cloth, set zir embroidery down, and rushed out the door.

"Whatever is the matter with *zir*?" asked Casamint.

"Zie had some fantastical and thoroughly romantic delusion that zie'd have a few moments of happiness in zir married life," answered Rajel.

Casamint shrugged, and started tossing his reeking bags into the closet without cleaning or unpacking them. The Sleeth lick-groomed her flank ostentatiously.

CHICORY'S GIFTS

A very small Herethroy girl with a very large basket-pack knocked on the door. "Boragette, are you there?"

"I am, truly." Zie opened the door. "Tansy? What are you doing here, so far from home?"

"Chicory sent me from Dorly with some presents!" Tansy took the basket-pack off, and swung her arms. "They're a little bit heavy! The little box is for you, the book in brown paper is for your husband, the bigger box is for your wife."

Casamint put an ivory skewer between two pages of his textbook, and peered over Boragette's shoulder at the girl. "Who's this?"

"She's Tansy, from Dorly. She and her family live right next to the main well. I know her two-thirds-sister Chicory quite well. Tansy, this is my husband Casamint."

Casamint gave Tansy an elaborate court salute which was properly only given to greater nobles who were either priests or scholars. "I'm Baron Casamint of Yazelton."

"You're the fourth-highest-titled person in Comblefree, and the only one who uses his title on little girls," said Rajel. "Even my father rarely mentions his title quite *this* early in the conversation."

"I'm very pleased to meet you, Baron Casamint, and you too, O warrior lady," said Tansy, clasping her mid-hands politely over her thorax.

"Are you hungry, Tansy, if you've walked all the way from Dorly today?" asked Boragette.

"Oh, just a little, Boragette ... Baron Boragette! I'll be all set to go home after a lunch," said Tansy.

"You shouldn't call me that except at fancy occasions, Tansy. It sounds as if my father were dead, and I very much hope he's not."

"Oh, no, he's all alive and fine, Boragette. Everyone is. Except that Nosteria fell off a tree and hurt her left knee and can't go farming. So Chicory's doing her work as well, so she couldn't bring these presents here," said Tansy.

"So, why is this Chicory person sending you and me presents, O my nominally-darling wife?" said Casamint. Rajel shrugged.

"She's a friend from home," said Boragette. "She's the best farmer in County Farwinn, or so everyone says." Zie picked up the small oaken box and opened it. "An antenna ring, and a rather nice one."

Rajel peered at it. "Ivory inlaid with lead — that can't be cheap."

"Oh, Chicory's rich, even for Dorly," said Boragette.

"Chicory and Boragette, with a little love-rune over the 'and'. When you say 'friend', O my darling mari, what sort of friend do you mean?" asked Casamint.

"Well, the sort of friend I would hope to marry someday," said Boragette. "But there's nothing improper about it."

"I would rather hope to have some influence in choosing your second marriage, Boragette. If you have to have one at all," said Rajel, working hard to keep her temper.

"I can't see why it should have anything to do with you, Rajel." said Casamint. "Zir first marriage didn't, after all."

"Oh, I haven't promised her anything at all," said Boragette. "She's delightful, though, and the best farmer in County Farwinn. I do hope you like her ... and she was thoughtful enough to send you presents, too."

"Sending presents to your lover's spouses does sound like a generosity," said Rajel, and opened the bigger box. Inside was a very nice trowel, with a magically-strengthened horn blade and a ring of inlaid teak Herethroy holding mid-hands around the handle. "A gardening implement?"

"Just the thing for a mighty warrior as my wife Rajel! Fierce as a Sleeth to the weeds, is Rajel, and armed with the Trowel of the Darksome Dooms," said Casamint.

Rajel shrugged. "I haven't managed to get a chance to do much farming lately, or even gardening." She had been avoiding it whenever possible.

Boragette was not fooled, but did not want to be antagonistic. "There has been a fair bit of this and that going on, what with Casamint and me showing up, and the harvest, and all like that. But Chicory means well, Rajel. She does love farming herself."

Casamint shrugged. "Rajel's as feminine as her pet Sleeth. Or so I conjecture, without having examined either of them in much detail."

Rajel scowled at her husband. "I'm a perfectly good farmer."

"Who am I to argue that point with your three-handed sword?" asked Casamint with a smirk.

Boragette held the book out to Casamint. "Chicory got you a present as well."

"Well, I'm sure that was very kind of her," said Casamint. "I must consult a manual of etiquette to see what the proper return gift for one's mari's adulterous lover is, when she is trying to be friendly to one."

"That's not how it is at all!" yelped Boragette.

"Oh, excellent. When you have the leisure time, please be so good as to explain to me how it differs from that, for I am afraid I cannot quite understand it," said Casamint.

"Don't be a pest. If anyone should be complaining, it's me, for Chicory is my rival not yours," said Rajel.

"Well, I defer to your mighty menace, O trowel-wielder," said Casamint. "I suppose I should look at this famous book she has sent me." He unwrapped the brown paper, and flicked his tailtip. "Well, it's a *pretty* book at least."

"What is it?" asked Boragette.

"It is *A Young Person's Guide to the Beasts of Forest and Field.* I did not realize that I was still counted as a Young Person." He flipped through it. "The print is large, and the amount of detail is small. Still, there are quite respectable brightly-colored pictures, so if I were to be unsure whether the beast in question were a small and harmless squirrel or a large and dangerous carcanofex, I could flip through this extremely noble *Guide* and tell which is which." He set it down on the edge of the bed, where it wobbled and crashed to the floor.

Boragette's antennae went flat. "I really do think she meant well. It's a beautiful book ... I'm sure she meant it for the art in it. At least she remembered that you're studying Natural Philosophy."

"Though, unaccountably, she thought I was fifteen years old."

Boragette shrugged. "That's Chicory for you. She's quite generous, but sometimes makes surprising choices. She's really quite wonderful, though."

"'Surprising'. I will grant you the 'surprising'. I will grant it to you several times over, and I might even be inclined to grant it to you with a few choice adverbs or qualifying phrases. Such as 'by reason of its foolishness'," said Casamint.

"Oh, put it on a shelf, Casamint," said Rajel.

Casamint put his lower hands on his hips, and his upper hands on his lower elbows, and faced his wife. "Is that some Comblefree way of saying, 'shut up'?"

"No, it's a Comblefree way of saying, 'put it on a shelf'. We'll give it to our children," said Rajel.

"Children are not imminent, unless the three of us have been intimate without mentioning the fact to me," said Casamint. He picked up the heaviest, densest textbook he had brought, and stomped out of the room.

Boragette sat heavily on the bed. "She's really not so horrid. Just a bit Orreny, a bit overenthusiastic the wrong way. She doesn't know you or Casamint, after all. *I* didn't know either of you when I told her about you, even."

Rajel fidgeted with the trowel. "I can't be insulted by a nice gift."

"I wish our husband would at least try to be pleasant. You're not so bad."

Rajel spread her antennae. "I wish he would, too. We'd be a lot happier."

Boragette drummed zir fingers on zir forearm a moment. "I hope Casamint meets her and likes her. It would be very convenient if he would marry her and me for his second marriage."

"He and she and you could be pleased enough, that way," Rajel said bitterly.

Boragette flinched. "We *will* get our marriage all fine before Casamint or I get married again. That's the only fair way." Zi was less determined than zie tried to sound.

"It's not you I'm worried about. You're a sweet little co-lover with a heart like a flowing fountain. I'm worried about our city-bug of a husband. If his heart is a fountain, it's flowing with ... that nasty bitter tea they give you to purify the blood. Yarrow or something."

"Well, we're stuck with him," said Boragette. "We'd better get a taste for yarrow tea."

"He'd better put his airs and affectations on a top shelf and get himself a better flavor," said Rajel.

"He just hates being rusticated, I think," said Boragette.

"We're country nobility. Does he plan to give up his title and move to the city and be a professor?"

"He's just my husband, Rajel. He doesn't tell me about his plans or hopes."

THE ENCHANTER'S INVITATION

Rajel twirled the letter by the stem. She recognized the big but precise handwriting on the leaf. Ilzatheinen was a wordy Rassimel; he would inevitably fill up the entire leaf, no matter how little he had to say, and have to write the last quarter of the letter crossways in a different color of ink.

> *To Rajel Rowns Tawlown of Comblefree and Corster, and Arrhwy of unknown provenance: I wish to engage your services as travel guards, from Lenkasia to a small village named Soohoon under the control of Byronny Mene, and, perhaps, to some of the cities of the Transwynt. This is not to be a dangerous trip; indeed, I am bringing my daughter. I have been hired for quite a good price to build defenses for Soohoon, as the residents there do not fully consider themselves safe. Not to put too fine a point on it, the village used until recently to have a defender, much like a knight although not strictly a member of any formal order, who has recently departed. I should think it safer to bring defenders of my own, and, as you have recently slain a nycathath, and as I doubt that there will be any greater danger present in Soohoon, I consider you to be more than adequate. But in light of our prior friendship please consider this offer, of two weeks and two days of my labor for each of you, or thirty thousand lozens.*
>
> *Your friend, Ilzatheinen*

Rajel looked at Arrhwy. "It sounds awfully pleasing to go away for a while and let Boragette and Casamint work everything out for me, I must say."

Arrhwy shook her head. "It sounds very the pleasing to get two weeks of work from Ilzatheinen. Very the odd too."

Rajel said, "Arrhwy, that doesn't matter. I *can't* go."

Arrhwy cocked her head. "And why is it that you cannot go?"

Rajel said, "I made Boragette and Casamint move here now, so I could have a proper triad with them. If I run off, I can't imagine they'll let me try again ... they might even divorce me. Teamary may want to have a Great Baron for a grandchild, or even for a daughter-in-law, but Casamint would rather go be a professor or something I should think. He acts like it anyways."

Arrhwy shrugged. "Ilzatheinen brings his daughter. You bring your husband and mari."

Rajel raised her antennae. "Now there's a thought. Not one of the three of us is having a good time in Comblefree ... and I don't think we'd do much better in anyone else's town. Spending a bit of time together, without other Herethroy around to bully Boragette, doing something halfway intellectual to interest Casamint. Let me see if I can talk them into it."

* * *

The three Herethroy sat on three corners of the bed; no two of them were really on touching terms. Arrhwy draped herself comfortably across a chest of drawers, twisted so that her hindquarters were right side up but her head was upside down. She only took that position around Herethroy, who were the least limber of the prime species.

"What, precisely, is he paying you, Rajel?", asked Casamint. "Two weeks of work? I trust he's more than a hairdresser or a tree-mage: what's a week's work worth?"

"He's an enchanter, and quite a respectable one. He made the most recent addition to the Girath city wall. He taught at Green for a year or two, but he's really a dreadful teacher. He'd rather be making things than telling other people how to," said Rajel.

"Years ago he makes an immortality talisman. Since then he is the Zi Ri of an enchanter, only no fire or wings. But he changes his name from Ilzath to Ilzatheinen, to sound more of a Zi Ri. Always he pays in time, not in money. He does the very good work though. Amulets he makes keep me alive fighting a nycathath," added Arrhwy.

"So a week's work from Ilzatheinen is worth, oh, tens thousands of lozens, perhaps," finished Rajel.

Casamint nodded seriously. "I have studied the Theory of Enchantment. I am thoroughly aware of what someone who can build an immortality device can do in two weeks' work."

Boragette glared at zir husband. "I don't know much about it, really."

Casamint said, "Here's an example you might appreciate: a device that sends everything in the room to the place you consider proper for it; a dozen uses a day. It would make light work of tidying up! But simply a trifle for him."

Arrhwy yawned a terrible, pointy yawn. "For my weeks I have him make The Gift of Seven Years. Sleeth do not live as long as Herethroy, and already I am not so young. A few more years of life are nice."

Boragette looked to Arrhwy. "Could he make an immortality device for you?"

Casamint snorted. "Don't be a fool, Boragette. That's a very individual enchantment. There can't be a dozen wizards on the whole World Tree who can make immortality devices for other people, and they don't ask third-rank adventurers politely to come with them. They only get the best, and they just *tell* them."

Boragette cringed, and Rajel lowered her antennae. Arrhwy smiled sweetly upside-down at Casamint. "Which is bigger of a fool: the one who does not know advanced magic theory from never studying it, or the one who insults everyone who is taking care of him in the danger time to come?"

Casamint said, "I told zir not to be a fool, not that zie *was* a fool. And you're not the greatest heroes on the branch (that's first rate), or even in a city (that's second rate), are you? It's not insulting if it's true, I shouldn't think."

Boragette glared at him. "You shouldn't think, no, not at all. It's quite bad for you ... gets you up to the mid-arms in a manure pond of trouble. You haven't the manners to do with what you've thought of."

Casamint blinked at zir, then brayed with laughter. "All right, all right, that's a sharp enough barb for me. This won't be a convenient vacation for me, nor an easy one, unless rich Rajel brings plenty of cash. I *had* hoped to get back to the academy."

Boragette spread zir antennae. "Do you really think it's safe, Rajel?"

Arrhwy answered, "He is the truthful Rassimel, so there is no lie in this letter. He thinks it is very the safe trip. But I think there is something he does not say so clearly. He is not the *honest* Rassimel, just the truthful one."

Rajel nodded. "He is bringing his daughter. I've met Zallarilla twice or thrice. She's quite nice and not a bit spoiled." She pointed an antenna distinctly at her husband, who ignored it. "But she's no adventurer or warrior. She's got some minor title from her mother's side."

"Baronet?" asked Casamint.

"Just esquire, I think. I don't quite know what she does, besides pilot her sky-yacht around and collect her allowance from her father," said Rajel.

"She's not a *young* daughter, then," said Boragette.

"Our age, more or less." said Rajel.

Boragette thought a moment. "We're not bringing anyone else?"

"You, me, Casamint, and Arrhwy," answered Rajel.

"Because I am hired," noted Arrhwy. "Beetheart is not hired, for Ilzatheinen does not know how fierce and terrible zie is."

Boragette grinned and said, "When do we leave?"

Casamint sighed.

> *Dearest Skirret,*
>
> *It seems I shan't be coming back to the academy next semester after all. Not that I am abandoning my studies to become a simple farmer, after getting my first taste of co-lovers — far from it! Indeed, I have not yet had those tastes, and may not for some time to come. Rajel is a harsh and brutal adventurer, handsome enough in her own way, but angry and rude. Borugette is actually well to my liking in most ways: usually sweet, but has a quick wit for a country cosi; and zie is quite pretty indeed. And rather shy. There's no use asking me what it's like coupling with a co-lover, much less a full trio, though I would tell you if I knew. In any case, never fear that they're stealing my heart; I don't even think they want to.*
>
> *But back to the academy, or, more accurately, not back to the academy. We have decided as a triad — and I use the word "decided" in the sense that, when a vote is taken, two may overcome one, no matter how good the one's reasons are — that we shall be going on a family vacation of sorts, to spend some months in the countryside of Araldy, as my fearsome hulking ogre of a wife guards some sorcerer as he makes ... I know not what, and care less. I daresay I'll be writing you often from the post office of Byronny.*
>
> *With all my love, I remain, your Casamint*

A FLATTERING WIND

A Flattering Wind was an elegant airship: a circular house of white wood, three stories tall, with four gleaming cupolas on top. She flew gracefully, pouring through the dawn air, just as though the gods had intended all houses to fly and only by laziness did most of them stay on the ground. She stopped, floating thirty feet over the middle of Comblefree. Farmers stopped working to look up at her: few skyboats visited Comblefree, and those that did were generally utilitarian sky-barges.

One of the cupolas slipped off the roof, drifting down to a meadow. A grinning young Rassimel woman hopped out, ringy tail perked behind her. "Hallo, hallo! I'm going far far away, beyond the primordial forest where the wooden goddess darkly stands, to mysterious cities of wicked magicians and to the homes of monsters! But before I left I thought I'd stop by to see if there was a farmer's daughter who might wish to come with me."

Rajel hoisted her three suitcases, and one of Casamint's. "There is one, at that, Zallarilla, but if you're always so melodramatic I shall demand a surcharge. "

Zallarilla giggled like bubbles in perfume. "Oh, I thought this would be a dullness and a boringness of a trip by your standards, so I might as well liven it up a bit."

"Don't liven it up too much! My husband considers my adventuring to be vulgar and undignified."

Casamint, standing by a pile of tapestry-sided bags, curtsied in the noble style. "Zallarilla, I take it? I am Casamint Imbarr Tawlown, and it is a deep pleasure to meet you."

Boragette gave Zallarilla a four-legged curtsey, after the fashion of the country gentry. "Boragette Norrow Tawlown."

Zallarilla returned his curtsey. "Casamint, Boragette, a deep pleasure in the high skies."

Boragette raised zir antennae. "Isn't there suppose to be something formal that you say to welcome us aboard? Or is that only in romance novels?"

"Oh, it's entirely real, but hardly anyone does it anymore." She grinned. "I think I remember the words, if you'd like... Boragette Norrow Tawlown, I do hereby formally invite you to come as a passenger upon *A Flattering Wind* and sail the skies with us, hither and yon, trunkward and outward, rollward and roll'gainst, beneath the eyes of the creator gods, until our paths do part us."

Boragette grinned and clapped her hands together. "I do accept this invitation, to be your guest and passenger upon *A Flattering Wind*, and ... and ..."

"It finishes, 'And to abide by all your orders as we fly, until our paths do part us.'" said Zallarilla.

"And to abide by all your orders as we fly until our paths do part us!" said Boragette.

"Oh, excellent," said Zallarilla. "Nobody's ever abided by even one of my orders before! Here's the first of them — put your luggage and yourselves in the big cabin on the second floor, the one with a stencil of a pie on the door. That's the only room I've got big enough for three."

The Rassimel and Herethroy loaded luggage, half of it Casamint's, into the cupola, and made their farewells to the Rowns and the rest of Comblefree. Arrhwy, physically incapable of lifting luggage and socially incapable of extensive friendliness, leapt to the top of the cupola and offered useless advice.

* * *

"Your father's not on board, then?" asked Boragette to the lace curtain fluttering in the kitchen window. Zie was chopping trompes-de-miel ferociously, and a leather pot was boiling with hosh grain on the hottest burner of the woodless, emberless ceramic stove.

"He's still in Lenkasia. We'll stay there tonight," answered the curtain in Zallarilla's voice. Zallarilla herself was in the pilot's chamber in the very center of *A Flattering Wind*, forbidden to all save members of the Sky Pilots' Guild. A dozen lace curtains on the outer windows of the skyboat had straightforward Illusidor enchantments, and she could see and talk from them.

Casamint was at the other counter, shredding leeks. "How did he entice you on this trip, Zallarilla?"

"He bought me *A Flattering Wind*, for starters, with a bit of the money from making the Girath wall. She's beautiful, even if she's slower than *Celestial Eel*." Zallarilla chattered on about her skyboats for a while, with the educated enthusiasm that few but Rassimel can achieve. The Herethroy waved their antennae knowingly: every Rassimel has some obsession, and Zallarilla's was clearly sky-piloting. It would be no harder to ask her to fly a thousand miles than it would be to ask Boragette to cook lunch.

* * *

Lenkasia, one of the greatest cities of Aradrueia, had two skyports. Doftree Port, the lesser of the two, flaunted Lenkasia's power: it was a single tall building, with a dozen towers branching off here and there. It could never have been built without much money, and it could never have stood without much magic.

A Flattering Wind docked at one of Doftree's upper branches. The Herethroy scrambled in their luggage to put together a single suitcase of one night's necessities. Arrhwy, who rarely wore clothing, sprawled over their bed, her tail flogging the pillows and any Herethroy who came too close in utterly simulated impatience.

At length they were finished, and they clambered down long dusty wooden staircases inside the arms of Doftree Port. Khtsoyis porters drifted beside them, calling, "Save your legs, buggies! We'll carry you to the ground for a bit of amber... Won't even charge double, for all that you've got twice as many legs."

Rajel laughed, and jumped out the next window they passed. Boragette and Casamint gasped. Rajel floated outside the window, surrounded by a Ruloc Corpador spell like polished ivory rings. She waved the glove that had been Oostmarine's. "We'll do it ourselves! I can carry one, and Arrhwy can also. Zallarilla, I've never heard of a sky pilot who couldn't at least levitate ..." The Rassimel nodded. "... so there's no need to walk."

The porters hooted. "Icky bugs, greedy bugs, stealy bugs! They seek to rob us of our proper jobs and our proper fees!"

Casamint beckoned Rajel back through the window. "They do have a point, noble wife. Let's just walk, or pay them to carry us."

Boragette blinked at zir husband. He waved his antennae. "I'm not a fool, Boragette. Whatever you think of me, do not think that. If mild Herethroy farmers will bemerde my luggage, there's no telling what Khtsoyis porters might do if I insult them."

"Well, my legs aren't so used to stairs yet. I *would* like to get down more easily," said Boragette. The staircase was wide enough to carry a banquet table up, and scuffed enough to suggest that many had been. But the dark wooden risers were irregular, their heights and widths suited to the curves of the dock's branch rather than the measure of any prime's pace.

A porter hooted, "That's the spirit, that's the spirit, noble bug! We'll carry any or all of you for three lozens the group!"

Rajel shrugged. "Whatever you like, Boragette. I'll fly, myself."

Zallarilla curled her tail, and stood on the window ledge. An old purple-scarred Khtsoyis in the midst of an argument about the relative merits of beer and narcotic tea curled two tentacles around her waist, and two more around her shoulders. The remaining three tentacles squirmed like drunken or drugged serpents, illustrating his argument to his fellows.

Boragette watched, and then allowed zirself to be carried as well. Zir Khtsoyis was much younger, and he turned his rubbery skin a muddy pink that matched zir rose chitin, to the most generous of eyes. His tentacles were warm and dry, and as smooth and strong as leather. He gargled, "Your first time t'Lenkasia, cosi?", his speaking mouth by zir ear.

"My first time away from the Pennypell countryside," zie admitted.

"Well, don't be scared, issa sweet city. If you want someone t'beat the students away from you, I can recommend a strong floaty guy with three good clubs..."

"Oh, no thank you. Look at my wife and her friend." Rajel had strapped her huge sword on her back, and Arrhwy's ears flickered around at every creak of a moored skyboat.

"They seem right dangerous folks, yes. Right fierce and fearsome, or I'm a flowering annual with interruptedly-pinnate leaves. If you want anything to calm 'em down and get 'em all friendly to you, I know a floaty guy who can help with *that* too."

Boragette blinked at him. He curled one tentacle as if holding a teacup, the tip elegantly aside, and pretended to sip from his talking mouth. The mouth he actually drank with was underneath, at the juncture of his tentacles. "*Special* tea. Good for married folk having a bit o'trouble, or even if they just want t'play a bit harder than usual."

Boragette scowled. "We are *not* having trouble."

The Khtsoyis wiggled a tentacle. "Didn't say you were, miss. Just illustrationating around my meaning. If there's any entertainment you'd like, your first visit to a city, it's I who knows where to find it for you... Hoi, we're aground now."

Boragette smiled. "No, but thank you ever so much." Zie curtsied country-style to him. He whirled in place in a Khtsoyis courtesy, the short green ribbons on his belt standing outwards.

Rajel gave him an amber octagon for the ride, and a small triangular third-lozen piece as a tip. "We'll be seeing you in three or four days, with a wizard and all his tools in tow, and I'm sure we'll be wanting a ride back up!"

When they got to the gate in Lenkasia's extravagant city wall, Boragette asked Rajel, "I thought we were only staying overnight?"

Rajel nodded. "Yes. Just I'm being a bit cautious. I doubt that the porters rob boats often, but *A Flattering Wind* is from Girath, we're from Pennypell, and you can never be too careful in a foreign city. If the porters *do* decide to sneak on board, I'd rather they didn't actually get around to it until we're gone."

Boragette spread zir antennae. "Do you always expect crimes and dangers, Rajel?"

Rajel nodded. "Always, Boragette. Better than being surprised."

Boragette shuddered.

FORBIDDEN CONVERSATION

Nethry was reading a children's story to seven children, as their parents perched on branches and watched. By prime law, she was committing a terrible crime; but there is no law in the Lenwynt, and especially not in the mid-Verticals by the Lenwynt.

"Flokin the fire god finished Its ice cream, and stretched, and sharpened Its claws on the lintel of her new ice cream parlor, and turned away and walked down the street, Its tail waving over Its back in some mixture of confusion and annoyance and laughter."

She set the book down on the spongy tree growing horizontally out from the side of the world-branch, and brought out a small bowl, sparky with cooling magic, from her pack. "And I brought some ice cream here for you to taste." The ice cream was already frozen hard on strings, which she tied to the upper branches of some bushes. The seven children chirped delightedly, and flew over to peck at it. They were conlee, sentient songbirds commanding respectable magical force; often friendly to primes, but more dangerous as friends than foes.

An adult flew and perched on a branch in front of her. Zir yellow feathers were quite ragged: zie was close to the end of zir four-year life. Murdering Nethry would have given zir several more years, and accepting a voluntary gift of some of Nethry's vitality would have given zir a few more; Nethry wondered how tempted zie was.

Zie did not seem tempted. "You're all kind with stories and treats, Nethry. Were you going to leave the books?"

Nethry nodded. "I surely am." Conlee learned quickly; with books, the chicks would be reading within a month. "Shall I simply leave them here, Tazca?"

Tazca nodded. "We are to move them someplace dry, from a spell. Not nests — they are not to fit in the nests!"

Nethry smiled, and leaned against a tree, watching the chicks peck at ice cream. "And what's going on in the ancient forest, Tazca?"

"I know what is to interest you, Inspector Nethry. You are to like knowing about Soohoon, the yes?"

Nethry sat back up, ears raised. "I am thoroughly to like knowing about Soohoon."

"From Soohoon you kill the great beast, the scyanturge. In Soohoon there is no sorrowing, for they fear the scyanturge most deeply. But in Soohoon there is no rejoicing, for the scyanturge is good to them. She brings them treasures from the boats she destroys. She keeps them safe from all the awful things that live in the deep Verticals, or further down. Now Soohoon has many treasures, and no scyanturge. They are the single ripe awbleberry on the bush, waiting for the first careful bird to come and to eat," said Tazca.

Nethry curled her tailtip. "They're a spiky little berry, though. A villageful of vorwi could put up somewhat of a fight, and you said that their Stop-Lord is a nycathath."

"Nherex-Dlostion is the Stop-Lord nycathath, the yes. Also there are a few perdithorne and a few ororosti. Soohoon is a tasty ripe awbleberry, but in the middle of the thicket. Safe this month."

Nethry nodded. "And...?"

"And they ask Vecsi over there to take a message. Vecsi can read..."

"I know!" grinned Nethry. Two years earlier Vecsi had been a chick listening as she told stories, studying other books she had left.

"So he does read the message. They want defenses! They will pay some of the treasure that Aulihemm got, and what they will buy is a city wall enchantment."

Nethry thought briefly. She knew something about most of the people who might have enchanted Soohoon's walls for several cities around, and none came to mind who would take such a job for a village of monsters. "I would rather they stayed an awbleberry. Who did the message go to?"

Vecsi fluttered his iridescent green wings, and chirped, "I carried the note to a thastryn. Wind wing spells, wing wind spells, it was a very long trip!"

"How long, Vecsi?"

"All the way to Lenkasia, at the other end of the Lenwynt! I have travelled farther than any decent conlee alive!" Conlee who murdered primes for extra life had the time to travel, but were, of course, not decent.

Nethry nodded thoughtfully. "Enchanters are plentiful in Lenkasia, what with Green there and all. And they would not care so much about what happens on our side of the Lenwynt."

Vecsi hopped on his branch. "I gave it to a thastryn, who gave it to a Herethroy, who took it to the city and asked it all around so delicately. I got a big bag, the thastryn got a mage's lever, the Herethroy got a lead torc! Lever and lead went into the big bag as its first carry." He showed off a tiny leather sachel worked with maps.

Nethry smiled, running a clawtip over the sachel. The sharp spikes of Locador were thoroughly evident to the magic sense. The bag was full of seeds, enough to feed the flock for a month, and two battered textbooks on magic theory and geometry that each outweighed the whole flock. She did not need to look further; they both had her name and her college address inside the front cover. "Very nice work, this bag. Only a few big bags shrink weight as well as size."

Vecsi hopped on his twig. "Nherex-Dlostion pays very well! She hopes to spend half the treasure so she can keep the other half — better than have it all eaten when a mighty monster comes to take the berry!"

A mighty monster, or a prime adventuring party, thought Nethry. "Nherex-Dlostion takes her Stop-Lordship quite seriously. Was there an answer, Vecsi?"

Vecsi spread his wings and bobbled his head. "The answer came on a little bone disk, and I put that in the sachel too! Ilzatheinen the Rassimel enchanter from Lenkasia will make walls for four months, and get the Tilmarth Note."

Nethry laughed aloud. "Nherex-Dlostion is getting robbed like a nose-deaf Cani in a perfume shop!"

Tazca cocked zir head. "Why is that, Nethry?"

Nethry thought a scowl at herself; as a matter of caution, she preferred not to tell her informants too much. But this was not Byronny's secret, and keeping this flock of conlee as her friends was more important than dropping a few minor details. "The Tilmarth Note is a Glory of Flokin. A professional enchanter would work four *years* to get one."

Vecsi bobbled again. "Not a prime enchanter, not four years in Soohoon down in the deep Verticals."

Nethry considered that. "A nine-times surcharge for having to work there? Fair enough."

Tazca said, "Tell us more about the Tilmarth Note."

Nethry put on her storytelling voice. "This is another true story about Flokin, though it's not in *A Child's Garden of Tales of Long Ago* that I just gave you. A thousand years ago Flokin fought a six-headed rat demon, the Omavrg. Flokin was a huge blazing Sleeth, and chased the Omavrg forward and back along outer Aradrueia, past the Transwynt. The two of them wrecked villages and set forests ablaze. After Flokin killed the Omavrg a few times and sent her home, It saw all the destruction. It is a destroyer, not a healer, so It asked some primes to fix things. Duke Tilmarth Mozentangus worked for seven years and nearly bankrupted his city-state, and most of the destruction was on his neighbor's land. Flokin wrote Tilmarth a thank-you note — it looks like Ilzatheinen's answer, except that it's copper, and misspelled, and the signature is a living flame."

"Why is that worth so much?"

"It's a Glory of Flokin. Each day someone can ask for one special favor of Flokin — not a big favor that It does in person, but a little favor. Like making a fire spell twice as strong," said the Rassimel.

"Oh, Lelka would like that!" Female conlee had Pyrador magic.

"An enchanter would like it even more, since those favors go nicely for enchantments," said Nethry. "I'm not surprised Nherex-Dlostion could find someone, at that price.

The conversation turned to other doings of the monsters of the Lenwynt. Nethry smiled to herself; a bit of ice cream, children's literature, and goodwill bought her more information than Pethiliant could scry, and far more cheaply.

* * *

Dear Casamint,

I'm very sorry to hear you won't be back soon. I need you, in ways that I cannot begin to describe. Not just your body on mine, but your beautiful, easy connection to our village and our whole species. Do hurry back as quick as you can, my love.

— Skirret

MEETING THE ENCHANTER

Ilzatheinen had a pair of apartments in the student quarter of Lenkasia, one for living and one for working. In most other cities, he would have been one of the greater sorcerers, and had a mansion and servants, mystical sculptures and a chariot of illusions. In Lenkasia, a great center of learning and priesting, there were dozens of comparable sorcerers and several greater ones, and such vainglory was socially unacceptable. Instead, he had bought *A Flattering Wind* for Zallarilla, and enjoyed having a mansion of sorts when he travelled.

Boragette smiled and curtsied. "A pleasure to meet you, Ilzatheinen." The pleasure was largely forged. Ilzatheinen was a fat, untidy Rassimel, with irregular rings on his face and tail. He did wear the traditional wizard's robes, but he wore them over a waistcoat and cummerbund of cheap, ratty azure velvet, and looked pompous and ridiculous.

Nor were his social graces perfect. "A pleasure to meet you, Boragette. I didn't know until quite recently that Rajel even *had* a family. She never mentioned you when she worked for me before."

Boragette shrugged. "I'm not sure she thought of it very often."

Casamint stepped in front of zir, and greeted Ilzatheinen as one scholar to another. "Good day, and good thy studies."

Ilzatheinen blinked at him. "And good thy studies as well." The tip of his tail twitched: he did not accept Casamint's pretensions of scholarship, but did not feel that the point was worth debating.

"Well then. Zallarilla, I trust you'll be staying here tonight?"

"Father, I will not be. It's the last night for many to come that I'll have to enjoy a proper city, and I mean to enjoy it quite thoroughly," said Zallarilla.

He frowned, and flattened his ears. "On one side, you *are* definitely grown up. On the other side, that Orren man of yours is scarcely a gentleman, and I wouldn't believe any claim he made to any other virtue either. Nor is it quite proper for a Rassimel girl to have ... entanglements ... with an Orren."

Zallarilla laughed. "Father, that was four years ago. I doubt me that Spirshash so much as remembers me; I doubt me that he remains in the city; I doubt me that you ever believed the true and overwhelming unscandalousness of our relationship. I shall, rather, dine at a fine restaurant to the accompaniment of flutes, my mother, my daughter, my daughter's father, and whoever he sees fit to practice contraception with at the moment. I shall attend whatever is being performed in the Undergreen Repertory Theatre; I shall sleep, alone, upon familiar silken sheets in *A Flattering Wind*, rather than upon equally familiar linen ones upon your couch."

Ilzatheinen threw up his arms, and showers of bright sparks coursed over his sleeves. "Alas! My daughter shall be slowly corrupted by the wickedness of Lenkasia!"

Zallarilla laughed. "As my parents were before me... and better that than the wickedness of Girath, I should think." She peered at the sparks. "Is that some new toy of yours? I can't see you wasting cley on melodrama that way."

He grinned, and showed her a silver pin he wore in his cloak. "A very old one from my academy days, which I rediscovered in a box of model ducks, of all things." He pinned it to her collar. "The command is, to curl your tongue in a tube: not a word at all."

Zallarilla winked at Rajel. "I come by my melodrama honestly, as you can see!" She added a shower of sparks to punctuate her words.

Rajel nodded. "I *have* worked for Ilzatheinen once or twice."

SOOHOON

A Flattering Wind was several days out from Lenkasia, and nearly across the Lenwynt. Casamint and Boragette were playing an unremarkable game of diamond-chess in one of the cupolas on top of *A Flattering Wind*. Boragette moved all three cani in different directions, taking Casamint's zi ri and orren. Casamint winced. "I wasn't expecting that. The books recommend against splitting your cani, if you've managed to get them together."

Boragette smiled. "I haven't read books on diamond-chess. Taking two pieces seemed good to me."

Casamint said, "Yes, but I get to take one of yours back. You're the exchange up, but less than you might think."

Boragette stretched and stood up while Casamint stared at the board, and then leaned over the cupola's railing. "Casamint, come look if you like. Zallarilla's taking us off the branch."

Casamint looked up, glad of an escape from a defeat at the hands of his uneducated but devious mari. "This Soohoon that we're going to must be on the very edge of the Verticals in Byronny Mene. And that would make sense: a town just next to the dangerous wilderness would be most likely to need defenses, I should think."

The edge of the world approached them, an endless cliff wall stretching forever to left and right. They could see over it now, to the steep steep wall of the Verticals, spongy horizontal trees sticking out of it, holding their inverted umbrellas of leaves to the sky, thirsty for rain.

Boragette and Casamint watched, leaving their half-finished game aside. "We're getting awfully close to the edge of the world-branch, Casamint."

Casamint laughed lightly. "I daresay our skyship can fly over nothing just as easily as over a branch. I shouldn't be surprised if there were some awkward haily weather inward of here that Zallarilla were going around, or some such." He pointed at the Verticals wall, where a dot of a beast was swinging from tree to tree on many arms. "There's a Jack O'Hooks, I imagine. Very dangerous."

The airship reached the edge of the world, and passed it, and started drifting down. Boragette frowned. "This is an awfully odd way for cutting around a storm."

Casamint spread his antennae. "I may have been wrong." He called to the lace curtain, "Zallarilla? We've gone off the edge of the world, you know ... what are we doing?"

Zallarilla answered, "Simply going down to Soohoon."

Casamint squeezed the rail in a mid-hand. "Soohoon's *in* the Verticals? In the Lenwynt?"

Zallarilla laughed. "You won't find a village of vorwi as a suburb of Byronny, I shouldn't expect!"

Boragette asked, "Village of vorwi?"

Casamint said, "Vorwi are floating tetrahedral people that live in the deep Verticals. Is Soohoon not a prime village, then?"

Zallarilla hesitated a minute, steering the skyship a bit further from the Verticals wall. "No, it's not." Her voice came from every curtain in the airship. "Rajel and Arrhwy, we're in the Verticals now. This might be a good time for you to be armed and armored and awake. No melodrama here, I'm afraid."

Boragette and Casamint looked at each other in alarm. "Casamint, I didn't think we'd be going on vacation in a village of monsters."

"I didn't either. I don't think it's such a good idea..."

Rajel clambered to the main deck, below them, strapping on her sword. "Zallarilla, why are we going into the Verticals?"

Zallarilla sighed. "We're going to Soohoon. It's a village of vorwi in the deep Verticals. Their Stop-Lord, who is a nycathath, wants some incendiary dangerous explosive defenses against all manner of wicked horrors around them. If you want more details, ask my father."

Rajel looked up to her spouses. "Casamint, could you make yourself useful and dredge Ilzatheinen up here? I have a question or two for him."

* * *

Ilzatheinen nodded. "Soohoon is, indeed, a nonprime village lead by a nycathath. There shouldn't be any trouble — after all, we are there to build something vital for them. In any case, you and Arrhwy are well capable of killing a nycathath in need, are you not?"

Rajel scowled. "You *should* have mentioned this earlier. We *have* killed a nycathath, but only with a very careful trap, and we lost a very good fighter when we did. A nycathath who's taking the initiative, on its own ground, with a village of vorwi to help out ..." She spread her antennae. "We start off by running away. In fact, I recommend that we do so immediately."

Ilzatheinen shook his head. "Don't be silly. This is a professional visit, not a military one. It's entirely safe."

Casamint raised a middle hand. "Vorwi aren't very aggressive nonprimes. I've read a fair bit of nonprime customs. I know."

Rajel crossed her middle arms. "I am not pleased at being hired for a much more dangerous situation than I had known at the outset."

Ilzatheinen shook his head. "It's not dangerous! Great staring gods, woman, it's not as if every nonprime were out to kill us."

"Be that as it may — shush, Casamint — as it may, Ilzatheinen, there are plenty of dangerous horrors and wicked monsters around here."

Ilzatheinen nodded. "I did not hire you at exorbitant rates to go on vacation in a tranquil suburb of Byronny! But between you, the defenses of the airship, the hordes of vorwi, and the nycathath who is their Stop-Lord, I doubt that we will be in any particular danger. I did, as you may have noticed, bring my daughter. I did, as you may have noticed, bring myself."

Rajel looked around. "Arrhwy? Casamint? Boragette?"

Arrhwy shrugged. "It is not the first time I am in the deep Verticals."

Boragette folded zir arms. "I should prefer to go home at once, or to prime lands at least."

Casamint smiled. "I do believe I know what we are getting into. It sounds adequately safe, and quite interesting."

Ilzatheinen shrugged. "This is not a matter for voting. My daughter is captain and pilot of this boat. It goes where she wishes, nowhere else. She is most devoutly concerned for her life, do you understand? She thinks it is safe."

Zallarilla's voice floated out from a lace curtain. "They certainly didn't kill me when I was here before — not that I noticed at least!"

Rajel stared at the curtain. "You were here before?"

Zallarilla said, "Making the arrangements for Papa. They're fairly friendly. They mostly hadn't seen primes before me, except for a wanderer or two."

Rajel threw her upper hands in the air. "Fine. Don't blame me if we all get killed!"

A MEETING WITH MONSTERS

Soohoon was most of a day's journey into the Verticals, down where the world-branch curved back towards the terrors of the Underneaths. The Verticals forest near Soohoon became stranger: epiphytes with great inflated bladders floating just next to the Verticals wall; vast nets of slithering vegetable worms; curling things like clusters of sharp curved horns, moving. Rajel and Arrhwy watched the sky, the Verticals wall, the horizon: this was not safe territory.

A trio of terrors rose towards *A Flattering Wind*: ororosti, people whose entire body was a single long strand of eyeballs and nerves. The adventurers watched them warily, contemplating their choices of long-range weaponry. But words sprinkled into their minds like drops of bitter rain: «*Be welcome to Soohoon, O primes, if you bring peace; but if you bring war ... know that we will rend your minds and terribly destroy you.*»

Arrhwy hissed angrily. "Mind-magic!" She invoked a defensive talisman against that most wicked of Nouns. Rajel had no such defenses, and so was helpless against their next words: «*Ilzatheinen must be among you. Bring him forth that we may ... speak with him.*»

Rajel shuddered, and shouted to the lace curtains, "Zallarilla, turn back this instant. Three ororosti are in front of us, and pouring words into our minds!"

Zallarilla laughed lightly from the pilot's cabin. "Give Rodents-At-Dawn my greetings, and tell it-or-him-or-her that all is well."

"You *know* these things, Zallarilla?"

"Well, of course. I *was* here before," Zallarilla answered.

"I see. Do you have any more disgusting surprises in store for us in this little village from the philosophers' realm of punishment?" shouted Rajel.

"One nycathath, five ororosti, five perdithorne, a few hundred vorwi, and sundry farm animals. I daresay you'll find the farm animals the most awful of the lot. Now do go be polite to them, won't you, Rajel? I can't talk to them from inside here."

Arrhwy flattened her ears. "Perdithornes are too much like Sleeth. Perhaps there are bickerings about territory if I talk to them."

Rajel poked the Sleeth. "These aren't the perdithorne. You talk to them."

Arrhwy blinked malachite eyes. "Rajel, I have Mentador protections up. I cannot take them down quickly. You, not I, must talk to them."

Rajel scowled, but Arrhwy peered back at her with a Sleeth's inexorable unconcern. The Herethroy shrugged, and stomped over to the edge of the boat, and shouted, "Hallo, monsters of Soohoon! Ilzatheinen will speak to you shortly!"

«*See that he does, O Herethroy!*» dripped into her thoughts.

Rajel growled, "Rude horrible telepaths!" She stormed off below to Ilzatheinen's suite.

* * *

Boragette stood on the deck, looking over Soohoon. "That's the oddest village I've ever seen." It was set in a wide round gall in the world-bark with a round opening some fifty yards in diameter. Inside there were dozens of wooden platforms, unfamiliar red-orange wood from some strange Verticals tree. Cables connected the platforms to each other and to the walls of the gall. There were no actual buildings, though the platforms closest to the gall's opening had screens positioned to block wind and rain.

The people were just as odd. Most were tetrahedral vorwi, floating around on minor Ruloc Corpador spells as Arrhwy often did. Boragette thought they had a dizzying variety of appendages on the ends of their four arms. Many had wide fans which they waved to help move them through the air; some had hands; some had large eyes, or mouths, or tightly curved claws just the size of the cables. As Boragette watched, a vorwi fanned himself to a platform, and his fans reshaped themselves to cable-grasping claws.

The other inhabitants were more disturbing. Five ororosti poured through the air towards *A Flattering Wind*. Several perdithorne watched from the platforms, sprawling out their Sleeth-like bodies — or the parts of them that were flesh. They were half-skeletal, as if everything but the bones on much of their bodies was simply invisible. There was no pattern or stability to the invisibility; as Boragette watched, a perdithorne's empty eye and cheek filled with flesh and fur, and its ear and neck became invisible.

The last kind of inhabitant was the nycathath, bat-winged and mighty. She flew towards *A Flattering Wind*, the air booming around her. "Hallo with you, Zallarilla and those who are come beside you. May I land aboard you?"

Zallarilla's voice answered, "And a good day to you too, Nherex-Dlostion. Come aboard, introduce yourself, be friendly and all of that."

Rajel was not a small Herethroy, but Nherex-Dlostion's eyes were level with the tops of her antennae. She looked at the diamond pattern of the nycathath's ribcage, thinking of how Bherva-Charion's similar ribs had shattered under her sword. She put that thought aside, and curtsied to the monster. "Hello, lord nycathath."

The monster's voice was as the striking of a wide drum. "Indeed, hello with you as well. Nherex-Dlostion I am, and Stop-Lord of Soohoon I am, and your host as well I am while you rest here."

Rajel paused, so Boragette smiled shyly and said, "Thank you deeply for the welcome. I am Boragette. This is Rajel, Casamint, Arrhwy. Ilzatheinen whom you have hired is belowdeck..."

"He is not!", chirped the enchanter. "He is sitting on the staircase, despairing over the breaking of a shoelace!" He tossed the scrap aside, and walked over with one boot loose to curtsey and introduce himself.

The nycathath crashed her wings together. "The sky-wide gladness is upon me that you have come here, for many are our future enemies, and greedy. Let us feast tonight, and our insidious plans prepare. I would not delay any further."

Ilzatheinen smiled. "I look forward to the exercise. Defending such a place as this, against such enemies as you may face, is hardly a textbook's case study from Green!"

Nherex-Dlostion looked to the Herethroy and Sleeth, then glanced back to Ilzatheinen. "Your servants and assistants are these? No chambers have we prepared for so many. What will be needful for their tending?"

The Herethroy frowned as one. Ilzatheinen quickly said, "They are companions and visitors: nobles and scholars among primes, mighty heroes for guarding me in the dangerous skies of the Lenwynt. Treat them as you would treat me, that they may speak well of you in the great courts of Araldy."

Nherex-Dlostion curtsied to them. "Then as mighty foes betruced shall we treat you. Small and rude against the courts of Araldy is Soohoon, yet what we have you shall not lack. Chambers shall be prepared shortly." She turned and shouted to vorwi, who air-swam to arrange matters.

Casamint whispered, "That should give us more respect." Boragette answered, "... or make the ransom higher." They looked at each other nervously.

NEGOTIATIONS

A formal banquet at Soohoon was a wild and primitive affair. Five platforms were set close to each other — no single platform they could make could hold everyone — and vorwi and ororosti brought segments of ancient treetrunks to make many small tables. There were no chairs: Nherex-Dlostion was the only native of Soohoon capable of sitting, and she simply sat on one table and ate from the next one. The primes decided to sit on the floor: the three Herethroy at one table, Ilzatheinen and Zallarilla sharing Nherex-Dlostion's table, and Arrhwy sprawled comfortably among the perdithorne.

The food was primitive but vigorous. In the central platform eight vorwi chefs performed, spending cley extravagantly to levitate a huge bonfire up so that it would not burn their platform, and more cley to hold the meats of the feast inside it and pull them out at the right time. The centerpiece was a pair of huge worms the size of horses, plucked that morning from the thick clayey moss of the Verticals-wall, cleaned and stuffed with leaves and petals. The Herethroy could not eat it; the other primes found it chewy and spicy, savory and gamy. There were bowls of pickled moss, of bark simmered until it was soft and sweet, of petals drizzled with honey, of fermented fruits. Afterwards the vorwi chefs, gleaming with sweat, brought out a long bowl hollowed from a single log and filled with water and leaves, and tossed the remains of the fire into it. The steam was fierce and fragrant, and the chefs scooped out gourd bowls of the liquid as a pungent bittersweet tea to end the meal.

Nherex-Dlostion called for her gourd and Ilzatheinen's to be refilled. "Prime enchanter, expert enchanter, expensive enchanter, now you see what situation we are in. How will you work to guard us?"

Ilzatheinen carefully scooped an ash-spangled petal out of his gourd on a clawtip and ate one quarter of it. "I have seen much, but two things are not yet here to see: your enemies, your payment."

Nherex-Dlostion silently passed Ilzatheinen a copper disk half the size of his hand. He read it: *"Duke Tilmarth: Thak you very much for all your work mending things."* The letters were melted into the copper, a bit awkwardly, written with a terribly hot clawtip. It was signed with a little picture of a cat, in flat flames. The flames danced as Ilzatheinen watched, and the cat's image turned to face him, and grinned a pointy fangy grin.

Ilzatheinen cupped the Note in his hands, feeling the summerwarm smile and distant regard of Flokin beating against his fur. Perhaps one of the great angels of fire could counterfeit such a thing, forging the god's signature and imitating Its presence, but neither nycathath nor scyanturge, nor the greatest of prime wizards, could do so, nor fool him with illusions to that extent.

Nonetheless, he smiled at Nherex-Dlostion. "You will, of course, have no objection if I test it?"

Nherex-Dlostion shrugged. "Ours is the presumption that you shall use it as you labor for us, insofar as it is suitable." She half-spread her wings. "But go some ways away from the platforms, for there is no power more dangerous than fire in a village made of wood, and Flokin is a cruel and a playful god."

Ilzatheinen nodded. Two cley left him floating in the center of Soohoon's gall, far from any wood. He conjured a swirling ball of flame in the ordinary way, with a third cley. He smiled at the Note, using its force the way anyone would use a cley ordinarily, and tried to shape the fireball into a bird with a simple, familiar spell.

As an expert mage, Ilzatheinen knew intimately how potent his spells were when he cast them ordinarily. The fire-shaping cast with the Tilmarth Note vastly exceeded the power he could achieve on his own, as his spell would ordinarily exceed the power of a child's unskilled magic. But the change was more than simply power. Ordinarily the spell required his full concentration. This one did not: it had its own spirit and intellect. It grinned at him with a half-opened beak, and spread its wings, and flew thrice around him trailing brilliant orange sparks.

He smiled, well-satisfied, and wasted another cley teleporting back to the feast. The firebird followed him unbidden: it could not teleport, but it knew where he was, and rushed to him in a whirl of wings. It circled his head, and the perdithorne and ororosti could not meet its terrible bright gaze.

"I have had the good fortune to use a Glory of this or that god eight times before, though never so casually as this. I have even used two Graces. This is genuine, never fear." Ilzatheinen was talking to his daughter as much as to the nycathath. He looked up at the bird. "This is a peculiarly obstinate glory, though, or I'm a small spotted five-legged snail-lizard who eats aromatic gums in the spice orchards. Have you, or anyone, used it before? Did it work properly?"

Nherex-Dlostion shook her head. "I have not, nor could I." She raised her voice and looked at one of the perdithorne. "Tlurrrien, come towards here and explain to the enchanter of that which transpired when you sought to use the Tilmarth Note."

Tlurrrien stretched a long clawsome stretch, then leapt casually from his dining-platform to Nherex's without much of a thought for the hundreds of feet of space beneath him. He regarded Ilzatheinen for a while from eyeless sockets, then rolled on his side and stretched fleshed and fleshless legs. "Squirmed it did, as a serpent who would not be eaten! Insisted I did! Let me use it did, but only after the argument."

Ilzatheinen raised his ears. "And you were trying to bind an attack spell, were you not?"

Tlurrrien chuffed, "No firebird like yours I did! Simply a wide and painsome explosion as a tlessat for an ororosti to toss."

Ilzatheinen nodded. "Just so. Nherex, what you have here is a very genuine Glory of Flokin, but not a particularly good one."

Nherex stiffened and narrowed her eyes. "Do you assert that it is inadequate as a fee?" The firebird spread its flaming wings and landed between her and Ilzatheinen, head cocked back, ready to strike at the nycathath should Ilzatheinen need the slightest defense.

Ilzatheinen ignored monster and firebird, and continued, "Pyrador is, of course, the most martial of the Nouns, and a great many Pyrador spells cast are cast in battles. But this is a thank-you note to someone for *defending*, and, as such, it is much more useful for protective magics than aggressive ones. My firebird demonstrates that. The basic fire-shaping I used would never take any action on its own; and the firebird of an aggressive Glory would, I daresay, be doing its very best to be grilling your liver at this point."

Nherex flapped her immense wings once, blowing the firebird far off the platform. "Do you assert that it is inadequate as a fee?", she demanded again.

Ilzatheinen laughed. "Do you imagine for one moment that any Glory on Aradrueia has fewer than a dozen books about it, in the libraries of Lenkasia? Or that I would neglect to look at them before I headed out? My good nycathath, I know seven competing and foolish theories about why the Note is spelled wrong!" He tossed it to Nherex. Tlurrrien winced, but Nherex caught it more quickly than Rassimel or perdithorne could see.

The firebird returned to the platform, and Ilzatheinen smiled at it and let it cease existing.

Nherex raised her huge ears. "So, the price is acceptable unto you?"

Ilzatheinen nodded. "Four months' work here, and up to another month for travel and other laboring at prime temples. You supply all materials. You are aware that enchantment is not subject to perfect calculation, and that this arrangement may fall a week or two short of finishing; these extra weeks will be paid at a lesser rate. Conversely, our first plans may be finished more quickly than we anticipated at first; in this case I shall perform other works for you."

Nherex and Ilzatheinen dickered over a few details here and there. Tlurrrien yawned, his tongue appearing in mid-yawn, and leapt back to talk with Arrhwy. After a time, Ilzatheinen smiled. "We are agreed, then."

Nherex curtsied again. "In all matters of substance, we are, indeed, agreed. You shall start work at tomorrow's dawning."

Ilzatheinen grinned. "There is one more matter..."

Nherex scowled. "Greedy enchanter, devious enchanter, wicked enchanter, you have just negotiated the entire price! Do you dare speak in bad faith to *me*?"

Ilzatheinen laughed. "Not a matter of price, but of what work you specifically want. Who, precisely, are your enemies? What, precisely, shall I build for you? Best against a scyanturge is one matter; best against a horde of nrex a very different one."

Nherex frowned, then laughed. "In all fairness we may well wish to answer that question. Unfortunately, today's friends may be tomorrow's enemies: a poor thing, as today's enchanted defenses will be tomorrow's enchanted defenses. Best, I think, to have very general defenses: good against anything, though best against nothing in particular."

Ilzatheinen nodded. "Then I recommend: a block against teleporting, a widespread protection from magic, a wall of flame that can cover the gap to the outside, and a very protective fire elemental."

"You have thought on this matter before this moment?"

"I am, indeed, a Rassimel. Never doubt it."

"Can you do all this in the allotted time? It seems a great deal."

"It is optimistic. I *could*, with luck and careful planning, finish it in four months, plus of course a trip to New Kottarnu. Most likely it would take two weeks or a month extra."

Nherex cocked her head. "By any measure, the fee we shall pay you for the extra time is less than you could get for just working the proper time. Are you not cheating yourself to do this?"

Ilzatheinen smiled. "Yes, but I have a creative approach to two parts, and a glory for two parts. I shall enjoy it!"

"You are, indeed, a Rassimel. I shall never doubt it."

* * *

Arrhwy pawed at Tlurrrien's foreleg, her pads feeling the invisible fur. She grinned at him. "Always that is very strange. When your eyelid is invisible, do you see through it as well?"

"See through it I do! Have you never met perdithorne before, longtail?"

"Twelve years ago I meet a tribe of scawn, all brave and berserk with more fury than a scawn often has. They rush at me, they scream, they strike poorly with spears — the spears explode with fire. I run away quickly, rrai! But that night I come back, floating, creeping, sneaking. Scawn watch the paths to their home, but the tree-canopy they do not watch. Living with them is a perdithorne woman. Vvakkahh is her name."

"Kill her, you did, longtail?" Tlurrrien flattened his one visible ear briefly, and presumably the other as well.

"I do not kill her! She smells me. She snarls at me. We discuss politely with much snarling until many scawn come with many explosive spears. I run away quickly again, rrai! And I come back with the knight and the healer, the deep-mage and the fire-mage. Many, many scawn die. Vvakkahh and I continue discussing politely with much snarling. Politely do we help Vvakkahh move to the mid-Verticals, away from all Cani and from all places Cani live. We do not pay her much. I am a fierce and vicious negotiator!"

Tlurrrien licked his foreleg, flattening invisible fur into shape. "Killing any of us, you do not do, longtail? Bringing Cani here, you do not do either..."

"We know there are perdithorne here. We bring no Cani. Civilization to civilization, we surely fight — Cani are the big part of prime society.

Person to person, Sleeth to perdithorne, we maybe do things that are not fighting."

Invisible eyes stroked through green-black fur, pondered the set of her ears, the leisure of her posture, the taste of her scent. "There are things to do that are not fighting. That tail so long, where does it go when a tom mounts you?"

Arrhwy spread her whiskers. "My tail goes behind the rest of me, wherever I go. Soon it goes to a private place. I am not the very romantic Sleeth. I do not like many people watching. Which way I bend it to get it out of the way is a thing I do not say. A tom would have to try and see."

"In the lower half of Soohoon gall there are thick tangles of bushes and low trees, as do grow happily with no sunshine. Privacy is there!"

"After eating, I too am there."

* * *

Much time and much happy caterwauling later, Arrhwy sauntered to the platform where the primes were to sleep. She prowled around, sniffing at the half-dozen low tents that the vorwi had set up for them. In the second she smelled and heard Herethroy, and she whacked the tent hard with her tail. "Rajel! Somehow I miss the tour. Get up and tell me which tent I stay in."

Rajel's antennae appeared from the tentflap. "That one. Where did you go?"

"I go to the bushes with Tlurrrien the tom-perdithorne." Arrhwy sprawled on the ground, spread her hind legs, and licked and groomed her lower belly a bit.

Rajel stared. "Arrhwy. You didn't."

Arrhwy peered back, a gaze as clear as emeralds in water. "Some things I do, some things I do not."

"You didn't go screw a perdithorne."

Arrhwy blinked. "He is the best thing to screw around here. You say no. Zallarilla says no. I am the polite Sleeth and I do not ask your husband or your mari. I am the marginally sane Sleeth and I do not ask Ilzatheinen."

Rajel frowned. "He is a nonprime, a monster."

Arrhwy shrugged. "Not many primes think I am much better than a monster. I do not *marry* him, Rajel. I do not have kittens by him: we are not the same species. It is not so different than me and an Orren, or me and a Cani. Except he is built more right, more like a tom-Sleeth."

Rajel shook her head. "Arrhwy, it's still disgusting. I don't even think it's safe. What if one of the other perdithorne is jealous and they decide to attack us?"

"Rrai, disgusting maybe, but not dangerous. The one who is envious is you. I think I am the only one on *A Flattering Wind* to get any sex this whole trip," snapped Arrhwy.

Rajel glowered at the Sleeth, who decided to continue her bath. "Arrhwy, that's not fair!"

Arrhwy lifted her head from her belly and blinked at Rajel. "If you want sex, talk to Boragette or Casamint. You bring them on a trip to be nice to them, after all." She yawned a big tongue-curling yawn. "I am stinging and sore, but happy and sleepy. Good night!" She rolled to her feet, and poured under the flap of her tent.

* * *

Arrhwy was off with the Rassimel, in principle to protect them as Ilzatheinen worked on plans for building magical walls. The three Herethroy sat together in dim light on the sleeping-platform. Hundreds of feet beneath them, a dusty lance of sunlight crossed the floor of the Soohoon gall, illuminating and feeding the few light-loving plants that grew inside.

"Had you intended this to be a *fun* vacation for us, Rajel?", asked Casamint in a vinegary voice.

Rajel's voice sounded like bitter skullcap. "I thought it was to be in some nice countryside somewhere. We've had this discussion four times already. Do you really want to make it five? You were the one who said it would be adequately safe and adequately interesting. Do something interesting!"

"What sort of interesting thing would you like, Rajel? Shall I ... conjure winged guntries from my tailpipe and send them flying about the gall? Recite the histories of the Thirty-Three Dread Wizards of Oorah Thrassen? Perform little duets with Boragette on the piccolo?"

Boragette spread zir antennae. "Please stop fighting, won't you? We're going to leave for civilization in a day or two. Rajel, you and your Sleeth have a contract, but Casamint and I don't. Perhaps we could get dropped off in Byronny and, I don't know, take a freighter back to Araldy when Ilzatheinen and you come back to do the enchantments?"

Casamint waved his antennae. "There's a smart cosi I married! Money might be a bit tight, but I imagine we could arrange it somehow or other."

Rajel nodded reluctantly. "I suppose that might be easier on all of us." She examined her dagger in the dingy light, then dripped pruss-bean oil on a bit of leather, and started polishing it. "Perhaps we can get a bit friendlier before then."

Casamint scowled at her. "So, Rajel. You think that you are likely to die here?"

She blinked at him. "No ... why do you even ask that?"

He said, "This 'friendlier' you say, my ears hear as 'three-way coitus', which is to say, 'engendering a child unless techniques are used to avoid such.' If you expect to die when you return to Soohoon, you will still have done your duty to the family, if Boragette is filled and growing with the joining of your flesh with mine."

Boragette flattened zir antennae. "Casamint!"

Casamint scowled in turn at zir. "I wish to know what our adventurous, dangerous wife's intent and plan may be."

Rajel scowled back. "Then ask her." When Casamint tried, she interrupted him with, "Actually you have already asked a dozen times, in all manner of different wordings, but the answer remains: fulfil the terms of my contract, collect mighty magic items, return home."

"And grow a family?", he demanded.

"In due course, I suppose," she said.

"Casamint, what *are* you going on after?" asked Boragette.

"Here we are, married as a pack of Cani, and I can't get a friendly caress *or* a friendly word from either of you," said Casamint.

"You might start by being more pleasant," said Boragette, and turned zir head away and stalked to zir tent. Casamint and Rajel heard the deep rasping sound of Herethroy sorrow.

Rajel stabbed her dagger between two coarse boards in the platform floor. "Excellently done, Casamint. The next time I need my mari driven off to cry, I know just the man for the job." Casamint shrugged, and strode off to his own tent, and looked through his books for something he felt like reading.

PREPARATION FOR A BETRAYAL

Wesk-Wesk scratched carefully on Boragette's tent, having unaccountably decided that zie was the best prime to talk to. "Please't you, Boragette, it's a Rassimel."

Boragette peeked out of Casamint's tent, where zie was slowly getting devoured at a bitter game of diamond-chess. "What's a Rassimel?"

Casamint bounced a captured orren-piece off zir back. "A Rassimel is a short, obsessive, mammalian, ringtailed, mask-eyed prime person, Boragette. If you weren't such a hick you might have met one or two. They might have been named Zallarilla, or Ilzatheinen."

Boragette tugged on three tent-poles with three hands, burying Casamint in leather, and, entirely coincidentally, ruining the chess game beyond all reconstruction. "Shush, Casamint, and let Wesk-Wesk speak to us."

"It's a Rassimel has come to us, and Nethry is her name. What shall we do with her, please't you?"

Boragette said, "Is there some problem with her?"

"She's had her wounding, somewhat, and she's wanting for unhurt clothes and new food."

"Bring her to *A Flattering Wind*, and I'll see what I can do for her, I suppose. And find Zallarilla — my clothes won't fit her much better than yours would, Wesk-Wesk, and I'd hate to give away a dearly beloved tunic of hers."

"Do it yourself, please't you? The sky-house is yours'ns, and I won't like to fly there all uninvited."

Casamint extricated his head from the tent. "Maybe you could go with zir, and carry Nethry? Boragette can't fly. Considering what she does to tents, I doubt that she can actually *walk*."

* * *

In the upper parlor on *A Flattering Wind*, Nethry rubbed her wounds, and her annoyed look was not entirely feigned. She had asked Tuku to stab her with his fearsome spiral horn, so that she would look injured and have some good reason for the primes in Soohoon to take her in. She was thus aching and wounded when the jack o'hooks swung silently from the forest and grabbed her in three tentacles like copper anacondas. It had ravaged her left arm and pierced her intestines with a pointed hook before she managed to teleport out of its long and insidious reach.

Boragette and Zallarilla were thoroughly sympathetic, and thoroughly impressed. Casamint was neither, but he had been banished to the kitchen to make suitable food for a Rassimel.

"So, what happened to you, that brings you to Soohoon to be wrapped in my best bathrobe?" asked Zallarilla.

Nethry sipped consommé before answering. She had had prepared a story that was eight parts of truth and four parts omission and one part of lies. "I'm a gatherer in the Lenwynt: a week or two of wandering in the right places and I can come back with a pack of amber and glirries, lead moss and bush-grown rubies. I was at the roll'gainst edge of the branch, and I went to look over — it's quite a view, you know. I thought I saw a stand of silver-bearing trees some ways down. I slipped down, and ... well, it wasn't silver-bearing trees; I'm not the first one to be fooled by ffugarian trees.

"Ffugarian trees don't look very silvery from inside, so I was casting about along the Verticals for exactly where I had seen them. I met a carcanofex, who did not take kindly to me intruding on his territory..." She described her fight with the carcanofex, neglecting only to mention that he lived elsewhere, and was a reasonably good friend of hers who stabbed her at her own wish.

"The best way to escape a carcanofex is to fly straight down. If you have a flight spell, that is, but you should have one in the Verticals anyway. They can jump horizontally and upwards, but they can't jump downwards very well. So that's where I flew ...

"And the next thing I know, a big cable of a tentacle has jammed a huge fishhook through my leg." She opened her bathrobe to show the bloodspattered place the wound had been before Rodents-At-Dawn had healed it, and much of the rest of her. Boragette simply looked at the bloody fur and shuddered, but Nethry was pleased to notice that Zallarilla stared a bit and spread her whiskers. Nethry artfully left the robe loose, giving Zallarilla occasional glimpses of Rassimel femininity as she told the full truth about fighting the jack o'hooks.

"And once I had escaped and gotten my bearings, I was very far down in the Verticals, and bleeding far too much really. The fastest way to the Flats was through the territories of two irascible monsters who had already given me drubbings once each today. Even if I got there, well, I'd be deep in the Lenwynt, which isn't too much safer than the Verticals. I had heard of Soohoon and didn't think there was anyone left here who hated Rassimel, so that's where I headed — I have a bit of amber and a few trade goods, so I thought I could buy healing or at least safety. I can't tell you how glad I am to see a pair of masked eyes and a cute ringed tail — or to have the chance to wind up in her ... bathrobe."

Zallarilla smiled wide. "Oh, the pleasure is all mine to meet such an adventuress! I'm quite glad to give you a bit of rest and food and clothing ... for that matter, *A Flattering Wind* is going on to Byronny and points outward, if you'd like to travel in comfort and pleasure."

Nethry leaned forward towards Zallarilla, careful to let her bathrobe fall open. "I'd be delighted! I suppose I should get a formal invitation from the captain... could you help me there?"

Zallarilla smirked. "I suppose I could help, just a touch. Just a moment..." She stood and strode towards the door. Boragette grinned after her. Nethry took the opportunity to improve her chances by slipping a few drops of tincture of wenezza, taken from the *Sensible Finch,* into Zallarilla's chalice of tea. She thought a bit and added one to her own as well, on the grounds that a seduction was easier when the seducer didn't have to feign lust.

In a few moments Zallarilla returned, wearing the formal crown and cowl of a skyboat captain, and spoke the ritual words. "Lady Nethry, I do hereby formally invite you to come as a passenger upon *A Flattering Wind* and sail the skies with us, hither and yon, trunkward and outward, rollward and roll'gainst, beneath the eyes of the creator gods, until our paths do part us."

Nethry feigned surprise and clumsiness, leaping up and letting her robe fall open again. "You're the captain of this beautiful and elegant skyboat, Zallarilla? That's wonderful!" She curtsied formally, sweeping the tails of the bathrobe wide. "I do accept this invitation, to be guest and passenger upon *A Flattering Wind,* and to abide by all your orders... and all your wishes ... as we fly, until our paths do part us."

Zallarilla smiled, and sat primly back in her seat, clinking the ivory crown against an iridescent wooden sconce. "Welcome aboard! We depart tomorrow or the day after, at the convenience of my father Ilzatheinen." She lapped at her chalice, and squirmed a bit without realizing it.

Nethry smiled. "Thank you! The wording of that response always amuses me. It's as if I should be crouching at your knees, or wearing nothing but a few ribbons and bringing you candied prens on a little amber tray."

Zallarilla laughed. "Well, the traditional response just goes, 'obey all your orders as we fly', and it's more that, oh, if I tell you to go below-deck because a storm's coming, that you should go. Not that I'd refuse a candied pren if you brought me one..."

Nethry lapped from her own chalice, feeling her breath quicken from the power of the wenezza. She grinned. "If I'd brought a candied pren, I'd be holding it to your muzzle to nibble, be sure of it! But it's not something I ordinarily go bushwhacking with. As it is, you're welcome to anything that I *did* come with..." She shifted in her seat, letting her robe fall open to make it clear what she meant.

Zallarilla finished up her tea. "Well, then, if you're feeling a bit rested and a touch healed, would you like a tour of the skyboat?"

Nethry nodded eagerly. "Nothing would please me more ... well ... perhaps one thing."

Boragette had not missed the exchange. Zie raised zir antennae. "Shall I show her around, Zallarilla?"

"No, thank you, Boragette. I've got plenty of time for a guest, especially a pretty one." The two Rassimel exchanged a sizzling glance, and stood and left the room together. There was not the slightest doubt where the tour would end up. Boragette drummed zir fingers on the table.

* * *

Casamint came in a moment later, with a tray of fruits and nuts, cheeses and fresh-baked bread. "Where did they go? I thought that Nethry was all hungry."

Boragette scowled. "Hungry for same-species kisses more than food, from the looks of things. And Zallarilla was glad to oblige."

Casamint set the tray down and picked up a fresh pren. "Better than Arrhwy, at least."

Boragette raised zir antennae high. "What did Arrhwy do? If she got Rajel before either of us did I'll ... oh, I don't know."

Casamint shook his head. "Worse. Well, a different texture of badness. She snuck off with one of the perdithorne."

Boragette's antennae went flat. "A *monster*? That's perverse!"

Casamint nodded. "I would say so. If I ever so much as kiss a nonprime, you are encouraged to thump me repeatedly with a trireme or something."

"What's a trireme?"

"It's a lake-boat with three banks of oars ... just a joke between Skirret and me. Use any weapon that comes to hand," asked Casamint.

"I think that's Rajel's job. Who is Skirret?" said Boragette cautiously.

"A friend from Pennypell Academy. Definitely a Herethroy! I checked. In detail," said Casamint, smirking.

"Detail? What sort of detail? And what sort of friend, for that matter?"

Casamint realized his tactical error a bit too late. "Well, rather the sort of friends you and Chicory are."

"I wouldn't say I knew Chicory's body in *detail*, though," said Boragette. "We never did anything in private that we couldn't have done just as well with you and Rajel watching."

"How wonderfully modest of you," said Casamint. "I, for my part, am required to marry twice, and so ..."

"So you decided to work on your second marriage already?" snapped Boragette, surprising both of them with zir ferocity. "We're your first one, and don't you forget it!"

Casamint clicked his fingertips on the tray. "I haven't forgotten. I almost wonder if you two have, sometimes."

Boragette curled zir antennae. "Don't be silly. How could we?"

Casamint chewed a mouthful of slightly-underripe pren. "Well, you don't act much like it. At this rate the only ones who won't get any interpersonal pleasure are the married people."

Boragette flattened zir antennae again. "Are you insinuating something, sir?"

Casamint sighed, hunting for some courage. "I'll ask outright then. I'm lonely, the woman I love best is far away, and I've barely been touched by another Herethroy in weeks. I know that Rajel doesn't like me much and I don't think we could consummate our marriage yet, but, well, would you come touch me?"

Boragette snapped, "No." Casamint looked so miserable that zie realized zie had to explain. "Not this time. I want to feel like I'm ... someone you care about at least a little, even if I'm not the Skirret you love. I don't want to be just the cosi that's easy to hand, and easier 'cause you're married to me."

Casamint spread his antennae. "I'm sorry... that's really not what I meant at all. I *do* find you attractive and appealing, and I'm getting to like you..."

Boragette stood up. "Casamint, it is exactly what you meant. Truth to tell, I feel the same about you — easy to hand." Zie had to work to say, "And attractive enough, though a co-lover's not supposed to say that. But you're not the Chicory I'm longing for, and I want to care more about you before we touch that way, as two or as three." Zie squeezed his hand. "I want to love you, I really do. It would make our life so much better ... please help me to, could you?"

He nodded, and started to say something, but zie turned and left the room on four legs. He shrugged, and poured himself a chalice of claret, and muttered darkly about romance.

MEETING HER FATHER

> *Dear Lord Muspis, Pardon me this note for its brevity. I have just now insinuated myself into the company of the Araldean enchanter Ilzatheinen — to be sure, I have not met the enchanter; that will come about in mere moments. His daughter Zallarilla is absolutely delightful; I could give an extensive report about that, but I shan't unless explicitly requested. In any case, I am in a position of considerable influence at this point, and if all goes well I shall dissuade him from granting defenses to nonprimes in no great time.*
> *With all service to Byronny, Nethry Chrestilium*

Nethry curtsied to her enemy of the month. "I am quite pleased to meet you, great mage."

Ilzatheinen nodded. "A pleasure, surely." Whatever pleasure he actually felt was quite vague; he was barely paying attention.

Zallarilla sat Nethry on the salamander-printed couch, and sat next to her. "Nethry will be coming with us for a time... Nethry? I forgot to ask you where we were to drop you off."

Nethry smiled. "I'm from Byronny, but I'm not entirely welcome there just now. Perhaps I'll take a break of a week or a month from foresting and gathering, if you don't mind?"

Zallarilla curled her tail around Nethry's ankle. "You're quite welcome!" The wenezza had long since worn off; Zallarilla's feelings were entirely her own.

Nethry smiled vaguely to the room of primes. "There's no obligation to answer — the staring gods know I don't talk about everything *I* do — but what are you doing in Soohoon? I didn't know primes ever came here."

Ilzatheinen shrugged. "The monsters here have hired me to build them some magical defenses. The price is high, the danger is low, and here we are. Rajel and Arrhwy are guards, in case there's need. Boragette and Casamint are tourists. I gather you've already met my daughter, perhaps at some depth."

Nethry flattened her ears. "Zallarilla is truly a wonderful woman." Several primes grinned, and Zallarilla took Nethry's hand.

Nethry looked to Ilzatheinen. "Do you think it's a good idea, building city walls for monsters?"

Ilzatheinen shrugged. "These monsters aren't too bad. They want to protect themselves, not go conquering or murdering."

"Still — the last Go-Lord of Soohoon was a scyanturge, who did go pirating. If she had had a fortress to hide in, she would have been harder to kill I should think."

"From what Nherex-Dlostion has told me, she was ambushed by an army of primes — seven or eight at least — when she was off pirating. The city walls would have been miles and miles away. No danger there!" said Ilzatheinen, actually paying attention to Nethry for the first time.

"True in this instance, lord enchanter, but not in all. If she *had* been able to flee, she would have had a place to recover and heal, and prepare for deeper revenge."

Ilzatheinen shrugged. "If she had fled into the Underneaths, she might well have found the same. I daresay she has a dangerous friend or two there — what monster would *not* take a scyanturge as a friend?"

"It is, indeed, a difference of degree rather than one of kind," admitted Nethry. "Still, it could be a considerable degree, even in the case of a scyanturge. More likely — consider a large flock of ulgrane, say. Ordinarily they make their nests on bits of sky-wrack, far away, unprotected save by distance and a few ulgrane. In a world-gall guarded by your own great magics, they could be much safer, much closer..."

Ilzatheinen nodded agreeably. "Another difference of degree. In any case, the monsters I am making this for are not ulgrane: they are vorwi and perdithorne, ororosti and nycathath...."

"Vorwi are not terribly dangerous. The others can be enemies as easily as allies. They've treated us well, certainly." noted Casamint.

"... and with good defenses, I daresay Soohoon will stay in vorwi hands ... blobs ... for a long time to come," finished Ilzatheinen.

Nethry shrugged. "Longer than your lifetime?"

Ilzatheinen held up a hand, his immortality bracelet gleaming. "You know what this is, I take it? That should be a good indication of my opinion, then. I do not expect to die, ever. I do not expect Soohoon's walls to cause me trouble, ever."

Nethry frowned. "With all due respect, I think *I* will have trouble from it, and I don't plan to live nearly so long."

Ilzatheinen smiled condescendingly. "If you do, come to talk to me afterwards, and I shall make it up to you."

"If I *can* talk, I will," said Nethry.

"Besides, half the defenses are permanently mounted inside Soohoon," added Rajel helpfully.

Nethry flinched inside. "That means that half of them can be moved ... could pirates use them as weapons too?"

Ilzatheinen shrugged. "Taking them out of Soohoon would be foolish; they could get lost. And only the flame bird would be useful as a weapon."

"Flame bird?" asked Nethry.

Ilzatheinen was happy to brag. "A substantial fire elemental, fierce to defend its master, capable of ... it remains to be seen precisely what tricks."

Nethry frowned. "How does that compare to a scyanturge? Or an extra ulgrane? How many primes could it kill, if misused?"

"I'm absolutely sure it won't be a problem," said Ilzatheinen, and turned the conversation elsewhere by force.

* * *

Most of the primes had left for the night. "Zallarilla, do you ordinarily grant people passage in exchange for their intimate services?" asked Ilzatheinen, with vinegar in his voice, after Zallarilla explained Nethry to him.

Zallarilla stamped her foot. "Not a bit so! Usually I grant them one or the other, for free!"

Ilzatheinen shook his head. "You are not being terribly serious, daughter."

Zallarilla scowled. "Why should I be? We don't have a family title or anything, and you're immortal now anyways. I'm happy to get a few presents here and there from you, and to spend whatever time and consideration it takes to keep my investments active and all of that. But you expect me to take a few months off now and then to cart you up and down Aradrueia! Well, I'm glad to, but I'll be amusing myself as I do."

Ilzatheinen shrugged. "Well, at least she won't get you pregnant."

Zallarilla all but shouted, "That was Darssell's fault! He botched that spell."

Ilzatheinen laughed. "I should think that any Rassimel man worth inviting between your legs should have a contraceptive spell *grafted* and hence not botchable. It indicates some forethought, and some adequacy of means and skill."

"You've mentioned that before. Perhaps twice before, or, conceivably, even thrice." said Zallarilla.

"Well, I *have* brought the topic up before, now that you mention it..." Ilzatheinen smiled.

"Once or twice a month for the last decade, you have," muttered Zallarilla.

"... But I *do* wish you'd find someone more suitable than a wandering woodswoman. And that the next time you find yourself pregnant, you do it intentionally."

Zallarilla glared. "Who are *you* doing, now that Mother does not make herself available for your convenience?"

Ilzatheinen shrugged. "Professionals, and not very many of them. It's not a great concern of mine."

"Well, it's not a great concern of *mine* either. I'm even saving money by *not* hiring professionals. I doubt that Nethry will cost me more than a few spare clothes."

Ilzatheinen snorted. "*That* is ridiculous. Fine. Enjoy your latest Rassy-toy."

Zallarilla hissed at her father, and left the parlor, tail lashing behind her.

* * *

IN THE PANTRY OF INIQUITY

Dearest Skirret,

I must apologize for not writing before, but the post office was less than convenient, as you shall see.

I do fear that I have gotten myself into an adventure ... gotten dragged into an adventure, to be more precise, by my hulking barbarian of a wife, and the hideous hissing quadruped she travels with. Actually Arrhwy is not so bad as all that, but I would still rather be with you in school ...

... than spending four months in Soohoon!

No, you shan't find Soohoon on a map of Byronny Mene. When we were told that Soohoon was on Byronny's territory, the dread and insidious enchanter Ilzatheinen used words wickedly. By 'Byronny's territory' he meant 'the lands which Byronny monitors and tries to exert some measure of influence on, and no other city-state does'. Which, in Soohoon's case means: the Verticals some distance into the Lenwynt. A more precise description of this might be, 'The territory of the goddess Lenhirrik', or, perhaps, 'the land on which those dwell who have recently been badly bashed and battered by the forces of Byronny.'

In any case, I have spent some days in the wild lands, surrounded by vorwi and perdithorne, ororosti and even a nycathath. I would joke that I found the perdithorne more appealing to me than I find my wife, but alas! it is not a good joke, for the Sleeth has indulged herself with one or two of them.

Fortunately, we are now flying to New Kottarnu for some cryptic, occult errand for the enchanter. Boragette and I plan to stay with Rajel until we get back to Byronny, and there find a sky-barge with cabins to take us back to Araldy. I don't know exactly what we shall do then, but it surely includes me returning to the academy by the start of the next season.

Perhaps Boragette will come with me. You would like zir, I think. I could well imagine ... I should not write this, for Teamary will think quite poorly of me mentioning the topic to you rather than her, and I am sure she has some other plans for me ... I am rather obligated to marry twice, after all, and we've got at least as many barons stuffed into my first marriage as any triad should have. Still, I do hope you don't go get married before I have a chance to influence everyone extensively.

Forgive me if this seems abrupt and untoward, and even presumptuous. Matters that seemed distant and trivial in the academy seem close and vital here.

With all my love, I remain your true,
Casamint

***

When *A Flattering Wind* got to Byronny, Nethry hinted at a few errands she had to do, and slipped away. She disguised herself to the eyes and nose, and went to the wealthy part of town.

Nethry clicked her claws on the Pororn door. Lord Muspis himself answered it, sniffing at her, looking at her curiously. "Good day to you, good Rassimel. Might I inquire what gives us the honor of your visit?" The tone of his voice and the set of his tail suggested that he found it more of an importunement than an honor; Nethry's clothes were not the finest.

Nethry smiled. "Not even you recognize me, Muspis. Excellent."

The nobleman frowned at her informal use of his given name. "I must say that you have the advantage of me, good Rassimel. I rarely forget a person's scent, and it strikes me as unusual that an honest Rassimel would wear so much juniper perfume that I cannot properly smell her. Now please be so good as to tell me why you have come here?"

"I'm Nethry, Muspis, and certainly not an honest Rassimel. Nethry Chrestilium, in disguise, and swimming in perfume." She grinned, and showed him signs by which he could recognize her.

"Good heavens! Nethry, do come in. You look exactly like nobody in particular! I take it that this is another serious visit, like that memorable one where you brought up the scyanturge?" said Muspis. Nethry nodded. Muspis wagged his tail and said, "Then let us repair to the pantry, where there are uncomfortable barrels to sit on, and the odors of vinegar and pickles shall merge noxiously with that of juniper perfume, and, of course, nobody shall overhear us."

"That sounds delightful, lord. Compared to the conversation, at least."

When they were in the pantry, the door closed behind them, Muspis turned to Nethry. "I imagine you have some sort of report for me?"

"A report, and a request for instructions," said Nethry.

"You have succeeded in shocking me, good inspector! I cannot remember a time where *anyone* in my department has asked me for instructions. I am, as you well know, little more than a figurehead — a position I relish like offirrah!" He patted the barrel he sat on, in which dead snakes packed in garlic were fermenting.

"Well, really a request for clarification of policy, Lord Muspis. Not instructions as such," she said.

"Much better then! Now, for your report?"

"I have insinuated myself into the company of the enchanter Ilzatheinen, whom Soohoon has hired for building defenses. Well, insinuated myself between his daughter's legs, to be specific." She described the circumstances with only four interruptions from the lord, and Ilzatheinen's plans.

"Well then. Just how dangerous are these things, Nethry?" he asked at length, interrupting her in the middle of a footnote to a tangential remark.

"The fire elemental and the protection from magic are, in my judgment, substantial dangers to us. They could easily be moved from Soohoon elsewhere — even mounted on a pirate skyship, say. The others are lesser but not trivial. We could not raid Soohoon quickly, not even with as strong as a force as we raised against Aulihemm Bremm. We could besiege it, but maintaining a siege on the very edge of the Underneaths would be extraordinarily difficult. I should say that, if Soohoon's next leader were so inclined, she could be quite an effective pirate — and, if she were suitably cautious, one that was all but impossible for us to root out."

Many questions followed. In the end, he said, "So I must agree with you, it seems. This enchantment project could resurrect a threat we quashed at great cost and great pain, and bring it back even worse. What do you recommend be done?"

"Well, we have to stop it," said Nethry.

"An excellent decision! How do you propose doing so? For I know that you never come here without a complete plan."

"Know fear and surprise, Lord Muspis! I have come here today without a complete plan," she said. "Remember that I am asking for clarification of policy."

"How so?"

"Casual and reasonable discussion has not dissuaded Ilzatheinen from his plans. Persuasion is futile. I know that part of the Rassimel psyche intimately. He wants the Tilmarth Note as devoutly as I want the safety of Byronny; the fact that primes may die because of it in some uncertain future time is of no concern to him. Should it be to me? Our policy is that we confront threats to Byronny with all suitable methods ... in this case, precisely which methods are suitable? I could, I suppose, murder Ilzatheinen in his sleep. That wouldn't even be illegal, as I could arrange to do it outside of any city-state's law," said Nethry.

Lord Muspis tucked his tail between his legs. "That surely must be a last resort! Murdering a Rassimel who is all but your father-in-law seems an extraordinary measure!"

"I thought so too," said Nethry glumly. "Still, I am low on options at the moment."

"Persuasion fails, and direct violence is excessive at the moment, so you must try indirect means. Could they be distracted into some lengthy and valuable side project? Could they encounter too many dangers along the way, and thereby decide not to return? Could they suffer some serious accident in New Kottarnu, perhaps? For that matter, could you acquire the Tilmarth Note yourself, and pay it to him for some other bit of work?" He thought a moment. "Ah, I have it. Persuade them by example that nonprimes are to be feared and hated, not trusted and bargained with."

Nethry smiles. "Lord Muspis, I must now demolish your career's hopes. If anyone ever asks me to recommend you for a figurehead's position, I will not be able to tout your incompetence in anything remotely like good faith."

Lord Muspis smiled. "These are helpful ideas, then?"

Nethry nodded. "That they are. You *do* know that some nonprimes are thoroughly trustworthy, and many can be bargained with?"

Muspis wagged his tail. "I have heard as much. From you."

"Still, a few encounters with the more vicious and terrible of monsters might help matters. I have some contacts, some friends who would be willing display their strength. And some enemies who I could perhaps trick into action. But this is best done before we return to Soohoon, so I'll need some luck — and, I'm afraid, some cash and other monster-bribes. And our best far-speaker. I can hardly visit monsters in person while I'm on *A Flattering Wind.*"

"Nethry, the far-speaker costs more than ten years of your salary, counting rewards and all. You shall have it, but be exceedingly careful to return it. Let us work out some details together..." For three hours the pantry was full of plotting and scheming, to the smell of rotting serpents and juniper perfume.

THE GRAND PADISHAH

The sun was flickering in the sky, still full of flame but starting to dwindle towards early evening. Boragette lost the afternoon's game of diamond chess to Casamint, and stood up and stretched. "Enough of that. We're in Byronny — let's go see some of Byronny. And eat some of it!"

"Would you like a slice of that cathedral, Boragette? It looks downright frosted, and with a thick sticky egg-and-sugar frosting at that," said Casamint with a grin.

"I think that's the winner's portion. I will content myself with plue and tarrissy and a few side dishes, as long as someone else cooks them. Wake Rajel up, would you?"

"I'm *sure* she needs her sleep. More than she needs dinner with us, at any rate."

"More than you need dinner with her, is what you're saying," said Boragette. Zie stood out of arms' reach of Rajel, and declaimed, "Rajel! We must dine, we must seek dinner, we must find dinner, dinner must be ours!"

Rajel opened her eyes, and stretched. "I suppose that's a good idea. A moment, while I clean up this and that."

Soon enough, the three of them were strolling in single file down a narrow hallway with a threadbare carpet runner that had been ornate and lavish the previous century. They turned left, descended stairs, turned right, and came to the hotel's lobby.

A tall, mottled Herethroy woman wearing a formal kilt leapt out of her chair. "Boragette! Lover! They said you were here, and here you are!"

Boragette stared. "Chicory! You're here!" Zie dashed over and entangled Chicory in a multitude of embracing limbs. Casamint and Rajel frowned at each other.

Chicory broke the hug first. "And you two must be the Baron Casamint and the Great Baron Marjoram."

Casamint gave Chicory an elaborate salute only suitable for use at ducal funerals. "And you must be my mari's adulterous lover and donor of children's books, Chicory."

"Yeah, that's me!", she said, and then grinned hugely. "Not just Chicory any-the-more. I'm Grand Padishah Chicory now, and as noble as any of you!"

"Grand Padishah? What's that?", asked Boragette nervously.

Chicory smiled broadly. "It's one of these Byronny titles. You can buy titles here, so I did. They think I'm foreign, so they only wanted to sell me foreign titles. Grand Padishah sounded good, so I got it, even though it was a bit more expensive than the rest."

Casamint flicked his tail. "Well, 'padishah' was the title of the ruler of Traegarraith, on outer Mrasteia, a few centuries ago. We'd use the word 'emperor', nowadays. And that's just an ordinary padishah. I don't know what a grand one could possibly be."

Chicory guffawed. "Pretty impressive, then, ain't it? Pretty cheap, too. You wanna be a Grand Padishah too, on top of Great Baron, Boragette?"

"I should advise you to stick with titles that mean something more than a souvenir, Boragette," said Casamint.

"Aww, my title means something, Minty-boy! It means that I had six hundred lozens yesterday, and I've got a little patch of the Nobles' Park that's almost big enough to lie on today. And that I'm a legally recognized noble anywhere on Aradrueia." She looked at him intently. "Even back in Pennypell."

"You'll be recognized as a farm girl and a gullible tourist, is what you'll be recognized as. *Our* titles are old titles, and full of promises to our subjects," said Casamint.

"Casamint, please stop teasing my, well, friend. I *do* want you two to get along," said Boragette.

Rajel smirked. "Well, *I* am pleased to congratulate you on your new title. Did you come to Byronny to get it?"

Chicory grinned at Rajel. "Nah. I wanted to catch up with you! I haven't seen Boragette in a while, and I wanted to meet you and Casamint. 'specially Casamint."

"Why 'especially' Casamint?" asked Casamint, in the strongest upper-class accent he could muster.

"Oh, I was hoping that we could meet up, do this, do that, fall legs-a-whirling in love, and get married, you, me, and Boragette."

"You have just proposed to me, haven't you? In almost as romantic a way as Rajel proposed to me last time," said Casamint. "I can hardly tell you how flattered I am. Unless you understand the mathematics of infinitesimals, of course."

Rajel laughed, then frowned. "Well, I don't think it's *quite* time to decide on Casamint's second marriage."

"Not before dinner, to be sure!" said Boragette, in a bright, artificially cheerful voice.

"Hey, let me take you out to dinner!" said Chicory. "There's a really good place, Cave Treasures. I found it a couple days ago. It's got the best grilled mushrooms I have *ever* eaten. And I grew up with the mushroom farmers of Dorly!"

Boragette smiled, "That's so sweet of you!" Rajel nodded, and Casamint curled his antennae down.

"Did you make your fortune in mushrooms, Chicory?" asked Rajel.

"Nah, not me. Dye plants."

"Dye plants?" asked Rajel.

"Lesser tythet, yavalle, and even puruulska," said Chicory proudly. Boragette beamed at zir girlfriend's prowess as a farmer.

"That's nonsense. I know for a fact that puruulska can't be cultivated. It's an underneaths-plant, a peculiar sort of vampiric epiphyte, and quite a touchy one. It can't even endure *light*." snapped Casamint.

"Well, maybe it can be cultivated and maybe it can't be cultivated, but I've sure got a lot of it growing in some split Verticals-trees in the back of some mushroom caves in Dorly," said Chicory.

"Split Verticals-trees, in a cave? I suppose that makes sense. How do you tend them, though?" asked Casamint, in the most pleasant voice he had used all day.

"Very carefully. *Very* carefully. And I studied enough Corpador magic to cast Sleeth Eyes. I can tend 'em in the dark. That's what really made it work."

"I'm just a warrior," said Rajel. "What's puruulska? And the others, too?"

"Puruulska is a crimson dye — there's nothing else quite like it," said Boragette. Zie showed Rajel a thin bright band on the rim of zir hat. "This is from thread dyed in Chicory's first batch. It's not very good, but you can see that it's more intense and rich a crimson than any other dye short of a very, very good spell. And people will pay more for it, because it's natural," said Boragette.

"Yavalle is this glowy green stuff," said Chicory, showing a little swatch of luminous cloth, the color and brilliance of noontime sunlight through an emerald. "You do *not* want to wear this when you're sneaking out to your secret sweetie at night! And lesser tythet is a sort of dull green, not that much to look at, but a few threads of it in a cloak or a bedspread'll keep the whole thing from burning."

"The yavalle is quite nice. I'm not sure why you'd bother with the lesser tythet — wouldn't a spell do just as well?"

"Oh, a spell'd work better if you want to build a bonfire on your bed, Rajel! But a few threads of lesser tythet is good enough to save you if you drop a candle on your bed, or let your hem get in the fire when you're warming your butt. And it's cheap. How many cley does a tailor have? And how many tailors are so good at Pyrador that they can fireproof a bedspread *forever*? Lesser tythet's a good sight less than a spell by a mage *that* good."

Rajel curled her antennae. "You don't need to sell it to me! I believe you!"

Chicory laughed. "I have visited *every* tailor from Girath to Green, trying to sell 'em my dyes. I can recite that stuff in my sleep — and I have, many times!" She abducted Rajel's elbow and marched with her to Cave Treasures, chattering to the bewildered warrior about the exotic and challenging plants that she had raised. Boragette walked with Casamint, and fretted.

* * *

"Zallarilla, I'd like to bring Chicory along with us on *A Flattering Wind*," said Boragette. Zie and she were sitting in the small parlor on the bottom floor. "Ground floor" seemed a wrong term for a building that rarely touched the ground.

"Well, if she's not a murderess or a Khtsoyis or some such, I can't imagine there would be any trouble," said Zallarilla, and lapped delicately at a chalice of port.

"Oh, not at all. She's a farmer — the best farmer in County Farwinn, back near Pennypell."

"Oh? I don't know that we're going to be back near Pennypell any time soon."

"No, she followed us to Byronny. Well, preceded us, since she took a passenger ship that didn't make a stop at Soohoon," said Boragette.

"So few passenger ships do! Still, if the passenger ship could endure her presence, or support her weight or whatever it is you're worried about, I daresay we can as well. Who is she?"

"Well, she's my girlfriend from Dorly," admitted Boragette.

Zallarilla smiled. "Well, it's a good thing that I seem to have acquired a girlfriend myself, or I would be envious. Still ... aren't you married to Rajel and Casamint?"

"Yes, you know that I am," said Boragette.

"That raises some vaguely rude questions to me, I'm afraid, Boragette. You needn't answer if you don't want to, but I *am* curious," said Zallarilla.

"Oh, ask all you like," said Boragette. "If my antenna curl up into knots you'll know I won't answer."

"I was under the impression that the country Herethroy didn't really approve of nobles having adulteries," said Zallarilla.

"No, we don't approve. And it's worse for co-lovers, we're supposed to be the modest sex," said Boragette. "And I have not done." Zie shrugged. "Which leaves me twenty-several years married, and thirty years a virgin."

"You don't need to tell me such details if you don't want to, Boragette."

"Oh ... I do want to. There's nobody else nearby to complain to. And I'd rather not complain to a Herethroy in any case. It's immodest, and un-co-lover-like. I should be quite embarrassed — my antennae *would* tie themselves in knots."

Zallarilla grinned. "I shall be glad to listen! I admit that I have been none too modest myself, and none too careful, even by the lax standards of the urban folk. I'm sure my daughter would agree. "

"You have a daughter?"

"Ten years old, now. She lives with her father, in Lenkasia."

"Oh! I didn't know. That's..."

"That's a sign that I shall not judge you harshly, even if, momentarily, you admit to not being entirely prudish. You may tell me any number of details. I shall nod and utter understanding words, for I have heard more shocking things from a double dozen of friends, and from my own muzzle," said Zallarilla. "Well, for anything you are likely to say. *Arrhwy* shocks me."

"Well, then ... I'm afraid I love Chicory. I have for years. She's everything I could want in a Herethroy woman. Rajel is very feminine too — so strong! — but she's so martial too. She's almost fearsome. She's almost like a Sleeth woman in a Herethroy body... Chicory is just as strong, strong of body and strong of will, but she's gentle, and she's *excellent* with plants. If she were a noble I'd try to marry her immediately, even if she were just an esquire. If we could find a man of course."

"I am just an esquire! Well, as a courtesy title, through my mother. It is a convenient title, with few obligations," said Zallarilla.

"Oh, I didn't mean to say anything bad about it, Zallarilla. I'm in love with someone without even that much! It's just that it would be much easier to persuade all the people who have to agree, if I were marrying another noble."

"She's a noble now, isn't she?"

"Well, she's bought a preposterous title. I don't think it would fool anyone in my family — it didn't even fool *her*." said Boragette.

"Well, that's one way to make soup, as the captain of the *Jartlaaf* said when he landed his flaming skyboat in Lake Laicrane."

"I was hoping that Casamint would like her, but he doesn't seem to," said Boragette. "That would be awfully convenient."

"He has to marry twice, right? And he's missing one?"

"He does. Not yet, though. Not until we've got our marriage all in order — or three years from last Lage, I think it is. And if he married Chicory and me, it would be a nice quadrette, which nobody could complain about."

"What could someone complain about, if everyone's married the right number of times?"

"Aristocratic extended marriages should be small. A quadrette is best. A quintette is acceptable — that's one man, two co-lovers, two women. More than that is *not* acceptable for anyone of rank. A pity, but there it is."

"Why is it a pity?", asked Zallarilla.

"It's a pity because it means that I can't marry Chicory easily. Well, if Casamint won't marry Chicory, then he has to marry sometwo else — there's a quintette right there. If I were to marry Chicory (she's number six), I'd have to marry a second man too (he's number seven). And the second man would have to marry twice, too. The best choice is that he marries Casamint's other co-lover as zir second marriage, but the woman in that triad is a new one (she's number eight). That's an octet, the third-smallest Herethroy extended marriage, and it's vulgar *and* all but impossible to arrange. What usually happens is that the second man has an entirely different second marriage, which has a new woman (number eight again) and a new co-lover (number nine), and that's hopeless. And if either of the co-lovers in those two marriages wants to marry, it can get bigger still."

"That's quite complicated!"

"Herethroy extended marriages are, I'm afraid."

Zallarilla leaned closer. "Now, in a quadrette or a quintette, who indulges themselves carnally with whom?"

"Oh, just the triads who are actually married. It's a bit of a scandal if anything else happens."

"Well, what *is* it like dealing with your husband's or your wife's other husbands and wives and maris?"

"Your wife never has any! And I have not done, since my husband isn't married yet. I suppose it's rather like dealing with your wife's parents."

"Don't you get jealous of them? They're not like your wife's parents — they're making themselves free with your husband's body!"

"That, and getting half his attention and half his money, too. You're not *supposed* to be jealous. But everyone is, a little at least. "

"That doesn't sound fun."

"It's not, or so I hear. For co-lovers especially — we're supposed to be sweet and kind to everyone, and keep the peace all around. If Casamint is ignoring Rajel and me, I'm to, well, give Rajel all the contentment and pleasure that two-person intercourse can provide, so that she's not unhappy. Hopefully that distracts me too, but if it doesn't, I am supposed to smile and be pleasant anyways. Oh, and if I've got a second marriage myself and my first husband is away too much, I'm supposed to ignore the second one mostly. Even if, say, I'm more in love with my second wife than my first, myself." Zie twitched zir tail, and poured zirself a half-chalice of port.

"That sounds hideously complicated! And rather painful. Rassimel usually marry in twos or sometimes threes, but never these overlapping triangles."

"If I could make *one* recommendation to our creator god, it would be equal numbers of the three sexes," said Boragette.

"Did anyone ever do that?" asked Zallarilla.

"Yes, or so a story goes. Virid just said that uneven numbers fit the aesthetic she intended for Herethroy," said Boragette. "I'm sure Casamint knows more."

"I'm sure he'll be glad to say that he does, at least," said Zallarilla, and licked the port off bottom of her chalice. "Now, forgive me? Nethry told me she'd show me this and that in Byronny while we're here, and the skyboat just told me that she's at the front door."

"Thank you for the gift of a pair of fuzzy ears, Zallarilla!"

"I'll be glad to chat any time you like, Boragette," she said, and bowed, and left to collect her lover.

* * *

"Ilzatheinen said he'd be here in one or two ninths of an hour," said Rajel, settling herself comfortably into the largest chair in the parlor. "He promised not to accidentally skip mentioning a nycathath or a Locador demon or another treat like that, on this leg of the trip."

"Ah, Ilzatheinen explains his plan for a new thing. This is good. Your mari should do the same!" said Arrhwy, her tailtip flicking.

"What has Boragette done?" asked Rajel, her antennae spread.

"Zie invites Chicory to travel with us!", said Arrhwy.

Rajel shrugged. "Well, yes. They were talking at dinner about asking Zallarilla."

Arrhwy paced angrily, swatting each cabinet door with her tail as she padded past. "Why does Boragette need a new woman? Zie does not use the one zie already has!"

Rajel laughed. "Well, there *is* that."

Arrhwy reared on her hind paws and swatted at Rajel's face, keeping her claws carefully sheathed. "You are the stupid! You go home to get sex from your mari! Instead you get no sex from your mari! Instead-instead you let your mari bring zir girlfriend along!"

Rajel caught Arrhwy's forelegs in two hands each, and lifted the Sleeth off the ground. "Chicory's not so bad. She's more of a proper Herethroy woman than I'll ever be."

"She is the rival! Instead of fighting with her you fight with Casamint! Casamint is not the rival! Casamint too should be the lover! You are the stupid!"

"Casamint is the rival of the whole situation. He'd rather be an unmarried student in Pennypell."

Arrhwy raked Rajel's belly fiercely with her hind legs, still keeping her claws sheathed. "Then divorce him and send him to Pennypell!"

"Now you're being the stupid. Herethroy women can't remarry. Also my title would devolve to my sister." She punched Arrhwy in the belly with a mid-hand.

Ilzatheinen peered at them from the door. "I trust that you are practicing your combats, albeit in as incongenial a location as my daughter's parlor, rather than trying to kill each other? I prefer my hired heroes to be alive."

"I am expressing concernednessess and protectivenesses for my partner! She does not concern or protective herself very well today!" said Arrhwy, and turned and caught Rajel's wrist in her fangs. "See? She should know where my fangs are and where her hands are! If we were fighting for real, I have one tasty hand now and she has only three."

"Well, perhaps you could concern and protect about our future, three or four days hence. I shall rely upon you to defend me in the Temple of the Dark Trinity in New Kottarnu."

"That seems like adventurer business, again. Do you have any more little jobs for us that you haven't mentioned?"

"I did indeed mention the Temple!"

"Yes, but you were talking to a monster at the time, not being direct with us. Be direct with us now. Any more dangers that we will have to deal with? Even small ones? Or unlikely ones?"

"Each other," snapped Ilzatheinen. "Marital discord. My daughter's new lover being rude. My daughter inviting yet another attractive ne'er-do-well be a passenger on the ship. No more dangers are in *my* plan."

"Good. Tell us now about this Temple," said Arrhwy.

"It's a temple of the Dark Trinity as understood in New Kottarnu: Flokin, "Here", and Iraz Varuun. If that's not the Dark Trinity that you learned about in grade school, with Arrhwy's creator god instead of Flokin, that's entirely predictable. New Kottarnu has very different customs from the rest of Aradrueia."

"What *is* the Dark Trinity? Or *a* Dark Trinity?" asked Rajel.

"The three most terrible of the gods, supposedly working together to defend the edges of the universe from wickeder things outside. Or, perhaps, planning to make the universe their plaything — instead of sharing it with the rest of the seven-and-twelve gods, I suppose. Or, perhaps, something else. It's an old story from the very early days, when the gods were more inclined to be chatty. I, personally, suspect that one of the more playful and less reliable gods, Hressh-Huu perhaps or Shaz Shay Shaz, was making it up entirely. In any case, we've got about seven or eight candidates for 'three most terrible gods', so there are lots of choices of Dark Trinities," said the enchanter.

"Well, what's the one in New Kottarnu about?"

"The city's two favorite gods, plus Flokin to make three. It's a very powerful temple, though: there's nowhere better on the branch to perform consecrations to those three gods."

"But they do not make it easy to do, rrai!" said Arrhwy.

"No: the Locador demon who runs the Temple prepares a changeable smorgasbord of troubles, traps, and dangers for anyone who wants to work consecrations there. I've been there once — I hired a very gentlemanly Rassimel named Vimirance to help me get to the top, and we didn't have much trouble."

Arrhwy and Rajel looked at each other. "This Vimirance had one ear replaced by an amber lens sort of thing, very enchanted?"

"Yes, he did. You know him?"

"By reputation. He's one of the great heroes of the Transwynt."

"I doubt that. He didn't charge as much as you two do," said Ilzatheinen. "Though he was entirely competent."

"He's also one of the great gamblers of the Transwynt. He usually needs money," said Rajel.

"Be that as it may, we encountered an assortment of burning statues, clawed darknesses, animated soap, Gormoror made out of wax with daggers for claws, and other incongruous horrors. Vimirance made short work of them."

Rajel and Arrhwy looked at each other again. "That sounds like we will make medium-long work of them. Best allow three days between trips, for us to recover," said Rajel.

"Reasonable enough. There's plenty for me to do in New Kottarnu — the city is a sorcerer's shopping dream, for one thing," said Ilzatheinen.

"Also you will need to recover as much as we do," said Arrhwy.

THE ULGRANE

The sun was almost full of fire, and thin extra flames reached up to lick at the lower stars. Clouds boiled underneath *A Flattering Wind*, en route from Byronny to New Kottarnu, but Zallarilla had taken the skyship high up to give her passengers a clear day. Arrhwy sprawled on the top of a cupola, sunning herself, her hindlegs dangling over the edge. Rajel sat inside the cupola, staring into a carved wooden box full of sparks; she had bought a copy of Blind Nut Mask in Byronny, and had two days of work ahead of her to graft it on her magerium and be able to cast it. Casamint and Boragette were on their fourth diamond-chess game of the day; Boragette was behind, one victory to two, but had some advantage early on in this game. Chicory had watched the first two games and offered her advice, which generally proved fatal when taken. She had slipped belowdeck for a nap, for the safety of the gamers.

Casamint peered at the board, and moved his orren all the way across the river, and his herethroy next to it. Boragette grinned, moving her cani and zi ri, cutting off the herethroy's retreat and giving Casamint a choice of three bad options. Casamint sighed, reached for the orren, pulled back his hand, thought a bit, and reached for his zi ri ... and a jagged line of eye-aching brilliance leapt from the sea of clouds and struck him, scattering chess pieces, blasting half his shirt to ashes, leaving him gasping in pain and astonishment.

Arrhwy and Rajel were alert instantly. "Someone's throwing lightning at us!", shouted Rajel, "Defend yourself if you can! Get inside the ship!" She rushed to the edge of the cupola, looking out and down to the clouds. "Ulgrane!"

Boragette shrieked in terror, holding on to a column. Arrhwy swatted zir with a forepaw, claws carefully sheathed. "Lie down now! Otherwise you are hit by lightning!" Zie stared at her, too stunned to understand. "Check Casamint!", hissed Arrhwy.

Boragette nodded mutely, and crouched by zir husband's side. "Are you all right?" zie asked, feeling that it was a ridiculous question: zie could see the crazing of scorched cracks in his chitin, the terror in his eyes that mirrored zir own.

He tried to smile at zir, but couldn't quite manage it. "Let's go inside. Let the adventurers do the fighting..."

Rajel nodded at them. "And get me my sword. It's in our cabin closet." She picked up a pole in her lower hands, and a heavy wooden deck-chair in her uppers.

"When they come, you threaten to sit on them!" grinned Arrhwy, as she turned one of her claws into a clattering hawk.

"Oh, pay attention to the fight," snapped Rajel. "Here comes the first one."

Boragette and Casamint crept towards the door, afraid to get up. Too slow: a huge eight-legged bird the size of a pony landed in front of them, smiling around a short jagged beak. It caught Boragette in one hand, stinging zir with the needles in its starfish-shaped forepaws. Zie wailed: the wounds bubbled with a horrible fierce ache of an itch.

The ulgrane's voice was soft and almost sweet. "Good day, good day! I trust your voyage through our territory has been pleasant hithertofore! I distinctly assert that it will continue to be pleasant once the toll has been paid!"

Despite his injuries, Casamint lowered his antennae and cast an incendiary spell at the monster, with all his craft and three cley. The spell built slowly: the ulgrane sparked and smoked, but would not catch fire for many seconds more. It swatted at him with its other starfish-shaped forepaw, leaving his face bubbling with itching venom.

The ulgrane smiled at Casamint, and said in a soft, almost apologetic voice, "In all honesty, I *must* recommend that you pay the toll without ill-mannerly violence! Unfortunately my fellow employees are, on the whole, capable of replying to violence with violence of our own — and, indeed, some of them may, perhaps, be eager for such things. I should prefer to disappoint them — shouldn't you?"

Arrhwy's hawk dived at the ulgrane, and Rajel swung the deck chair at the ulgrane's face. It dodged both attacks, but was sufficiently distracted that Arrhwy leapt on its left wing, claws and teeth rending feathers and bones. Casamint's spell finally went off, scorching the ulgrane's body. The ulgrane raised its forehands against Rajel and Arrhwy, releasing Boragette, but the co-lover was too stunned to move.

The ulgrane's attention was sufficiently diverted. Casamint grabbed Boragette's middle hand and yanked zir towards the doorway. Zie nodded, and ran for it — and, when zie got there, stopped and shoved zir badly-wounded husband through it, and slammed it behind them.

The two Herethroy held each other in the hall for a moment, shaking from the sudden blast of violence in a peaceful afternoon. The sound of smashing wood and crashing lightning drifted around them.

Boragette yelped, "Rajel needs her sword!" Zie darted for the staircase on four legs.

Nethry dodged around zir as she ran up the stairs. "What's going on?"

Casamint leaned against a wall, stinking of burnt cloth and chitin. "Ulgrane demanding tolls. Rajel and Arrhwy are fighting them."

Nethry nodded, put on a blood-streaked glove that moaned with bitter Destroc potencies, slipped out the door, and slapped the ulgrane's rump. The monster howled as her device opened deep fissures weeping with blood. She grinned at Casamint, and went out to join the battle. Another ulgrane was circling overhead, tossing lightning bolts; Rajel warbled to Nethry, glad of another ally.

Casamint panted softly, then turned to the lace curtains on the nearest window. "Zallarilla, if you can hear me, tell your father that we're being pestered by ulgrane, and that we could use a great sorcerer conjuring firebirds and woe-winds."

Zallarilla's voice snapped, "I know, Casamint. He'll come if he's needed, he said. Thanks."

Boragette rushed back up the stairs, panting under the weight of Rajel's immense sword. Casamint tried to take it from zir, but zie said, "You're badly hurt already, Casamint. I'll do it ... I don't think a lightning bolt would kill me. It might kill you."

He nodded, regretfully. "Come back in immediately, mari. I don't want you hurt." He grinned a bitter grin. "Their lightning is not comfortable."

Zie smiled at him, and ran out of the door with the sword. Rajel's deck-chair was a splintered mess by this point, though the ulgrane's head and shoulders were bludgeoned and bloodied from it.

The ulgrane reached for zir with a forepaw. "We have been discussing the toll, your friends and I, and at this point in the negotiations I can safely say that we have agreed that the toll is reduced to one single large magical metal weapon. How fortunate, indeed, that you have so quickly fetched it! Once I have it, I shall write you a receipt, and let you go on your most pleasant way!"

Nethry slapped the ulgrane's forepaw away from zir, her enchanted glove wounding it terribly. The ulgrane protested mildly, "Excuse me! Perhaps I have been a touch optimistic regarding the measure of agreement our negotiations have achieved to date — but rest assured, I seek only to save you further trouble!" As it spoke it raked her with lightning and swatted her with the clubs of its mid-claws. The lightning did almost nothing: Nethry was thoroughly prepared for it, since she had sent tempting messages to the ulgrane in the first place, and knew all their tricks.

Boragette held the sword out to Rajel, hilt-first. Rajel grabbed it in her left hands, dropping her chair. A third ulgrane took this chance to land by her and assault her. She turned away from Boragette to fight it. Boragette ran back to the door, slamming it behind zirself.

Casamint asked, "How is it out there?"

Boragette slumped against him. "Bloody. I think we're winning though."

"Is there anything more we could do to help?"

Boragette thought a moment. "Cast spells through the windows?" Casamint conjured a puff of powdered pepper in the first ulgrane's eyes. The next moment Arrhwy's hawk sank its talons into the ulgrane's shoulder, and the Sleeth herself raked its back.

It wailed, "Honorable guests, noble primes! Here, what is this? I must protest this treatment! We simply seek to collect the customary tolls for this corner of the sky, yet we are met with disparaging words and acts which could, if uncharitably interpreted, be considered aggressive! Be assured that a protest will be lodged in our embassy!" As it spoke, it leapt sideways off the edge of *A Flattering Wind*, wincing as its wounded wings caught the winds.

"Do ulgrane even *have* an embassy?", asked Boragette.

"I can't imagine so," said Casamint.

The three prime warriors turned on the remaining pair of ulgrane. Rajel, with her flying-glove and three-handed sword, took the battle to the ulgrane which had never landed. Nethry and Arrhwy, with a few minor spells from Casamint and Boragette, assaulted the ulgrane which still remained on deck.

"Oh, what deeds of iniquity do the primes do now?", hooted the ulgrane as Nethry and Arrhwy struck it by turns, "They defy the honest toll-gatherers, they resort to warcraft, the work of bitter blades and subtle spells, rather than the honorable honoring of treaty-signed obligations, or even the sweet harmony of negotiation! Alas, for the state of the World Tree nowadays! The primes are little better than pirates!" So saying, the two ulgrane followed their comrade. Rajel flew after them for a ways, cleaving a great gash in the lightning-caster's flank, but when the two of them whirled and turned on her she fled back to the ship, and let the ulgrane make their escape.

"In one way the ulgrane are right," Arrhwy remarked to Rajel. "We are a little better than pirates. At fighting, at least."

* * *

Zallarilla kept *A Flattering Wind* close to the ground for the rest of the day, barely above the tops of the highest hills, far below the clouds. The three adventurers healed themselves and Casamint as best they could, then stayed on deck, watching the skies nervously.

Boragette tucked Casamint into his bed, and sat beside him. The venom had worn off over two hours, and Nethry's Heal Once had taken the worst of the sting out of the wound, but he was still injured.

"I think you saved my life, when the ulgrane grabbed me and you set it on fire," said Boragette, trying to keep zir voice steady.

"Rajel and Arrhwy get most of the credit, really... I didn't do very much. And you were pretty brave yourself, running into the battle to bring Rajel her sword."

Zie smiled at him. "You're nicer when you're hurt. Not as arrogant."

He winced. "I try to be honest ... that's not arrogant, is it?"

Zie flattened zir antennae. "I don't mean it badly, Casamint. I expect Rajel to go fighting things. She's a woman and she's an adventurer; she's killed worse than ulgrane. You're a man and a scholar ... you were wonderful. Very brave."

Casamint took zir mid-hand in his left hands. "You were too. You kept your head most of the time ... you didn't do that much compared to the warriors, but what you did was all very important. Getting Rajel her sword, I think that turned the tide of the fight... I just tried to get that enchanter up on deck..."

Zie put zir fingers on his lips. "And you got me to safety. We both did pretty well, really. Stop insulting yourself."

He stopped insulting himself, and found another use for his tongue, of licking zir fingers. Zie giggled, and crouched over him, twining the tips of zir antennae with his, touching his belly with all a co-lover's sweetness. He responded in kind, in the ancient Herethroy rhythms. They had to be careful to avoid his wound, and neither of them was very experienced with the other's gender, but they were both well satisfied in the end. Afterwards he leaned his cheek on the chitin of her chest, curled one antenna across a sensitive stripe, and they slept in happiness.

* * *

"Boragette? Boragette? Are you there?" Rajel rapped at her mari's door.

The noise awoke Boragette, next door. "I'm with Casamint, Rajel," zie replied sleepily.

"Well, we're all hungry on deck, and we won't get to Morthavon for another three hours..." She opened Casamint's bedroom door and saw her spouses tangled up as lovers. "It's like that, is it? Well, *if* you can pry yourself away from that man and be a bit pleasant to the people who spent blood and cley to save your chitin — and are still working on it while you're down here getting laid — we *would* appreciate some food." She slammed the door and stomped back to the deck.

Casamint blinked at Boragette. "What a Sleeth-woman! You'd think she would be *happy* that some of us were finally starting to act a bit married."

Boragette spread zir antennae. "She does have a point ... I should get something for her and Arrhwy and Nethry now." Zie lifted his left arms from zir side and stood up. He started to stand, but zie put a mid-hand on his forehead. "No, no. You're wounded. You should rest. I'm the only one who wasn't hurt much. I'll take care of people now."

He nodded, and squeezed zir hand. "Thank you ... my sweet brave mari."

Zie grinned at him. "My pleasure, my sweet brave husband."

* * *

Nethry sprinkled grated cheese and dried peppers on a bowl of roasted nuts, and scooped up a dozen dried pitted prens, and smiled to Boragette. Arrhwy lapped guinea-pig soup from a big tureen, and brushed her flank against Boragette's leg. Rajel accepted a bowl of plue prepared in the Comblefree style from her mari without acknowledging zir.

Boragette watched zir wife eat for a moment, but Rajel would not meet zir eyes. Finally zie asked the room, "What are we going to do now?"

Nethry answered, "We talked it over with Zallarilla. We're going to stop for a few days in Morthavon. I'm used to this sort of thing — I know what kinds of monsters the nonprimes are — but I think many people would be glad to have city walls around them for a few days. And time to recover."

"We're not going all the way to New Kottarnu?"

"Morthavon's the nearest city on our way. We're not in such a hurry, are we? No need to discomfort ourselves to rush and make powerful magic items for monsters, not when we've just been attacked by monsters," said Nethry.

"I suppose that makes sense," agreed Boragette. The three ate quietly for a moment, and Boragette nibbled on a few shreds of tarrissy uncomfortably. "Do you think we're going to get attacked again?"

"We do not think so. Earlier today we do not think we will get attacked even once, so today we are wary," said Arrhwy.

"Oh." Boragette's word fell into a pool of thick silence, broken only by the sounds of chewing.

Some minutes passed in raspy quiet. Finally Boragette touched Rajel's shoulder. "Rajel? Would you come inside with me for a moment?"

Rajel nodded curtly, and turned to the other adventurers. "I won't be long. Make lots of noise if you need me in a hurry, OK?"

"Any reason we need you soon makes a lot of noise, even if we try to fight so quietly!" grinned Arrhwy.

* * *

Boragette and Rajel stood in the corridor where Boragette and Casamint had been during the fight. Rajel refused to go any further away from deck.

"What's wrong, Rajel?", asked Boragette.

"Nothing. Not a single, dead-ulgrane-futtering, live-mouse-eating, vaguely cataleptic thing."

Boragette spread zir antennae. "I'm sorry if I did something that offended you ... I was trying to be helpful in the fight, but I'm not much of a warrior ..."

Rajel glared at zir. "The best place for you on a battlefield is off the battlefield. You were where I wanted you. Then."

Boragette's gaze fell. "It's about me and Casamint, then ..."

Rajel shrugged. "I don't care what one person you fuck, as long as it's not a trio. Go two-play with a dozen men and a dozen women if you want." Her voice was as bitter as gall-wine.

"Casamint saved me, Rajel."

She scowled. "A little. Other people did most of the work. For that matter, *you* did more of the work than he did: you ran back into the fight with my sword." She patted the hilt of the weapon on her back.

Boragette spread zir antennae. "You saved me too, Rajel.... I'd be glad to two-play with you too." Zir voice was a bit shaky.

"You'll two-play with your wife, after she saves your life, without even making her beg **too** much for it? How generous of you, after weeks of barely touching her. Did you make Casamint beg for it?" said Rajel.

Boragette winced. "Rajel, I honor Casamint as a scholar and like him as a man. I honor you as a warrior and like you as a woman."

"Well, *I* detest him as a jerk and dislike him as an asshole. If he's got male bits inside that chitin, I haven't felt like noticing them."

"He is a bit abrasive at times, but he's our husband, Rajel. We ought to try to like him ... try to see his good sides. For he does have them."

Rajel leaned on the wall. "And there's not much but contempt he's said to you ... ever, really. He thinks you're his cook, his seamstress, and, when he's in the mood, his diamond-chess partner. And I guess now, when he's in the mood, his bed-partner. I've been trying to be your friend, Boragette ... I know you're a whole person, not just a convenience for me when I feel like it."

Boragette took zir wife's lower hand; Rajel's hand, so weighty in battle, was limp and unresponsive. "Rajel, I do know that. I'm trying to love you, to want you, really I am."

"You're trying harder with Casamint, though. He counts ahead of me, I suppose." "

Boragette gasped. "I don't count you behind or ahead of Casamint, Rajel! That's not how a triad is supposed to be!"

"You do *futter* him ahead of me, though," she snapped.

Boragette fumed inside: how could zir wife be jealous of zir husband? That was a terrible thing for a marriage! Zie kept zir voice low and steady, though, trying to damp the argument as much as zie could. "Rajel, would you like to go to bed with me, now?"

Rajel folded her upper arms. "I'd like you to *want* me to go to bed with you, now or any time. If I wanted someone who didn't want me back, I'd hire someone." She laughed. "You feel just as empty afterwards, but at least the quality of the copulation is better."

Boragette spread zir antennae wide. "I'll try, Rajel. I want to love you, I really do..."

Rajel reached out to squeeze her mari's shoulder. "Go rest, Boragette. I can handle days like this a dozen in a row, but you're a sweet pretty protected village cosi, and you shouldn't have to see a fight up close even once. Go rest. Even with our husband if you really want."

Boragette fled back to the kitchen. Dinner was salted with zir tears, and Casamint could not understand why zie refused to sit next to him and hold his hand under the table.

SOME APPLES OF ANGER

> *Dear Lord Muspis,*
> *I cannot say that the ulgrane attack was a great and instant success. Ilzatheinen, I think, barely noticed it; he remained below-decks, and had his warriors do the actual work. The poor newlywed-ish passengers were caught abovedecks, though, and I hope that their stories and their obvious distress shall break through the thick walls of Rassimel obsession around his spirit. Fortunately for the thick walls of Rassimel obsession around mine, Zallarilla was in the pilot's chamber at the time. I am a touch worried, nonetheless — I do wish you or I could come up with a somewhat safer approach. I am at a loss, however.*
> *In duty to Byronny,*
> *Nethry Ch.*

Zallarilla and Nethry had preferred to stay aboard *A Flattering Wind*, for privacy, but everyone else had gone to a hotel of Nethry's recommendation, Some Apples of Delight. That is where the quarrels began.

"We don't need to take a private room," said Rajel. "We don't want to spend that much on the hotel — after all, we don't have any idea how much it will cost you to get passage back to Araldy."

"You *could* lend us the money yourself, you rich and powerful adventure-bug, you," said Casamint.

"I made one set of arrangements for you, aboard *A Flattering Wind*. If you don't like them, I don't feel any responsibility to take care of you," snapped Rajel. "Or you could ask that Grand Padishah who keeps offering to marry you."

"I was hoping to find a pleasant, civilized, compassionate, and educated wife. If, in fact, such a thing is possible," said Casamint.

"I'm sure we could get the money somehow," said Boragette in a low, discouraged voice.

Casamint took his mari's side, as he had been doing quite diligently all day. "There must be some way for merchants to get money from Araldy to here, short of carrying it in big heavy suitcases on skyboats. Some of my classmates from Drysselwyn and New Kottarnu seemed quite well-off after some quick visits to the bankers' street."

"We're not in Drysselwyn and we're not in New Kottarnu yet," said Rajel. "And we don't know how they set it up — it could have been, say, a deposit of a few big coins in a bank. Hundred-lozen pieces aren't so hard to carry: it's a weight and a volume that many people rather enjoy."

"Rajel, mighty on the field of battle, but not mighty in the classroom. Morthavon is more commercial of a city than either Drysselwyn or New Kottarnu. I'm *sure* that we could get a money transfer from Araldy — or a loan, for that matter. Secured by Yazelton, if need be: I may not be the heiress of a Great Baron, but I *am* a nobleman of Araldy in my own right. And so is my mari," said Casamint.

"*Our* mari," said Rajel, in a voice like a swordstroke.

Arrhwy's tail had been twitching for several minutes, as the Herethroy argued. Finally her patience was gone, and she crouched and leapt onto the hotel's counter. The young Orren working there shrank back. Arrhwy hissed, "For me, you provide a bed in a public room: near the fire. For these three married Herethroy, you provide a private room. To the best sleeping of your other guests, make it the best-quieted of your private rooms. For the other Herethroy who comes along soon, a public room bed also. But a different public room than for me. I see her too much already."

"Arrhwy! What nonsense is this?" demanded Rajel.

Arrhwy flapped Rajel's face with her heavy tail. To the nervous Orren, she added, "I pay for both these rooms, but not the room for the other Herethroy who comes along soon. Also you must tell me: is there better entertainment in Morthavon than quarreling bugs?"

"OK! Twenty lozens the night ... Twenty-one if you want your breakfast alive, O Sleeth. We're not really set up for that as a regular sort of thing," said the Orren. He avoided the question of entertainment.

Arrhwy opened her left saddlebag with her innate magic, and levitated a small leather purse out — with difficulty, as the coins inside it were amber and weakened her Ruloc Corpador. She tugged it open with a fang, and dropped it in front of the Orren. "Take three of twenties of lozens. Maybe we stay longer; I pay for more then. For breakfast tomorrow I will have the cooked eggs and the blood pudding. If you give me blood pudding that is still alive, I pay the extra lozen for the sight of it, rrai! That is a new thing."

The Orren counted coins, shivering under Arrhwy's emerald gaze. Rajel poked Arrhwy in the rump with a finger. "What is this? What are you doing paying for my room?"

Arrhwy kicked her friend in the face with a hindpaw. "I am stopping you arguing. I am helping your quest."

Casamint asked, "Quest? Rajel, are you doing some other adventure that you haven't happened to mention to us yet? Perhaps one that attracts ulgrane?"

Rajel growled, "I am doing no such thing. Arrhwy is just being ridiculous."

Arrhwy turned and glowered, baring her fangs. "I am doing no such thing. Rajel is on a quest for a vacation of pleasing and relaxing! Her training leaves her ill-suited for such a thing, so a Sleeth must help. We know the pleasing and the relaxing!"

Rajel tugged Arrhwy's tail. "Get off that counter. You're scaring the attendant."

Arrhwy chose to drift like smoke up to the ceiling. "Now you may scare the attendant yourself, Rajel. Or scare your spouses. Or, if you are feeling newly sensible, scare Chicory."

Rajel glowered up at her partner. "You are no help at all, Arrhwy."

* * *

Breakfast at Some Apples of Delight was huge and surprisingly elegant. Arrhwy's eggs and blood pudding (dead) were served in a bowl of butter-gravy, at the center of a tablecloth on the floor; the waiters did not trust a Sleeth to eat neatly. The Herethroy ate biscuits and grilled squash and pastries stuffed with peas, and drank much kathia spiced with rosemary and lemon.

"Another pitcher of kathia, if you please," said Casamint to a waiter. He yawned, wriggling his antennae. "I'm afraid I didn't sleep all that well last night."

Arrhwy pricked up her ears. "Is this the good not-sleep-well, or the bad not-sleep-well?"

"It's the Rajel-on-my-right not-sleep-well," said Casamint in a light voice. "She insisted on taking the middle of the bed, and, from that tactically-favorable position, invaded and ultimately conquered about three-quarters of the territory of the bed, and collected all the sheets as her booty and loot and tribute."

Arrhwy flattened her ears briefly. "No better tribute than that? I think she could have gotten a better!"

Rajel glared in mid-yawn. "Just because you couldn't find a ... whatever ... to screw doesn't give you the right to prod at *our* marital arrangements."

Arrhwy grinned. "Rrai, why do you think I ask for the quietest room for you? So you do not hear me yowling outside your window three times with three different people!"

Rajel just shook her head, snagged the kathia that the waiter was bringing to Casamint, and poured herself and Boragette full glasses. Boragette blinked at Arrhwy. "Did you?"

Arrhwy smiled at zir, licking butter-gravy off her whiskers. "I am not on heat. Last night I just sleep. I am not on heat, but I am bored. Maybe tonight I look for more."

Boragette flattened zir antennae, and Rajel glowered. Casamint just smirked and looked superior.

Chicory strode up from her public room, wearing a dignified vest and jacket of burgundy cloth. "Hey there! Did you finish off all the grilled squash in the hotel yet, Rajel, or is there a bit for me?"

Boragette hopped up and touched antennae with zir girlfriend. Rajel laughed. "No, there's a bit more on the table. After that's done, well, you're a mighty farmer. I'm sure you can grow some new ones in no time."

Chicory took a squash, flicked a seed out of it into Casamint's kathia cup, and cast a straightforward spell that farmers only use in emergencies. The seed sprouted and rooted, drinking kathia, spreading vines, and, soon, bearing three squashes.

Casamint scowled. "Am I supposed to be delighted with your skill, Chicory?" He picked a squash and took a bite. "Well, better than I had thought, but it's still woody and bland. It takes a *lot* of skill to create food that's actually worth eating." He created a head of cabbage, with the same spell he had used on Wilsamander much earlier.

Chicory said, "Yeah, I know the veggies aren't any good. But the seeds are just fine, that's what the spell is for." She cut a slice of Casamint's cabbage. "This is not half bad, though. What *is* that spell?"

Arrhwy peered at the cabbage, and laughed. "Casamint is the cheating bug! Two spells are there. Leaves on the Shoulders to make a cabbage, and Tasty Treat to make it taste good. Also it is not the permanent cabbage. It is the temporary cabbage. In two hours, or three, it is the no longer existing cabbage. If you are a farmer, you are a starving farmer, Casamint!"

Casamint glared. "I'm a scholar, not a farmer, and a rather good one."

Chicory slapped him on the back. "A rather good one halfway through your first cycle at the Academy. Gotta get back there and finish your studies before you can buy real cabbages from anything you earn as a scholar!"

Casamint glared at Boragette. "Did you arrange something about travel funds with her?"

"I did not do!" said Boragette.

"Nah, Zallarilla's flying me around for free, 'cause she's a sweetie," said Chicory. "That means I can spend some money on something else, and I think it might be a good time to do just that."

"What do you want to buy?" asked Boragette.

"Weapons, Boragette. Weapons and armor. If we get attacked again, I want to be all armed up, and protecting you with my shield and my quarterstaff," said Chicory.

"Bah. I did perfectly well with just my spells and my cleverness," said Casamint.

"And your wife," said Rajel. "*Mostly* your wife."

Chicory grinned at Rajel. "And what a wife! I'll leave the fighting to you, Miss Assassin Bug. But I'll keep the Boragette all safe while you're doing it."

"Dubito, dubito," said Casamint. Nobody else at the table spoke ancient Ketharian, so his meaning was lost, as he intended.

* * *

After breakfast, the five wandered around Morthavon. Being in a city was a relief to Boragette. Not that zie was used to having the strength and danger of enchanted city walls around her; zie had only been inside city walls a handful of weeks in zie life. Half of the relief was the familiarity of the people: ringtailed Rassimel, eager brown-furred Orren, chattering groups of Cani with their tails a-wag, and the shining chitin and expressive antennae of zir own species. Once zie saw a Gormoror, shaggy head standing out of the crowd, feathers tied in his fur, the handle of a huge sword on his back. Boragette grinned privately; for all the Gormoror's evident strength, he still had only two hands, and his sword was smaller than zir wife's.

Casamint insisted on browsing in bookshops on the Street of Trapezoids, and pulled Boragette and even Arrhwy in after him. Rajel stayed outside, scowling at the diagonal-cut logs of the boardwalk, wondering what her husband was up to. Chicory ogled the natives and the architecture in equal amounts.

After a very small eternity, they came out of a bookshop, a packet wrapped in green paper in Boragette's mid-hand, and Casamint's mid-hand in zir other. Casamint was babbling happily. "The Vermifuge of Tessoria is absolutely delightful, Boragette. It's a classic, but it still speaks to the modern Herethroy — all of the triumphs and disappointments of agriculture, and with a light happy style of writing."

"What do you know about agriculture, Casamint?" asked Rajel. "You, who ran off to the academy as soon as your parents could afford it?"

"I *am* a scholar of natural philosophy," said Casamint. "In training," he added with a nod to Chicory.

Rajel shrugged. "As you will. Let's go see weapons-shops now. My left upper greave got a bit damaged when I was saving you from the ulgrane, and of course Chicory wants something or other. I don't imagine that a classic novel or whatever else you got would be quite so good in a battle."

Casamint smirked. "Perhaps not, but perhaps so. We shall see in just a few days."

"Hey, Rajel. I'll bet you know weapons. What's good for me for, oh, six hundred lozens or so? That's what I paid for the funny title, I figure I should pay about as much to defend it," said Chicory.

"For defense, mostly? Are you any good with a sword?" asked Rajel, tapping the hilt of the tremendous one she wore.

"Nah. Just spear 'n quarterstaff. Proper farmer style stuff," said Chicory.

"Not that there's anything *wrong* with a Herethroy using a sword," added Boragette hastily.

"Oh, nothing at all, of course!" said Casamint. "Indeed, it has one signal advantage. It provides the single and solitary bit of evidence that she knows she is not a Sleeth." He raised his kathia cup to his mouth.

Arrhwy flicked Casamint's cup with her tailtip, splashing hot honeyed kathia into his face. She whirled and caught her tail in her forepaws before Casamint could react. "Oh! Excuse me!", she said to him. "It must be an accident though. A Sleeth cannot use a weapon, not even a cup!"

Casamint dabbled furiously at his face with the corner of the tablecloth, and folded his antennae as everyone laughed at him.

* * *

The five set off, turning left on Dulcet Street, following some vague directions Rajel had gotten from a city guard. Casamint and Rajel continued trading barbed comments, with Chicory ignoring or missing the whole thing. Boragette let go of Casamint's hand, and then dropped behind. When the others turned right on Arshtway Street, zie continued straight, dropping to four legs to dash ahead. She turned left on the Avenue of the Gargoyles, and then left again on Drunken Banker Street, and made herself alone in a crowd.

Now and then someone would glance sharply at zir, noting zir foreign clothes. On the whole, though, zie was simply another person in a cosmopolitan city: when zie was worth a second glance, zie was not worth a third. There were no vorwi or ororosti there, wondering everything about prime civilization; no husband and wife and girlfriend bickering about everything...

Zir relief was broken by a cuff from a clawsome paw on zir calf, a rolling Sleeth voice saying "Boragette! You slink away from everyone, you are hard to track on city boardwalks!"

Zie scriffled Arrhwy's head with a midhand. "My everyones are full of arguments and quarrels with each other. I had no great desire to listen to them."

Arrhwy purred a deep rusty purr. "They fight about you."

Boragette's hand dropped. "No, they're fighting about what to do and how much to spend and where to eat." Zie looked around. "And, speaking of that, I haven't. Would you like anything?"

Arrhwy smiled. "Buy me scorched bird bits, on cinnamon skewers! But you are wrong. Two nights ago, Rajel sits on my bed for the very long time, and there she explains at considerable length why she hates Casamint."

Boragette paid a handful of seashells with dots of amber in their folds for three skewers of meat for the Sleeth, and a huge steamed bun stuffed with minced greens and garlic for zirself. "I wish she wouldn't hate Casamint. He's not the most likeable man I've ever met, but there's a lot of good in him. And I wish he wouldn't hate Chicory."

The Sleeth levitated a skewer with difficulty, and carefully tugged a chunk of spicy, fatty bird off of it. "Do good and bad matter for liking or hating? Or for coupling or not coupling, even? I say they do not. Tlurrrien is not a good man, not by the thought of most people here, but he is a good screw."

"It matters to me, Arrhwy," said Boragette.

"So you think Rajel is a wicked person?" asked Arrhwy.

"Not at all!"

"Then why do you not screw her instead of your Chicory?" demanded the Sleeth.

"Arrhwy! How can you ask me such things?" yelped Boragette.

The Sleeth's heavy tail twitched. "Someone should ask you that. You are now married with Rajel as long as my son is alive."

"Did she put you up to this?"

Arrhwy snorted, and ate another chunk of bird before answering. "No and yes. She does not ask me. Likely she does not think that a Sleeth would do any good a job of it. Likely I will not! But she does complain at great length — also at substantial depth, and at wearying width, and with a low mopy acrid stink all over. She does this in my bedroom two days ago. Evicting her so that I can sleep is hard! So I think I make my own sleeping easier by talking to you."

Boragette bit zir bun fiercely, and green juice squirted over zir chin. "Talk then."

"Remember, I am the Sleeth. I boink who I will, I do not care how unprivate it is, I have kittens without asking the tom. I am the old Sleeth: if there are surprises of sex left for me, they hide themselves well. I am so immodest that I barely tell the difference between the shy blushing Herethroy noble-cosi and the brazen forward Herethroy noble-cosi. So you can be coarse with me. I think fine words are not so good for talking about lust!"

Boragette flattened zir antennae, thoroughly embarrassed, but zie laughed a bit. "I suppose that's true."

Arrhwy sat on her hind legs, sprawled awkwardly against a cobbler's front door against the edge of the boardwalk. She held the skewer awkwardly in her forepaws, and nibbled the last bit of meat off of it, then let it drop because she had no way of holding it further. "I ask again: why do you not screw Rajel?"

Boragette fidgeted with the leaf zir bun had come on. "I don't think she and Casamint and I are ready for actual intercourse yet."

"Of course you are not, and if you do not screw Rajel you never are, but I do not ask you this thing and you know I do not ask you this thing. Why do you not two-person-play with Rajel?"

Boragette stuffed the rest of the bun in zir mouth and chewed slowly. The Sleeth stared at her with fierce malachite eyes, and ostentatiously spread the claws on one big paw and licked between them, her ears following zir closely.

"Rajel scares me a little. She's all hard and fierce and merciless ... more feminine than a woman should be, more like a Gormoror warrior or something."

Arrhwy grinned. "Or a Sleeth, but you are careful not to say that."

Boragette continued, "And I want some bits of romance from both my spouses. We've been married as long as we could talk. We've always known it. They never had to work to woo me and win me. My parents took care of that long ago. Casamint wasn't quite sweet to me yesterday, but he showed he cared enough to try to keep me alive. And Chicory *has* worked to win me. She's been endlessly sweet to me for years. And patient too, for I never did anything improper with her."

The Sleeth tried to protest, but Boragette spoke on. "I know Rajel did too ... but ... that's what she does. She's an adventurer; she fights. For her that's nothing special. She's done it for money, for boredom I suppose. I'd like her to do something that's special for *me*."

Arrhwy chuffed. "Boragette, you are the cosi with the odd opinions of things. Still, you want what you want. Are you upset if I tell Rajel of this? I do not think she guesses it fast by herself ... but maybe you prefer to make her think of it all alone, and to keep her fighting and miserable until she does."

Boragette frowned. "Arrhwy! I am not so cruel as ... all that!" The actual idiom was "so cruel as a Sleeth", but saying that directly to a Sleeth was perhaps rude.

Arrhwy's tail thumped on Boragette's ankle. "You are not the definitive of an answerer of all that either."

Boragette glared at Arrhwy. "First you intimidate and humiliate my heart's secrets out of me, now you go tell them to Rajel?"

Arrhwy shrugged. "You and she are both maybe happier if I do. But if you ask I do not tell. Maybe instead you tell her yourself?"

Boragette shuddered. "I can't *imagine* that conversation going well. I'd rather have a quick social call on some ulgrane. Would you tell her?"

Arrhwy grinned triumphantly. "I tell her. Maybe she listens, maybe she does not listen. But maybe you and she are not so badly unhappy after this."

Boragette spread zir antennae. "Arrhwy ... thank you."

Arrhwy laughed. "I am entirely selfish here. I wish to sleep on *A Flattering Wind*, without your wife ruding mopily at me in my cabin for the many hours!"

Boragette looked at Arrhwy closely, but had no idea if she was joking or serious. Quite likely Arrhwy herself didn't know. "Well, Arrhwy ... shall we go see the Vermillion Temple? It's supposed to be the most impressive sight of Morthavon."

"Good! We go!"

LOVE AND LOCKSMITHS

> *Dear Inspector Chrestilium,*
>
> *If a clever and mighty Inspector, in the middle of the situation, cannot discern a better plan, then an overweight henpecked figurehead of a Lord Secretary could hardly do better. I grow increasingly worried about this issue. Your colleagues have explained to me that great monsters, like the simplest of grasses, abhor emptiness; when one is killed, another may well move into its territory. Wherefore, if money or influence may be required — up to a small fraction of what we paid for the fight against Aulihemm Bremm — please do not hesitate to ask.*
>
> *Cheerio!*
>
> *Muspis*

"Zallarilla, sweetie, if you don't move your fingers, there's not the slightest chance I shall want to get out of bed," said Nethry.

This was not true: Nethry was fretting inside about how she was going to arrange the next bit of evidence to turn Ilzatheinen against nonprimes. Her best contact among the predatory monsters of the area had flatly refused to attack a skyboat, not even for the promise of a magic item. Her second-best contact, a pack of perdithorne, were obstinate and cowardly and not actually willing to put themselves into a fight. Nethry needed to find some monsters who were aggressive, persuadable, and not overly clever or dangerous. It would have been difficult enough in person; trying to do it by far-speaker was a trouble and a half. 'This is stretching my skills at subterfuge and diplomacy to the limit,' she thought to herself, 'Fortunately Zallarilla is so easy to like, or I'd be quite beyond my depth.'

Zallarilla wiggled her fingers familiarly. "Observe! My fingers are now moving. Surely you wish to escape?"

Nethry curled her tail backwards and wriggled in unfeigned pleasure. "That *really* isn't helping. Don't you have some laborers coming to the skyboat this morning?"

"I suppose I do. I suppose I don't want to share you with them, too..." Zallarilla sat back and wiped her hand on the sheets. Nethry rolled over and nuzzled a pillow for a moment, then reluctantly slipped out of the bed.

"Hallo? Hallo, *A Flattering Wind*? Is anyone there?" A deep Herethroy voice called at the front door of the skyship.

Zallarilla popped her head out her bedroom window. "One moment!" She struggled into her captain's jacket, then looked around frantically. "Where's my kilt, Nethry?"

Nethry paused from scrubbing sticky spots of her bellyfur. "Someone, perhaps a wicked foreign spy or a nonprime monster, persuaded you to remove it in the breakfast room. Unless other forces of evil have been at work — outside your bed that is — it's probably still there." She frowned at herself inwardly: 'I shouldn't even joke about that. I don't want anyone connecting me with anything.'

"Oh, seven great staring gods!" Zallarilla trotted off to the breakfast room, with Nethry grinning at her bare rump and formal jacket. "Gah, it's all inside-out and tangled. What did you *do* to it, Nethry?"

"I didn't touch it a bit. I was just dancing at you ... from the other side of the room, as you will recall. You could have taken it off and folded it neatly on a sideboard. You could even have left it on," said Nethry.

"Hah! Not likely! You were exercising your wiles at me — the whole breakfast room is full of leftover wiles! Come look!"

Nethry said, "Um ... that doesn't make much sense, Zallarilla," but she obediently padded to the breakfast room. Zallarilla, dressed in full sport-captain's regalia, caught Nethry in a warm kilted embrace. "That's nice, Zallarilla, but shouldn't you be answering the ... mrow!" She yelped as Zallarilla's hands snuck around and touched her quite intimately indeed.

"See? You left all sorts of wiles in here, Nethry. We're going to have a job and a half cleaning them up this evening." Zallarilla glared fiercely at Nethry. "And don't you *dare* try to clean them up without me. Now go get dressed."

Nethry laughed, picked up a couple of abandoned bits of clothing, and headed back to the bedroom to dress — and, of course, try to arrange for monsters to attack her lover's skyboat.

Zallarilla sauntered downstairs to the front door. "Sorry to keep you waiting, O Herethroy. You are from ...?"

"I'm Darkspots, here from the Caterer of Nomune Avenue." The Herethroy woman showed a battered leaf covered with Zallarilla's writing. "I've brought most of this as you asked. Tillard greens are out of season, and the bitegrass harvest was quite poor this year. I've brought a few packets of alternatives."

Zallarilla nodded. "I'm not used to buying food for Herethroy, and I've got three aboard on this trip."

Darkspots waved her antennae. "This became apparent from your order. I have taken the liberty of bringing certain other common choices for Herethroy, in case you don't wish your passengers to be miserable from poor nutrition."

"Ah, thank you very much, Darkspots! Indeed I am not in charge of making my Herethroy miserable. They take care of that for each other."

Darkspots gave Zallarilla a leaf itemizing a dozen kinds of greens and vegetables in big blocky handwriting. "How is that?"

The Rassimel looked at it quickly, and nodded. "I'll take all of this. Oh, they're a married trio, but it's an arranged marriage and they're being together for the first time."

Darkspots nodded sympathetically. "I was married as a child too. There were some peculiar times growing up ... I never exactly felt that my marriage *started* at any particular time, you see. My husband wanted to have children starting when he turned twenty-seven, and to start practicing for it much earlier ... My mari was waiting for some big event to lose zir virginity. Of course the big event had happened when we were six ..."

"Did you get it all straightened out?"

Darkspots waved her antennae in big circles. "Oh, I suppose so. Most co-lovers' parents lecture them to encourage them to stay at home and remain chaste at that age: Bandazure's parents encouraged zir to move in with us and perform. After a while zie listened to them somewhat." She shrugged. "It's not too bad, really. Our husband spends most of his time with his other triad though. I would too if I were a male or a co-lover."

Zallarilla listened, her ears going flat in embarrassment. "My passengers didn't grow up together."

"Ah, I don't know if that makes it better or worse. Bandazure and Umber and I grew up together. I always thought of them like siblings, which didn't make marriage too easy. Umber always thought of Bandazure as, well, someone he could grab when he felt like, and *that* didn't help either."

Zallarilla shrugged. "Well, my passengers are trying to figure out who does what to whom, and to get used to each other at all. Not my business, really."

"Ah, I shouldn't be dripping my own troubles on a stranger's ears, really," said the caterer. She got out a round wooden tray covered with big leaves. "Here's the rest of your order ... I gather your own romance is better than your passengers', O Rassimel of Araldy?"

Zallarilla grinned, and peeked under the leaves. "Oh, that looks beautiful!" She flattened her ears. "You know what it means? I didn't think that the Transwynt used these designs..."

"Oh, that we don't, O Rassimel, but the Caterer of Nomune Avenue is a Rassimel too. There's not much he doesn't know about food, or the preparation of food, or the secret meaning of food."

Zallarilla gave Darkspots a handful of amber as payment, and a couple coins extra. "Well, he certainly got the details right. Can you help bring this upstairs?"

Darkspots waved her antennae. "Certainly."

* * *

The sun filled with fire, and *A Flattering Wind* filled with supplies. A pair of Orren men came with boards and screws, spells and nails, and Zallarilla set them to work on the doors to the deck.

Nethry asked, "You look downcast, lover. What's wrong?"

Zallarilla curled her tailtip. "They'll be doing adequate work, but it won't be pretty."

"What are they doing?"

"Putting locks and bars on the doors. If ulgrane land on deck again, whoever doesn't feel like fighting can hide safe inside... safer, at least. And everyone will sleep better, knowing that there's stout wood and Sustenoc keeping monsters out."

Nethry smiled to herself: the Araldeans were starting to worry properly about monsters. She nodded. "Now that's a wise thing, truly. I hope it's worth a bit of inelegance... maybe only for a short time? Could you get to a shipyard and have more stylish bars installed?" She was not particularly interested in skyships, but she understood the Rassimel drive for excellence and perfection.

Zallarilla nodded. "I think I'll wait until I'm back in Girath. It's not an actual problem with the ship, just a cosmetic matter." She turned Nethry's muzzle towards her, and kissed her fiercely. Nethry moaned and leaned towards her, but Zallarilla hopped up. "Lunchtime!"

"Tease of a flirt, to leave me after such a kissing!"

Zallarilla's eyes twinkled. "I have a shipful of crafters and carpenters! It's not an afternoon to lie pleasantly together in bed! Lunchtime, lunchtime, lunchtime ... In my cabin with the door closed."

Nethry smirked. "And precisely how much management of the crafters and carpenters will you be doing, in the cabin with the door closed?"

Zallarilla grinned, closing the cabin door behind her. "I will stay entirely dressed." She tore the leaves off the round tray from the Caterer of Nomune Avenue, revealing an elegant symmetric array of mushrooms and fruits and sweet cheese biscuits, surrounding sliced smoked pink fish in the shape of two interlinked circles.

Nethry looked at it. "Good heavens, you do not perform lunch lightly! That's quite pretty."

Zallarilla sat on a stool, and flipped her kilt up "It's a design from Araldy: the story is that smoked fish brings energy and enthusiasm: Orren food for Orren style.

Nethry laughed. "That's a bit silly. *I* bet that it's a myth some Orren fish-seller made up to sell a salmon to a newlywed Rassimel couple a few centuries ago, or some such."

Zallarilla grinned. "Oh, probably. It's one of our little customs, though. If you were a boy one of the rings would be a line instead."

Nethry giggled. "That's direct and enthusiastic. Now I'm sure it's an Orren thing."

She reached for a piece of fish, but Zallarilla stopped her. "No: I feed you, and you feed me. With one hand." Zallarilla picked up a bit of fish and held it to Nethry's lips. Nethry nibbled it, and smiled. "Oh, this is delicious. You didn't get low-grade fish, I must say. Why one hand, though? What's the other one for?"

Zallarilla smirked. "Whatever you like ... hey! Whatever you like as long as we stay dressed! This is usually served in restaurants, you know!"

Nethry looked as innocent as possible considering the circumstances. "Restaurants with long tablecloths?" She wrapped a bit of fish around a sliver of underripe pren, and held it up for Zallarilla.

"Just so."

Their lunchtime conversation was bright and delightful, and spoken with fish and fruit and fingers rather than words.

* * *

Dear Lord Muspis,

Thank you for your offer. This seems to be a case requiring considerable persistence and attention, for both its difficulty and importance; but I am a bustard in a bottle if I know how more money could help it along. Also — forgive me — the company of Zallarilla is distinctly pleasant. I fear me that I must count at half the time I spend on it as vacation. Fortunately I seem to have neglected to use most of the vacation due me for the last seven or eight years. Nor, as I understand, is there a spare scyanturge applying for the post of Go-Lord of Soohoon, at least as of a week ago. Therefore I shall let matters proceed at their own comfortable pace — and give Ilzatheinen his own chance to become comfortable with me and, perhaps, listen to me more closely.

In duty,
Nethry Ch.

ROMANCE

The sun's flames were guttering low, except for two long red-orange tongues curling towards each other but not quite touching inside the solar globe. Boragette strolled along halfway-familiar boardwalks, tapping zir midhands on the heads of the fantastical wooden beasts carved on the fenceposts around Some Apples of Delight. Arrhwy poured on the walkways behind zir, tail arched high over her back. She had been smirking an insidious feline smirk since mid-day, and refused to explain why. As they approached the hotel, she became even more cryptic: she slipped off in mid-sentence. When Boragette turned to look for her, she was already bounding from rooftop to rooftop, her fur as dark as blood under the deep sunlight.

Boragette shrugged, "There's no accounting for Sleeth." Zie walked alone into the hotel.

Of course Rajel had taken charge of the key to their room. Boragette walked to the counter, where two adolescent Orren were thoroughly engrossed in a game of matching cards. After a moment zie rapped on the counter. "Hallo?"

One of the Orren grinned and hopped up. "No looking at my cards Twizzelfry! What d'you want, O Herethroy?"

"The key to my bedchamber: the pale blue room on the third floor. It would likely be under a Sleeth name, of Arrhwy."

The Orren laughed. "Oh, that room! It's all popular today."

"What do you mean?" Zie accepted a carved wooden bar the size of zir hand, and with as many fingers.

"Well, three or four porters came there, and a Herethroy man who's staying there has come and gone and come and gone, and ... I don't know the half of it. It wouldn't surprise me one bit if someone had moved a great swimming finfianc into the room while I wasn't watching!"

"I hope not that," zie said, and climbed the two flights of creaky hardwood stairs to the light of a few perpetual candles. The wooden lock on the door was awkward, and took zir several tries to open.

* * *

Rajel was sitting on the bed, looking quite miserable. She set aside her breastplate and the gritty cloth she had been polishing it with.

"Hallo, Rajel. Where's Casamint?"

Rajel frowned. "He's off drinking with some junior priests or some such. He won't be back until late, or until tomorrow. We spent half the afternoon together, after you left us. He was a bit angry by the end."

"I seem to have misplaced Arrhwy too. Last I saw she was bouncing about on the rooftops — hunting pigeons perhaps, or terrorizing servants in their top-floor chambers."

Rajel nodded. "Arrhwy does that now and then. I shouldn't worry about it." She fidgeted with the corner of a pillow. "Boragette? I bought you a present."

Boragette smiled, starting to feel nervous zirself. "How sweet of you!"

Rajel crouched by the side of the bed, opening a squeaky wooden drawer. She presented zir with a bouquet of candied wheat stalks, their spiky heads frosted into the shape of a fountain's spray, glittering with white and blue-tinged sugar.

Boragette took it, and spun it next to a candleflame. "Rajel, that *is* sweet, and not just with the sugar." Zie looked closely. "Are you supposed to look at it or eat it?"

Rajel shrugged miserably. "I don't really know. I asked the confectioners' for something romantic ... it didn't come with instructions!"

Boragette waved zir antennae. "Don't worry, Rajel. It's very nice, even if we use it to ... to ... cudgel ulgrane with, I suppose. It's spiky and hard enough!"

Rajel's antennae spread. "Is it gone stale and hard, Boragette? I really tried to get a nice one of ... of ... whatever it is. I thought you'd like it."

Boragette smiled. "I do like it, oh my wife, even if its true nature is a mystery to me still. And even more I like that you thought of me that way." Zie sat next to her, twirling the spiky confection.

Rajel mumbled, "Well, Arrhwy sent me Silent Words that I should get you *something*."

Boragette put zir hand over zir wife's mouth. "Stop making it sound bad. I'm really very glad of it, even if great Virid stepped out of the sky and thumped you over the head with it and told you to go be romantic."

Rajel smiled a ragged smile around Boragette's fingers. "Well, nothing quite that exciting."

Boragette looked at the confection again. "Some of the ears are already getting broken. They don't build houses of structural sugar, do they? So I think it's meant to be admired and then eaten. I have done the first, and I shall start on the second. And you shall help me!" Zie broke off two glistening ears of candied wheat, and put one of them into Rajel's mouth.

Rajel chewed awkwardly. "It's for you, O my mari!"

Boragette's antenna-chitin glittered. "For me to use as I wish, I should hope! But you can't expect me to eat the whole thing by myself, not tonight."

Rajel smiled. "It does taste good though. That's not just wheat, is it?"

Boragette crunched zir own piece. "Pren-flower extract, I think. And the wheat's been toasted some. Quite nice! I should get a recipe for it. When we have children I shall teach them to make it, for holiday decorations and treats."

Rajel flinched. "Not for a while yet..."

Boragette smiled. "There are a few things we'd have to do first. You and Casamint would have to help out a bit."

Rajel nodded miserably. "Do you really think we should get pregnant before we're back home?"

Boragette laughed. "I'd like to do some several of things before I'm tending skittering children! One of those is to make good friends among the co-lovers around where we live... An even more important one is to make good friends of you and Casamint."

Rajel looked pained. "I'm trying, Boragette. I really am."

Boragette peered into zir wife's face. "I know you are, Rajel." Zie leaned over to kiss her cheek, clicking antennae together.

Rajel whined, "What can I *do*?"

Boragette sighed to herself: Rajel had only the barest idea of how to behave with a spouse, but she would never learn without encouragement. Zie broke off another pair of wheat-ears. "Have some more candy, and let me sit up against you."

Rajel sat stiffly as Boragette snuggled against her side, but relaxed a bit when zie tugged her lower arm around zirself. Zie waved zir antennae. "Holding me isn't so bad, is it?"

Rajel shook her head wordlessly, and, quite nervously, stroked a finger across one of Boragette's junctures, where the chitin is thin and the flesh is sensitive. "Is that all right?"

It was hardly the caress of a superb lover, nor as passionate as Chicory's eager fingers, but Boragette leaned down to kiss zir wife's fingers. "Yes. Married people can do that if they want."

"And do you want to? Did I bribe you with candy, like a child?", asked Rajel.

"Oh, hush. We both should learn how to be nice to each other ... we should both exert ourselves to fall in love, even, if we can manage it. Candy and cuddling are bits of nice for us to enjoy; treats so we can learn to find happiness in each other." Zie drew Rajel's arms tighter around zir chest, and tried to force zir own nervous body to respond to hers. They did little more than hold each other, leaving Rajel aching for more, but they held each other and hummed village hymns in harmony until the sun went out, and fell asleep comfortably tangled together.

THE AFTERMATH OF THE ROMANCE

Dear Nethry,

You certainly do have vacation due to you, and I can hardly deny it to you. Still, be careful in this instance! Too great an entanglement with the Araldean enchanter's family may prove a difficulty and a half in the completion of your distinctly urgent mission! I shall make you this offer: if you dissuade Ilzatheinen promptly, you may take a sabbatical of seven months (in addition to the vacation currently due to you), perhaps at the Vermillion Temple in Morthavon or some other place learned in the ways of nonprimes.

Take care, be careful, let caution be the glove on your left hand to match that extraordinarily dangerous one on your right hand! I never fear when you go among monsters, but now you are among people, lissome and delightful and pleasant — and, of course, currently embarked in a course of action which may well doom dozens or hundreds of citizens of Byronny.

Your most respectful but worried,
Muspis.

* * *

Rajel and Boragette came down for a late breakfast, hands in hands shyly. Casamint was there already, wearing yesterday's clothes all spotted with dust and dried wine, scowling into a large chalice of kathia next to a plate with four steaming pastries stuffed with garlic and cheese. Rajel smiled at him, as bright as sunshine. "Ah! There you are, O my honored husband! And where did you find to spend the night? Some out-of-the-way public boardwalk, perchance? Or the bed and the arms of some cute drunken scholar-boy?"

Casamint looked past Rajel. "Oh, good morning, Boragette my dear mari. I'm ever so glad to see you. I was worried when you wandered off yesterday with that Sleeth. But I guess you like them feminine, don't you? I got in a bit late last night, and you looked so cozy up with some brawny beast of a swordswoman that I thought I'd hire a bed in a public room. Of course I *would* end up next to that Sleeth. We did have a nice quick chess game though. You're better."

Boragette laughed, tugging zir scowling wife to Casamint's table, and kissed Casamint on the cheek.

Rajel sat down as hard as she could manage, making the spindly chair creak and rock under her weight. She snatched the four pastries from Casamint's plate, giving two to Boragette and keeping two for herself. "I'll just take charge of these. I fear me that my husband is still too drunk to be trusted with money *or* hot food."

He turned away from her, and called to an Orren carrying a tray of used wooden plates. "O Orren, please to bring my wife a pot of your largest, sludgiest porridge, for she is hungry past all etiquette. And bring my mari candied mushrooms, for I know zie loves them well."

The waiter peered at him. "O Herethroy, well ... could you tell me which is which?"

Casamint laughed. "The dreadfully feminine one with muscles like a nycathath and manners like an ulgrane — for she has slain both in battle, and I believe eaten their spirits in some hideous primitive ritual — is my wife. The thoroughly pretty one with iridescent rose chitin is my mari."

The Orren nodded, "Rose chitin gets candied mushrooms. I can do that!" He scampered off towards the kitchen, losing an egg-stained napkin from his tray. Rajel shouted, "No! Cancel that order!" after him, but too late.

Boragette laughed like bubbles bursting in wine, and smiled brightly at Casamint. Rajel tensed next to zir, so zie squeezed her upper hand which zie still held, and ran a lower-hand finger over her calf under the table, and she relaxed. "Candied mushrooms and candied wheat, singing and compliments. My life has become sweet indeed!"

Rajel muttered, "I may not be as good with words as the schoolboy over there, but I'll bring you candy *and* cheese pastries. I'm not only dessert for your life."

Boragette kissed zir wife on the cheek. "I know you're not, O my beloved wife." Zie glanced out of the corner of zir eye to see Casamint scowling at the kiss. His jealousy tingled in zir antennae. Zie felt filled with a mighty power, that zie could ensnare three people with zir own beauty and charm, that zie could make them crave zir and compete for zir.

Casamint winked at zir. "And you know I'd never dessert you, for I did not when the ulgrane came! And behold! The candied mushrooms have arrived!"

Boragette giggled a bit at the weak pun. Rajel snorted. "Child's humor. I'm surprised you don't use spontaneous magic, child's magic, too."

Boragette waved zir antenna coaxingly. "Oh, don't be cross, Rajel. He's just being pleasant company!" Zie held a candied mushroom up to Rajel's lips, watching Casamint's smile darken for a moment.

Rajel smiled at the sign of her mari's momentary favor. "We shall not need minstrel nor jester, with him in the triad! Not every noble household is so well equipped in its husband."

"Nor shall we need a pair of great oxen and an enchanted plowshare to plow our fields, for our wife is here! One swipe of her great huge sword, and the trees are cloven and the ground will yield to her." He glanced at Boragette on the word 'ground'. Boragette winked at him.

"I'm not going to pull a plow, Casamint," glowered Rajel, "And I'm not blunting my sword on trees and roots."

Boragette grinned. "You've set yourself a task, and you've set one for Rajel, but what about me?"

Casamint smiled and waved his antennae, and spoke in an extravagant storyteller's voice. "For you, Boragette, we shall construct a tall, tall spire of rosewood and teak, and make for you a throne atop it upon a platform of glass. And you shall ascend to it in the early evening, so that your beauty illuminates the entire valley, and all Herethroy may work late ... and our animals too shall be inspired, and their numbers shall grow greatly."

Rajel frowned. "That's just being silly."

Boragette beamed and giggled. "Ooh! What then?"

Casamint grins. "We shall sell many, many guntries to the Cani. We shall buy you carapace inlay of copper, and a crown of copper and rose quartz, and cushions of spell-softened glass for your lofty throne."

Boragette grinned, and leaned over to kiss his cheek. "That's *so* sweet of you!"

Rajel rolled her eyes. "Boragette, I'll buy inlay for you *now*, not with some foolsome phantasm to pay for it. I've won plenty of money, using my sword better than our japing husband could ever imagine."

Boragette touched Rajel's leg with the lower balls of zir tail. "Would you really? I'd *love* that." Zie smiled to zirself; there were rewards for being pleasant to zir spouses!

Rajel caressed zir tail with her lower hand, and took a few big bites of porridge. "Very well then. Are you ready?"

Boragette blinked. "Ready?"

"We're going shopping for inlay jewelry," said Rajel.

Casamint stared. "Just like that?"

Rajel grinned. "Just like that. I am not some weak vacillating confused Orren of a man, Casamint. I am a woman, strong and brave and decisive!"

Boragette finished the last of the candied mushrooms. "Very well then! I am indeed ready!" Zie shoved zir chair back and stood on four legs.

Casamint shook his head. "Not so long ago you were fussing about a few lozens more or less for a hotel room. Today you're spending a dozen times that buying jewelry. What's come over you, Rajel?"

Rajel glared at her husband. "Come over me? Do I need to be overtaken with hallucinations or ethereal vapors or some weakness of the spirit in order for me to buy jewelry for my mari? Do you, perhaps, suggest that zie is unworthy of it? Perhaps zie is not beautiful to your eyes, and worth only stories about metal and not the actual metal itself. But to my eyes zie is most glorious. Spending some lozens here or there to enhance zir natural beauty would hardly be wasting them!" Boragette beamed at her, and she beamed back.

Casamint shook his head, knowing that he did not have enough lozens to match Rajel gift for expensive gift. "Last night must have been a truly excellent one for you, Rajel. Perhaps it was your first time with someone else? What could be more natural than saving your virginity for your mari ... even if the saving of it was, perhaps, inadvertent. Even if nobody you weren't married to would take it."

Rajel frowned. "I've never lacked for lovers."

Casamint smirked. "I thought not. You have the air of a slut about you, you know? Well, good day to you, and enjoy the shopping ... and whatever you can buy with it. I'll be at the temples."

"Collecting a cute priest-boy or two, I shouldn't doubt," snapped Rajel. Casamint just grinned, knowing better than to say yes or no.

Rajel and Boragette got directions to the street of jewelers from the Orren at the front counter, and walked off. Casamint's last barb had stung, though. Rajel fumed about Casamint the whole way. Boragette tried to distract her with the business of picking out a design and the wire for it, but Rajel, in the usual feminine style, had little concept of adornment and less love of it. She wound up snapping at Boragette the fifth or twentieth time zie asked for her opinion.

In the end Boragette got a squared double spiral of some pinkish copper alloy inlaid into zir left shoulder, a classic design that matched zir chitin's color and ridges nicely. Zie was grateful and volubly delighted, and held Rajel's hand and sang to her; but the morning was only pleasant where it could have been wonderful.

Boragette danced in Chicory's cabin, zir new inlay gleaming. Chicory spread her antennae. "That's kind of pretty. You got yourself a pretty good wife there, getting you stuff like that." She grinned. "But your blouse is getting in the way of it."

Boragette turned away from Chicory to latch the door, and then to slip out of zir blouse. Zie turned and smiled shyly at zir girlfriend, zir four arms crossed over zir mating-siphuncles

Chicory's smile was anything but shy. "Now you're looking even better, and that's a *really* cute inlay. Y'know, this is the closest I've ever gotten to *seeing* your thorax. I guess married life is suiting you nicely, getting you all less shy!"

"You're not jealous, are you, Chicory?"

"Me? Nah. A girl can't be jealous. I know to the frumbles that I'm gonna share you ... well, I mean, I'm *sure* to share my husband, and like as not share my mari as well. No point in being jealous! Gotta just take what you can get." She gently lifted Boragette's lower hands, and put her own lower hands in their place, her thumbs moving intimately.

Boragette spread zir antennae. "That feels good ... I should stop you, shouldn't I?"

"You always have before right about now. Right about a bit before now, even. Said you were saving it for your first marriage." She touched antennae with zir. "Guess there's no point in saving your *second* time for them too?"

"Well, I've let Casamint touch me, and I've let Rajel touch me. It's about time I let the woman I actually love touch me." Zie uncrossed zir upper hands, and tugged at Chicory's belt: the most forward thing zie had ever done in zir life.

Chicory's reaction was immediate and substantial. The two of them sprawled on the floor, moving together in ancient ways, with Boragette's lower mid-hand taking the role that would be played more satisfactorily by a male in a full mating.

* * *

"Now *that* was worth waiting for, Boragette," said Chicory. "But let's not wait so many years before we do it again, huh?"

Boragette shamelessly cupped the smallest ball of Chicory's tail in a hand. "No, let's not."

"Heh. Only one thing better, I hear."

Boragette flattened zir antennae. "I wouldn't know."

"What? You wouldn't know? All those nights you three have spent together, and you wouldn't know?"

"Really, no. I'm doing my best to be friendly to them both, but they're all fighting and bickering at each other."

"Aww, still? I thought that was just for show. My parents were always like that in public, but at home they were plenty sweet to each other," said Chicory.

"No, it's real."

Chicory tapped Boragette on a chitin plate covering an intimate region. "That is *so* wrong. You go get them both at once, soon as you can. And then you drag that scholar-bug down here and let me try."

"You like Casamint that much?"

"Hey, he's here, he's your husband, he'll do. My old mom always told me not to pay attention too much to what men say, anyway. They're rare, so they think they're special, but *you* don't need to be fooled."

Boragette laughed. "He certainly thinks he's special." Zie did not want to spoil zir first time with Chicory by arguing, but zie thought to zirself that zie would be happier loving zir husband, if that could be managed somehow.

CODA TO ADULTERY

Arrhwy sniffed as Boragette entered the trio's bedroom, and then tasted the air after the style of felines. She grunted, and ostentatiously cast a spell to amplify scents, and sniffed Boragette from knees to throat. The Tawlowns all peered at the Sleeth curiously.

"What are you doing, Arrhwy?" asked Casamint.

"I am smelling pornography!" proclaimed Arrhwy, and flicked her tail up lasciviously.

"Pornography?" asked Boragette.

"I am smelling of what you recently do with Chicory. It is very much a pornography smell!" She pointed at Boragette's abdomen with her muzzle. "Your twef is very well-used now. Not just by your wife."

Boragette gasped at the vulgarity. "Arrhwy! How can you say such things?"

"Rrai, it is very the easy to say them, when next to a cosi who does them! Since you are now the indiscriminant adultery bug, perhaps you do me next?"

"Arrhwy, please stop pestering my mari," said Casamint.

"Hah, I think zie challenges me as Ship's Slut. She has the hard challenge, for I am very experienced. But I think a few more afternoons like this one for her and maybe I give her the title! She is as pure as swamp water!"

Boragette's antennae curled to knots. "That's not it at all."

Rajel stared at her mari. "What **did** you do?"

"Well, I *did* spend a while with Chicory, cuddling and such," said Boragette.

Arrhwy interrupted, "When *I* cuddle like that, everyone can hear the climax-yowling for three blocks around!"

"Well, we *did* get a bit carried away," admitted Boragette.

Rajel calmly took all the chalices off of the lacquered wooden tray the hotel provided, and snarled, and smashed the tray in three hands. "I work and work and work to get a *little* lovemaking with you — I buy you metal inlay! — and *she's* the woman who you get carried away with."

"I didn't get *all* the way carried away. I *did* save the last degree of intimacy with a woman for you," said Boragette in a very meek tone.

"Did zie, Arrhwy, can you smell it?" snapped Rajel in an adventurer's voice.

Arrhwy laughed, and sniffed a terribly embarrassed Boragette carefully again. "Zie only bilfs her off, nothing more! Your mari is as pure as *boiled* swamp water."

Casamint pushed Arrhwy's head away from Boragette with two hands, and took the broken tray from Rajel. "You are not apprehending a murderer here. You are menacing our mari, who, from the sound of it, has only been a bit excessive with someone that zie is hoping to marry. And I'm sure zie was coming here straightaway to apologize to us, as is only polite." He smirked at Arrhwy. "As you *must* be able to smell — or are intentions beyond even *your* keen nose, O Sleeth?"

Boragette stood halfway behind Casamint. "Thank you, O my husband. I knew I should tell you as soon as possible..." Zie certainly knew the general etiquette, though zie had not had time to realize that it applied to zir.

Rajel glared at her spouses. "We're on this trip for each other. I don't particularly want to share either of you with anyone. I especially don't want either of you picking up your second marriages now." Her voice was harsh with distress. "I don't get a second. If this one doesn't work, I will see to it that your others don't work either."

"If you kill Chicory, I shall never forgive you," said Boragette, rather nervously.

Rajel's antennae went flat. "I shan't murder anyone. I'll just ... I can't think exactly what. Protest the unfairness of the situation to everyone who will listen, I should think, in the company of other women doing the same."

Boragette took zir wife's hands. "I shan't be unfair to you." The two of them smiled tentatively at each other. Arrhwy pushed Rajel towards Boragette. Rajel blinked at the Sleeth, blinked, and took Boragette in her arms.

"Boragette? Come sit on deck a bit with me?" asked Rajel nervously.

"Of course I shall, O my wife!", said Boragette, and slipped zir left arms around Rajel's waist and shoulders. The two of them left.

Arrhwy smirked. "If Boragette is two-thirds the clever Herethroy I think she is, Rajel finally gets what she was hoping from the marriage."

Casamint snorted. "And if you are two-thirds the tactically-minded Sleeth I think you are, you will apologize extensively and intensively to Boragette. You said some quite rude things to zir, your words as sharp as your teeth."

Arrhwy's tailtip flicked uncertainly. "I am very cruel to zir? This is unfortunate. I intend to be only moderately cruel to zir. She is moderately cruel to my friend."

"You used descriptions more suitable to, oh, your own self, than to a refined country noble co-lover. And some quite rude words besides."

Arrhwy snorted. "'Twef' is the fine short word for it! The biology word is much longer. If I have it right at all — I only study the biology words for boys and for girls."

"I shan't enlighten you. It is not a matter I care to discuss with a Sleeth. My recommendation of apology stands."

Arrhwy thought for a minute, thinking about whether she needed to care about Boragette's opinion of her. "I am living with zir for some years more, I think. I suppose I do not want zir to be the anger cosi with me. Well enough, then, I apologize soon enough. Perhaps after zie finishes up with Rajel. Zie is smiley and floaty from so many lovers then, I think!"

"Don't talk about my mari so rudely, Arrhwy," warned Casamint. Arrhwy gave him a wide-eyed kittenish look, and stalked elegantly out the door.

MORE ULGRANE

Dear Lord Muspis.

There is some reason why I have not taken leave from my job in the last seven or eight years. I shall not accept a sabbatical in Morthavon! I shall do this errand at its proper and deliberate speed, without applying haste in any way that risks its ultimate success. And I certainly shall not let affection for Zallarilla do the slightest thing to slow it down or compromise it. Never think that!

Remember your ambitions to be a figurehead! You can never fulfil such ambitions if you recommend courses of action to me!

– Nethry

When the rains started, the Herethroy dashed around the airship, slamming windows and locking them. When the rugs were safe, they retired to the lower parlor for vervain tea and deep-fried cabbage leaves and diamond chess. "I should have thought that rain would be softer up here," remarked Boragette, "for it doesn't have so far to fall."

"That's not how it works at all, truth to tell, Boragette," smiled Casamint. "The air elementals mainly manage the weather on the surface of the branch. Up here they pay less attention, and so the winds are wilder. We can fly so high because *A Flattering Wind* has a transvection engine: A skyboat with sails might well lose its sails. Things only fall so fast through air, and a little raindrop will fall fairly slowly; but the wind whips them about and sends them crashing and clattering on our windows." He waved his antennae benignly.

Boragette looked over the board, and took the zi ri with zir herethroy. "If the winds get worse and worse the farther off the tree you go, wouldn't the sun get blown off its track? To say nothing of the star-serpent and all the moons and even the gods' eidolons."

"Oh, not at all. I shouldn't think that the winds were worse a million miles up than a hundred. Not that we know for sure ... though I *have* seen studies that say that the sun stirs up terrible winds around the circumference of the universe, as it rolls about. If it weren't for the Tree itself, we'd be in the middle of a perpetual cyclone." Casamint casually took Boragette's herethroy with his own.

Boragette grinned, and captured two of Casamint's pieces with zir khtsoyis. "If they didn't make anything for us to stand on, would the gods have made us at all?"

Casamint frowned at the board, and leaned his head on three hands. "I did those two moves in the wrong order, didn't I? You are distracting me with questions. Which, honestly, are at least as good as chess. Only you and Ilzatheinen on board have any spirit of curiosity, and Ilzatheinen rarely wants to talk."

Arrhwy, who had been asleep in Rajel's lap — and much of the couch on either side — woke suddenly, ears swivelling around. "Mrarow! That is not a noise of rain!"

Casamint looked up. "What is it, Arrhwy?"

Boragette tapped zir husband's chest. "Back to the game, you. I am about to give you a fearsome drubbing, and I wish to enjoy it fully."

Arrhwy shook her head. "Play fast, O Herethroy! Heavy feet are walking on the roof."

The lace curtains swore. "Oh, anal intercourse with Accanax. More ulgrane. Lots more."

Rajel shoved at Arrhwy. "Get up, you inert Sleeth. Time for more work." Arrhwy hissed, batted at Rajel's face with retracted claws, and teleported to the top storey of *A Flattering Wind* to check the newly-barred doors. Rajel ran for her cabin, to get her weapons.

An ulgrane flew across the window, the storm breaking around some weather-ruling spell it wore. It clutched at the window frame with four taloned legs, and peered in. "Good day, good day! We were just strolling about the neighborhood, stretching the old wings you know, and saw a skyboat in a storm. We thought to ourselves, 'Oh dearie me! It's ever so dreadfully unsafe to fly about in weather like this — perhaps we should go check to see that they're all right!' And so here we are." It reared back and struck the windowpane with all its strength.

A Flattering Wind was more heavily strengthened than most skyships would be; the window rang like a bell, and the ulgrane's head bounced back painfully. "Oh, dear," it said, "You do seem to be having a touch of navigational difficulties. Well, never fear — we'll set everything right in half an instant!" It started to conjure a bolt of lightning at the window.

"Get inside, Boragette!" shouted Casamint, and ran over to draw and tie the drapes.

"We're beset by ulgrane again!" shouted Zallarilla through every curtain in the skyboat. "Stay inside! Hold on to something solid!"

* * *

A Flattering Wind thrashed in the air like an angry serpent. Boragette, Casamint, the tea-set, and the surviving chesspieces were flung around the parlor. Through the tattered drapes they saw the ulgrane get torn free from the window frame.

Boragette caught a couch with a mid-hand, and helped zir husband to crouch behind it. The skyboat lurched again. The ulgrane started to fold its wings, hoping to drop out of the way, but it did not have enough time. The alarmed Herethroy saw it slam against the parlor window, hard enough to leave its starboard legs and wing red and ruined. The ulgrane fell, fluttering, trying to work a wind-mastery spell strong enough to fly it to safety.

Zallarilla flicked *A Flattering Wind* this way and that, bringing three more terrible crunches from the sides and top of the skyship, and a torrent of mild ulgrane complaints. "We are simply coming to investigate possible problems or troubles with a prime airship flying through a terrible storm! We risked giving our feathers the great soaking! Nonetheless, your driving is terribly hazardous — if you continue, we shall have little choice but to file a complaint with our lawyer in New Kottarnu!"

Zallarilla's voice snapped from the curtains. "Nethry, Arrhwy, look outside — *carefully*. All the ulgrane I can see are leaving. Is it a trick? Everybody else, hang on."

An angry yowl answered from the upper floor. Boragette untangled zirself from Casamint and couch. "Arrhwy's all hurt!"

Casamint ran after zir. "Boragette, come back! Zalla said hang on!"

Arrhwy was crouched at the bottom of the main staircase, fur bristling, tail thrashing more fiercely than the skyboat had been, eyes gleaming with anger. "That was not the delightful fight! I do not taste any blood. I do not even see an enemy. Instead a Rassimel I am trying to protect breaks some of my bones with a banister!"

"Oh, Arrhwy! Are you badly hurt?" Boragette rushed to her side. Casamint ran off the other way.

"I am angrily hurt! Zallarilla flips me from one end of the staircase to the other and back again! Are you the healer Herethroy, Boragette?"

"I have a little spell..." Zie cast Kiss the Stinging Cut, a minor Healoc spell more suitable for children's knocked antennae than warrior's wounds.

"That is the very little spell, Boragette," snapped the Sleeth.

"I'm sorry, it's the best one I know," apologized Boragette.

Arrhwy licked her foreleg, wincing. "Well, I cannot bite you for not knowing any more." She tried to get to all four legs, and whined. "This is not so comfortable! Bruises and hurts are now all over me!"

NEW KOTTARNU

> *Dear Lord Muspis,*
> *That didn't go at all well. Zallarilla is clever and fierce! And, I know you are thinking it: I am quite sure I gave her no hint or inkling of any coming danger, for all that we share a bed and much more. I am afraid that today's events have not encouraged matters even a little; further delays are likely.*
> *— Nethry*

Zallarilla rushed *A Flattering Wind* to the skyport at New Kottarnu. The captain of the Byronny military ship *Striking Weasel* howled in rage as Zallarilla took her berth.

"Privilege of emergency," Zallarilla shouted back. "We'll be going to the healers as quick as we can."

Of course that was not very quick. Arrhwy could not walk, or would not walk, and crossly refused to levitate. "A broken leg is not so good for concentration. I fall and hurt it more!" Rajel and Casamint built a haphazard litter out of blankets and deck-poles, as Zallarilla made apologies to an increasingly sarcastic *Striking Weasel* crew.

After the better part of an hour, the litter was solid enough to support Arrhwy's weight in a style which she was willing to accept. The Araldeans made an odd sight in the streets of New Kottarnu — and a lengthy one, as the people they asked for directions sent them on a twisty and perplexing route to the Healers' Guild.

New Kottarnu made an equally odd sight to the visitors. To the magic sense, the city ached with the straight black spikes of Locador magic. The houses were towers, ridiculously thin and often bent or twisted, made of black wood inlaid with peculiar runes, topped by three or four crooked spires. Doors were surrounded by arches in the forms of distorted gryphons or anguished lizards, or pillars of bone surmounted by skulls.

"This is quite eerie," said Boragette, as they walked through a city park. Most of the trees were natural enough, if odd choices for a city: pain-willows and umbral ash, or hazillits laden with beautiful, poisonous fruit. A few trees were dead, wrapped in indigo leather carefully inscribed with detailed maps of a country that could not possibly exist, held to the wood by an extravagance of corpse-nails. Nethry was reminded of the Big Bags her friendly conlee had carried.

"There is a house or two like this in Pennypell," said Casamint. "Xhant Tandanza's for one."

"The deep mage?" Boragette shuddered.

"The very one," said Ilzatheinen, who seemed quite at home in the distressing city. "This is all very practical, to the proper sense of practicality — but that of a sorcerer concerned with magical effectiveness, and not traditional aesthetics."

"How is that?" asked Chicory.

Ilzatheinen tapped one of the dead, wrapped trees. "This, for instance. By itself the park would be a small thing, a clawtip in the middle of a tiny city. New Kottarnu was built in a hurry, for the survivors of Kottarnu in the Holocaust Wars, and was never intended to be a large city or the center of a city-state. The Kottarnami use Locador magic quite extravagantly, stretching their tiny clawtip of a town into a great huge city. This tree is enchanted, one of the four pillars that keeps the park large enough to be worthy of the name." He indicated certain coils and angry meditations in the tree's magic to the other primes.

"Effective, I gather, but hideous nonetheless. There's something pleasant about real space that's simply *wrong* about all this Locador-made emptiness," shuddered Zallarilla.

Ilzatheinen laughed. "Perhaps to an artist's eye, but not to reality. Natural space and the interior of New Kottarnu are made of the same stuff: all from the substance of the Locador god. And I predict that in no great time, perhaps as soon as seven centuries, all of Ketheria will look like New Kottarnu. There is simply not enough natural space here for all the people who want to live here."

Zallarilla shook her head. "No great time now that you have your immortality. I don't want to live to see it! It sounds hideous and wicked."

He smiled indulgently. "You will, though, in your next incarnation if not in this one."

Zallarilla shuddered. "Father, that's quite an unpleasant concept. I shall take care to enjoy this life thoroughly while I have it then!" She slipped her arm around Nethry's waist, and got an answering squeeze from her lover.

Casamint shook his head. "Not necessarily, O Rassimel. There are other ways to make space. Already there is the half-mile balcony around the main trunk: using existing space, to be sure, but taking empty air and making it something that primes can live upon. In the academy the school of architecture was making plans for a floating village in the air rollwards of Lenkasia. A great deal of magic, yes: but Herbador and Corpador mostly, not this horrid Locador."

Ilzatheinen smiled indulgently. "Perhaps I exaggerate. New Kottarnu was certainly done in a hurry, and with much recourse to that huge pyramid thing up ahead."

"Excellent," groaned Arrhwy melodramatically. "Now take me to the unnaturally-expanded Healers' Guild. Better if they had used Locador tricks to make the streets go more quickly!"

* * *

The hall of the Healers' Guild was a bulbous building, glistening with black lacquer, half-buried; its four knobby towers looked horizontal from the street, but cast long shadows as if they were vertical. A pair of black chalices taller than Ilzatheinen flanked the door, spilling darkly glittering water as slow fountains. They caught the enchanter's eye immediately.

"Look at these, all who doubt the beneficence of New Kottarnu. Name for me one other city on Aradrueia in which there are healing fountains available for free outside the Healers' Guild!"

Nethry peered at the leftmost chalice, and the enchantment like a sea of heavy cream upon it. "I *have* never known a doctor that healed for free before." She leaned over, letting the chalice's power pour over her treachery-earned bruises. "Not a great healing, though, for I still ache somewhat, and I've only got a few thumps here and there."

"Try the other one. It's an analgesic."

Most of the primes splashed themselves with Healoc-charged water. Arrhwy refused to stir from her stretcher. Rajel splashed towards the Sleeth. "You don't hurt that much. You simply don't want to get wet, you coward."

"I happily flee from any enemy I cannot defeat!" protested Arrhwy. "And water is surely such a foe: more than a few mouthfuls, and it will remain, unconquered and unconcerned, after my greatest attacks."

"Water isn't *concerned* about anything anyways," noted Casamint.

"Just so! There is no fun in fighting an enemy so apathetic! Now take me to the healers. Ilzatheinen, you must pay for this, as these were wounds earned defending you or trying to."

* * *

The healer had cast spells to mend Arrhwy's bones and flesh, and the primes bore her to their hotel. The Arch of Night was a pair of towers leaning towards each other.

"It's comfortable enough, but it's so *dark*," said Boragette.

Zallarilla threw herself on the bed that she and Nethry were to share, and tugged Nethry's tail until she sat next to her. Nethry ran one hand over Zallarilla's belly, and the other over the black velvet bedspread. "I suppose that's why they call it Arch of Night. You'd hardly expect a symphony of pastel yellow and pink from a place named that!"

Boragette picked up the one lit candle, and strode to the candelabra of shaped indigo-dyed bone. "Well, they could at least have windows, not just candles for light." Zie held the flame to a candle, and glared. "They've enchanted this thing so it won't catch fire. No windows and dark candles!"

Casamint looked more closely. "Not that perverse; it just lights on command."

Boragette handed the whole candelabra to him. "Well, what command? If we can't get any light in here I'm going out shopping 'til the sun goes out!"

Casamint looked at a tag tied to one the candelabra's twisted, clawed feet. "To light, speak the Kottarnami word for 'flame'. To extinguish, the word for 'darkness eternal'. Delightful."

Nethry looked up from petting her girlfriend. "Do you speak Kottarnami?"

Casamint mused, "Kottarnu was on Remseia, during the Holocaust wars ... maybe Kottarnami is Calanchian?" He looked at the candelabra and intoned, "Lirir". Nothing happened.

Boragette giggled. "You sound like a ritual mage from some bad historical romance!"

Casamint wiggled his fingers, then held them in odd positions of feigned arcane significance as he tried more words. "Liltan! Lirlith!" At his third word, the seven irregular candles burst into flame. "Well, that was remarkably easy. I was afraid I'd have to go ask the bellhop."

Boragette embraced Casamint, cupping the base of his tail promisingly in a lower hand where the Rassimel couldn't see it. "It's good to have a scholar in the triad!"

Casamint grinned. "The light of knowledge dispels the night of despair!" He caressed zir tailbase, more openly than zie had done to his.

Zie slapped his hand. "None of that! I'm not a Sleeth, I don't want an audience!"

Casamint wiggled his antennae unrepentantly. "Apologies, apologies."

Nethry looked up from the circle of Zallarilla's arms. "We were looking elsewhere — we saw nothing! Still, if you'd like to be excused, we would be hideously insulted but, possibly, find some way to divert ourselves and assuage the insult in due time."

Boragette patted Zallarilla's foot, "Have fun!"

Casamint added, "If our wife or Chicory comes by looking for us, tell her that we told you we were ... going shopping down the street and she should join us."

Boragette thumped zir husband's chitin-armored belly. "Casamint! That's not nice!"

"I want a bit of privacy with you, O dear my mari."

Zie giggled, and left the room with him.

* * *

Rajel, Arrhwy, and Ilzatheinen sat on couches on an upper balcony of the Arch of Night, or sprawled half-twisted over them, as each preferred. Arrhwy's tail was twined around Rajel's ankle, and her eyes were closed.

"It concerns me, all these ulgrane. I have made a dozen trips in the Transwynt, and Zallarilla has made three dozen in *A Flattering Wind*, and never a single ulgrane did we see. On this trip: one attack is unusual, and two is more than unusual. It is alarming."

Rajel shrugged. "They didn't say what they were after. They just threatened us in their meek little way."

Ilzatheinen nodded. "The presence of a mighty talisman might, possibly, alert them from some ways off. The Tilmarth Note is such a thing ... but Nherex-Dlostion kept it in Soohoon. The skyboat and this or that on it are valuable, to be sure, but not the sort of thing that grins with eyes of flame across the leagues of the sky."

"Perhaps Nethry is more than she seems?"

"Perhaps she is — my daughter evidently finds her so! — but to the magic sense she is simply a well-equipped adventuress, not greatly different from the two of you. And I do not think that ulgrane are seeking her for the presumed mind-swaying sweetness of her embraces."

Rajel flattened her antennae. "I'll leave comments on your daughter's choice of consort to you. Perhaps it's something else entirely — could we have been mistaken for a similar skyship carrying some interesting cargo? Could there be some wide assortment of ulgrane attacks on all skyboats in the area?"

"Worthy questions, for which I have no answer. Rajel, when you are adequately rested, please extract my daughter from her huntress, and the two of you go to the skyport and ask such things? I would like to know."

Rajel nodded. "That I will, Ilzatheinen."

Getting Zallarilla and Nethry out of bed and dressed was a half-hour's hard argument, and asking around at the skyport was another two hours' work. In the end, Rajel and Zallarilla were none the wiser. Nethry drooped inwardly, but reminded herself of her duty to Byronny: better for her new friends and lover to have a few hours of pain and a few weeks of fear than her city to live with a fortified pirate base next door.

IN THE RESTAURANT OF DOOM

Dear Inspector Nethry,

I quite understand the occasional activity that is less than entirely successful — I simply imagine how I would have done under the circumstances, which is to say, worse than any Inspector has ever managed.

Forgive me, but I am starting to become worried that you are paying too much attention and devoting too much affection to this Zallarilla. If you were Cani, I would know that you were becoming loyal to her, but I would know that you would know how to balance that loyalty against your other loyalties. As you are Rassimel, I fear you are becoming obsessed with her, but (I have little choice but to say it) Rassimel are not, on the whole, experienced in moderating their obsessions.

Please do be careful. Please do not hesitate to ask for any sort of assistance, should need arise.

Your concerned figurehead,
Muspis.

* * *

Dinner at Diflannu's seemed in order, for Rassimel and Herethroy both. "It has been a bit of an exciting trip," said Zallarilla, "and I don't see why we shouldn't have a peaceful and delicious evening somewhere excellent or at least famous."

From the outside, Diflannu's was a squat bulging globe of a building, the husk of a gourd grown to an immense size by excessive magic, then lacquered in a deep lustrous black, and tied about with cords and with snaking lines of engraved runes. When the irregular doors had been opened, and shut behind, the inside was predictably far larger than the outside, pricked through by Locador enchantment. The restaurant seemed a vegetable chasm, with seeds and immense membranes still hanging to the walls. A dozen square wooden platforms with snarling mantichorae carved at their corners floated precariously in the void, connected to each other by wobbly inadequate wooden bridges, upon which waiters in skeletal armor hurried with trays of soups thick with viscid perfume and roasts tied in distressing shapes.

"A pity Arrhwy didn't want to come. She'd have bounded from platform to platform, terrifying the diners," said Nethry.

"I daresay the Kottarnami are inured to fear," said Boragette in a low voice, "if a place like this is a popular restaurant. I understand about the Locador enchantments and all, but surely the waiters could get by with kilts and vests?"

Casamint said, "Look more closely at the diners. I see the emblems of Morthavon, of Byronny ... that table of uniformed Cani surely comes from

Drysselwyn ... those Herethroy may be visiting from Lenkasia, for they wear priestly robes of Lenhirrik and have sacred acorns at their throats. Those Orren look Kottarnami, at least... and that table of sorcerers is half local and half Araldean, or I'm a picnic. I doubt that the locals eat here often; this is a restaurant for tourists."

"For hungry tourists — among which I number myself!" said Ilzatheinen, and stepped forward without hesitation to the rickety uneven balcony floored with the rib cages of wicked beasts. Boragette winced, but the balcony held; it did not even wobble beneath the fat enchanter's weight.

On the balcony loomed a figure, cloaked in heavy-draped robes, with a steam of bitter herbs masking its face and scent, so that not even its species could be told from outside. "A table for six, please," said Ilzatheinen. The figure raised its arm heavily, extending a monstrous nine-fingered hand covered with short black feathers and bearing a rune-inscribed staff. It gestured arcanely to a circular table on the third balcony.

Casamint stared closely at the hand with magic sense. He whispered to Boragette, "Just a scrap of an illusion spell there. I can't see through it, but if it's weak enough for me to tell that it's an illusion, it can't be very big."

The draped figure turned to him, and spoke in a deep whisper that seemed to echo up from the depths of ancient tombs. "You must be new to our ... *circle*. I trust you shall ... *enjoy* your evening at Diflannu's." It laughed, a rusty broken sound as of a creature that had not felt true amusement in many tormented centuries.

Ilzatheinen set off towards the indicated table on one of the inadequate bridges, which swayed terribly under his weight. Zallarilla followed; when she looked down, the floor of the restaurant was a vast distance beneath her, and she saw the vague shapes of vorwl and ororosti — looking as if the illusionist who must have cast them was working from pictures, rather than the live ones that she knew — cavorting there, circling a struggling Rassimel woman bound to a hideous amber altar. She regarded it sharply with magic sense. It, too, was an illusion, well-crafted and changing and sentient, but with its power unnaturally low so that the unnerved could see its falseness and be comforted.

The seven achieved their table, after two bridges and one shower of viridian sparks from some horrid flying thing above. Their masked and armored waiter gave them menus written in bloody letters on the sides of archaic-seeming battered ceramic vases, in which dried bits of a dark sticky substance best not identified still remained. The waiter stood in thick silence as they read.

"I'd like the ...", said Ilzatheinen. The waiter put its finger to the lips of its mask, and hissed loudly for him to be silent. The enchanter frowned, then yelped in surprise.

All his companions turned to him. He blinked, and grinned at them. "Nowhere on Aradrueia but New Kottarnu could a restaurant get away with such thing — nowhere!" He did not explain.

The waiter's gaze passed heavily over the table; not a word was spoken. Nethry hissed angrily when it looked at her, but Ilzatheinen put a hand on her shoulder. "Look at the bottom of your vase," he said.

The waiter indicated by ritualized gestures of its bloody-clawed hands and short scythe that their appetizers would arrive shortly, and glided off, not having spoken a word.

Nethry turned her vase over, and read aloud, "If you wish the waiters to use spoken words rather than evil Mentador magic to take your order, place your napkin in this vase. I missed that."

"Well, *I* missed noticing the Mentador magic at all," said Boragette. "How can they *do* such things? It's terribly rude."

"It's a theme restaurant. Almost everyone who comes here knows about it, expects it ... except when their companions accidentally neglect to mention it. Accidentally!" said Zallarilla, smirking.

"Are there any other horrid surprises coming?" said Casamint, protective of his mari.

Zallarilla grinned. "Wait 'til you see the plates."

Rajel sighed. "Oh, delightful. This sort of thing is annoying enough to encounter professionally. How can they make a silly entertainment of it?"

Chicory said, "Not everyone is in your profession, Rajel! Boragette, if you'd rather eat with your eyes closed, I'd be glad to feed you..."

Boragette peered at Chicory. "Thank you, I suppose, but I shan't. In a place like this I'd much rather have my eyes open!"

"It's *not* really dangerous," said Ilzatheinen. "It's mostly illusions; and when they do use more substantial magics, like taking your order, it's all harmless."

Boragette grinned. "I understand! I want to have my eyes open so I can see all the creepy illusions!"

"Ah. Excellent," said Ilzatheinen.

The waiter brought them thick, turgid ghoul-goose soup in bowls that appeared to have been fashioned from the skulls of long-dead beasts, and they ate of it. The soup bowl had been heavily perfumed with haa-mleng, but the soup was a familiar if well-made soup of lentils and grilled sweet vegetables.

* * *

The meal progressed in a series of uncanny courses. When a grinning apparition brought small bowls of deep-fried apple slices in a sauce of prens to clear the palate between heavier courses, Nethry pressed her mission again.

"It seems fitting, in such surroundings as this, to consider again your purpose in coming here, and the dangers of it. For now you have seen for yourself, just this afternoon, the wickedness that non-primes are capable of. They are dangerous! They seek to rob us, or kill us, or worse!"

Rajel shrugged. "Ulgrane, yes, of course. Vorwi and ororosti, no, or not particularly, those silly illusions down there to the contrary. For that matter, back in the Pennypell area I know a dozen gentlemen who would be glad to rob us, and two or three who would just as gladly kill us for a very reasonable price. And these gentlemen are all as prime as prime can be. In a few days I'm sure I could find such in New Kottarnu as well — and not mere actors would stake you out on an altar and plunge a dagger at your breast, only to have the dagger turn out to be a cunningly-shaped rusk of bread, for the centerpiece of a tourist attraction."

Nethry nodded. "There is truth to that — but I would recommend against giving such gentlemen succor as well, and a place to plan their iniquities and to carry them out in safety. But for ulgrane, at least, piracy is the flavor of the eggs they hatch from, and piracy the winds that bears them aloft. Nor are they the worst of nonprimes: Soohoon had its scyanturge until very recently."

"I see the time has come again in which my daughter's concubine presses me to break my obligations. I do not fully understand why she cares so much, nor yet why I should have any reason to attend to her at all; but nonetheless, it shall make a fitting topic of conversation for surroundings such as these," said Ilzatheinen in a heavy voice.

"I would hardly press you, great enchanter! But I have lived for years in the wilds of the Lenwynt, and I know the secret minds of the monsters who dwell there — I know their myriad hatreds for us! Vorwi are harmless enough, to be sure. But perdithorne, ororosti, even nycathath are dangerous and insidious. If a Cani had come with us, we would have had no peace from perdithorne — and, of ten primes, two or three are Cani!"

"Twenty-four percent Cani, in Araldy at least, or so say the scholars," added Casamint.

"Thank you ... And that's just the monsters who are there *now*. Last year a scyanturge was there: they hate all primes with a terrible passion, baked into them by terrible Accanax their creator!" said Nethry.

Ilzatheinen shrugged. "Soohoon has no wish for another scyanturge to rule it. In any case, none is there now; the defenses I build may well help them to keep one out, or at least make it a more challenging target than any in the neighborhood."

"A more valuable target, worth a young scyanturge's effort!" said Nethry.

"And it needn't be a scyanturge. Consider a nendrai: smarter and more gracious than the average scyanturge, much more helpful to a town, and nearly as dangerous to us," added Zallarilla.

Ilzatheinen speared his last apple slice on a thin skewer of bone. "Consider a karcist who can cast Paw of the Fire God, and thereby destroy a city with a week's easy labor. Consider an skilled official of the Department of Flowing — no wizard she, but a person who could arrange to turn a city into a lake on a moment's notice. Consider being in a city anywhere but Ketheria: any month a leaf from a world-branch above may fall and blanket your city and countryside too. Consider a bonstable slipping into your city in the guise of your duke, and ruling wickedly for years before being discovered. Consider someone making a mistake with too many Locador spells — something that worries me about the very city we are in now! — and having some great terror from outside our universe enter the city, worse than any monster created by our own gods. Consider terrible Flokin, idiot god of fire, who has destroyed cities by mistake at least twice." He paused to eat his apple, and crushed the bone skewer against the side of his bowl.

"Nethry, there are many, many dangers in our world; the gods seem to delight in them. Safety is an illusion; we are born to peril, and endure it until we die of it. Against peril, we have our strength and our skill, our cooperation and our magic. Magic is no less important than anything else. And bear in mind the price I shall get for making these walls: the Tilmarth Note. With this I shall build protectives and even weapons for many primes. Whatever danger an enemy in Soohoon might bring to prime civilization, be assured that it will be balanced by power and safety for such as Rajel and Arrhwy."

Nethry sighed. "For prime civilization as a whole, you might be right or wrong, Ilzatheinen. It is a matter of comparing a myriad possible futures. For Byronny, you are certainly wrong: your future creations would benefit Araldy, not the Transwynt. Byronny city and Byronny people will be in more danger. Distant foreigners, such as yourself, will be in less danger."

Ilzatheinen waved his hand. "Point the first. Byronny is situated on the very edge of the Lenwynt. They have survived for many centuries — and prospered greatly, from the look of the place. I'm sure they pay close attention to all the deeds in the near Lenwynt, just as any city does to the Verticals and whatever other perils lurk in their domain."

Nethry nodded. "I'm sure they do. I've sold them a tip or two myself, and know something of the matter. This is precisely why I am so worried! I know how difficult it is already!"

Ilzatheinen charged on. "Point the second, the mathematical one. I will induce a certain fixed amount of danger to primes by making this all. Arguendo, I can entertain the hypothesis that it is a large amount. But you must concede that the benefit I provide to primes from the Tilmarth Note will increase over time, and that some fraction of this benefit will accrue to Byronny. Ergo, at some time, Byronny's benefit from the Tilmarth Note will, at some point in the future, exceed the danger. In the long run, even Byronny is better off from this!"

Nethry curled her tailtip. "One never knows how long the long run will be. If it exceeds the current age of the universe, say, your argument is less than persuasive."

Ilzatheinen laughed. "Ah, well, four thousand years is quite a young universe; I am given to understand that some worlds can go for a hundred times that without a notable event occurring. In any case, my point the third and last, the economical one. I shall be quite happy to provide further magical defenses to Byronny, should Byronny ask."

"And should Byronny pay," added Nethry.

"Well, of course they should pay. I imagine they might pay well for a defense against the fire elemental... It is no rare thing for an enchanter to supply both sides of a war: a weapon to the first, a defense to the second, a stronger weapon to the first, a thicker defense to the second. It has always seemed a touch on the ethically dubious side to do so. In this case, Soohoon is not prime, so it is only half so dubious; and Soohoon could hardly afford me a second time, so it shall not go on for long. Nethry, O my daughter's lover, your worries are very little ones, in full truth."

She did what she could. "That may be as it may be. But remember, local monsters have attacked you twice already, and may well do so again. I urge you think about this in more detail. Your own daughter may be killed by your plan! Neither you nor I would be pleased at that."

Ilzatheinen sighed. "The ulgrane seem quite capable of attacking Zallarilla even without a base at Soohoon. Nethry, I understand Rassimel obsession as well as any ringytail. I do hope that you are not so obsessed with this topic that you have no other to bring up at dinnertime?"

Zallarilla patted her knee under the table. "I know you're rattled by all these ulgrane, lover. I can't promise there won't be more, but we really *have* been safe enough from these. I hurt more primes than all the ulgrane did, last attack! Besides, we checked with the other sky-pilots and sailors: it was just coincidence that we got two of them. Coincidence and bad luck."

Nethry nodded. "It must have been nothing but bad luck." She started musing on what still worse luck she could arrange, to terrify her girlfriend and thereby defend her city. Every wonderful day of love simply made her mission that much more painful.

A waiter garbed in tomb-cerements in the style of the ancient hierophants of Oorah Thrassen (or, at least, a passable imitation) brought them small pentagonal plates heaped with shreds of the black-turban mushroom, sautéed with the blood of moles and with bitter spice (or, for the Herethroy, a salted garlic broth and bitter spice). "It is said, in the mystical herbals of Tassisp Tsarne, that these mushrooms induce a turgid sleep tainted with dreams of unnatural prophecy; yet those who eat of them too deeply are drawn under their terrible spell, and crave no other food. Eat, and observe!" The plates were passed around in near-silence.

"That *would* explain why Beetheart was so upset when I used trompes-de-miel in the plue," whispered Boragette to Rajel. Rajel giggled, and fed Boragette a bite of supposedly-doomed mushrooms.

THE GROOMING-GIRL

> *Dear Muspis,*
> *I am not in love with Zallarilla. I am not obsessed with Zallarilla.*
> *No further discussion on this topic is acceptable.*
> *– Nethry*

* * *

Nethry wanted colors more emphatic than the far-speaker could make. She paid extra for vermillion paint at the post office, and wrote in big angry letters on the mailing-leaf, too upset for her usual small precise brushwork. She waved the leaf around to dry it quickly, ripping it along the word "discussion", and had to pay another lozen for a drop of suitably enchanted glue.

She left the half-dry letter with the postal clerk, and stalked out of the post office. "Curse him with an infestation of red-hot copper fleas, for making me lie to him!" Her tail was bristling, and she snarled and stomped and snapped her teeth. Aboard *A Flattering Wind* she did not permit herself to behave that way; now she granted herself the luxury of two minutes of it. Three young insectile Herethroy children wearing smocks embroidered with death-masks and runes of dreadful significance squeaked as she stormed by, and hid from her behind the talisman-encrusted corpse of a tree.

Nethry's two minutes were soon over. She sighed, trying to calm herself, and raked futilely at her tail with her claws.

A Cani girl at a grooming-shop called to Nethry, "O foreign Rassimel, if it's grooming you seek and calming touches, come here! I have rongon-bristle brushes and combs of arken wood. I have the scent of hazillit blossoms captured in spirits of wine, and the scent of vertcorn captured in spirits of oil. I have calm fingers, and a velvet couch stuffed with fresh straw!"

Nethry blinked at her, then called back, "For two lozens, will you make me beautiful for one I love?"

"For four lozens, he will never resist you, he will forgive you any lie you have told him!"

"Was I shouting to the whole street?" Nethry shook her head, thinking that she was being dangerously careless. "I *do* need that grooming, I'll never deny it. Three lozens, O Cani, and tell nobody of what I have said!"

"Three lozens, O Rassimel, and fear not: a knight may reveal a secret, or a wizard most dark, but never will a grooming-girl!" She wagged her tail, and held a curtain aside for Nethry to enter.

Nethry removed her jacket and lay on her crossed arms on the couch. The grooming-girl sniffed her carefully, and picked four bottles of essential oils from her shelf, mixing an impromptu perfume to go well with Nethry's personal odor. Only Cani and Sleeth could smell the subtleties of the perfume, but it was part of the groomer's standard services.

"What has your beloved man done to make you so angry, O Rassimel, and to lie to him?", asked the grooming-girl in a light voice.

"Oh, I don't love him. Nothing but my employer is he. He thinks I am spending too much time and attention on someone else."

"Ah! Is that what he made you lie about? Turn your head." The grooming-girl sprinkled a brush with a few drops of the oil blend, and ran it lightly over Nethry's muzzle.

Nethry breathed deeply, smelling sage and bitter lavender, and closed her eyes. "I suppose so. If it was a lie."

"You're not sure? I think you're in love with *someone*. You've been crying. I'll have to wash the salt off." The grooming-girl scooped a bowl full of steaming water, dipped a square of thick white cloth in it, wrang it out, and dabbled at the corners of Nethry's eyes.

"I have been? Great staring gods..."

"Crying, or digging with your muzzle in the salt-bowl. Your choice!"

"I must choose crying, then. But I'm really not in love. Just a bit of an infatuation."

The grooming-girl went back to brushing. "You don't believe that one bit."

Nethry sat up, snarling. "Does *everyone* in New Kottarnu use Mentador, without permission?"

The grooming-girl stepped back and wagged her tail. "No Mentador in here! I'm no great wizard with cley to use and to lose! But your back went all tight when you said that, and your scent came all muddy and dark."

Nethry took the hot towel and rubbed her face. "There's no keeping your feelings secret from a Cani, is there?"

"Not one who's grooming you, truly! But we don't have to speak of it if you'd rather not ... Nothing but chatting while I work, am I!"

Nethry lay back on the couch. "I've nobody else I can speak of such things with, for all my friends care too much about my employer, or about her."

"'Her' being the one you perhaps love and perhaps do not?"

"Just so."

The grooming-girl added a drop or two of orange-spike to her perfume blend. "It seems like a great hard trouble to you ... your employer does not approve of your involvement with this woman?"

"That he does not. I am an emissary of sorts, and he prefers me dispassionate and undistracted." Nethry looked up at the grooming-girl. "And no, that's not entirely true, but I'm not going to tell you the entire truth."

The grooming-girl laughed, her tongue lolling out the side of her mouth. "True as family, or concoct up a story out of pure oils, it's all the same to me! How important is this job?"

"People might die if I fail. Or they might not."

The Cani's eyes widened. "Oh, my. I certainly hope you're lying to me a lot!"

"I wish I were."

The grooming-girl drizzled her perfumed oil on a brush, and started working on Nethry's tail, long strokes perpendicular to her rings. "Well ... does you being in love really make it so much harder to do?"

"Maybe a bit, but I don't think so, really. My employer *does* worry about it though. I seem to be well on my way to failing, love or no love."

"I don't blame him for worry, then, if he's worried about people dying. But I think you're the one who knows the matter best ..."

Nethry laughed. "I am here, and my employer is far away!"

"... so *I* think that you can be in love as much as you like, so long as you do your duty loyally and well. And if he doesn't like that, tell him to come talk to me!" finished the grooming-girl, with more bravado than practicality.

Nethry smiled. "I hope I can. First I need to decide if I am, in fact, in love."

"You may be, and you may not be... but after I finish with you, and you go to your beloved, there is no question but that *she* will be most thoroughly and completely in love with *you*." The grooming-girl grinned. "And there's no Mentador there. Just brushing and perfume to brighten your own natural beauty."

Nethry raised her tail, and looked over her shoulder at it. "No burrs and tangles? I wonder if she'll even *recognize* it."

The grooming-girl patted the small of Nethry's back. "And just remember this. Jobs may come and jobs may go. But love isn't so common or so cheap to be thrown away lightly. Especially for a Rassimel, for you're the most given to monogamy of any primes."

"There is that...," said Nethry. "I certainly haven't met her like before."

"Sit up now..." The grooming-girl brushed Nethry's chest carefully, and traced a line between her breasts with a drop of a spicier perfume. "See? If I were you, I'd choose the love. But I'm Cani. You'll have to decide in your own Rassimel way."

"I'll think it over very carefully," said Nethry, fishing a three-lozen piece and a handful of terch out of her pouch.

"That's the Rassimel way! Thank you, I hope you enjoyed the grooming, and I wish you good luck deciding. I *know* you'll have good luck with her tonight!"

The grooming-girl was right about Nethry's night. But as Nethry lay beside a sleeping Zallarilla, she thought hard, without any conclusion whatever.

THE TEMPLE OF THE DARK TRINITY AT NEW KOTTARNU

Dear parents,

Despite your worries, this is quite the safe adventure. I am currently, for example, ensconced inside of city walls — and far better walls than Pennypell's, even! — and preparing to walk with my employer into the heart of a temple. A temple, in particular, into which primes have walked for some centuries now. Fear, or even nervousness, at this point would be ridiculous.

Father, I can hear your words now: "Are you quite sure that you are not cheating this enchanter, this Ilzatheinen? For an annoyed enchanter would be a poor addition to our family's alliances." And I have already earned my pay. We have had a brush or two with ulgrane, which Arrhwy and I quite effectively dealt with. Also we have been negotiating with some nearly-civilized nonprimes. So, yes, I have upheld the family reputation for honesty (if we have one — nobody outside of Comblefree and Corster seems to know about it) and our alliances are quite safe in my hands.

To answer your other question, just as directly as you asked it: Boragette isn't carrying my egg yet, either. If you talk to zir in person, please be kind enough to use some sort of euphemism — or, better still, avoid asking it entirely. She is both meek and modest, as befits a co-lover of high station from a proper country town, and finds the topic dreadfully embarrassing.

Your remarkably dutiful daughter, regardless of your opinion of the subject: Rajel (Marjoram)

Boragette peered over Rajel's shoulder at the post office. "I'm meek and modest?"

"Well, compared to ... um ..."

"Me," grunted Arrhwy. "You are the very strange woman, Rajel. Every time you know you are going into a dangerous place, you write your parents a letter. I think you say goodbye. But never do you actually say goodbye. Usually you are very rude. Also usually you are very leaving out of many important details."

Rajel shrugged. "Details, like fighting a whole nycathath or guesting with one? If I don't get killed by those details, then there's no sense in fighting with my parents about them — worse than a nycathath some days! And if I do, at least I don't have to go have the argument with them. That'll be *your* job, Arrhwy."

Boragette squeezed Rajel's hand. "Don't you go get killed, O my wife. And not just because I don't want to explain to your parents how it happened ... Arrhwy is *sure* to leave it to me."

Casamint snorted, "I'm sure she had intended to be careless — as a way of getting unmarried to *me*, if nothing else — but from your so personal and touching request, she will now take steps to survive."

Rajel shook her head. "Casamint? Please don't even joke about that, just now."

Casamint scowled, and turned aside.

* * *

"At great length, we come to our actual work in New Kottarnu. This is the reality of which Diflannu's is just a mockery and an exploitation," said Ilzatheinen in a subdued voice. The Temple of the Dark Trinity at New Kottarnu towered over them, a tetrahedral pyramid of fibrous black wood bound together with gleaming translucent leather. The single entrance was a tiny pentagonal portal near one point, set irregularly so that none of its sides was parallel or perpendicular to boardwalk or temple wall.

"Do we just go in?" asked Rajel. Arrhwy simply tasted the air, which was heavy with many flavors of smoke: some from wood, some from incense, some from more troubling things.

"To start with. The bottom floor is simply an ordinary temple — though it gets more traffic than the temples of Flokin, 'Here', and Iraz Varuun do in most cities. But we must go to the top of it, where the three great altar rooms of the three gods are. The middle levels are the domain of Ymru-Wyxyhyr, whose tastes are fairly pleasant as the tastes of Locador demons go."

Arrhwy looked up to the top of the temple. "Three small isosceles great altar rooms, if they fit up there! Why not leave them down below, where they can be larger and be reached by less work?"

Ilzatheinen shook his head. "No; each of the three takes up the entire top part of the pyramid. They could hardly deny any one of the three the whole of the top place: all three gods are touchy in their own way, and more likely than most to take a distressing revenge. Keeping all three temples there at the same time is, I daresay, a big part of Ymru-Wyxyhyr's part in the matter."

Arrhwy shrugged. "Gods are stupid and touchy. Even smart, gentle gods are stupid and touchy. And these are not the gentle gods, even if Iraz Varuun is the smart one."

"Unfortunately they made the world and supply it with magic. If you wish to perform the greatest of enchantments, there are few alternatives."

* * *

The public altar room was square, and predictably larger than would fit in the triangular base of the temple. Images of the three gods of the Dark Trinity towered over altars on three sides of the square. No side of the square was without its idol, however; the idols did not visibly move, nor was there more than one idol to any of the gods. The room was thick with Locador magic. "That's a bit overdone." muttered Ilzatheinen.

An Orren priest wearing a spiky black cowl, a delicate black kirtle, and a rope belt ending in a huge knot nodded to him. "The geometry of the temple, you mean, surely? I would not call it overdone. I would call it tacky. However, the long-dead architects of this building — and those few who are not dead, and are not likely to die any time soon — called it modern and progressive, when they built it."

Ilzatheinen bowed. "May future generations judge our works less harshly!"

The priest grinned. "Especially if they are us — there surely must be no humiliation quite like that of deciding that your tastes in a former life are tacky." The other primes grinned. "I am Sodosma, by the way; priest of the Dark Trinity. Judging from those packs you bear, you are here for something beyond simple worship?"

"I am Ilzatheinen: these are Rajel and Arrhwy. I wish to perform four consecrations for enchantments, including the construction of a rather particular fire elemental."

"For the basic consecrations, such as any might be performed in any temple without much loss of quality, you will find our prices high but not extravagant," said Sodosma cheerfully.

"Those are not the consecrations I require, however. I plan great workings!"

Sodosma nodded. "As ever foreign enchanters do. One might almost suspect that, for the ordinary workings, they preferred the lower prices and greater convenience of their local temples ... unaccountable, utterly unaccountable. Do you know what you must do?"

"I have been here before! I must pay quite a high price, and then manage to get myself to the altar rooms, preferably without being fatally injured or driven mad by whatever unpleasantness your pet Locador demon has on the menu today. For this reason I bring two strong companions," said Ilzatheinen with a touch of irritation.

"You sound like a gentleman who would prefer that the gods were more straightforward. Alas! In universes where the gods are more straightforward, they supply little magic. The project you have is in mind is challenging on the World Tree; in a kinder universe, it would not be possible at all," said Sodosma in a sweet voice.

"How do you know what I have in mind? Is everyone in this town using Mentador magic? This is not Diflannu's!"

Sodosma laughed, a light laugh like the sounds of insects. "Oh, I have no idea what you have in mind — save that you found it worth your time and effort to come back here. My hypothesis was categorical, not specific to you."

Ilzatheinen shrugged annoyedly. "As you wish. What will the price be?"

"Let me see your designs," said Sodosma. "For most, the price is one thing; heinous or particularly clever enchantments are charged higher prices, and those that threaten the city are charged a price which will cover the likely damage they cause..." She lead the Araldeans beneath the amber wings and writhing copper serpents of the image of Flokin, to a more private room.

THE TRUTH ABOUT SKIRRET

Dear Casamint,

I recognize that it is hideously rude to write upon a leaf what one must properly say in person, but what choice remains to me? I am here and you are there; you will be there for some great while; I can hardly spare time or amber to come to you. And what I have to say is as week-old cream: currently it reeks, but the longer it rests the more wicked and pernicious will its reek become.

Having written that, O Casamint, I daresay I do not need to write the rest. You are a clever man; you know what is to come, or enough of it. I truly think you might well tear this leaf up now, or cast it into a flame, and you would miss only the least bit.

Well, Samand is looking over my shoulder, and says that I am delaying matters. So this: I regret to inform you that I can no longer maintain our love and affection for each other in the form in which we once practiced it. The fault is mine and mine alone. I must only hope that you can somehow forgive me, in the depths of time, and that we may maintain some echoes of friendship and commonality of spirit despite the loss of physical connection.

Oh, futter that the wrong way 'round. What I really mean to say is that Wilsamander and I have somehow managed to fall in love, and that I'm a horrible transaffectionate pervert now and really always was, and I daresay I shan't be allowed in polite Herethroy society ever again. I had been hoping for weeks that you and I, and he and I, could arrange something — but when I read your tentative sort of marriage proposal hinting consideration mention thing I knew I could not live such in a dishonesty.

I am unfit — I am improper — I am degenerate — I am hopelessly beneath you. Not just in rank, as we always knew, but in sheer purity of character. I cannot return to Yazelton; my parents have disowned me; I cannot enter the life of any Herethroy village again, never. This is no passing whimsy, such as anyone might have. For as long as I can remember I have craved the touch of fur, admired the quick movements of the mammals, longed to swim with Orren and wrestle with Cani... There are no words for it, Casamint. It is a bitter violation of natural law, and I shall suffer its many penalties my whole life.

I realize that I must apologize for all manner of things. I used you. I tried to bury myself in Herethroy arms, in the right and decent forms of lust and of love. But I failed. Never think that I did not try: I strove hard to love you, to wash away the foulness within me in the cleanness of your kisses. But I could not. When we lay together in my room, I would look at the prints of Tessara's nudes on the walls. Did it ever occur to you to wonder why I was more passionate there than anywhere else?

There is no good in me, Casamint. Forget me. You are well-married, you are honorable and honest, you shall be a paragon among Herethroy. I am nothing and worse than nothing. You shall despise me for this, and you shall be right.

Your miserable friend, or, I shouldn't blame you, former friend,
Skirret.

"Hallo there, Rajel. How was the Temple today?" asked Boragette.

"I'm earning my wages, Boragette, I'll tell you that. More after I change my clothes... and why are you sitting out in the hall? Did you and Casamint have a fight?" said Rajel. She tried not to sound too hopeful.

"Not at all, but he did get a rather unpleasant letter from Pennypell. I was with him for a while, but he wanted to be alone for a bit."

"Oh? A death in the family or something?" asked Rajel.

"Nothing so bad as that." Boragette tugged helpfully at Rajel's sword-buckles, which were crusted with a viscid blue gel. "Rajel, oh my sweet wife, I've a favor to ask of you today."

Rajel sighed exhaustedly. "Can I change first, and rest? The cursed Locador demon decided that up was up and down was also up, so I've been climbing hard all day."

"Oh, it shouldn't be so effortful a favor. Just be kind to Casamint today. His girlfriend Skirret from Pennypell left him."

"Clever girlfriend, that. She's got a good idea in her head."

Boragette tapped zir wife intimately. "That's just the thing I'd like you not to say to him."

Rajel spread her antennae. "Touch me there, and I'll be as quiet as you like — or as noisy!"

Boragette stretched to kiss Rajel on the lips, tapping antennae with her. "Later."

Rajel nodded. "Not too much later! Is it safe for me to go in there to clean off, or must I give our husband his solitude and go expose myself to Arrhwy?"

Boragette tapped on the door. "Casamint? Rajel's back, and needs to use the washroom."

"Shortly, shortly," groaned Casamint from inside. He opened the door, his limbs floppy and his eyes bulging from too much crying.

"Casamint? Boragette told me about Skirret. I know a proper wife would be happy when her husband possible other marriage turns to ashes, but ... I *am* sorry to hear it. And not just because that means you'll be spending more time with our mari."

Casamint smiled a very ragged smile. "Thank you."

Boragette slipped zir arms around Casamint's back. Rajel rather nervously did the same. Casamint hugged them both back, his face-chitin clicking against their chests. "I'll be fine soon enough, Rajel. You can go clean up if you'd like."

She smiled at him. "I rather need to, don't I?" She drew her sword and laid it on the bed, and poured a chaliceful of water over the bemired scabbard and started scrubbing blue gel off of it.

Casamint got up. "Could I help you, Rajel?"

She blinked at him. "Well, surely you could, if you'd like to. Look at my shield there — is it ruined? Should I get a new one, think you?"

He splashed water from the room's pitcher onto the shield, and washed blue gel off of it. "It's stuck with any number of little wooden darts."

"So was I," said Rajel. "Pull them out, if you could?"

He nodded, and started plucking them. Boragette joined him in a moment. He sighed. "I never had even half a chance with Skirret."

Rajel cocked her head. "How's that? I thought you'd been rather close with her."

"Close in body, but not in everything, it seems..." He rubbed the shield fiercely with a towel, and many darts came off in it. "If she knew it all along, how *dare* she waste my time and go candy-jigging all over my heart!"

"Knew what?" asked Rajel.

"Knew that she didn't like Herethroy," said Casamint in a hollow angry voice.

"She was Sleething around Casamint's Rassimel friend," said Boragette.

Rajel splashed her belt with clean water, and patted it with a towel. "That sounds awfully hard, losing a Herethroy lover to a mammal."

"It's not something I'd recommend, no," said Casamint.

"I'm sorry to hear it," said Rajel.

"It's just as vile as Arrhwy rolling around with that perdithorne. Or worse: Skirret's a Herethroy, a proper village-raised Herethroy at that, even if she did move to the city with Casamint. She should know better than to take up with a mammal!" Boragette snapped the tip off of a dart angrily.

Neither Rajel nor Casamint wanted to press the point. Casamint dunked a bracer into soapy water, and hunted for a different conversation. "What was your day like? Your armor's all messy in the most peculiar sort of ways."

Rajel laughed. "It was like being the plaything of a demigod with the inventiveness of three Orren and the viciousness of three Sleeth."

"Ymru-Wyxyhyr, I take it?"

"So Ilzatheinen said."

"What happened?", asked Boragette.

"The lower floors of the temple were ordinary — well, as ordinary a place as there is in the heart of New Kottarnu. All twisted corridors lit by cressets in the shape of skulls of spike-horned beasts. Which are probably use for nursery decorations in New Kottarnu. Even that part of it is a maze — one wrong turn will dump you into the acolyte's lounge, where seven coal-robed junior priests are practicing some arcane chant, and give you seven very dirty looks when you interrupt them.

"Then you come to the big door marked, 'TO THE UPPER TEMPLE. VERY DANGEROUS!'. Past that door things get unpleasant. There was one corridor that looked flat, but was as tiring to walk on as climbing straight up the Verticals wall. Another one was full of long hair, and we got jumped by worm-headed scorpions swinging around in it. Ilzatheinen got stung, and burned all the hair up around us — that's all these scorchmarks on the armor."

"Are you hurt?" asked Boragette. "You don't look scorched yourself."

"Rather. I'd be roughly dead except for a Temporary Health. Not all from the burning hair, though. There were also some glass-headed teak statues running around on spiked legs, spitting burning nails at us. They took *forever* to die, too."

"Ithphanabuli?" asked Casamint.

"They didn't introduce themselves," said Rajel.

"They sound like ithphanabuli; I did some reading on the Temple and the Dark Trinity. They're one of Ymru-Wyxyhyr's creations," said Casamint.

"We figured as much out, though we are no expert scholars such as yourself," said Rajel.

Casamint grinned. "Did you know that they are blind?"

"They're not blind. They could see most excellently well, which they proved several times by several quite accurately-aimed burning spikes."

"But they are, indeed, blind — or at least, they do not see by light. They see by sound. Daflamasorto interviewed several of them. One of them even wrote poetry about fighting, seeing its opponents dimly by their voices, brightly and briefly when mages set off thunderclaps," said Casamint.

Rajel set down her oilcloth and raised her antennae. "Really? That would have been good to know. Arrhwy knows Ward for the Napping Kittens."

"That would have effectively blinded them," said Casamint. "According to Daflamasorto, each kind of guardian has its own characteristic flaw."

"How did Daflamasorto interview them?" asked Boragette.

"By fighting them slowly, and chatting with them as he did. He used every defensive spell and device he could get his hands on, and kept the fight going for a good twenty minutes. They were glad to talk, too; they're almost friendly. If a bit bizarre — they enjoy having visitors come and kill them or be killed by them; that's what they were created for, and that's their passion. So they think of intruders the way that Sleeth think of prey, or the way that we think of gardens."

Boragette shook zir head. "If I think too much about that, it will make sense and then I shall be officially a lunatic."

Rajel smiled to Casamint. "You do seem to have learned something useful. Could you lend us your books?"

"I'll do better than that, if you'd like. I'll come with you," said Casamint.

Rajel nodded. "Let me ask the others, but I daresay you'd be welcome. We'll go again the day after tomorrow, if everyone's all healed and resupplied."

Boragette shook zir head. "Casamint! If you get yourself killed over Skirret, I shall be quite cross with you!"

"It's not so dangerous as that, Boragette, really. Only a dozen or so people have died there in the last twenty years, and they mostly didn't know how to escape properly."

"*I* don't know how to escape properly, Casamint," said Rajel.

"Throw down a cord that's all tied up into a big tanglesome knot, and say, 'Ymru-Wyxyhyr has granted me my choice of death, and I choose to be strangled by this cord.' The guardians will stop to untangle the cord, and you can flee. Oh, but if you see that guardian again the next time, be sure to destroy the cord first thing. One careless Rassimel forgot that, and *did* get strangled by it."

"Oh! All the acolytes and priests had big knotted lumps of rope. I thought it was a peculiar and foreign religious symbol," said Rajel.

"A very practical one!" said Casamint.

"All these odd little rituals. Is Ymru-Wyxyhyr trying to keep people out of the upper temples? If he is, why does he give the guardians all these weaknesses? If he's not, why does he have guardians there at all?" asked Boragette.

Rajel shrugged. "Ymru-Wyxyhyr is mad. It doesn't *need* a reason."

Casamint shook his head. "Ymru-Wyxyhyr is not particularly mad nor particularly wicked by the standards of Locador demons. Daflamasorto tried to interview it as well, though casual conversation with such a distressing entity is less than safe ... its purpose in this instance is to discourage frivolous use of the upper Temple, perhaps saving the gods the necessity of judging those who come before them. The tormenting of primes who come through is a part of its salary. It is very Sleethlike and cruel, as you had noted, Rajel. Also bored, I should imagine."

Boragette said in a small voice, "This is all making too much sense. I don't *like* thinking of demons and monsters and gods as people... I wish they'd just run the universe gently and not bother us."

Casamint squeezed zir hand. "Well, in this instance, Ymru-Wyxyhyr isn't rampaging around New Kottarnu, much less around Dorly. We're going into its domain, for reasons of our own. Village-folk and city-folk can live their whole lives without ever meeting the personality of a god or angel, much less wandering in one's domain, and I daresay you will. For my part, I'm interested enough to look..."

Rajel smiled. "The day after tomorrow, then."

Boragette lowered zir antennae. "Do be careful, both of you. I've no wish to be a widow, or even half a widow."

Casamint nodded gravely. "Nor I, nor a corpse. We shall take all precautions — even ones that Rajel skipped the first time 'round. Shall we go procure some food?"

* * *

"She left him for a mammal? Frumbles of misery, that's harsh," said Chicory.

"I can't imagine it myself," said Boragette.

"Nah, I think you never will. I doubt anyone would leave *you* for whatever reason," said Chicory. "I sure won't."

"Well, except for Dittany and Macewain. Oh, and Tansy," said Boragette.

"You were a kid when you were with Dittany, and not much older with Macewain. You and Tansy had a thing going? I never knew about that," said Chicory.

"Oh, he sang love-songs at me every time he could for two months, last year! I never encouraged him, though. I had my hands full keeping *you* off."

"Yeah, well, sorry about that," Chicory said with a grin. "Good thing everything's all sweet with your husband and wife now, so you don't have to keep me off." She cupped zir uppermost tail-ball in a mid-hand.

"Anyways, now that this Skirret is out of the way, d'you think Minty-bug and you and I can get married?"

"Well, two of us are in favor of it. Casamint doesn't seem to like you as well as I do, though."

"Well, I don't like him as much as I like you, either. I figure you gotta put up with him anyways, and the more help you've got, the better.

"You still don't have to persuade me, Chicory. Maybe the two of us can talk to him together?"

"Maybe the two of us can seduce him together, and get him to say yes when he's all happied up afterwards."

Boragette's antennae drooped. "That might be a good plan, but we *can't* do it yet."

Chicory asked, "Why not?" She saw Boragette's expression. "Oh, you three *still* haven't? Get *on* with it, sweetie! Or does that Rajel of yours have some problem with it?"

"Rajel and Casamint aren't that comfortable together."

"What's Casamint got, ivory skewers up his tailpipe? Who *does* he get along with?"

"Me, and the Rassimel."

"You sure his girlfriend's the transaffectionate one? He's acting like it himself!"

"Well, he's acting like it a lot. Except that he's eager with me, and eager with Skirret. And the pillow-book he brought is all of Herethroy, too."

"Oh, double frambles. 'cause I think transaffection is grounds for divorce," said Chicory.

"I don't want to divorce him!"

"It's just a joke, honey!"

"Well, don't joke that kind of joke. He's got a good title, and he's got a good body, and he's even got a good spirit once in a while," said Boragette.

"Hey, I'm sorry!"

"And if we're considering trying to marry him, we'd better not be thinking of divorcing him. It'd be awfully inconvenient," Boragette continued.

"I get the point! But why'd it be inconvenient?"

"Divorce, for whatever reason, means that you and I couldn't get married again."

"Oh. That's bad!"

"It's bad. I was looking up Herethroy divorce laws a couple months ago, but they're quite harsh. We'd all lose our titles — our inherited titles at least. I think you'd keep yours."

"Heh. We can all be Grand Padishahs!"

"Well, let's not get divorced. Let's see what Casamint thinks about you as a wife, now."

* * *

Chicory strode across the hotel's porch to a white-cushioned bench in a gazebo, where Casamint was trying to persuade himself that he was studying. "Too bad about Skirret, Minty-bug. But, well, how about it?"

He looked up at her. "How about what? If the 'what' is the 'what' I was just reading about, I must admit a certain hesitation."

Boragette walked up behind Chicory, and peeked at her husband. "What *are* you reading?"

"I am reading about a disease called the thewks. It renders the victim's bones flexible and elongated, and causes convulsions. Usually the victims tie themselves in knots and strangle."

"Oh. That doesn't sound at all nice."

"No. It fits my mood of the day, at least." He flattened his antennae. "Unfortunately Rassimel are immune to it, and nearly everything else." He glanced at Chicory. "Herethroy can't get it either, or I might take you up on your offer. At least, if you sampled it first."

Chicory took a step back. "Um, no. I wasn't talking about anything like that, Casamint."

He shrugged. "Perhaps you should have been. I'm sure it would please me better than whatever you *are* going to talk about."

She peered at him closely. "I'm proposing marriage to you. Not talking about diseases."

"I can't say which one I prefer to talk about with you. For that matter, I can't say which one I'd prefer to *have*."

Boragette put a midhand on zir girlfriend's shoulder. "Perhaps we're being a bit hasty here. Casamint, I know you're a bit upset, but I do wonder if we could talk about it again in a week or two?"

Casamint stared coldly at zir. "Perhaps when I am studying about *chronic* diseases."

Chicory squeezed Boragette's hand, and looked hard at Casamint. "It's a pretty good idea. You get a nice decent quadrette marriage. I'll give you a big allowance. You can even live in the city most of the time, and study and stuff."

"So, the biggest virtue to marrying you is that I shall be barely married to you? Ah, but I have a trick worth two of that: I shall not marry you at all," said Casamint.

Chicory glared at him, and drew herself up to her full height. Casamint waggled a finger at her. "You *can't* intimidate me into marrying you. I'm married to *Rajel*, for Virid's sake."

"Don't you want Boragette to be happy?"

"Certainly. But, more specifically, I want Boragette and myself to be happy in marriage together. I even want *Rajel* and myself to be happy in marriage together, at least in principle, though I'm a candied carcanofex if I know what to do about it. That's quite enough wantings-to-be-happy for me for now. After my wife and mari and I are satisfied, I shall find a marriage whose merits suit *my* style and aspirations."

Boragette tugged at Chicory. "Chicory, you're not helping. Casamint, O dear my husband, I *am* sorry for pestering you with this, and I *do* hope we can find some arrangement where everyone is happy."

He shrugged. "I'm sure we'll come up with something tolerable sometime. Perhaps even something that doesn't require periodic social calls on terrible monsters and insane godlings." He stood, and gave Chicory a formal court bow ordinarily used for the illicit lovers of greater nobility.

* * *

"That didn't go at all well," said Boragette.

"Aw, we just picked a bad day. I don't really get it though. I know that if **I** had just gotten dumped, I'd be **more** than happy to have sometwo else come and propose to me."

"Well, Casamint's a moody scholar sometimes," said Boragette.

"Nah, I'm just not used to thinking like a boy," said Chicory. "Married's a luxury for a girl, but a job for him."

"Married's a job for everybody. Love's the luxury," said Boragette, and sought zir luxury in Chicory's arms.

* * *

The group assembled in front of Some Apples of Delight. "Shall we eat at Diflannu's again?" asked Boragette, struggling to keep amused malice out of zir voice. The sun's flames were dwindling, and the party had gathered in the hotel lobby.

"I've had quite enough eldritch and uncanny horror for one day," groaned Rajel. "Perhaps there's a very ordinary porridge bar or some such?"

"Off on the Street of the Canopic Urns, five or six blocks rollward, there were a half-dozen places that looked plausible. Nethry and I did a bit of scouting," said Zallarilla.

"Scouting, is that what you call it now?" said Ilzatheinen.

Zallarilla frowned. "Technically, I would call it, 'Wandering about the uncanny city with my girlfriend, enjoying a few moments without teasing or scowling from my honored but overly worried father.'"

Ilzatheinen met his daughter's eyes, then lowered his ears. "Forgive me. It was a fatiguing and difficult day."

Zallarilla blinked in surprise. "Well then, don't mention it."

"Let us wander back rollward, and see what restaurants may lurk there. In New Kottarnu, I daresay that's what restaurants do," said Casamint.

At the front door, Rajel looked dubiously at the carved heads on the posts of the boardwalk. "I like those less after today's work."

Arrhwy snorted. "Fortunately these do not vomit stinging blueness upon us. Fortunately also the horizontal-seeming boardwalk is, somehow, unnaturally, horizontal."

Ilzatheinen nodded. "That was not my favorite experience of the day. You two are good at climbing, but I am a personage of considerable stature even when I am not carrying a pack of sorcerous supplies and sacrifices."

"That sounds hideous and horrid, Rajel," said Boragette. "Are you sure you want to go to that temple, Casamint?"

"It will be memorable," said Casamint.

"I had not thought of bringing an expert in the Temple's inner structures ... Last time I had a more skilled hero than I do now, who seemed to deal with eventualities as they arose. I had thought that Ymru-Wyxyhyr's conceits were simply its terrible whimsy, and beyond thought or pattern: to be endured, nothing more. Since I am wrong in this, and since I have an expert to hand, of course he shall come along," said Ilzatheinen.

"That's no way to treat a baron," snapped Boragette.

Ilzatheinen stopped to peer at zir. "Baron?"

Boragette drew zirself up. "Each of us is a pro-Baron at least: heir to a village in Darinny Mene. Rajel is a Grand Baron, with two villages. We are not simply adventurers whom you have hired to do your dirty work ... you have not hired Casamint at all!"

Ilzatheinen stared at Rajel. "Is this true?"

Rajel shrugged. "My title has proven itself worthy of every terch I paid for it, just precisely. Not a terch, not a use. I gather Casamint's gotten more use from his."

Casamint hissed in a wormwood voice, "I'd have gotten more use from a pelt of brown fur." Boragette slipped zir arm around his waist, and held him a moment.

Arrhwy grinned at Ilzatheinen. "You and I are the only commoners here. *We* know what a title is worth."

Ilzatheinen shook his head. "I gather that there is more to this band than meets the eye. Any other surprises? One of you is a shifter hybrid, a Herethroy and a Zi Ri in alternate hours, but I happen to have only looked in the Herethroy ones? A cley vampire? User and victim of a terrible sentient spirit-eating sword from the Holocaust Wars? No? Then ... which of these fine restaurants shall we choose?"

Boragette frowned at Ilzatheinen. "Don't change the subject. If you're taking my husband into that Temple, you should pay him a decent adventurer's wage, at least. He doesn't just come with Rajel and Arrhwy."

Arrhwy thwacked Rajel on the back with her tail. "For adventuring next time, you bring your whole triad! Casamint untangles the ancient mysteries, Boragette confronts the wicked insane wizard-priest!"

Ilzatheinen sputtered angrily, words failing him. Casamint smiled. "No great fee is necessary. Perhaps you will simply pay for food and lodging on this trip, for myself and Boragette?"

Ilzatheinen nodded. "Excellent, my lord scholar. I repeat my question: which of these fine restaurants shall we choose?"

Zallarilla grinned to Nethry. "More of a scholar then a lord, by the purse of him."

Nethry grinned back, "And not likely to change that any time soon, if he negotiates his fees like that!"

Casamint shrugged. "We're guests on this trip. It seems fair to help out a bit."

Ilzatheinen harumphed. "It seems that, as party leader, this important decision devolves to me: that my experienced warriors and devious scholars have no advice on the matter..."

Arrhwy smirked, "A look at waistlines shows us who has the expertise in food!"

"... and so I choose the restaurant to our left, 'A Garden of Expansive Biscuits', for our dinner, on the grounds that it looks the least sorcerously-inclined of any establishment on this street," said Ilzatheinen.

"It's called 'A Garden of Poisonous Hazillits'," observed Zallarilla. The two words looked similar in the swooping New Kottarnu script.

"Delightful," said Ilzatheinen, not a bit delighted. "Well, let us go see if this garden serves anything that is not poisonous."

* * *

The dinner was not poisonous; indeed, it had been refreshingly ordinary, served in round wooden bowls by lazy Rassimel waiters wearing street clothes. Boragette, convinced that Casamint had sold himself too cheaply as an adventurer, had ordered the most expensive vegetables on the menu, and discovered that roasted fern-heads, though pricey, were bitter and acrid out of season.

When they got back to their room, Rajel started stuffing a few bits of clothing in a bag. "I'll see you in the morning, Boragette, Casamint."

Boragette said, "Where are you going?", rather surprised.

"Arrhwy's room has a couch," she said.

"We've got a bed for three," said Boragette. "I had thought you'd stay here."

Rajel lowered her antennae. "Not to put too fine a point on it, but I am trying to give you and Casamint the night together. I know you prefer him to me, and I know he has had a most terrible shock."

Casamint bowed his head. "Rajel ... thank you."

Boragette snatched zir wife's bag and shook the clothes out of it. "Don't be ridiculous. I am getting fond of you both. Stay here!"

"I don't think she wants to watch the two of us together," said Casamint. "I don't blame her ... *I'll* go sleep on Arrhwy's couch."

Boragette turned zir back on them, talking to the carved vaguely-Herethroy faces around the fireplace. "My husband and my wife are now bickering about which one of them does not have to sleep with me. What a humiliating situation!"

Casamint winced. "That's not what we're doing at all..."

Boragette turned back. "I have it. *I* shall sleep on Arrhwy's couch. You two figure out how to be happy with each other. After all, your life rather depends on it: you are adventuring partners now, as well as spouses."

Husband and wife said, "No!" in unison.

Boragette smiled. "You're agreeing on something: that is good. So: everybody stays here. I will devote some attention to first one of you, then the other, and then I shall sleep between you with two hands on each of you. It shall be rather as if we were a happy trio. All *sorts* of people will be fooled! And nobody has to go sleep with the Sleeth."

It was not the most comfortable of evenings; all three were self-conscious and awkward, and Casamint and Rajel gave each other occasional sharply jealous glares. In the end, though, Rajel quite shyly reached over Boragette's belly to hold Casamint's hand, and that is how they slept.

A SHOPPING TRIP

Boragette watched zir spouses stroll off towards the Temple of the Dark Trinity, and sighed a bit. "Rajel looks as confident and feminine as always, no surprise there; but Casamint looks almost eager. What does *he* have to prove? He's not a girl!" Zie twisted zir napkin nervously in zir mid-hands.

Zallarilla buttered a biscuit stuffed with curried peas. "It always tickles my ears the wrong way to hear Herethroy. You talk almost as if men and women and co-lovers were three different species."

Boragette smiled a wide, false smile. "Oh, I daresay we're more different than Orren and Cani and Rassimel. You city-folks are really the same: missing a third of the limbs and a third of the genders, and all covered with rugs to boot."

Nethry refilled two chalices and a cup of kathia. "Most people would call that 'fur', Boragette. And there are a couple of subtleties you don't take into account. Imagine what it would be like in a species where, say, the males go small and swimmy when they get wet, and females are all loyal and social, and the co-lovers stay up all night working on their favorite silly projects."

Boragette threw the back of zir hand to zir forehead. "Alas! It is not so far off. We must stay up all night. It is the price of our beauty."

Nethry blinked. "I know you're called the beautiful ones, but what the staring gods do you mean?"

"Well, you two stay up half the night, when you're pleased with each other — don't deny it, for I've heard your mattress groaning its exhausted complaints. Well, *I've* got two spouses to attend to. And don't you imagine that either one will accept less than a full share!"

"What about me?" asked Chicory in a peeved voice.

"When I am married to you, I am quite sure I'll need to get something that stretches time the way all these Kottarnami corpse-trees stretch space. And even then I doubt I'll get much sleep. I imagine you're more vigorous than Rajel and Casamint combined."

"I thought Herethroy only mated in trios," said Zallarilla, her tail tucked between her legs in embarrassment.

"They're not up to that yet," said Nethry. "Somebody's got to learn a childproofing spell first, I daresay?"

It was Boragette's turn to be embarrassed. "That, and get Casamint and Rajel to like each other better."

"Ymru-Wyxyhyr may do some of that for you. Nothing like shared danger to get people to trust each other, at least," said Nethry.

Boragette nodded enthusiastically. "I hope so. And I hope it's not too dangerous."

"People don't die there all that often. And Casamint sounded like he knew what he was doing," said Nethry.

"And what's the chance that Casamint is wrong? He's a good scholar for a second-year Academy student who read a book on the subject once ... but even if he does know as much as he thinks he does, he could panic. Or get killed by some horrid spiky protrusion that Rajel or Arrhwy would just laugh at," said Boragette.

Zallarilla stood up. "There's no cure for worry like trying on gowns and waistcoats. Even if the local styles are a tad on the archaic and rune-encrusted side. Come on, I'll take you shopping while your spouses go swimming up stairways dripping viscid blue vileness."

Nethry yawned. "Forgive me, but I've a bit of sleeping to attend to." She gave Boragette a very innocent look. "From which I forbid you to make even a *single* disreputable inference!" In fact, her efforts to arrange another attack on the skyboat were going poorly; word had spread among all the ulgrane a thousand miles in either direction, and among their many friends.

Zallarilla patted her girlfriend between the ears. "Sleep well, poor tired ringytail. And when you awake, I shall be attired as the radiant noonday sun, and you shall look upon me and weep from the little tiny needle-darts of beauty piercing most sweetly and metaphorically into your helpless eyes!"

"I shall look upon you and wish most devoutly that you were not attired at all, that's more likely. Now be good and keep Boragette thoroughly distracted, will you?" The two Rassimel kissed fondly, and Nethry slipped off, yawning.

Boragette looked to Chicory. "And you? Would you like to come clothes-shopping with Zallarilla and me?"

Chicory looked pained. "If you *really* want me to, I guess I can. I'm a girl, not a co-lover. No offense, Zal."

"How could I possibly be offended? I am borrowing your lover for company at shopping!"

* * *

There were few tailors in New Kottarnu who would make clothes for both Rassimel and Herethroy, so Zallarilla and Boragette took turns. Boragette stared at a wall full of hats, fringed and decorated extravagantly.

"The hats of Pennypell are modest about the antenna-holes, as necessary breaks in the symmetry of the hat. But this is New Kottarnu, and it is almost as if the antenna-holes are the most important bits, with the rest of the hat simply a necessary accompaniment which they would dispose of if they could," said Zallarilla. "Try on that one, if you would? Not that it could possibly look good on you, but I want to see it."

Boragette said, "There is a price for me trying it on. You'll have to put it on my head. It's too complicated for a Herethroy to put on zirself" Zie crouched, and Zallarilla carefully fitted it around zir antennae. Zie stood and looked in a mirror.

"Now that is New Kottarnu in miniature. It manages to be kitschy *and* alarming at the same time." Zie nodded zir head. The fishing rods wielded by tiny Cani figurines around the antenna holes bobbled up and down, with the crabs and three-headed lizards they had caught.

"Good crafting, though. I would have expected their lines to get tangled together," said Zallarilla. The Rassimel haberdasher looked up from the jungle of leather and silk and tools that was his worktable, and smiled.

"Not a practical hat for travel, though. Far too delicate," concluded Boragette. "And I imagine my spouses would find one of their scanty moments of agreement in mocking me about it. Also it's hideous. Could you take it off of me, before one of the figurines comes alive and fishes out half my brain, please?"

Zallarilla took it off carefully, not wanting to damage it and have to buy it. "I wonder what Nethry would say if I bought her the Rassimel equivalent."

"I'm finished here. Let's go see what the Rassimel equivalent is. She's not quite your wife, is she? Have you got any plans for that?"

They left the Herethroy hat shop, pursued by the haberdasher's annoyed glares. "We're not married now. Do you think it would be a terrible thing if I asked her, though?"

Boragette's antennae drooped. "I'm hardly the best one to discuss marriage with."

"You're far and away the best one on *A Flattering Wind*. Who else can I talk to? Casamint, with all the romance of a porcupine? The Sleeth? My father?"

"Casamint has his moments. Though he does take care to separate them greatly, so that each one surprises you." said Boragette.

Zallarilla spread her ears. "I shan't try to steal him from you. It's Nethry I'm fretting about now."

"I don't have a thought about it exactly. Perhaps you could tell me a bit more, and I'll give you an opinion then?"

"Well enough. Over tea, though; it's a perplexing conversation to go with shopping."

* * *

The balcony was wide and stout, and the railing around it sprouted clusters of clawlike blackened wood spikes. Snarling chromodon's heads leered from the corners from folds of shimmering blue-black fabric. Everything on the menu had a disturbing name: Zallarilla's honeyed kathia was "The Kathia of the Pit of Darkness", and Boragette's berry tea was described as "A recipe from Old Kottarnu, City of Iniquities, justly destroyed in the Holocaust Wars." All in all, the cafe was the least alarming one in that part of the shopping district.

Boragette sipped zir tea. "It tastes just like ordinary berry tea."

"Perhaps the Old Kottarnu recipe spread to all Aradrueia?"

"Or perhaps the Aradrueian recipe spread to Old Kottarnu and was brought back here. Or perhaps the cafe is being pompous. Well ... why do you want to marry Nethry? You certainly seem to have your tails tied together."

Zallarilla flattened her ears in a Rassimel blush. "Pleasure's a bit of it, but just a bit. She and I are comfortable together ... we can talk about anything. I could trust her with my life, *or* to sweep my cabin. And she me, I think."

"Sweep your cabin? Is that a sky-sailor's euphemism for something naughty and mammalian?"

"Sky-sailor's expression, but it's not naughty. Lots of people you can trust with your life — if the waiter were suddenly getting clawed and raked by a perdithorne, say, you and I and everyone in here would rush to rescue him. But getting a friend to sweep your cabin — and not think it was an obnoxious request to make, and not resent it, and not to make a poor work of it, and all of that — only a close sort of friend would do that kind of errand."

"Or a servant, of course."

"A servant would be paid. A friend wouldn't be."

Boragette sipped zir tea, thinking. "There's some distance between a friend and lover on one pair of hands, and a wife on the other, isn't there? You're minor nobility of Araldy, and I understand she's a fairly wild and untitled woman who barely spends time in cities even in the Transwynt."

"She's got a title — she's a marchioness of Byronny. A reward for helping out against some pirate monsters not long ago," said Zallarilla.

"That's all for the best, I imagine. But Transwynt titles aren't real titles, are they?"

"Neither one is as real as, oh, an airship. Hers is *better* than mine, really. She earned it directly, by rescuing people from some terrible monster. Mine's just from my mother, because some long-ago ancestor was a particularly delicious consort to a duke and agreed not to tell anyone about it, or that's our family story." said Zallarilla.

"Well, *would* she be comfortable living in Pennypell?"

"I live in Girath — or, rather, I live on *A Flattering Wind*, now, though she and I are more likely to be found in Girath than most other places. And Nethry's not *that* devoted to the wilds."

"Rassimel are usually devoted to *something*. I can't recall a single conversation with you where skyboating didn't show up sooner or later..."

"I have had no such conversation these past dozen years!"

"... But what *is* she devoted to?", asked Boragette.

"She's a bit unfocussed for a Rassimel, I must say. She likes meeting people, making friends. She didn't so much gather things in the Lenwynt as trade them with the monsters and wildfolk. She's told me that she'd like to retire to a city, and not too long from now. And keep on meeting and manipulating people there, I imagine."

"She'd have a bit of competition from the Cani, wouldn't she?" asked Boragette

"I imagine that's why she's in the Lenwynt. I daresay a Cani could do the same brokering and trading she does, and perhaps do it better, but a Cani would hardly move away from family and friends. If she's simply doing it for fun, though, what matter if the Cani are doing it better? And travelling around on *A Flattering Wind* would give her plenty of variety of people, which is what she likes best I think."

Boragette sipped zir tea. "If I understand Rassimel at all, the best marriage would be when your hobbies fit together well, and they certainly seem to. Is there some urgency, though?"

"Well, in two weeks or so we'll be back in Soohoon. I would like her to stay with me, not fly her to some convenient spot in the Verticals where there's not even a post office I could write her at, and never see her again. But if I'd like her to stay, I should have something to make the request sweet, shouldn't I? I can't order all manner of romantic foods in Soohoon, or any such thing. I think I'd ask her eventually, if we were together for a while. Why not ask her soon, when it's a good tactical move as well?"

"You're hardly being as hasty as I was, at least. I got bribed with a storybook," said Boragette.

"Well, I don't think I'd want my father to arrange a marriage for me. I've always rathered that he not poke and prod about my life that way."

"Poking and prodding it is, truly, Zallarilla. Being married didn't stop that from my parents. Being in the Transwynt didn't either. There was a letter waiting for me requesting that I be pregnant when I return."

Zallarilla nodded. "I never gave him the chance to demand that — he was very upset that I had a daughter by mistake. I don't need to worry about that kind of mistake with Nethry, for two reasons."

Boragette blinked. "I know one reason. What's the other?"

"Oh, the other is that we're both female."

Boragette stared. "That's the one I know."

Zallarilla grinned. "The more important one is that Nethry is very very careful — in all things — and would never make a mistake the way Darssell did. That's a much more important part of her personality than simply being female, and that's the one you *should* have thought of first."

Boragette curled zir antennae. "Have you been taking lessons in conversation from Casamint?"

Zallarilla smiled. "Maybe one or two ... I should apologize for that."

"Oh, think nothing of it. I should be very, very used to it. I'm condemned to it until the day I die. Or get divorced ... which, according to my parents, will only be after I die."

"They'll kill you for asking for a divorce?"

"No, they wouldn't, but they'd steam and storm and seethe about it."

"Do you want one?"

Boragette waved zir antennae. "Yes and no. The 'yes' is down to half an hour every other day. Like clockwork, whether Casamint has done anything smarmy or not."

Zallarilla patted zir midhand. "I hope this vacation has helped matters."

"Oh, immensely. I've seen them both at their best, and I'm truly glad to be married to both."

"May they someday be glad to be married to each other, and a soon someday!" Zallarilla raised her chalice.

"And may you and Nethry someday be glad to be married to each other, and a soon someday!" Boragette raised her cup as well.

Zallarilla smiled, and they both drank. "Thank you for listening. Shall we be back to shopping?"

"I hardly think I gave much by way of advice!"

"Hearing *someone* sensible say that I'm not being the Grand Fool of Girath about the topic is plenty of help, truly, and that you have done."

"HERE", AND BACK AGAIN

"How was your day, O my spouses?", asked Boragette, waving zir antennae at the sight of them — around a spiky confection of pink-dyed leather and a few glittering slivers of glass, which they had not seen before.

"And what happened to my father?", asked Zallarilla, tail curled. "I thought he would be back with you."

"We took him to the Healers' Guild," said Rajel, her voice tired, her antennae drooping.

"How badly is he hurt?" Zallarilla was quite alarmed. "I knew there was some danger, but I didn't expect *that* ... whatever *that* might be."

"If you lead him into some writhing danger that you thought you understood from books, Casamint, I shall disembowel you," hissed Nethry. She meant to say it lightly, but Zallarilla's worry gave Nethry's voice an edge she had never intended.

"Nothing of the sort," said Casamint. He looked much amused by the whole expedition, though almost as tired as Rajel. "I, personally, arranged for him to be delivered from ithphanabuli, scarthedon, hideous glowing silverware, and a carcanofex made of silk and ivory that our dear friend Ymru-Wyxyhyr has evidently acquired since Daflamasorto published his book. Or perhaps I do not have the most recent edition."

"Casamint, I rather wish you would leave off praising yourself until *after* you have told me whether my father is alive or dead," said Zallarilla in as mild a voice as she could manage.

"Oh, that. Forgive me! He's alive, of course," said Casamint.

"And what, then, is he doing in the Healer's Guild?"

"Coughing a great deal, I should think, accompanied by mucus and blood and very valuable black spiky burrs. He started as soon as we left the temple," said Casamint airily.

Arrhwy snorted. "Casamint rather tells about his triumphs than explains to Zallarilla about her father's triumphs. The Locador god is the cruel god; also he is the god who enjoys spikes. This afternoon he blesses Ilzatheinen's enchantment, but viciously. The spiky black burrs that Ilzatheinen coughs are how "Here" provides his blessing." She shrugged. "To me it seems like the pointless torture, but what does a Sleeth know about cruelty?"

Rajel looked at her partner dubiously. "Quite a bit."

Arrhwy grinned dangerously. "When I am as old and powerful as "Here" is now — then I am as cruel as he is now! By then he is probably worse, though."

Zallarilla watched the bantering adventurers, her tailtip flicking. "Is my father going to recover?"

"Tomorrow at dawn, according to the priest Sodosma," said Rajel.

"It's one of "Here"'s better gifts," said Casamint. "Ilzatheinen was quite pleased to get it; it will help more than he expected with the enchantment."

Zallarilla shook her head. "My father must feel right at home in New Kottarnu. *I* would not consider a rending cough a pleasing thing!"

Casamint smiled kindly. "Well, be glad he didn't get the highest gift that "Here" provides in this temple! That would be a spiky ball, somewhat too big to fit in the muzzle but stuck in it, with spikes piercing the eyes and ears and nose from the inside. When you get it out it's quite helpful indeed."

Arrhwy nodded at Casamint. "My kitten Lyonder is now grown to be an adult. When he is still a kitten, he climbs a tree, and jumps to the next tree, and falls, and breaks his foreleg. I take him to the Healers' Guild to have it tied in sticks. Unfortunate to me, but you are not there then. Otherwise I have you tell hurt kitten Lyonder comforting stories to take his mind off being the hurt kitten!"

Boragette laughed, and took zir husband's lower hand. "Why don't you tell Zallarilla all the comfortable things you can think of now, then we'll go get dinner and you can tell about all your heroic deeds." Zie looked carefully at zir mari. "And Rajel's as well."

Arrhwy looked up at Boragette, her eyes wide and green. She mewed like an oversized kitten. "Not mine?"

Boragette scriffled Arrhwy between the ears. "I have heard you tell stories before. I think you will tell your own."

* * *

'The Spiral Plate' was next door to 'A Garden of Poisonous Hazillits', and run by Cani. Only Arrhwy had the precision of taste to appreciate the subtleties of the six amuse-bouches and their sauces that came on a double spiral of a tray, and she refused to even taste the ones that were not meat or greens. The Rassimel and Herethroy ordered the simplest foods on the menu, grilled birds and fishes with fruit, porridge, plates of steamed tubers and berries and thick succulent petals.

"I told you how to defeat the blind ithphanabuli, with silences," said Casamint. "It worked excellently."

Rajel nodded seriously. "It did, truly. It is considerably easier fighting an enemy who cannot see."

"Rajel fights one of them to pieces with her very the large sword," said Arrhwy. "I have more trouble, for claws and teeth are not so good at hurting wood. So Rajel kills mine too. At the same time Casamint has knocked the last one down, and Ilzatheinen sits on it until the bug with the big sword comes to chop it up."

Boragette giggled. "Really?"

Casamint beamed. "I stuck my staff between its legs, and over it goes! Ilzatheinen didn't want to waste cley, and the fighters were busy, and he *is* quite large, so it made sense. I sat on it too."

Arrhwy looked kittenish again. "Is it the comfortable seat?"

"Under a chitinous rump, most seats are comfortable!"

Rajel shook her head at her husband. "Chitin is better armor than a Rassimel's or a Sleeth's hide, but you *should* wear more. I think that someone should spank you hard enough so you can feel it and learn."

Boragette nodded. "You certainly should wear armor! I will take you shopping for some tomorrow. Zallarilla and I scouted and surveyed every boutique."

Rajel shook her head at her mari. "Good armor does not come from a *boutique*."

Boragette smiled at Rajel. "Well, I imagine you'd know best! What happened next?"

"A shower of poisoned glowing knives, spilling out of a tapestry of jugglers. They were intangible, too, to most things. But they got flesh well enough!"

"And what did you do there?" asked Boragette.

"Snuck behind the tapestry. Which was not the easiest thing to do, as it was glued to the wall. But there was a hanging-loop on top, almost big enough for a finger; Ilzatheinen stretched it wide enough to walk through," grinned Casamint.

"How?" asked Zallarilla.

"Stretch the Hole, or some variant on that. What would you expect? You *know* your father is good at Locador," said Rajel.

"I do know, in fact. I was also under the impression that using powerful Locador spells in the presence of a terrible Locador demon like Ymru-Wyxyhyr was less than entirely safe. I was wondering if Father came up with a variant approach," said Zallarilla, somewhat archly.

Casamint shrugged. "Nothing much came of it, in any case."

Rajel shook her head. "No: the silk carcanofex with all the needles following behind came of it. It certainly came the next minute, popping out of the next cabinet, and skewering Arrhwy."

"As I am creeping out of the widened tapestry, and with a scholar-bug too close behind me, so I have no room to dodge!" protested Arrhwy.

"A silk carcanofex? What an odd conceit, even for an angel," said Zallarilla. "I should think you could cut it to shreds with a few swats of your forepaw, Arrhwy."

"But it came with a thousand little ivory needles, Zallarilla. Whenever Arrhwy slashed it, the needles would sew it back together, as good as new," said Casamint. "But I have a trick worth two of that."

"And he'll make you ask him what it is," muttered Rajel.

Casamint flattened his antennae. "Oh, I created a big heavy log in its left leg. Fifty pounds of wood, which is more than an animated scrap of silk can lift. We ran around it, and left it whispering 'Come back here and fight like some clothing!' behind us."

Boragette laughed aloud. "And that wasn't in your books?"

"Not *this* edition! But I shall write to Daflamasorto tomorrow," said Casamint.

Rajel shook her head. "After that was a seven-headed giant mherobump sort of thing with a spear that could have been carved out of a whole arken tree. In a corridor that was too low for me to even stand up properly. Casamint didn't have a trick to deal with that one!"

"The scarthedon? No, Rajel and Arrhwy had to kill it. With a few spells from Ilzatheinen and me. But I did have a cheerful polite conversation with it while they were killing it — *and* got directions through that labyrinth," said Casamint.

"Yes, Casamint. You were very clever," said Rajel unenthusiastically.

Arrhwy cuffed Casamint's side with a forepaw. "Now you say, 'And you are very the strong, Rajel.' From this kind of politeness, maybe Rajel is happier to... ow!" She gave her partner a reproachful look, for Rajel had just kicked her in the side.

Casamint nodded cheerfully, missing or ignoring the sarcasm. "Rajel did quite an impressive job hewing and slashing away. She's better on monsters than I am on weeds! Arrhwy too — the ones that claws worked on, at least."

Boragette waved the tips of zir antennae in circles. "I am glad to be married to two such great adventurers! What happened next?"

"Next, we got to the great altar room of "Here". Now that's a sight and a half. It has no floor, for one thing," said Casamint.

"Just rafters of the ceiling of the room below?"

"No — no rafters, no foundations, no Aradrueia. Nothing at all. Just empty sky, above and below. That was unnerving! No gods in the sky above, no stars. Just the flaming sun, bright enough so you could see sky above and sky below. The temple room had a door, a wobbly bridge of planks, a platform for the actual temple room, and the sun. That's all," said Casamint.

"Also the sky is not smooth. It has rings, darker blue on lighter blue," added Arrhwy.

Boragette struggled to imagine it. "It sounds thoroughly unnatural and distressing."

"It was: stark and beautiful, in its own way. It would be thoroughly terrible at night, truly! Darkness in all directions, and that's all.

"The altar itself was very ordinary. That was also disturbing: it didn't fit the surroundings; it looked just like the altar to "Here" in Pennypell. Until Ilzatheinen started working, at least," said Casamint.

"I've never been to the temple of "Here" in Pennypell. What's it like?" asked Nethry.

"A very plain table, striped black and white, square, with a statue of the god behind it. In his Herethroy shape, with windows opening through his carapace. Except, when Ilzatheinen started working, the windows started showing things," said Casamint.

"Did the god show up in person?"

"No, "Here" didn't show up in person. I'm not sure if the window trick was ordinary illusion, like a very fancy version of Diflannu's decor, or something more real ... I think it was real. I can't believe that a prime mind sane enough to cast a spell could imagine what was on the other side of some of those windows."

"What sorts of things?"

Casamint shuddered. "An empty place, emptier than anything; there were monsters there, sentients even, without body or mind. Thousands fought over a grain of dust as I watched, and most died... That window slid off to the side, of the statue, and I didn't want to watch it any more.

"The others were more pleasant; just very strange. A world made of stone, a big disk of stone, tipped on its side, in a small limp universe, with a huge glowing orange moth the size of all Aradrueia climbing on it. People lived inside the stone: there were tunnels, like you could make in soil."

"That's pleasant? Valuable, maybe, with all that stone, but it doesn't sound pleasant," said Nethry.

"After the void, it was pleasant ... anything would have been, if it were just a thing. There was a cityscape, where Rassimel and vorwi lived together, slaves to some intelligent trees; they drew them around in huge flowerpot carriages."

"How could you tell all that from just a glance?"

Rajel shook head. "It was obvious from a glance. I stopped looking after a second, and Casamint was staring and staring, but I saw it too. There was probably more than just illusion there: mind-magic, maybe, or some trick of "Here" or Ymru-Wyxyhyr."

Casamint shook his head. "Not Ymru-Wyxyhyr's. I doubt that he would use his power to praise and magnify his master. Locador demons aren't supposed to be so nice."

"Casamint? How about not telling me any more about what you saw?" said Boragette in a small voice.

Casamint raised his antennae. "I will gladly tell, or not tell, as you wish, O my mari. Tell me about your day, if you would be so kind!"

"One moment, first, if I may. Tell me about my father's workings?" said Zallarilla.

"Oh ... it was complicated and theological. And ugly — doing things that "Here" approves of, which aren't nice. Ilzatheinen could tell that it had worked, and worked well, right afterwards. He was bouncing on his toes! The way out was easy enough, just uphill. As soon as we got out the door, he collapsed in a fit of coughing, as though he had breathed in a flock of choking burrs."

"Do burrs come in flocks?" asked Boragette.

"These must have! We brought him back in, and Sodosma explained some of the physical manifestations of "Here"'s enchantment blessings. Most gods don't do that... Sodosma told us to save all the burrs, so we went and scraped Ilzatheinen's chokings off the boardwalk. Rajel had to fly under it where something had dripped... then we hurried him to the Healers' Guild. They'd seen that before."

Zallarilla shuddered. "I hardly know whether to admire my father, or name him a fool for putting up with such things."

"Do both, then," said Casamint.

THE ASSAULT OF THE CARCANOFEX

> *Dear Tuku,*
>
> *I am very sorry to have a violent favor to ask you, but there is nobody else I can turn to. I need to have a skyboat attacked by someone of significant power. I do not need any particular result from the attack — I simply need someone to bound in, cause a few injuries, scare a few people, and leave. Three of the skyboat's passengers are moderately dangerous, but only moderately, and there is no reason at all why you need to confront those three. Indeed, it would suit me perfectly if you attacked someone else and fled when the dangerous ones came.*
>
> *I am one of the three; a Herethroy with a big three-handed sword is the second; a Sleeth is the third. The specific dangers involved are [...]*
>
> *If you do me this favor, I shall thank you with all my heart, and with some of my pocketbook as well — I shall give you a talisman that protects reasonably well from claws and teeth, and the bone battleaxes and leather nooses of the War-Bannu Gormoror as well.*
>
> *Your apologetic but desperate friend,*
> *Nethry*

It was a fine day for a lazy flight from Byronny to Soohoon. The sun's fire was dripping, teardrops of white brilliance that streaked the edge of the universe and made the noontime glow bright and innocent. Zallarilla had stopped *A Flattering Wind* over the crest of a line-hill; she and Boragette were preparing a lunch to eat on deck.

"We could always eat on deck while we're in Soohoon," said Boragette. "But the sun will be on the other side of the branch, so we'll have shade and indirect light for half the month. It's bad enough when the trunk's shadow falls over Aradrueia, and that's only for a few hours!"

"I generally enjoy that myself, truth to tell. It's the one time of month when you can fly at noontime, and, no matter which way you look, your eyes will not get dazzled," said Zallarilla.

"I suppose you have to look all around you when you're piloting," said Boragette.

"Well, yes. Why the gods couldn't have put the sun to stay in one place I do not know — on top of the universe, so it would shine on us from above."

Boragette pointed at the sun through the window. "Just imagine where the sun-drips would fall if they had done that." Zie peered out. "What's that?"

Zallarilla set a leather bag of water on the stove to boil, and measured dried cherries into a wooden mixing bowl. "What's what?"

"Something hopping towards the skyboat!"

"Hopping?" Zallarilla looked out the window herself. "A carcanofex? *This* high up?" She poked the enchanted lace curtain, and called out,

"Everyone, a sharp-eyed Herethroy cosi spotted a carcanofex approaching from below! Warriors, to the deck!" Boots and claws scrabbled urgently on the parquet floorboards elsewhere in the ship.

"Should we do anything?" asked Boragette. "I don't know much about carcanofex."

"Oh, they're not very dangerous, and they're not very aggressive," said Zallarilla, who did not know much more. "I imagine that Arrhwy will snarl at and it'll flee. We're safe indoors ... and if there *is* a fight, I daresay our beloved warriors will want lunch immediately afterwards. So we shall cook the excellent dried cherry sauce for them!" She checked the bag of water on the stove, which was now boiling, and poured it over the cherries.

The carcanofex leapt through the hull of the ship, no more solid to his special magic than any other wood. He looked at the two of them, and grunted, "No swords or gloves or Sleeth — excellent! I shall injure you both!"

Boragette grabbed down the curtain rod as an improvised quarterstaff. She waved the enchanted lace, and shrieked to it, "It's in the kitchen! Help us in here!"

Zallarilla tossed the bowl of boiling water and cherries into the carcanofex's face, and ran around the counter away from it. The carcanofex yelped in pain, and grunted, "That hurt! I'll start with you!"

He leapt through the wooden counter, and impaled her on its heavy horn. The force of his leap drove the horn entirely through her chest. Zallarilla felt her ribs crack, as Nethry ran through the door, and she died for an instant.

A Heal the Awful Wound spell brought her back to life almost instantly. The carcanofex had not had time to extract his horn; her face was buried in the coarse dusky fur of his chest, and the pain was terrible.

She heard Nethry's voice yelling, "Not her! You're not supposed to hurt *her*, for all the gods' sake!"

The carcanofex turned his head to face Nethry, thick tail lashing, his voice petulant. "But you didn't say not to hurt her! And she threw boiling water in my face!"

"If you hurt her any more, Tuku, I shall kill you," shouted Nethry. Her glove's power broadened menacingly, like a bouquet of vipers. Arrhwy leapt through the door, hissing at Tuku, and other primes were behind her.

Tuku's horn shrank from a huge spiral lance to a delicate toothpick, and he carefully lifted Zallarilla off of it and set her on the counter. Zallarilla fainted from the pain. "Sheesh, Nethry, have a calmness! I'm doing you a favor! If you wanted something else, you should have told me!" He waved a sharp cone of a shell six inches long at her, with a spiral of words engraved on it. Nethry bent over Zallarilla, casting the best healing spell she could on her lover. Boragette darted over and took the shell from Tuku's paw.

Nethry's knowledge of medicine was more practical than professional, but she poured three cley into the spell for extra power. Zallarilla felt at her chest, where the impalement was only the ghost of a wound. She opened her eyes and smiles at Nethry. "You saved me, beloved."

Boragette shook zir head. "I'm afraid not, Zallarilla. The carcanofex is her servant or ally or something ... She had it attack us." Zie held the shell to Zallarilla to read.

Zallarilla blinked pain-blurred eyes at Boragette. "I beg your pardon?"

Tuku nodded vigorously, perhaps because Arrhwy was bristling in front of him, obviously considering disembowelling him. "Nethry and I have been good friends for years — and any friend of hers is a friend of mine! Sorry about your ribs there, missy ... count it as payback for that boiling water, and we're even to even with each other."

Arrhwy prodded Tuku in the belly. "If she is your friend, why do you attack us?"

Tuku stepped back, half-penetrating the wall. "Nethry asked me to, is why. No killing, just scaring, like. I figured it for some kind of practical joke, maybe. Or a holiday — maybe it's Sleeth Feast today? I dunno the prime calendar that well."

Arrhwy's tailtip flicked. "Today is *not* Sleeth Feast holiday. But if you lie to us or fight us any more, I feast on your liver and brain."

Tuku shook his head. "You are all so touchy today!" He looked to Zallarilla. "I don't blame *you* for being touchy, miss ... I have to apologize for skewering you so hard. It's the boiling water, you know ... I haven't been fond of boiling water since a conlee family scalded me thoroughly a while back. Not that I'd expect you to know that! But I'm very sorry anyways." His voice trailed off into babbling incoherent apologies.

Zallarilla was not paying attention to Tuku. She turned to Nethry, and asked in a low voice, "Lover? Why did you have your friend the monster try to kill me?"

Tuku hopped. "Not kill! She said, no killing!"

Zallarilla sat up, cupping her hands over her half-wound. "If you wanted to break up with me, a simple 'I'm sorry, Zallarilla' would have worked just as well."

Nethry collapsed against the counter. "I don't want to break up ... I didn't want you hurt ..."

Tuku waved his forelegs. "Then you should have said, 'Don't hurt the Rassimel cook!' I'm a genius and a half, but Mentador's for ororosti not carcanofex!"

Casamint had taken the letter from his mari, and glanced over it. "Not Zallarilla, and nobody dangerous. That would seem to leave Boragette and me, and perhaps Ilzatheinen if you caught him by surprise. Nethry? Why were you trying to have *me* injured?"

Nethry stood up, "Let me finish taking care of Zallarilla. I'll answer every question after that." She needed the time to think. By rights, she should escape, her mission most likely in shreds, but at least Byronny's name not sullied by her failed plans. She could not bear the thought of leaving Zallarilla, though, and especially not with no chance to explain and justify herself to her lover.

Zallarilla shook her head. "I'm not dying, now. I'm sure my father can heal me the rest of the way. For now I'd like to hear your story."

"Why not fly back to Byronny?" asked Chicory. "We're not too far away."

"Because Nethry knows Byronny very well, Rajel." Zallarilla took Nethry's muzzle in a shaky hand. "Unless, perchance, that too is a bit of a falsehood? Do tell!"

Nethry stripped her glove off. "I'm from Byronny. I'm an Inspector of Affairs of the Lenwynt, there."

Zallarilla looked at her with a gaze as clear as boiling water. "I don't quite see the connection from that fact to a carcanofex's horn through my heart." Tuku flattened his ears embarrassedly.

Nethry tucked her tail between her legs. "You know most of it. It's just what I've been talking about with your father. It would be very bad for Byronny if monsters and pirates got a stronghold as Ilzatheinen is building. I've been trying to remind him of why it's such a bad idea to give mighty magic to nonprimes."

Casamint rolled the letter up and pointed at her like a weapon. "You have tried and failed to persuade him several times."

"So I thought I'd give him some first-hand experience. Nonprimes can be very dangerous, without any obvious reason."

Tuku barked, "I had a reason! You asked me to! Besides, I thought Rassimel *like* that sort of thing! You asked me to stab *you* not so long ago! And you got those Gormoror to stab you a lot too!"

Zallarilla curled up miserably on the counter. "You had me stabbed through the heart to make a philosophical point with my father?"

Nethry nodded. "I didn't expect Tuku to go after *you*."

"The Sleeth you told me to stay away from was on the top of the skyboat! So I started looking for people at the bottom!" shouted the carcanofex.

Zallarilla regarded Nethry with a bitter gaze. "And the rest? When you seduced me, when you told me of your love ... was that another kind of stabbing me through the heart to make a philosophical point with my father?"

Nethry took Zallarilla's hand, though Zallarilla held it limp, without giving Nethry any sign of approval. "Not since the first day ... I seduce people for work now and then, yes. I love you on my own time, though."

"I love you too, Nethry," said Zallarilla, out of the near-instinctive habit that lovers often get. She thought a second more. "But I have no idea what to do with you, now."

Casamint said, "Impale *her* and toss her off the skyboat. Right back to her job the fast way, and good riddance!" Chicory nodded her fierce agreement.

Zallarilla glared at Casamint. "Sir, I am captain of this boat, and insofar as there is law or justice here, it is *my* law and *my* justice."

Casamint glared back. "It was *me* she was trying to have stabbed, me and my mari! I am the aggrieved party, I have a strong opinion to express!"

Zallarilla shouted, "It was *me* that *was* stabbed! Cram your strong opinion up your sheath-cavity!"

Arrhwy nodded sagely. "Nethry is very the attractive Rassimel, then? She lies to you, she betrays you, she sends the carcanofex to stab you. No matter! As long as she continues to delight you with copulations, you are happy to keep her to hand!"

Zallarilla kicked Arrhwy in the chin. "You know nothing about love, Sleeth." She glared at Nethry. "I'm not sure about you." She gingerly got off the counter, and Boragette helped her to the pilot's chamber. The others tried to follow her, but she turned them away with a ferocious teary glare.

Nethry sat in the kitchen, slumped over the counter, crying bitterly. Tuku left through the wall as he had come, complaining "Every prime here is crazy!" The others took biscuits and dried fruits from the kitchen, and sat on deck to argue about who had to explain the matter to Ilzatheinen.

* * *

Ilzatheinen was, reasonably enough, furious at the news. His tailfur bristled like a brush, and he lashed it against the side of a cupola. "My daughter is the greatest fool on all of Aradrueia! I shall roast Nethry over a vast fire of hazillits. If she is lucky the smoke is poisonous, and she will die fast!"

Arrhwy shrugged at him. "Several of us make suggestions for disposing of the betrayer. But Zallarilla decides that she is the captain and she judges Nethry. If you disagree with her, you go to her cabin to discuss the matter with her. I do not think she is very happy with two mutinies in one day."

Ilzatheinen snarled. "Is it mutiny to correct your daughter's mistake, when she invites a saboteur and a traitor to travel with you?"

Casamint shrugged. "If she is captain, yes, it is. Sky Pilot Guild law. They do like to be in charge on their own ships, the sky pilots."

Rajel shrugged. "I think she's only settling on a punishment. She seemed fairly upset. I imagine she'll come up with something that hurts more than your best effort, Ilzatheinen. She knows Nethry better."

"Or thinks she did! Her opinion of Nethry was not wholly accurate!", added Casamint.

Arrhwy snorted. "If you mistake your lovers for your friends, you risk disappointing sex or disappointing loyalty. I avoid this particular piece of unwisdom!"

Casamint sighed, and sat down, antennae curled. "I can't quite argue with you, Arrhwy. Skirret didn't come off all that well in either way, in the end."

Ilzatheinen sputtered, "Arrhwy, Rajel, you are hired to protect me. Nethry is more of a danger to me than all the unfriendly monsters we have met so far — a fortiori, for she brought them all. This would be an excellent time for you to do your duty."

Arrhwy and Rajel glanced at each other. Arrhwy stretched, and poured liquidly off of a tabletop. "I go intimidate the evil villain of a Nethry. Rajel, you stay here in case Nethry also sends the invitation out to a scyanturge to stop by for tea and murder."

"I didn't mean for you to watch her. I mean for you to kill her," said Ilzatheinen.

Arrhwy snorted. "I protect your tomorrow, not just your today. I watch her." She trotted belowdeck, claws scratching the white planks.

"Rajel, perhaps you are less cowardly than the Sleeth?"

Rajel shrugged. "For bravery and battle-lust you should have hired a Gormoror. Arrhwy and I will keep Nethry from killing you, and we will keep you from offending your daughter beyond repair, and we will keep up whatever other defenses need defending."

"Offending my daughter? Nethry has offended her beyond repair, I should say, not I!"

"And I imagine she'll have Nethry properly executed. But if you go do it first, I doubt she'll forgive you easily, even if she was going to do it herself a minute later."

Ilzatheinen nodded curtly. "There is that, yes."

* * *

Arrhwy snuck into the kitchen, silent as a green-black shadow. Nethry was slumped on a stool, her head on the counter, breathing raspily and sobbing now and then. Arrhwy leapt onto the counter and swatted the back of her head with a heavy forepaw. Nethry's face hit the countertop; she yowled and looked up, blood streaming from her muzzle.

Arrhwy growled, "Good afternoon, traitor wicked Rassimel! I am the extremely nice and kind Sleeth now, or else when I hit you I use my claws too. Do you send out any other extremely nice and kind invitations to monsters to come and kill us?"

Nethry absently brushed her face with a talisman that healed wounds inflicted by wood. She shook her head miserably. "No, no more invitations. I really wasn't trying to kill anybody. I picked only monsters I knew we could deal with."

"Rrai, that is the stupid plan, Nethry! A monster we can deal with might bring a friend who is a monster we cannot deal with."

Nethry wrung a dishtowel in cold water, and started cleaning blood off her face. "I *am* more careful than that, Arrhwy. I picked monsters that don't like to share. And I shared your danger, you know. If the monsters killed us all, they would have killed me too."

"That is a stupid of an argument! If we want to fight with monsters, we pick fights carefully and we do not bring Rajel's triad! Also you do not take an even share of the injuries! When we fight the second ulgrane flock, only the Sleeth is hurt."

Nethry sighed. "I didn't have any better choices, Arrhwy. I could hardly kill Ilzatheinen. Stealing the Tilmarth Note was a possibility, but I didn't see how I could get it away from Soohoon without the monsters there chasing us and killing several."

Arrhwy shrugged. "You do not have to do any of these things. Let Soohoon have defenses! They are only defenses."

"I've argued that point with Ilzatheinen no end. You know what I think."

"I have heard you arguing! I do not think you are right. I do not think you are wrong either. I do not know much about this topic. But I am not here to argue onto you," said Arrhwy.

"What are you here for? A spot of cruelty, perhaps?" said Nethry bitterly.

Arrhwy grinned. "Ilzatheinen pays me! Perhaps Ilzatheinen has some opinion about you! Think of what it might be. Imagine perhaps that he is distressed to think that some harm might come to his daughter's lover!"

Nethry regarded Arrhwy closely. "If you, alone, try to kill me, you will be achingly surprised, several times."

"If I, alone, am trying to kill you, I remember to use my claws when I sneak up behind you. Also my fangs, and also some spells. In fact I am not here to give you your killing. Ilzatheinen simply wishes you to indulge in no more mischiefs!"

Nethry shrugged, and wiped her face with the dishtowel again. "I have a busy schedule this afternoon, including crying, weeping, mourning, regretting, and contemplating spending ten thousand years studying Tempador so I could redo the last few weeks. I have no time for mischief."

Arrhwy prodded Nethry with a forepaw. "Also no time to argue with the Sleeth, then. Pray continue, while I watch you! I recall that you have gotten no further than the crying when I come in."

Nethry sat on her stool, glaring. "It's hard to cry properly when someone is watching, and a Sleeth in particular."

"I do not leave you alone now! You must cry badly, or not at all."

Nethry sighed, and brewed a pot of tea. She sat quietly, staring into the black steam, wondering what could possibly remain to her.

ZALLARILLA'S JUDGMENT

Boragette stopped at the door to the pilot's chamber. "Guild law says I can't go in there, doesn't it?"

"Oh, guild law can go get futtered by a ... a ... Rassimel spy. Anyways, guild law says I can let someone in an emergency, and this cursed well is one. I'm angry enough to slam *A Flattering Wind* into a hillside," said Zallarilla. She grabbed Boragette's lower wrist and pulled zir inside, slamming the door behind them.

Boragette took a quick glance at a table of the cryptic implements which must have controlled the skyboat: a hinged globe of grey glass, a copper bowl of hazelnuts, a knitting needle with silken cord wrapped around it.

Zallarilla shoved an armchair at zir, and threw herself on the floor. "Just a week ago you talked me into thinking of marriage. Just last night I was trying to find the courage to propose. Now I almost wish I *had* found it."

Boragette cocked zir head. "You do?"

"If I had, I could break it to show how betrayed I am!" Zallarilla shook her head. "That doesn't make sense, does it?"

"I don't think you're obligated to make sense just now."

"When, then?"

Boragette pretended to look at the sun. "Tomorrow, shortly before midday."

"A whole day I'm allowed? How generous."

Boragette nodded. "A whole day, less ten percent. The Duke of Girath's taxes, you know."

Zallarilla stared at zir, then shook in mixed laughter and tears. "That makes no sense at all! And how long are *you* allowed to do that? After taxes?"

Boragette smiled. "I'll make sense at you as best I can, any time you like, Zallarilla."

Zallarilla rubbed her cheek on the polished teak leg of the table of controls. "It *would* be a good time now, come to think of it."

"You'll have my best thoughts now, then. No more guarantee on them than last time, of course."

"That's plenty. What *should* I do with her, Boragette?"

"If you want her killed, I rather think Arrhwy could be persuaded to help. If you want her married, I think you'll have to do it yourself."

Zallarilla looked up. "Are those my only choices?"

"Unfortunately not. You could send her away. You could deliver her to Drysselwyn I suppose — they might be glad enough to do something with an agent of Byronny. You could have her crippled. You could demand a huge fine. There must be some other choices."

"I'd rather have just two, curse it. Two choices I could think about."

Boragette stroked Zallarilla's headfur. "I'm afraid you've gone rather beyond my experience."

Zallarilla snapped, "Well, do you think *my* lovers try to kill *me* constantly?"

"No ... if you put it that way, we could ask Arrhwy for advice."

Zallarilla laughed bitterly. "I take your point, insect. As we are both dancing on this frozen lake for the first time, could you *please* say something useful instead of apologizing and making stupid jokes?"

"I'll do my best, Zallarilla." Zie bit back another apology. "Well ... what would you most like to have happen?"

"That I wake up and have this be some sort of fear-induced nightmare in the aftermath of getting engaged to her," roared Zallarilla.

"You want her to stay with you, then?"

Zallarilla picked up the glass globe and fidgeted with it. "How could I possibly want that? It makes no sense at all. Seven staring gods! She nearly tried to kill me!"

Boragette looked at her closely. "You still don't have to make sense. That's no part of a joke. But you *do* have to answer me, and clearly, with a yes or a no. You want her to stay with you, then?"

Zallarilla spun the globe. "Yes and no are my only choices, no shades of meaning or subtleties?"

"Those come later."

The globe fell out of her hand. The skyship groaned in the air, and Zallarilla leapt for the globe and caught it on the second bounce. She put it on the table carefully, and petted it until the skyship was calm again.

"Well?"

Zallarilla sighed. "I haven't loved very often or very deeply. I threw my other one away over a silly careless mistake of his. I'm sure I did worse for myself by flying off the once. I think I'll be doing worse for myself by flying off again."

"This wasn't a careless mistake, Zallarilla. You know Nethry doesn't make careless mistakes."

"No, this wasn't."

"You said you could trust her to sweep your cabin. That you could talk to her about anything," said Boragette. "You obviously can't still."

"I want that back!" Zallarilla's shout surprised even the Rassimel herself.

"How could you possibly trust her again, after this?" asked Boragette.

Zallarilla sighed. "I hope she can answer that. I certainly can't."

Boragette nodded. "And even if you could, would you want to?"

"Do you love Rajel and Casamint?"

"I haven't thought about that lately. I like them both now. The things I thought were horrid about them, I now think are just part of their idiosyncratic charms. I'd certainly share body-play with either of them again ... I'd even ask for it. I suppose I'm creeping up on love. Maybe some time I'll be sure I'm all the way there."

"If they did something like this, would you wish for them back?"

Boragette winced at the question. "I really don't think so."

Zallarilla stood up. "Excellent. My decision is made."

"Oh, good. I think Casamint and Arrhwy will be pleased. Everyone, really."

"They will not be, for I have decided to try my most intense and severe best to stay with her," said Zallarilla.

"I'm afraid I don't quite understand," said Boragette.

"I want real love in my life if I'm going to have it at all — love as strong as a scyanturge, fierce harsh intense love. Not like your feeble meek Herethroy villager maybe-slightly-sneaking-up-on-love."

Boragette winced. "It's not like that at all!"

Zallarilla glowered at zir. "If it's not, that's between the three of you. It certainly sounds like it from everything you've said." She took a deep breath, and lowered her ears. "I'm sorry, Boragette. You really have helped me understand this. I don't imagine that anyone else will really approve of what I'm going to do, or anyone but a Rassimel could really understand what obsession is about."

Boragette nodded sagely. "This is where Rassimel and Herethroy cannot agree."

"It is."

"Zallarilla, I suppose the choice is yours to create or destroy; the heart is yours that risks recovering or ravaging. I wish you all the best, however you choose."

Zallarilla smiled. "I'll perfume my whiskers with your wishes, then, and go corner my soon-to-be-fiancée. I wonder if she'll cooperate with me?"

They left the pilot's chamber, Boragette shaking zir head worriedly.

* * *

"How can I trust you?", asked Zallarilla, her voice like water spilling over broken glass. Salt frosted the fine black fur of her mask. Boragette sat beside her, tracing curves and jagged spirals on zir leg-chitin with a fingertip.

Nethry twisted her tailtip in her hands. "You can understand why I do whatever I do. Everything that wasn't for you was for my city ... for the long-term good of my city."

"And that would be just about everything, would it not, Nethry?"

Nethry flattened her ears. "That would be everything bad I've done to you."

"And what, exactly, is everything bad you've done to me? Another surprise like the first would be less than delightful."

Nethry said, "You know everything now. I tried to influence your father. I lied somewhat about my history. I coaxed two sets of ulgrane and one carcanofex to attack you... I lied and betrayed you."

"Nothing else?"

Nethry thought about a few drops of tincture of wenezza from the *Sensible Finch*. Nothing short of very deep magic could discover them after such a long time, and if she tossed the bottle off the edge of the world at

Soohoon, there would be nothing to raise Zallarilla's suspicions. She would figure out later how to make peace with herself for this lie. "Nothing else, Zallarilla."

"I have a judgment, then."

Nethry stared. "Already?"

"Already. You must do two things, or I shall call the Sleeth and the Herethroy woman to escort you off the deck of *A Flattering Wind*, and I shan't land first. The first is preparation for the second. You must betray Byronny more thoroughly than you betrayed me. You must exile yourself from there forever, immediately, without returning."

Nethry curled her tail. "You were torturing me when you asked how you could trust me, were you? Leading me forward to the branch-edge, where you could shove me off?"

Zallarilla's voice was as harsh as lead foil ripping. "Second: you must marry me as soon as possible. And swear to give me all the loyalty that you once did to Byronny." She accompanied her words by a shower of bright sparks, from the talisman Ilzatheinen had given her.

Nethry stared at Zallarilla for a moment, and fell into her arms. The two Rassimel cried together, embracing. A thoroughly embarrassed Boragette crept out of the room, to try to explain matters to everyone else.

* * *

There were practical matters to arrange.

"I've got a full dozen of talismans and suchlike, starting with that glove and getting more important," said Nethry. "They belong to the city. I should arrange to send them back, somehow."

"Don't you *dare*, Nethry," said Zallarilla. "Stealing them shall be part of your severing of ties. Indeed, you shall make sure to mention that you are absconding with them when you write to poor Lord Secretary Muspis."

"I had planned to get you a metal pendant in the shape of a sail as an engagement token, Zallarilla. Would you like an exceedingly expensive far-speaker instead? As a symbol of where I have chosen to put my loyalty, in the end?"

"And an extraordinarily useful device for a travelling skyboat, too! I can't think why it's not common equipment."

Ilzatheinen scowled, or rather continued to scowl, as he had done since he learned of the carcanofex attack. "It is not common equipment because it costs rather more than *A Flattering Wind*. It slips through a loophole in the gods' laws of reality, to be able to send messages so far; such workings are difficult and hence expensive. There is nothing a whisker of such difficulty in *A Flattering Wind*: it is all routine work."

Zallarilla glowered at her father. "I appreciate the gift of the skyboat, never doubt that. But I am fully adult, and fully capable of making my own decisions ... and of paying the price for them, should they prove doomful."

"They already have, daughter!"

Nethry flattened her ears. "Zallarilla, I don't deserve defense in this. But, Ilzatheinen, you know what I am paying for the love of your daughter. There will be nothing in my life but her ... I shall protect her with everything."

"Your past deeds condemn you! Your promises are worthless!"

"The first, yes. But the letter I write is the first promise I break, and I think the last."

Ilzatheinen folded his arms. "Daughter, you shall have the customary gifts from a father at a wedding. Nor shall I disinherit you. But know that, however hard Nethry has to work to recover your good graces, she must work seven by twelve times harder to recover mine."

Zallarilla barked, "You are on the very edge of being a lout!"

Nethry curled her tail. "I would call it generous."

Zallarilla swatted Nethry. "Stop insulting my fiancée. You challenge my taste, you cast aspersions on my good fortune! I won't have it, I say!"

Nethry and Ilzatheinen both blinked at her. Nethry recovered first, and leapt on her, kissing her fiercely. Ilzatheinen stalked voluminously out of the room.

FAMILY MATTERS

Boragette collected Casamint and Rajel, one in each lower hand, and towed them to their bedroom. "I have an important announcement to make. You get it first, O my lucky spouses."

"That sounds bad," said Rajel.

"Oh, on an ordinary day, I should be quite terrified, to be sure. I don't think zie's going to say anything quite so bad about us as zie did about Nethry, though," said Casamint.

"Not so bad, no, but you may care in any case. I am going to marry Chicory," said Boragette.

Casamint's antennae went flat. Rajel dropped Boragette's hand, and stared at zir.

Casamint recovered first. "I suppose I should have been terrified after all. What man will be involved in this?"

"And when did you arrange it?" asked Rajel.

"And, well, don't you need our consent?" said Casamint. "If I've given mine, I've quite forgotten about it. Perhaps I did it in the rush of battle frenzy this morning?"

Boragette waved zir hands. "Stop, stop. I have no specific plans. I haven't even *asked* Chicory yet, much less found a husband for us. I'm asking you *first*."

Casamint relaxed enough to raise the tips of his antennae. "Well, that sounds much more proper. I suppose you should say a bit more, though? I must admit I'm not entirely persuaded that we should have such a big marriage, nor am I quite willing to marry her myself."

Zie tangled a lower hand into the bedspread, cringing a bit at how uncoloverly a thing zie was about to say. "There is one more thing to say, and it is this: that I shall marry her, one way or another."

Rajel curled her tail as much as she could. "What will you do, if we refuse? Elope with her to the Transwynt, and bribe a count ... or whatever they have in place of counts ... to perform the wedding?"

"I don't need a count to make a legal wedding there — they don't have real nobility, so there aren't any customs about who can perform nobles' weddings. For that matter, Zallarilla could do it, if we're flying over the Lenwynt."

"Ah, you already investigated how to elope. Clever cosi you are: clever enough to be quite dangerous," said Casamint.

"Chicory checked when she was hoping you'd marry her and me on the spot," said Boragette.

"Boragette? I do know you've loved Chicory for a long while. Why did you just now decide to marry her?" asked Rajel.

Boragette sat on the bed, zir limbs folded demurely. "Zallarilla inspired me. No, that's not right. Zallarilla stung me. *She's* doing something very brave to get the woman she loves..."

"'Brave' is perhaps the meekest word I would choose for it. 'Foolhardy', or, perhaps, even 'utterly mad' come to mind as better phrasings," said Casamint.

Boragette ignored zir husband. "She called our marriage loveless. She's right, too, isn't she?" Zie stared hard at zir spouses in turn, and they lowered their antennae.

"She's not right. Not very right. I could say I loved you," said Rajel.

"But you have not done. You have never done," said Boragette.

"It's never come up," said Rajel, her antenna curled tight.

"How can you say it's never come up? It's what this whole insane and monster-infested trip is about!"

Rajel lowered her gaze. "I'm a woman, and such words do not come so easily to me."

Casamint, hoping to avoid the same accusation, pointed an upper finger at Boragette. "We are working on love. With some success. I love you. I even love that half-Sleeth we somehow got ourselves married to, despite all the inconveniences and ridiculous situations she's gotten us into. Married love takes time and attention — and work, curse it — and your Grand Padishah has a few years' head start on us."

Boragette snapped, "That's quite a stupid thing to say, Casamint. How long did you know Skirret before you loved her? How long did Zallarilla and Nethry know each other before they fell in love?" Casamint flattened his antennae, and had no answer.

"Boragette? You *do* know what having a big sloppy family will cost us? Cost *my* children, in particular? Our firstborn will be a Great Baron of four villages, but whatever wealth we have will get smeared all around to, oh, children of your second husband's second triad, and maybe further if that triad's co-lover wants to marry too. Your parents may have been rich enough to be proper nobility and hire knights when Dorly got troubled by monsters and all, but mine and Casamint's had trouble. I'd rather that we had a few children, but ones in a better situation than us, not a worse one," said Rajel.

"Well, you're fairly well-off, and Chicory's downright rich," said Boragette.

"At the moment, on both of those. Adventuring is mischancy work, and I imagine that dye prices aren't wholly stable either," said Rajel. "And Chicory is quite a spendthrift."

Boragette nodded, and hugged zir legs in zir mid-arms. "I'm afraid so."

Rajel pressed her advantage. "And you can't vouch for the character and position of your second husband, because you haven't one in mind yet."

"No ... Well, maybe Casamint would be willing to consider her?"

"I *have* considered her. I have considered her provincial. I have considered her crass. I have considered her distasteful. I have considered her, as you noted, a spendthrift. I have even considered her ridiculous. If I have any say in my second wife (and second mari if it comes to that, though I truly would prefer a tight little quadrette), it will be someone with education and good manners and good sense. I am *not* so concerned about marrying a strong girly farmer sort of person."

Boragette glared at him. "She is going to be your mari's wife. You be nice to her."

Casamint glared back at zir. "She is my mari's adulterous lover. She is destined to be the source of most of the troubles in our own marriage over the next several months. I will be precisely as nice to her — and, more to the point now, *about* her — as the situation warrants."

"You're not going to do it," said Boragette.

"I am certainly not going to marry her myself," said Casamint. "I may yet give my consent to you marrying her, but only once I have been satisfied on many matters. Imprimus, that *our* marriage is all in order and proper and solid. I have said that I love you, you will note, but you have not managed to say that to me. For one instance." It was Boragette's turn to look ashamed.

Rajel sighed. "I can't imagine giving my consent either, not any time soon at least. For practical reasons, and, well, for a bit of jealousy too."

Boragette sat upright. "Then I shall elope and not ask you."

"I think we might find a compromise, though," said Rajel.

"Ah, a compromise," said Casamint. "What is it? Half a marriage? I shall marry Chicory's lower half? Which, on the whole, is where she keeps her more desirable aspects. Or her less undesirable ones. As I think of desire, at least — I gather that our energetic little mari has explored the matter more." That got him glares from both Boragette and Rajel.

Rajel continued, "I don't mind Chicory herself, or not enough to complain about her. I *do* mind having her involved in our family enough to hurt *my* children. So how about if we let Boragette keep Chicory as a consort?"

"Consort?", said Boragette, her antenna flattening in embarrassment.

"Gallant. Concubine. Gigolo for whom you have arranged a bulk discount," said Rajel.

"That's hardly decent," said Boragette.

"Eloping, too, is hardly decent," said Rajel. "Indeed, if you elope, I should consider divorcing you, no matter the personal cost. If you have a consort with my consent, well, I shouldn't do that."

"*I* think it's shameful," said Casamint.

"Well, *you* already had one," snapped Boragette. "And you weren't nearly as restrained with her as I have been with Chicory."

Casamint glared at Rajel. "Well, I must admit, you *did* find a compromise. One that satisfies no one!"

Rajel shrugged. "It satisfies me. Though I'm the furthest off. I only get the one marriage, now or ever. If it takes being cuckolded to make it work, well, that's better than *not* making it work."

Boragette looked up. "It satisfies me too, I suppose, except that it *is* awfully immodest."

Casamint crashed his forearms together. "Well, then, it satisfies everybody except me. It is awfully immodest, truly. I see no good in it."

"There's the good of having a happy mari, for one," said Rajel. "And one who isn't eloping."

"I can put some good in it for you," said Boragette. "You want a quadrette, you said?"

"I would prefer one. Not with someone like Chicory, as I have said many's the time."

"Well, how about if Rajel and I give you the mastery in finding your second wife? I'll marry pretty much anyone you choose, however scholarly a bug she is, if she's halfway reasonable, if I can keep Chicory."

Casamint looked at his mari, and thought a moment. "That is not a small offer. I was worried that I'd have to settle for some tedious farm-bug or other."

"Is it worth the price of your mari sleething around on you?" asked Boragette.

"Well, a single lover of the same species and different sex is hardly *sleething*, not by Arrhwy's standards," said Casamint. "I think this compromise is very compromiseful. I find that I despise one half and crave the other half."

Rajel laughed. "I respectfully point out that, well, Boragette is getting what zie most wants in love outside of our marriage, and Casamint is getting what *he* most wants in love outside of our marriage."

"Do *you* have a surprise lover that *you* haven't mentioned to us, too, Rajel?" asked Casamint.

"Hah, a few nights or two with this or that hirable co-lover or woman. Nobody I'd introduce in polite society," said Rajel.

"Hah, if *I* know polite society, they've all hired them a dozen times over," said Casamint.

"Hah, there is that. In any case, I have no actual plans. I simply think that Boragette got a nice something, and Casamint did, and I have ... nothing I haven't had for most of my life. So I'd like *something*. I don't know what, though, so I'll ask for a promissory note... I simply would hope that, as we're going to be a shocking bunch of libertine aristocrats, that I have a certain amount of tolerance for anything shocking that we do. " said Rajel.

"One more thing," said Boragette.

"And what would that be?"

"That we stop making plans for our adulteries *or* our second marriages until this one is all working and proper and right," said Boragette.

Rajel regarded zir archly. "This is a remarkable statement, since you are our principal adulterer."

Boragette groomed zir antennae briefly. "Well, yes. I'll leave off with Chicory for a while, if the both of you leave off your scheming."

Casamint shrugged. "I would be looking at Pennypell Academy in any case. And Rajel's stuck in Soohoon for a while."

"Ah, now there's what I want as my branch of the compromise. I want you two to come to Soohoon with me. Which is pretty much what Boragette asked for, really."

"I asked no such thing!" said Boragette.

Which started another discussion as long and nervous discussion of just what to do. In the end, though, Boragette and Casamint agreed to stay with Rajel.

SEALING THE DEAL

Boragette woke Chicory with a hand on her tail. "Lover? I have some good news for us."

Chicory wiggled her arms and legs, and then gathered Boragette close for a tangly embrace. "What's your news, sweetie?"

"Casamint and Rajel have agreed that you and I can be lovers, even after we're home and everything!" Boragette did zir best to sound delighted with it, for all that it was a compromise to zir true wishes.

"Well, now, that's mighty generous of them," said Chicory, who was not fooled. "Any day now they'll give us permission to eat plue and drink water."

"You know it's not a little thing," said Boragette.

"What gives them the right to give you orders? Even if they're ones you like?"

Boragette folded zir mid-arms. "I give them the right. They're my spouses and I'm responsible to them. And they are to me. We spent **hours** negotiating so that everyone would be happy."

"So that every Tawlown would be happy. I wasn't there, Boragette. You're telling me I should be happy?"

"If you're not happy being my lover, then ... how dare you be my lover?"

"I don't **have** to be your lover any-the-more, Boragette. You tell me to stop, I'll stop, just like that."

Boragette sat on Chicory, arranging a few of her limbs for comfort. "You'd better not stop! I had to promise some big things to get to keep you!"

"Oh, no. What'd you promise?"

"Casamint and I will stay with Rajel in Soohoon. And, well, Casamint gets to pick who else he's marrying," said Boragette.

"I don't think he'll be choosing me," said Chicory. "Look, I don't mean to get angry at you, Boragette, but ... if you were negotiating anyways, couldn't you have asked for, like, having him marry me?"

The compromise which had satisfied all the Tawlowns suddenly looked meagre and lopsided in the presence of Chicory. "I did try," said Boragette in a small voice, and told zir lover what had happened.

Chicory thumped her fists on her chitinous thighs. "That's all dreadful! They're not letting us stay lovers — those two scoundrels are keeping us from getting married! And keeping us apart for months now! And as your good little adulterous lover, I'm supposed to take whatever leftovers they leave over!"

Boragette turned and looked into Chicory's opaline eyes. "Not two scoundrels. Three scoundrels, or no scoundrels. I'm a Tawlown too. I took my share in arranging things for the good of my triad. If there's blame to be blamed, I get a full share of it."

"You're just like Nethry, you know?"

Boragette gasped. "What?"

"Betraying your older promises for your new marriage."

"My marriage is **not** new. I've been a Tawlown all my life."

"Well, you just noticed it, anyways. You just took up with Casamint and Rajel," said Chicory.

"Chicory, I **am** sorry I can't have you and them both, the way I want, but I can't."

Chicory folded her hands under her chin. "Might be best for me to go back to Pennypell and find a real mari, if I can't marry you any more than that."

"Find one who doesn't mind adultery, then," said Boragette, a bit desperately. "One who'll appreciate the connection to a Great Baron and who won't fuss about just what the connection means."

"If you won't *be* my mari, I don't see why you get to *pick* my mari, either," said Chicory morosely.

"This is why!" said Boragette, and tugged at the belt of Chicory's kilt. Modesty was a luxury for less desperate times.

Chicory looked at zir, and opened her mid-arms to let zir reach the buckles. "Guess that's a reason," she admitted.

"Chicory, I love you, and more itchily and severely than I love my husband or my wife. Maybe I won't abandon everything for you, but I *will* abandon a lot for you: my standing in polite society, for one instance."

"Heh. And your kirtle?"

"For the moment!", zie said, and tugged it off in such a hurry that a sleeve caught on a spike in zir chitin, and ripped.

"Well, if I'm to be your official adulterous lover, I might as well start now," said Chicory. She suited actions to words, with a ferocity that surprised them both.

PARTINGS

"Rajel, strong insect woman, I think you can carry the more. Also I think that on that table is the more you can carry, wrapped in mnenorzion wire! Boragette! On the left side of Rajel's basket-pack is the space for it!" It was time to move Ilzatheinen's workshop onto one of Soohoon's platforms, and all the primes were called upon to help. For Arrhwy, help was largely supervising, and supervising was largely ordering people to add to Rajel's burdens.

"I'd rather not," said Rajel. "This is plenty heavy."

Boragette looked at the object wrapped in mnenorzion wire. "What *is* it?"

Casamint answered, "It looks like a sex toy from New Kottarnu. I wouldn't touch it if I were you, Boragette. Arrhwy probably used it on an ulgrane while we weren't looking."

Arrhwy swatted him with her tail. "You think if I put it in Tlurrrien he gets more eager? Perhaps I do not do it then! Already he is pestering me for a second round!" Boragette folded zir antennae and retreated demurely to the other side of the room.

Ilzatheinen wrapped it in cloth and added it to Rajel's burden. "Not so far off. It is the generative organ of a male jack o'hooks, smoked over a ffugarian fire, mummified, and wrapped. For the Locador enchantment, naturally."

"Naturally! Who could imagine any other thing! Casamint is the fool to suggest any other thing!"

"Shush, Arrhwy, or I'll have Rajel stuff it in *you*," said Casamint.

"Politely I decline this offer! Rajel and I are not on such intimate terms! Yet!"

"Don't do *anything* with *any* of my instruments, Casamint. They are in suitable states of ritual purity," said Ilzatheinen.

Rajel struggled to four feet. "The person who adds another item to this burden had best be on exceedingly intimate terms with me, for I shall surely insert something somewhere into him. Most likely a sword-blade. This is cursed heavy already, and I'm taking it to the cupola."

* * *

Zallarilla slipped out of Nethry's lap, and the two Rassimel helped Rajel take the basket-pack off her back. "They didn't half load you up, did they, Rajel?"

Rajel stretched, pounding on her chitin as best she could by way of self-massage. "Rajel thinks that the stronger I am, the better a fighter I shall be. True enough. The next time we encounter enemies who are best vanquished by being loaded into a basket on my back, I shall be mighty indeed."

The Rassimel started putting boxes and odd-shaped parcels on the floor of the cupola. "I should have thought to buy two dozen basket-packs, not just one. Then we could just cart them into the cupola, fly over, and cart them out, without packing and unpacking and packing and unpacking," said Zallarilla.

"Truth to tell, O beloved, I am happier this way. It's an excuse to be alone with you and the occasional Rajel. I don't think the others have forgiven me yet."

Rajel frowned at Nethry. "I don't think *I* have done. The fewer times I am attacked by ulgrane, the better."

Zallarilla nodded. "Yes, of course. After all these things are moved, Nethry and I will remove ourselves to Araldy for some weeks. Delivering Chicory to home, first, I think makes sense."

Rajel's antennae uncurled. "That, at least, I approve of."

* * *

Dear Lord Muspis,
I herewith do resign from your service. I herewith do abandon my former name. I herewith do betray my home town of Byronny. I herewith do embezzle every implement and enchanted item that you have provided me with. I herewith warn you that you cannot confiscate my personal accounts, for I have already emptied them. Feel free to dock the wages due me for my latest mission; I have been amply and more than amply paid by foreign parties for it. Indeed, you have no choice in the matter: I shall not return to Aradrueia again, and I shall live my life so far from Byronny that Pethiliant's best location spell cannot cover the twelfth part of the distance.
No, it's nothing you did. I simply got a better offer.
With insufficient regret, Nethry

* * *

Boragette's kitchen in Soohoon would not have met Beetheart's standards, nor Boragette's before zie came to Soohoon. It was far better than it had been at the beginning, though, and boasted a long flat counter raised two feet over the floor. Originally it had been higher, as Boragette preferred to stand as zie prepared food, but that had shaken the platform too much.

Zie was working there now, slicing bark thin in preparation for pickling it. A six-inch cone of a seashell appeared on that counter in an aching twist of spiky Locador magic. Zie picked it up and read the spiralling letters engraved around it.

To Boragette, from Nethry aboard A Flattering Wind, greetings. Is this a good time for us to come and bring the all of you home? Speak into the bottom of the cone, and I shall hear you.

Boragette set down zir cleaver. "It must be a good time now. Ilzatheinen will take a week longer than he intended, but come as soon as you like. Or sooner! It will be good to see primes!"

A second cone appeared. *Well then, we'll be there mid-tomorrow. How have things gone?*

"I needn't have worried about a boring vacation: it's scarcely been the one and scarcely been the other. I daresay we'll tell you everything when you get here, though."

A third cone appeared; Nethry was using the far-speaker's power extravagantly. *Is everyone still upset with me, think you?*

"Ilzatheinen is determined to be perpetually upset with Zallarilla's lovers, you more than most. Casamint has taken to blaming everything that goes wrong on you, but if he can joke about you I daresay he's not actually upset. Rajel, Arrhwy, Rodents-at-Dawn, and Tlurrrien are bored of the jokes, so I don't think they are either. Nherex-Dlostion will never trust you again, but is not angry. Wesk-wesk has promised not to lead the village against you." She paused, and added in a sweet voice, "And I agree with Nherex. You're as perfidious as any Rassimel: very much or not at all, and it doesn't matter to you, it's just a coincidence from doing whatever it is you need to do. I do not hate you, I think. But I am as protective of my family as anyone should be, and I certainly do not fully trust you either ... nor Ilzatheinen, nor Zallarilla, nor anyone who has some grand plan to do and thinks that Rajel or Casamint or I will fit nicely into it. But come here and take us home, and we will be most grateful."

Nethry took a moment to answer. *Perfidious. I had thought you'd be the most forgiving of the primes there. Well, we shall be there tomorrow early, perfidious or not.*

"Until tomorrow, and give my best regards to Zallarilla," said Boragette, and wondered how rude zie had been.

* * *

A Flattering Wind danced and dodged half a mile from Soohoon, and a terrible seven-headed firebird spat blazing javelins at it. Ilzatheinen flew to the bird in a desperate rush, shouting, "No, no! They are friends!", and the bird immediately became calm.

Zallarilla let her skyboat drift closer to Soohoon, cautiously, ready to flee if the bird attacked again. She shouted from every curtain, "That would be your new elemental, O father? It seems quite mighty and thoroughly dangerous!"

Ilzatheinen flew to the skyboat and ran downstairs. "O daughter, you are a welcome sight. Or you will be when you come out of the pilot's room. I haven't seen a Rassimel in months, much less a relative!"

Nethry waved to him from the parlor. "Well, I can supply a masked face and ringed tail to see, though I daresay your daughter has some minutes of pilotry left. Good day to you!"

Ilzatheinen sighed. "Nethry. Good day to you, I imagine. How have you been treating my daughter?"

The curtains answered him, "She has been treating me quite adequately, to be sure. Wealth can do that!"

"She's wealthy, is she?"

Nethry curtsied. "Between my earlier salary from Byronny, and my more recent embezzlements from Byronny, I could sell a few things and replace *A Flattering Wind* if need should arise."

Ilzatheinen frowned. "I have better things to do than engage in a contest of wealth to keep my daughter's interest."

"Just as well, for that's not how I hold her interest."

A Flattering Wind shook violently. Nethry grabbed a bookshelf to steady herself. Ilzatheinen's flight spell suspended him in mid-air. Zallarilla shouted through the curtains, "Be friendly, the both of you! And if you can't be friendly, be civil."

Nethry smiled. "In any case, we have treated each other quite well indeed — which is fortunate for me, now there's nobody else in the world for me."

Ilzatheinen landed, and curtsied. "Well, then ... the secret to dealing with Zallarilla is, quite simply, to give her whatever she wants."

"Father!", wailed the curtain.

Nethry grinned. "I am beginning to realize that, truly. Fortunately she is satisfied with a single skyboat at a time."

"Lover!", wailed the curtain.

Ilzatheinen smiled a bit. "Her demands are, after all, modest: a skyboat here, all your money and honor there..."

Zallarilla stormed out of the pilot's chamber and stood in the doorway, glaring, hands on her hips. "I suppose I should be glad that you two have found something in common to talk about. Still, talk about it too much and I shall fling a tureen of ghoul-goose soup at you!"

Ilzatheinen landed, and hugged his daughter. After a moment she relented and hugged him back.

* * *

The Herethroy had built themselves an actual table and chairs, and Boragette had insinuated versions of several country Herethroy recipes into the Soohoon cooks' repertoire. Otherwise the farewell feast was much the same as the welcome one.

"How has your vacation been, then, Boragette?" asked Zallarilla.

"Rather more exciting that I had expected, truly. Soohoon's neighbors didn't like them getting great enchantments any more than Byronny did, and they were more direct about it. We've had half a dozen raids, and a pitched battle two weeks ago," said Boragette.

"I should think that seven-headed spitting firebird would make short work of nearly any raiders!"

"It did! We sat inside the wall of fire and watched it pierce and broil hugeng and ulgrane and perdithorne with spears! But that was three days ago, after Ilzatheinen had finished making it," said Boragette.

Nethry quirked her ears. "It dealt with them all by itself? How many of them?"

Zallarilla poked her lover in the ribs with a clawtip. "*You* are still worrying about your ex-city."

Nethry tucked her tail between her legs. "As a matter of academic interest only!"

"When they come they are five hugeng, eight ulgrane, one perdithorne. When they go they are two hugeng, six ulgrane, no perdithorne. Wesk-wesk tells us to kill them all. Nherex wants us to let the firebird do every work. Nherex of course gets her way."

Nethry looked at the tables of vorwi. "Wesk-wesk was a child-tender when I was here before, and occasionally a guest-tender. Zie has come up in the world, I take it?"

"Wesk-wesk is voted Go-Lord of Soohoon to replace the mighty scyanturge. In this vote she wins over Tlurrrien the aggressive of perdithorne. Most of the time zie is still a child-tender. Soohoon is very the stop village, with the mighty Stop-Lord and the meager Go-Lord."

Nethry sighed. "Excellent. For the next few years I shan't feel guilty about failing so thoroughly." She looked at Zallarilla. "Not that I'm going to *do* anything about it one way or another. But do let's move to Girath after this, or Vheshrame, or somewhere far away."

"Once everyone is all returned home, love."

* * *

Zallarilla and Boragette sat at dusk with chalices of tea and bowl of incense, on a platform by the hole in Soohoon's gall. Ilzatheinen's wall of fire protected them: though it was currently in abeyance, waiting and watching for danger, they could feel its terrible force and fierce attention with magic sense.

"How is your marriage going, Boragette?"

"Well, there's nothing like a long expedition to the lower Verticals to improve things. At least, I hope I never experience anything like it ever again. I've had to do *surgery* on my husband ... In any case, I do think we're quite the good triad now. We never exactly fell in love, but I think we climbed to somewhere near it."

Zallarilla smiled. "That's good to hear. I'll stick with love at first sight myself. It's *much* more convenient."

"Ah, well, I've bargained away **that** convenience already, to earn more convenient adultery. Speaking of which, any news of Chicory?"

"Your Grand Padishah was delivered to Dorly, all full of eagerness to find two status-craving and morally adaptable Herethroy to marry as soon as ever she could. She gave a long expository discursion on how she would spend her wedding night with you and without her husband and mari. I don't think she's planning on love at all, much less love at first sight," reported Zallarilla.

"That's a pity ... I must give her lessons in proper care and love for one's spouses, then," said Boragette.

"Your first triad is going so well that you are now an esteemed teacher of marital romance?"

Boragette shook zir head. "My first triad is going so adequately that I want to keep matters both happy and scandal-free. Well, as scandal-free as the arrangement allows, which isn't much. When we have children I want them untainted, socially!"

"Will *that* be soon?"

Boragette flattened zir antennae. "Not so soon. We'll live in Pennypell for three terms of the Academy, then go live in someone's home village — the choice is not yet made — and start trying there. Some time yet. I'd like to study a bit, and enjoy the city a bit, but it's better to raise children in a village."

Zallarilla nodded. "Nethry has decided to get pregnant, too ... sooner than you, I think."

"How will you manage that, with two girls? There's a ritual spell, but I hear it's awfully expensive."

"Nothing so fancy as that. I had *my* daughter by someone who's not her. She can have hers by someone who's not me. We'll fly to somewhere — it could even be Pennypell, if you could recommend a suitable Rassimel man to help — and do the necessary physical preludes, then fly somewhere else and actually have the child there. She thinks it will help take her mind off Byronny."

"I should think it would! Does she still feel bad about that?"

"Yes, rather," said Zallarilla. "And that's the last I shall say about *that* topic tonight. You said you are now rich?"

"Well, we have been adventuring in the Verticals for months now, and tolerably successfully too. We've got a box of lead from moss we gathered in one spot, another box of silver snail shells; we've got rare glirries and magic resins, a few beads of world-amber and a carcanofex's horn, and all sorts of less valuable things."

"You killed Tuku?"

"Oh, not at all. Tuku has come to visit several times. He's a gentleman of a monster; he apologizes every time for what he did to us. This was a different carcanofex, Ghargha-something, who was in the second raiding party. He speared Casamint something awful, and then Rajel and Nherex and I ganged up on him. Casamint was only alive by temporary healing spells. The ororosti had to work hard to rescue him."

"You were fighting?"

"Casamint and I were in back, with some of the vorwi and some of the ororosti, sponting little spells here and there, and then getting jumped by the carcanofex coming through the world-bark."

"You're getting to be quite an adventurer!"

"Rather too much. My next adventure shall be within city walls! And not require healing, I most sincerely hope."

Zallarilla smiled. "In not so many days, I shall fly you home."

"That you shall not do, Zallarilla."

Zallarilla blinked. "You're staying in Soohoon?"

Boragette laughed. "Hardly! You shall fly us to Pennypell, and we shall be glad of it. But home for me is officially Rajel and Casamint, be it in a Herethroy village, or a prime city, or a tent surrounded by monsters."

Zallarilla smiled. "That's a pleasant way to think about it."

"And a pleasant way to live it, too."

GLOSSARY

CANI	Dogfolk (prime).
CLEY	The fuel of prime magic. Most spells cost one cley; most people can use a half-dozen cley a day.
CO-LOVER	The third sex of Herethroy.
COSI	A co-lover child; parallel to "boy" or "girl".
GORMOROR	Bearfolk (prime).
HERETHROY	Cricket-folk (prime).
KHTSOYIS	Aerial cephalapods (prime).
MARI	A co-lover spouse of a Herethroy; parallel to "husband" and "wife".
MONSTER	Any creature which is not a prime or harmless animal, the primes call a monster.
NYCATHATH	A powerful, brawny, batlike monster.
OROROSTI	A monster like a levitating string of eyeballs, with considerable magical power.
ORREN	Otterfolk (prime).
PERDITHORNE	A monster like a panther with half its flesh invisible.
PRIME	One of the eight species comprising the main World Tree civilization: Cani, Gormoror, Herethroy, Khtsoyis, Orren, Rassimel, Sleeth, and Zi Ri.
RASSIMEL	Raccoon-folk (prime).
SATHER	The co-lover parent of a Herethroy; parallel to "mother" and "father".
SCYANTURGE	A very powerful monster with great destructive force.
SLEETH	Non-anthropomorphic sentient panthers (prime).

VORWI	Weak floating four-armed tetrahedral monsters.
WORLD TREE	The world on which this story takes place; a very large tree, with branches fifty miles wide and tens of thousand long. Prime civilization is on the flat tops of the branches.
ZI RI	Miniature dragons (prime).
ZIE	Pronoun for co-lovers and others who are neither male nor female, parallel to "he" and "she".
ZIR	Pronoun for co-lovers and others who are neither male nor female, parallel to "his" or "him" and "her".

ACKNOWLEDGEMENTS

I thank Limyaael Alaydarie, Elizabeth Barrette, Vicki Bloom, H. Clower, Brent Edwards, Gabrielle Harbowy, Maggie Hogarth, Mel. Smith, Cheryl Urbani, Jo Walton, and May Wasserman for help, comments, and editing. Mistakes and infelicities are my fault alone. And thanks to the World Tree Role Playing Game community and the readers of *Sythyry's Journal* for enthusiasm and joy.

BIOGRAPHY

BARD BLOOM is one of the authors of the ***WORLD TREE ROLE PLAYING GAME***, the world in which *A Marriage of* Insects is set. Zie lives in suburban not-quite-NYC with zir wife and fellow gaming designer Vicki Borah Bloom and their son Rhys, who enjoys rolling dice and talking to bugs. Bard spends much of zir time as a computer science researcher and occasional attack logician, but may also be found making pottery, cooking, gamemastering, or writing Sythyry's Journal (http://sythyry.livejournal.com) and other works of fiction and gaming.

CRYPTO-CRITTERS
EDITED BY
BRUCE GEHWEILER

TIME CAPSULE

Know The Lore!

by Patrick Thomas

www.padwolf.com/mlseries.htm

VALLEY OF THE ANJELS

the first volume in a new fantasy series by best selling author
Judith Tracy

Three magical sisters searching for their hearts' destiny find
themselves in a battle to save their world

ISBN 1-890096-23-7, $14 US

<u>Praise for Judith Tracy</u>

"INVENTIVE, WILLING TO TAKE CHANCES... AND A CLIMACTIC TWIST." -Paul Di Filippo,
ASIMOV'S

"A REMARKABLE SCIENCE FICTION NOVEL." -Leann Arndt, **BUZZ BOOK REVIEW**

*"ELEGANCE, A REALLY GOOD COMMAND OF BASIC STORYTELLING... AN AUTHOR TO
WATCH."* -Andrew Andrews, **TRUE REVIEW**

DESTINY'S DOOR

The bestselling novel from Judith Tracy

Here's to those that hope and pray.
Fate has led you here today.
Have we the power to grant you this,
Search your heart and make one wish.
Click here to Enter

ISBN 1-890096-08-3 $14.00 US

THE STARSCAPE PROJECT

BRAD AIKEN

The Teconean Empire, a civilization of Neanderthals, is determined
to retake Earth, their homeworld. The rogue starfighter pilot that
once stopped their plans, is now framed and running for his life
over a crime he did not commit. Danny Stryker finds himself on
an unexpected path that will alter the balance of power in the
galaxy, and forever change man's definition of life.

$14 US ISBN 1890096202

DECONTRUCTING TOLKIEN A Fundamental Analysis Of The Lord Of The Rings
Edward J. McFadden Trade Paperback ISBN 1-890096-24-5; US $16;

THE 2ND COMING *The Best of Pirate Writings Vol. 2* & **THE BEST OF PIRATE WRITINGS VOL.1**
Ed. by Edward McFadden; 1-890096-13-X, $14 US SBN 1-89009604-0; US $12.95;

EPITAPHS ed. by Tom Piccirilli & Edward McFadden; $14

THE WILDSIDHE CHRONICLES™: $6.99 each
BOOK 1: WELCOME TO THE WILSIDHE Patrick Thomas
BOOK 2: DOUBLE CROSS   Patrick Thomas
BOOK 3: DARK PROPOSAL   Judith Tracy
BOOK 4: LEGACY   Judith Tracy
BOOK 5: THE UNDERCOVER DRAGON   Tony DiGerolamo
BOOK 6: CAR TROUBLE   Myke Cole

MURDER & MAYHEM IN THE GOD BOX ON A BILLION DOLLARS A DAY

RICK NEUBE
ROBERT B. SCOFIELD
JUDITH TRACY

THE TITLE SAYS IT ALL